PIRATES OF WORLD WAR II

BY

BRYAN CANTRELL

A PIRATE TIME TRAVEL NOVEL

Storm of Time series
Book One – Pirates of the Wild West
Book Two – Pirates of World War II

Also by Bryan Cantrell
The Bellevue Boys

Pirates of World War II is a work of fiction. Names, characters, places, and incidents are the product of the author's imagination. Historical figures and events appear only in fictionalized form; they are not intended as factual representations but as narrative devices for dramatic effect. Are pirates and outlaws public figures? Absolutely. But for the record: there are no verified accounts of pirates, cowboys, soldiers, or other rogues time traveling, nor of their involvement in theft, murder, or mayhem as described here. Again—fiction.

Published by Dark Gravity Studios

www.bryancantrell.com

First edition: Oct 2025

Contents

CHAPTER 1 – DAY OF INFAMY

Edward Thatch was only moments from drowning as his lungs felt close to bursting and his heart thundered like a drum inside his chest. His jaw was clenched, and his lips sealed shut to keep the seawater from rushing into his oxygen-starved lungs. The light was fading as he desperately felt his way along the metal walls of the turret he had climbed into by way of the gunport just before the ironclad was swallowed by the swirling vortex of ocean water. The turret quickly became flooded as the ironclad sank deeper and deeper into the sea. Darkness enveloped the chamber as any light from the sun was extinguished by the depth and murk of the enormous whirlpool the ship had been caught in. Thatch's disorientation was so severe that he couldn't tell if he was clawing his way up to the deckhead of the turret or down to the floor.

His hands felt a sensation change as they emerged from water to air, and he kicked his feet to propel his face to the newly acquired pocket of life-saving oxygen. His lips found the bubble and he sucked in as much as he could before the shifting of the vessel sent the air pocket moving to a new space. He strained his eyes to pick out any details in the darkness, searching for a feature to orient himself. Abruptly, the motion of the vessel changed again, and he was thrown, pressed to what may have been the floor, as the ship accelerated on its new course. The speed and motion were so powerful that he could do nothing but lie prone with his back against the unyielding metal and pray that he was ascending rather than descending further to the bottom of the Pacific.

Edward held tight to his breath as the dimmest of light was beginning to shine through the portholes and gunports. He was indeed lying on the floor of the turret, the big twin guns mounted in the center becoming visible as more light spilled into the chamber while the ironclad raced to the surface. His mind played out the scenario of the ship surging up to break dramatically through the waves and burst out of the water, throwing its occupants forward as their motion would continue as the ship's ceased. Thatch wrapped his arms around a stool that was bolted to the floor and prepared for the eventual stop the vessel would arrive at.

The speeding ironclad launched out of the sea, rising just past its stern propeller before its momentum ceased and the *Comanche* dropped to the ocean's surface with a wide splash of water as if it were a breaching humpback whale. Inside the fifteen-foot diameter turret Thatch's body was sent thrashing toward the deckhead in the flooded room. His arms strained to keep himself in place. He held tight to the bolted stool as the initial inertia peaked when the vessel stopped its forward movement. His eyes bulged as he spotted the water pouring out from the holes in the walls, and he kicked off the floor to swim toward the growing pocket of air at the top of the turret. He gasped for breath and sucked in a great lungful once his head broke the surface. Treading water, he looked around the now sunlit room. The water was thick with oil and flotsam. He swam to the gunport and gingerly stuck his head out to see the outside world.

The once-torrential storm that had raged only minutes before was gone. The sun that shone on his face and caused his eyes to squint in its brilliance was warm and strong. He quickly circled the interior moving from porthole to porthole, feasting his eyes on a glimmering ocean with a lush coastline only a mile away. As the seawater drained out of the turret, he began to hear clanging from below deck. The pirate hunter, Woodes Rogers, and his militant crew were one level below him. He patted his coat sleeve, discovering he still had his cabin boy's small Derringer pistol on his person. The pistol would be no match for the heavily armed men intent on ending his charmed life. He squeezed himself out though the gunport, not wanting to be trapped in the small compartment any longer.

Thatch fell to the deck of the low-drafted ironclad and crouched on all fours, spitting, and coughing up the remaining seawater that had filled his mouth and throat. Water poured and dripped from his drenched hair and dense black beard. His wet clothes were heavy on his vastly fatigued body. He rolled over on his back to rest a quick moment and noticed that the air was hot and humid, completely changed from the icy cold he had experienced only minutes before, prior to the watery vortex swallowing the vessel he was on. A far cry from the stormy seas off the coast of Northern California.

He lay, letting the sun begin to warm his face and body, trying to recall the recent events leading to his predicament. Thatch had offered himself to the pirate hunter in exchange for the freedom of Colette Dallaire, the golden-haired beauty he had fallen for. Colette had saved him from a noose after only knowing him a mere week or so. She had unfortunately been captured by the pirate hunter en route back to her saloon, The Paris, to be used as leverage against Thatch.

He had watched as Black Caesar had rescued Colette from falling overboard in the wild storm and safely saw her delivered to the *Queen Anne's Revenge*. Thatch had given himself up to Woodes in exchange for her freedom in a standoff on the deck of the *Comanche*. Luckily the fierceness of the storm had intervened before Woodes was able to put a handful of bullets into him.

He pushed himself to his feet and scanned the seas searching for his beloved 200-ton frigate. There were fishing boats, sailing vessels and a densely packed harbor off in the distance. Thatch narrowed his eyes at what he first took to be large buildings lining the docks before realizing that what he was seeing were ships the like of which he never dreamed existed.

A clanking sound from underneath the deck brought him back to his problem at hand. Armed men would soon be coming topside to escape being trapped inside this iron beast should it be sinking. He quickly moved to the edge facing the coastline and looked for some escape. The *Queen Anne's Revenge* was nowhere to be seen but a hundred or so yards away was a bobbing skiff that must have broken away from his ship. It was the same one that had transferred him to the ironclad. He gave one glance at the still-shut hatch of the *Comanche* and dove into the water. The swim was difficult in his clothes and boots, but he was loath to lose them. Thatch with great effort pulled himself aboard the little boat and found that a set of oars remained inside. He stripped off his soaked coat, shirt and boots, stowing his only weapon in a pocket of the finely tailored coat, and began rowing toward the harbor, eyes watching the *Comanche* to see if anyone emerged from below to see him as he made his escape.

Henry Jennings trudged through the waist-deep water inside the *Comanche* to reach the ladder that led to the main deck. He pushed aside a man floating face down as he came to the line of men waiting for the hatch to be opened. He, along with everyone else inside this floating iron pot, had been thrashed about and violently spun around as it was sucked into the whirlpool that had claimed Blackbeard's ship as well. The sound and flood of water overwhelmed the senses to the point of causing a complete blackout of consciousness making it difficult to determine how much time had passed while they were underwater. Jennings had come to, bruised and battered, but alive and unbroken—unlike several less fortunate souls that littered the oily, bloody water trapped in the interior of this warship.

"Open that damn hatch! I need air by God!" yelled Woodes Rogers as he made his way toward Jennings and the ladder.

Jennings looked up at the two ironclad sailors standing on the rungs straining to open the hatch. Both men had intense, desperate looks on their dirty and bleeding faces.

"It's stuck God damn it! Wedged tight," said one of the men.

There was no room on the ladder for Jennings to climb up and assist. In truth he was dead on his feet with fatigue and would probably add no extra strength even if he could squeeze himself into a position to help.

"Move! Make way," called out the voice of Bill Cooper.

Jennings stepped aside as the stocky Wells Fargo man reached the ladder and pulled on the first man's leg to come down. His arms were thick with muscle and power, his deep commanding voice sending the ladder men sliding down to make way.

Woodes hurriedly pushed the men aside to make room for Cooper to climb up and get his hands on the wheel securing the hatch. All the men stood back and waited as Cooper ascended the rungs and braced his back against the wall of the narrow chamber.

Cooper grunted with effort as he strained to move the wheel. Beads of sweat coated his forehead and the veins in his neck and arms bulged as he struggled to open the hatch. Jennings looked at Woodes in worry that they might be trapped inside this iron coffin, doomed to sink, imprisoned within for all eternity.

Cooper changed his footing in hopes of getting more torque and power against the wheel. One foot left the rung of the ladder to brace against the wall and he let out a yell of frustration as he cranked all his strength against the lever.

CLANG! Cooper's boot slipped off the ladder to slam against the wall as the wheel broke free and turned to release the hatch. Cooper hung on and kept himself from falling, putting both feet back on the metal rungs, and twisted the wheel completely so that the hatch could swing open as the men standing below him cheered.

Cooper climbed higher and eased his head and shoulders out into the sun-warmed air, taking a big breath and relishing the freshness of it. He could feel the crowd of men following him up, so he finished his climb and fully emerged to stand on the deck of the ironclad.

He turned in a circle to orient himself with his surroundings. Gone was the storm and so was the California coastline. His relief at surviving the ordeal and surfacing from the confines of below deck was tempered as he made his way to the starboard railing. He stared at the island a short distance away and became increasingly unsettled as he took in the harbor and city that lined its coast.

Woodes, Jennings and the rest of the men who were able, joined him to gaze at the view.

"Where the devil are we?" asked Woodes.

No one answered.

Cooper watched the boat traffic moving about in the distance including a boat being rowed by a man with long dark hair. His unease deepened in his gut as he noticed the unusualness of the craft that traversed the waters. There were none of the common steamers he was familiar with in the harbor or on the seas that he could see. There were enormous ships, gray in color, with guns of a size and scope that defied logic. What set his mouth agape wasn't what floated on the waters though, it was the engine noise that his eyes followed coming from a yellow-winged contraption flying a few hundred feet above the water as it moved along the coastline toward the harbor.

His peripheral vision picked up the pointed finger of Henry Jennings as he too followed the… flying machine. Woodes made a gasp, but none of the men said a word as they watched the wings tip, and the machine made a wide turn to fly inland over the city. The silence of the men on the deck of the *Comanche* was deafening as they all crowded around the railing, mouths agape, staring at a sight their 1700s and 1800s minds struggled to comprehend.

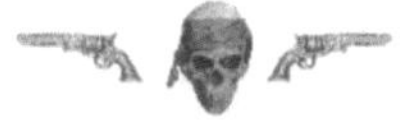

Edward Thatch struggled to quicken his pace of rowing as he watched the water level in his little boat rise. The battered tender was sinking and there was no bucket aboard to bail the water out, so he gave himself an order to 'put his back into it' and kept pulling hard on the oars.

A quick glance toward the bow caused him to do a double take as a large metal ship was going to cross his path. Painted a solemn gray, it boasted four towering smokestacks, emblematic of the steam-powered vessels of the new era he found himself thrust into. Upon its deck, numerous men bustled about amidst an array of machinery and cranes, while smaller boats were neatly stacked, ready for deployment. Thatch realized he was minutes from sinking and decided if he desired not to have to swim the rest of the way to shore, he needed a bit of rescuing. He turned toward the oncoming vessel and waved an oar to get the attention of the sailors on the deck.

"Oy! Oy! Ahoy, mates!" Thatch called out.

One of the sailors noticed Thatch and pointed him out to another man holding a set of strange goggles to his eyes. The man trained the goggles in Thatch's direction.

"Me ship is sinking! Lend a fellow sailor some aid?"

Thatch watched as the two men exchanged a few words then the man with the goggles in his hand rushed to the midcastle hopefully to give word to the captain to pick him up.

It was getting harder to row the waterlogged boat and Thatch gave up the oars for one of his boots. He used it to bail out water as the metal ship adjusted course to intercept him. The two men were back at the rail watching him do his best to stave off sinking before they could reach him. Thatch breathed a sigh of relief; even if he had to swim for the vessel, he was sure to survive.

Several more sailors arrived at the railing to look down upon Thatch as the ship slowed to come alongside. Thatch estimated the ship was three hundred or so feet in length with a beam of thirty. He gathered up his belongings and carefully stood in the calf-deep water as a ladder was lowered down the side for him to grasp.

His little boat knocked against the metal vessel before slipping underneath the water as he climbed up to receive a helping hand to board the ship.

Thatch stood in his bare feet and chest before a crowd of sailors dressed smartly in dark blue uniforms. His wild hair and beard were in a state of chaos, his face and body battered and beaten from the ordeals of the past days. He looked around the deck of the ship, spotting six mounted guns, even larger than those of the ironclad.

"Me thanks to ye," he said with a toothy grin. "Aye, where be your captain? I'd like a word with him."

A man with thinning dark hair and glasses strode up from midship with an air of authority.

"What have you fished out of the water today, Mr. Stanton?"

"Might be a pirate from the looks of him, or maybe Robinson Crusoe," one of the men who helped Thatch aboard piped up.

"Edward Thatch, at your service," Thatch said with a flourished bow.

The captain put his hands to his hips as he looked Thatch over.

"Looks like you've had a time of it, Mr. Thatch. I'm Lieutenant. Commander Outerbridge, welcome aboard the *Ward.*"

"Me thanks for saving me from a long, tiring swim to shore."

"Mind telling me how you ended up out here in that leaky old boat?" Outerbridge asked.

Suddenly a young man ran breathlessly up with a paper in hand.

"Sir! Sir! Jap sub spotted three miles off the coast!"

Outerbridge took the report the young man handed him and read the contents.

"Alright, men, let's get this ship turned around and on the hunt. Stanton, get Mr. Thatch some dry clothes, we can drop him at Pearl later this evening. Everyone back to their stations and look sharp." Outerbridge then led the way back to the midcastle with a trailing of sailors.

Thatch watched as the crew rushed about with high enthusiasm to their duties.

"Follow me, Mr. Thatch. We'll get you some new clothes," Stanton said, leading the way below deck.

Thatch followed the man, eyes taking in everything that his senses could process. The narrow hallways were illuminated by flameless lanterns, and he passed machinery and mechanisms that completely baffled him as to their purpose. They squeezed by several men as they made their way further below, the ship's engines roaring to life in Thatch's ears, and he felt the power of the ship as it changed course and pushed through the sea.

Stanton led him to a long narrow room that was lined with tall, thin metal closets. He opened several, glancing at the contents before finding what he was looking for.

"You can change your clothes and store yours to dry in here," Stanton said, indicating the closet.

"What sort of hunt are we on?" asked Thatch as he took the offered dry clothes. He held them up and saw they were the same as those the men of the ship were wearing but without the insignias or embellishments of rank.

"We've been getting reports of Jap subs all throughout the island chain. The peace talks keep continuing but no one trusts the Japs, they're looking for a fight after all the embargoes."

"Japs? Who be the Japs?" asked Thatch as he changed his clothes.

"Japanese. You Brits don't call them Japs? Guess you guys have too much to deal with fighting the Krauts and the Macaronis."

Thatch looked up from his dressing with a confused look on his face.

"You a Brit, right? You sound like a Brit."

An alarm sounded at that moment, and a red light near the door began to flash an ominous warning.

"Shit. We need to roll up our flaps and get up top. Sounds like they got eyes on something."

Thatch hastily finished buckling a belt around the waist of his dark blue dungarees and half buttoned his light blue shirt.

"Maybe you should stay down here," Stanton said as he leaned into the hallway with sailors rushing about.

"I've spent many years in the Queen's Navy, I know when to help or stay out the way."

Stanton couldn't hide his excitement and eagerness to be up where the action was.

"Alright, don't do anything that's going to get me in trouble with the big wheel."

Thatch wasn't sure what the term 'big wheel' meant but he nodded his head and said, "You have me word."

The two men made their way back through the belly of the ship and up the stairway leading to the deck. The frantic nature of the men rushing below was gone. They were all business now, each attending a station. Stanton arrived at one of the enormous swivel guns being manned by two men. He turned to Thatch.

"Stand here, Mr. Thatch, try not to get in the way."

"Aye, just watch'n," answered Thatch.

"You brought Crusoe up top?" asked one of the sailors, glancing back at Thatch.

"He's in the British Navy, figured he could see how we deal with Jap subs in the good old USA. Anything spotted yet?"

"Periscope maybe a thousand yards out that way," answered the other sailor.

"Let me in that seat, Kent," Stanton said, and the sailor reluctantly gave up his position at one of the two seats manning the gun.

Thatch watched as the man named Kent put thick goggles that hung from a strap around his neck to his eyes.

"Let's hope this periscope doesn't turn out to be a seal just having a look around," said Kent, scanning the horizon while the ship knifed through the low swells.

"There she is! Nine o'clock!" A shout rang out from a deck above on the midcastle.

"Brockman!" Stanton yelled out and the man in the second seat operated the gun turret to swivel to the nine o'clock position.

"I see it!" Kent exclaimed as he peered through the goggles.

Thatch moved his tall frame to stand just behind Kent and squinted his eyes to make out a thin black rod protruding from the azure waters. The tip seemed to have a rectangular eye which glinted in the sun as it faced them.

"Can we take a shot?" Stanton yelled out.

An officer from the mid-deck yelled out in answer, "Confirmed it's not ours…"

"Fish in the water!" one of the men screamed out from his position at the railing.

Thatch looked off to where the man was pointing to see something just under the surface of the water moving fast toward them forming a V-shaped wake behind.

"Fire at that sub!" the officer from the mid-deck yelled out.

Stanton was already moving the long barrel of the gun into position to target the periscope. Thatch watched as wheels were spun to operate and aim the turret.

The ship decreased speed and steered hard to port to avoid whatever was rapidly approaching them just under the surface of the water.

KABLAM! KABLAM! KABLAM! The noise of the big guns firing was all but ear-shattering. He felt the concussion as the gun manned by Stanton fired its round, and a split second later two more of the ship's guns fired as well.

Three tremendous geysers of seawater shot up in the air around the area of the periscope. When the water cleared Thatch couldn't see the scope cresting the water anymore.

"Did we get it? Do you see it?" Stanton excitedly asked Brockman.

"I can't see it. It submerged. Looking for wreckage…" Brockman's goggles never left his eyes as he answered.

Thatch's ears were still ringing as the *Ward* sailed toward the region of the vessel they had just attacked. He could see the strange fast-moving tube that had been fired at them from under the water passing harmlessly by.

"What the devil was that thing?" he asked.

"Torpedo," Brockman answered as he trained his view on the submerged missile.

"Drop depth charges!" was shouted out from somewhere above deck.

"Ash cans away!" was the shouted response.

Thatch wandered to the ship's railing and gazed out on the waters. He searched for some sign of a vessel below the surface. He couldn't imagine what such a ship would look like that would travel underneath the water instead of on the surface. As the *Ward* moved past the position of the enemy vessel, he could see cylinder-shaped objects dropping into the sea from somewhere at the ship's stern.

He watched them fade from view then a moment later, a safe distance away, came an explosive concussion from deep under the sea. These eruptions brought a large bubble of air mixed with smoke to the surface. These explosions went on for several minutes while the ship paced its way, randomly targeting a foe it could no longer see underneath the surface.

Thatch gazed around the metal ship and watched the young crew as they congratulated each other and went about the business of searching for the remains of their foe, vigilantly looking for any further dangers. He looked back toward the now-distant island and watched the boat traffic on the horizon. He once again felt the disorientation of being out of place and out of time. He knew in his gut that he was no longer in the 1800s. The same vortex that had sucked him out of 1718 a week before had now deposited him further into the future, further in time, along with the pirate hunter, Jennings and the ironclad called the *Comanche*.

His eyes were drawn to an odd sight in the distance. On the horizon, flying in the direction of the island, was a large bird-like object, its metallic wings gleaming in the radiant sunlight as it gracefully traversed the heavens. Perplexed and captivated, he struggled to comprehend the enigmatic sorcery behind this magnificent aerial display. Thatch's eyes were fixed on the avian contraption while it soared over the shimmering sea, and in that moment his heart leaped with joy. As he gazed at the distant flying machine, it passed over the three tall masts of the majestic *Queen Anne's Revenge*.

CHAPTER 2 – BIRDS OF WAR

The pirates slowly rose from their crouched positions as the flying machine roared past the *Queen Anne's Revenge*. Only the short figure of Philip Edward Albert had remained standing, an expression of awe fixed to his face as he watched the machine defy the laws of gravity. In his mind's eye he calculated the sophistication of such a vehicle in comparison to the technology of 1873 and quickly concluded that the validity of the pirates he now surrounded himself with traveling through time was no longer in question. He was indeed not only caught up in their adventure but was now a traveler through time himself. Instead of feeling the shock of the loss of his own time, his pulse quickened with excitement. Philip's gaze followed the… *Air Engine, yes that was what he would call it if he were to have built it*, as his pirate and cowboy companions slowly rose to their feet.

Their clothes were all soaked with seawater from their ordeal of being sucked under the Pacific by the torrential vortex that had claimed the *Queen Anne's Revenge*. They had emerged dazzled by the brightness of the sun and their good fortune to have survived not only the drowning of the ship but the battle against the ironclad that had been dragged to the bottom of the sea along with them, though it was now nowhere in sight.

Charles Vane shook his head like a wet dog as the flying vehicle shrank into the distance. Anger and frustration, added to the shock of the sight, was too much for his short temper and he turned to Philip. He strode quickly over and grabbed the man by the scruff of his shirt and pushed him halfway over the ship's railing.

"What the devil was that, scientist?" he spat.

"I don't… know. I've never seen such a sight," Philip stuttered out as his upper body was now hanging over the azure sea. He wasn't in danger of dying from a fall but believed he was inches from a throttling by the brutal pirate that clutched him.

"You be standing there smiling like a damn lark! What do you know?" raged Vane.

"We've traveled in time again. *You've* traveled in time again. The vortex from your story in the saloon the night we met, it must have been the same," Philip said quickly as the crew began to crowd around them. He looked at their faces—Black Caesar, Anne Bonny, Mary Read, Sam Bellamy, Charlotte De Berry, Bart Roberts, and his crew. He saw Jesse and Frank James shoulder their way closer to him.

"That beast, in the sky…" Vane started to ask.

"I don't know! I've never seen anything like it, an air engine. You saw the man inside driving it? We must be in a future time where such a thing is possible, common even," Philip said teetering on the edge as Vane pushed him further off the deck.

"Mr. Vane, please unhand Mr. Albert. His insight will be most valuable if we are in want to get home," said Colette from behind Black Caesar.

Vane scowled at Philip and tightened his grip, wanting to take his frustration out on this skinny little worm of a man, helpful or not.

"Charles, let him be!" Black Caesar commanded with a heavy hand clenching Vane's shoulder.

Vane glanced back at the looming pirate behind him, then back at the frightened Philip. He let out a snort of exasperation, gave his victim one more push, then picked him off the rail and set him roughly to the deck and strode away, shoving people aside as he sought space from the crowd.

"The man's a mindless brute," Philip said rubbing his aching neck.

Black Caesar set a consoling hand on Philip's head and patted it. It didn't help as the hand was big enough to crush his head, so all it did was stir up thoughts of mortality. And his mortality had been in constant question since he met these men and women such a short time ago.

He anxiously reached into his pocket and pulled his metal cigarette case out, flipping it open and extracted the paper-rolled tobacco. He popped the cigarette between his lips and realized it was soaking wet. The figure of Colette Dallaire, wet blonde hair, rouge still in place accentuating her high cheek bones, a calming smile on her lovely face, took the useless cigarette from his mouth and discarded it.

"Are you okay, Mr. Albert?" she asked with genuine concern.

Philip saw the young Chinese boy, Tom, next to her with eyes full of apprehension. The grown men and women aboard this ship were barely holding themselves together; how could this adolescent scamp be expected to have a clear head? Philip took a deep breath and pulled himself erect.

"I am, Miss Dallaire. I'll be quite fine. A grand adventure this is," he said with a nervous snort.

"Yes, grand." Colette moved to the railing and took in the coastline of the island before them. Philip turned and joined her; his hands gripped the solid wood of the railing tightly for the sake of security, and she watched his head turn to make sure Vane was not behind him. "You're confident we have traveled to a new time?" she asked.

"All evidence presented points to that conclusion."

This was how his new pirate friends had traveled from their time of 1718, he realized. It wasn't an easy story to believe when they entered his life a week ago in the saloon called The Paris, but facts were facts, and these men and women were indeed pirates of another age.

An idea was forming in the back of his brain that he struggled to bring forth, to comprehend… why were they not in the same location as the one they left? They were clearly in a tropical zone far from the coast of San Francisco. He remembered the pirates telling him they had arrived in the bay of San Francisco from the Caribbean Sea, thousands of miles away. Philip closed his eyes forcing his thoughts to pick out the answers, something to do with the earth rotating…

"What in the Sam Hill was that?" Jesse James exclaimed, hitting Philip's shoulder with the back of his hand.

"It sounded like one of your trains but moves through the air without tracks," said Charlotte as she glanced from Philip to the distant flying machine. "Your time has more marvels than the Spanish have gold."

"Not our time, Miss Charlotte. No such device exists," Colette said, then turned to face Philip. "I'm I correct in saying so?"

Philip just stared back at the many faces gathered around the deck of the ship looking to him for answers. The interruption had caused the inner workings of his time travel location solution to fade back into obscurity. His brow knitted but no words were forthcoming from his lips.

"I'll say you're correct, miss," Chester piped up. "There are no such things as flying machines, at least where we come from."

Sam Bellamy sank down to sit on the floor, back against the railing. He looked up at the sky then put his head in his hands, overwhelmed and distraught. The group was silent as they started to process their situation. A great unknown lay before them, both in place as well as in time. Most of the crew was not equipped to comprehend their predicament but felt fortunate that they were alive after their last battle and near disaster.

"Is there any sign of Edward or the ironclad?" Colette asked, setting her hands on the railing as she scanned the horizon. Her chest tightened with longing, heart aching for even the faintest sign that Edward had survived—that fate had carried him with them through the storm of time.

"That ship went down the spiraling sea, same as we," Mary Read said as she squeezed the seawater out of her dark red locks.

"Edward? Did he…" Colette asked with trepidation.

"I'd seen him before we went under, crawling into the turret, but then we all were taken by the sea," Anne said.

"The captain is alive?" asked the cabin boy, Tom, hopefully.

"A charmed life as any rascal I've met. Blackbeard has assuredly defeated the pirate hunter and Jennings alike, either with his wit or his brawn, dear boy," Roberts said with a flourish. He glanced at the hopeful yet wary face of Colette, the woman used by Woodes Rogers to capture Blackbeard because of their budding feelings toward one another, or so he'd been told by his precious Charlotte.

"Ain't that right, Caesar? Your dear captain's been in worse scrapes, probably taken that iron bucket as a prize," Roberts finished in an effort to steady Colette's and Tom's worried hearts.

Black Caesar cast a look down at Robert and quickly picked up the rally.

"Aye, the many lives of a cat with still more to spare," he said with forced jolly.

Bart Robert's extended his hand to the seated Sam Bellamy who sighed and allowed Roberts to help him to his feet. Roberts then leaped onto a crate with athletic agility and turned to address the entire crew.

"That island before us is called Hawaii. Sam and many of us were in these waters only days ago. That may very well have been in some distant time by a magic or divine intervention but there it lies, with fresh water, food, and supplies. Let's make fast repairs to the rigging and hoist any of the spare sails in the hold. Then we make port and spend some of the plunder we are all entitled to! Huzzah!" he yelled with a fist in the air.

Many men took up Roberts' shout of huzzah. This speech got the crew going and out of any dark mood they had fallen into. The thought of dividing up the silver and gold erased any fears or depression that might have become entrenched in their psyches.

"You heard him, get movin' you sad lot!" Black Caesar bellowed, sending everyone scampering for a job to perform.

Within minutes Tom and the lithe Charlotte De Berry were high above the deck climbing the rigging and masts like spiders on a web. Though Tom had only begun his training a mere day ago he was a natural at navigating the ropes, knots, stays and crosstrees. He watched and listened to Charlotte as she pointed and called out orders to him, feeling a surge of pride as damaged sheets were lowered and fresh ones hoisted up in their place. From his vantage he was able to use the knife he was entrusted with to cut loose lines that had snapped from the storm or been cut by the shrapnel in their battle with the *Comanche*.

Down on the deck the dashing Bart Roberts rolled up his sleeves and lent a hand where necessary. The crew of the *Queen Anne's Revenge* was now large enough with the addition of his men from the sunken freighter *Charlotte's Fortune* to function as a 200-ton, forty-gun frigate should. Maybe they lacked the skilled sailors of his day, and the ship may be shy of a dozen or so gunners to man all forty, but it would be an easy sail into the Hawaiian harbor today.

He strode up to the little fellow everyone called 'the scientist'; Philip was his name, he remembered on approach. The man wasn't helping at the moment in the ship's readiness, instead he stood squinting toward the tremendous ships that crowded the distant bay.

Roberts stood next to him and pulled a spyglass from his belt; it was a well-made brass unit with finely ground glass that greatly enhanced one's view through it. The ships were indeed enormous and armed with cannons the like of which he'd never seen. He handed the spyglass to Philip so the man could assess the docked and moored fleet with a magnified view.

Philip gazed at the ships then focused his attention on the surrounding city. It was clean and organized, unlike any place he'd ever been. So much perfection and precision in the engineering of ships and buildings, even the houses. He handed the spyglass back to the current captain of the pirate ship.

"Are the natives going to receive us with goodwill, Mr. Roberts?" he asked.

"'Twas not the reception we experienced last time we were in this port, but I dare say they had warrant to be discontented with our arrival." Roberts paused in thought. "Eighteen seventy-three... are you of the mind we are a far cry from that year?"

Philip didn't take his eyes off the coastline when he answered, "I am. A very far cry."

Roberts nodded. He looked at the placement of the sun in the east— close to eight in the morning.

"We shall make port far before the midday sun. I shall see if there is dry powder just in case we humble traders are unwelcome."

Philip watched Roberts stride away to confer with Black Caesar. He knew it would be ill-advised to start trouble with the likes of an armed fleet such as was sitting in the Hawaiian harbor, but he held his tongue. These pirates may be lacking in education and scientific knowledge, but he had learned they were not without intelligence and savvy. He didn't doubt for an instant that the new captain of the *Queen Anne's Revenge* understood the folly of starting a battle with a ship of the 1700s against ships of... whatever distant future date they currently resided in.

A soft sound of thunder brought his attention to the south side of the island. The clear sky in that direction was dotted with winged craft buzzing low along the inland shores like bees in a flower garden.

More thunder pattered to his ears with no lightning or clouds visible in any direction. Philip longed for the spyglass as he strained his vision to see the distant air engines, his mind quickly counting many dozens soaring above the terrain. Smoke. Smoke and explosions erupted underneath the craft as they passed. Being a man of science, one specializing in combustibles and incendiary devices used in mining, he quickly realized he was witnessing an attack on the island.

The flock of air engines dropped their bombs and continued on their course from west to east, heading directly toward the quiet harbor the *Queen Anne's Revenge* was sailing to. The destruction in their wake, while distant, grew in smoke and flame with each passing winged craft.

"What the devil are those?"

Philip pulled his eyes from the scene to see the comely face of Anne Bonny who had silently arrived to stand next to him. Her brows knitted as she glared at the island, hand resting on the grip of her hip-holstered pistol, finger tapping it with anticipation of aggression. Her scent of sandalwood and huckleberry clouded his thoughts momentarily.

Philip glanced around as more crew members caught the sounds and sight of the violence.

He met Anne's spirited eyes with his own. "Those are... birds of war, my dear."

CHAPTER 3 – CRUSOE

"Hey, Crusoe!" the sailor named Kent called out as he, Stanton, and Brockman approached Thatch who was standing at the railing, watching the distant *Queen Anne's Revenge* raising her sails.

"First day on the *Ward* and you get to watch us sink a Jap sub, ain't you one lucky bastard," Brockman said.

Stanton whistled. "Look at that old beauty." He moved his lanky frame next to Thatch. "Eighteenth-century replica I bet."

Thatch turned and narrowed his eyes at the man. "That be me ship, the *Queen Anne's Revenge*. Launched in 1710, she be one of the finest ships ever to sail."

"Bullshit. Crusoe, a ship that old would have rotted away a century ago," Kent said dismissively.

Thatch looked hard at Kent, sizing him up. The young sailor was a few inches shorter but a good two stones heavier with a mixture of muscle and thickness to his arms and chest. Thatch aggressively moved toward him and confronted him just the same. "A man calls another a liar, he best be ready to bleed or draw blood."

Kent's face went from a witless grin to genuine fear under Thatch's dark, severe glare. The other two sailors stood in shocked silence as the pirate drew himself up, standing inches from Kent.

"I don't know who or what a Crusoe is, but I am starting to believe it to be unkind, an insult. I'm thinking you don't want to be insulting me again, sailor. And ye can start addressing me as captain, Captain Blackbeard."

"Like the pirate Blackbeard?" Kent softly stammered.

"Aye, like the pirate Blackbeard."

Kent looked from the wild-eyed bearded man to the distant eighteenth-century frigate with confusion and awe on his face.

The sounds of muffled explosions caused the four men to slowly turn toward the southern coastline of the island. A silence among the sailors quickly enveloped the entire ship as all attention turned toward the squadrons of planes dropping their munitions on the airfield and buildings.

"Battle stations!" The call came from an officer standing mid-deck with a desperate yet angry note in his voice to bring the crew to action. The clanging of a bell rang out as men ran across the decks, slid down ladders, and dodged other crew members to reach their stations.

Blackbeard watched as the winged craft continued their way toward the east after dropping their grenades, leaving clouds of smoke from the fires raging below. His thick, dark brows knitted together as he saw the path of the craft would be toward the *Queen Anne's Revenge*.

"Bloody hell."

Thatch charged up the ladder toward the midcastle where the pilot house was located while the engines could be heard, noisily accelerating the ship to intercept the flying enemy. He couldn't fathom the time and materials it would take to build such a ship as this. The power and strength surging under his feet was unlike anything he had ever encountered.

When he reached the top deck he could see Captain Outerbridge through the window, goggles held to his face, watching the flying craft in the distance. Six other men moved around him with the precision of hands on a clock, each one focused on their task.

Thatch burst through the open door and stopped as he took in the strangeness of the pilot house: gray metal and brass everywhere; the thick glass windows so clear as to be nearly invisible; the large wheel manned by a sailor turned with little effort from the thin, young lad like the great beast of a ship was lending a helping hand. Several men stood staring out the windows and moving knobs and switches mounted on cabinets while calling out navigational headings and statuses.

"Great Poseidon," Thatch said under his breath as he paused to let his eyes roam the metal and brass fixtures that dominated the room.

"Mr. Thatch, I will ask you to please confine yourself below deck. You've unfortunately found yourself in a dire situation in which we can't drop you off and we can't have you getting in the way," Outerbridge said then turned to one of the sailors in the room. "Ensign, escort our guest below deck, he can stay in the crew's quarters for the moment."

Thatch switched out of the stupor that had overtaken him. "You need to take me to me ship, it's a mere league off the port side."

"The Japs just declared war, man! Taxiing you to your ship is not a priority. Yeoman, sound general stations and make sure those .50-calibers are ready for action." Outerbridge put his goggles up to his eyes and followed the winged craft through the window.

Thatch watched as the yeoman took a black handle with cupped ends off the wall. The handle was attached to a black cord connected to a box mounted to the metal wall. He brought the handle to the side of his face, one cup pressed to his ear, the other to his mouth.

"Alert! General stations, all hands general stations."

Thatch spun in place as the man's voice could be heard not only in the room but echoing loudly outside. *The wonders of this ship…* His mind snapped back to the issue at hand. He moved toward the window where he could see the *Queen Anne* in the distance. The flock of winged craft were moments away from it.

"Captain, me crew, me woman… they need me. I must get to my ship!"

Outerbridge watched the scene with his binoculars. The eighteenth-century sailing ship was a sight—beautiful lines, ornamental woodwork throughout the large three-masted frigate. He could see a sizable crew working the rigging bringing the ship to full sail. Outerbridge had done his fair share of sailing in his youth with his father and uncles. The largest boat he ever experienced sailing was a forty-foot sloop back in Boston. It was an exhilarating feeling when the sloop had a brisk wind at its stern. Sailing aboard the vessel he was now staring at would be something else entirely.

He shifted his focus back to the Japanese planes flying toward the ship Thatch claimed to captain. It might be possible to reach the ship and intercept those bombers and Zeros before they made their way toward Pearl, which was undoubtedly their next objective. The entire fleet of US battleships was harbored there in the sleepy bay like sitting ducks. He turned toward his helmsman: "Set a course toward that tall ship and let's see if we can take out some birds on the way."

"Aye, aye, Captain."

"You have me thanks," Thatch said and turned to rush out the door of the pilot house.

"I'd still like you to wait below Mr…" Outerbridge got out as Blackbeard made his exit. He looked at one of the ensigns and gestured for him to go after the man.

Thatch hastened down the stairs to the main deck and came to a stop at the bow. The *Ward* had quickly been brought to speed. Thatch looked down as its V-shaped hull cut through the seas like a knife. She must be sailing close to thirty knots, faster than Thatch had ever traveled in his life, that is if you didn't count his travel through time. He smiled at that thought, as well as the thrill of cutting through the wind and water at this accelerated pace. Unfortunately, that smile faded fast as the flying craft approaching the *Queen Anne's Revenge* began spitting out their munitions at her.

Black Bart Roberts had claimed his spot at the large, polished wheel of the *Queen Anne's Revenge* from Black Caesar, the big man reluctantly yielding the position. The ship moved swiftly under full sail… well, close to full sail. There were still several damaged sheets that were not able to be replaced by the spares stored in the hold. Roberts watched as the graceful and lithe form of his newly beloved Charlotte swung to the deck near the bow to adjust a line, hence giving one of the sheets more wind.

"She rides high and fast on the water, Caesar!"

"Aye," Black Caesar answered without emotion, muscular arms crossed, sea legs keeping his big frame steady.

"Think Blackbeard be letting me keep her?"

Black Caesar turned toward him with a heated look.

Roberts smiled wide and laughed.

"I say in jest, mate. She is a fine ship though, and the old rogue may be lost to time. We may never see that magnificent beard again."

"I'll be damned if I…" Black Caesar's response was cut short by the shouting of Philip as he and Colette rushed toward them from the stern. Philip strode with a limping gait and Colette ran beside him, both hands hiking her dress to allow her legs to move with longer strides. Caesar narrowed his eyes in an effort to surmise the reason for these two landlubbers to be storming the pilot deck. They were yelling something about wings and a word he couldn't place as they rushed toward them.

"The air engines! We need to go faster!" yelled the little scientist.

Chaos erupted at that moment for the crew and passengers of the *Queen Anne's Revenge.* Thundering shots sounded and shrapnel of wood exploded from the decking as the roar of one of the winged craft tore through the sky a mere hundred feet above the masts. Two men fell to the deck in a spray of blood and ruined flesh. A twin set of rounds chased across the aftcastle as a winged craft spat fire from its nose.

"Man the swivel guns by God!" Roberts screamed above the deafening sounds of the craft flying overhead, their guns raining down destruction as they passed.

Anne Bonny slid to a stop upon reaching the aft swivel gun before anyone else. She reached down and flipped open the secured wooden box next to the rail-mounted cannon. She hastily started the breech-loading process as Jesse, Frank, and Mary arrived to assist. Anne stared into the sky as she gave way for Mary to take charge of loading the weapon for firing. The sky was filled with winged craft spread out over the coast heading for the same harbor as they were. Several had taken aim at their frigate as they flew by. She watched as another one dropped low to take a firing run at them, launching its attack many yards distant, sending two by two violent splashes marching toward the ship.

BLAM! BLAM! BLAM! Anne flinched as Jesse and Frank James began firing their pistols at the craft. BLAM! A third gun fired, and Anne noticed the small cabin boy, Tom, his shoulders and arms kicking back as he squinted his left eye and fired one of Thatch's big revolvers held tightly in both hands.

"Ready!" yelled Mary holding the smoldering linstock next to the fire chamber. This brought Anne's eyes back to the sky. She took aim at the flying beast as its rounds of shot were about to reach them.

"Fire!" Anne called and steadfastly held the swivel gun in line with the oncoming craft.

KABAM!

The driver of the craft tipped his wings to port when he saw the discharge from the cannon. Anne's shot missed but the craft gave up its combat run and flew past the port side of the ship out of their view. They all looked back at the oncoming flock and began the process of reloading their weapons.

"What the devil be those beasts?" Mary asked as she finished reloading.

"Dragons." Tom looked up at her as he shook out the revolver's chamber, empty shells bouncing off the deck and rolling with the pitch of the sailing ship.

The adults exchanged quick furtive glances as they all finished reloading their weapons.

Charles Vane was shouting orders to the green sailors that struggled with their stations as he made his way toward the pilot deck. Black Sam Bellamy followed in his wake.

Bart Roberts shouted out an order to Charlotte while pointing to a sheet that had been damaged in the attack. The woman was moving swiftly through the rat nest toward the thrashing sail.

"Turn to port and give them bastards a broadside!" Vane shouted at Roberts as he arrived around the crowded wheel.

"They ride too high, you clodpate!" said Sam irritably.

Vane turned to the younger man and shoved him backwards. "You'd have us sit with our thumbs in our arse?"

"We need to head further out to sea," Philip said to them. "They are not after us. Look, they are heading toward the harbor."

"Aye, we are just an easy target on the way," Roberts said as two more craft roared overhead. He looked aft and saw them drop low for a firing run on the frigate.

"Let me at the helm." Vane pushed to take the wheel from Roberts who pushed him back.

"Stop! There are too many captains and other jobs to be done," Colette scolded the ornery men.

Roberts looked aft again, eyeing Anne, Mary and the cowboys training their weapons on the incoming craft.

"I'll turn hard to port," he said, "that may bring up our starboard side guns to have a chance, seeing how they drop low when attacking. You two get to the gun decks and ready the crew."

"Grapeshot if you have it," suggested Philip.

Sam and Vane nodded and rushed from the aftcastle to the gun decks where the new crew stood waiting for orders.

The *Queen Anne's Revenge* had a total of forty guns. The main deck held twenty cannons, some mounted on swivels, most were fixed three-, six- and twelve-pounders spread out evenly on the starboard and port sides. The lower gun deck was located one level below the main deck. The wide hold had been constructed with ten gunports on each side that allowed cannon to be moved forward so that the deadly barrels could be maneuvered and unleashed once the port covers were raised.

Charles Vane left Sam Bellamy on the main deck while he descended the steps two at a time to the gun deck. Twenty-seven men manning the cannons all looked up at his arrival. Vane felt a surge of pride and excitement as he strode into the hold.

"Open the ports, you scallywags, and load them guns with grapeshot. We're going to hunt us some birds this fine day."

The men raised the covers on the ports and by cranking the rope braces they moved the barrels to protrude out of the gunports. The cannons were of varying design, some breech-loaders, some muzzle-loaders, but these men had been able to quickly pick up on the process.

"We's going to give 'em a black eye from the starboard side, so make ready," Vane ordered as he paced the line before kneeling to gaze out through one of the gunports at the view. The crew could hear the roar of the flying engines overhead and cringed as their munitions began to sound while they took aim at the frigate from the sky.

The ship abruptly turned hard to port, and their entire world tilted sharply, causing everyone to brace themselves and hang onto anything near before they slipped across the deck. Vane held a hand to the porthole and kept his eye on the sky as the starboard side tilted up, losing site of the water below. He gestured his other arm up to ready the gun crews. The men stood at the ready with linstocks poised above the firing holes.

Vane leaned his face further out the port, aware that he would quickly need to move away before giving the order to fire the cannon whose barrel was inches from his face. The ship was close to completing its sharp turn and the starboard-side walls of the hull were at their apex. Vane saw three of the winged monsters come into view. He swung his head back inside and turned toward the awaiting gun men.

"Now!"

The ear-rattling sound of ten cannons firing almost at once boomed through the enclosed gun deck, followed seconds later by the concussion from the cannons on the deck above where Vane had left Sam Bellamy.

The heavy guns slammed back against their braces and smoke from the powder wafted throughout the hold. Vane pulled himself toward the porthole and sought a view of the battle.

Sam Bellamy had a much better view from the main deck. His ears rang from the blasts and his heart soared as grapeshot ripped into one of the flying craft sending it careening off, smoking, spitting fire as it dived down and crashed into the sea.

A great cheer erupted from the entire crew watching as the two other winged craft dodged further away, giving wide berth to the forty-gun vessel.

"That will teach the monsters, lads. Prepare to give 'em another taste!"

Sam's optimism faded with his smile as he turned to see dozens more of the flying beasts headed toward them. One of the three they had targeted also circled around to make another run at the fleeing pirate ship. The *Queen Anne's Revenge* even at full sail was no match for the speed of these craft. Sam guessed that they were flying three to four times as fast as their ship could sail. Their deafening roar drowned out all calls coming from the aftcastle warning of the incoming attack.

Sam screamed for the cannon to be reloaded but that job was violently interrupted by rounds ripping across the deck as the flying vessels dived out of the sky toward the wooden frigate desperately trying to make an escape. Round after round ate up the wood and iron as they raked the ship. Men and equipment were struck by the bullets and shrapnel. One round burst against the barrel of the cannon which Sam stood close to. It shattered against the iron, ricocheting the projectile into his abdomen.

CHAPTER 4 – FISH IN THE WATER

There was no need for the captain to give the order to fire. Once the *Ward* was in range for the anti-aircraft guns to target the Japanese fighter planes the gun crews opened with one of the three-inch, .23-caliber cannons firing at a rate of nine rounds per minute. The *Ward* was equipped with three such weapons. They had a range of eight thousand yards and the *Ward* was closing on the fight surrounding the wooden tall ship at thirty knots.

For Edward Thatch, the anger was rising to the boiling point. He had watched as the *Queen Anne's Revenge* managed a hard turn to port that brought the starboard side of the ship to an almost forty-five-degree elevation allowing a full broadside to target the deadly craft. It was a maneuver that was unlikely to be effective twice.

The winged craft were now swooping around his frigate like vultures, unleashing a fury that the ship wasn't equipped to withstand. He stood at the most forward position on the *Ward* with the booming blast of the long-barreled cannons sounding behind him in a satisfying tone of destruction. They had yet to hit the nimble targets but the speed of their reload was giving him hope. If this ship was his he would have quickly outfitted it with dozens more of the breech-loading guns.

Thatch had left Black Bart Roberts in command of his ship before he disembarked to confront the pirate hunter Woodes Rogers. Rogers had held the lovely Colette Dallaire at gunpoint on the deck of the ironclad offering an exchange of her life for his. Roberts had only joined his crew moments before along with a full complement of able-bodied seamen. If Roberts was still at the helm, he was doing his damnedest to escape this onslaught. Thatch could conceive of no options that Roberts hadn't tried to avoid the attack he was under. They were outgunned and outmaneuvered. There was no defense the *Queen Anne's Revenge* had against a flying adversary such as these.

A second gun, located amidships, joined the fight. He noticed its loud bark booming in his ears amid the shots from the first gun. He glanced back at the four men manning the cannon closest to him. They were well trained and practiced, working in harmony to load the next projectile once one was dispensed. The gun rose and swerved to track its target. Thatch burned the motions and mechanics the sailors used to operate the cannon into his memory.

The roar of the enemy craft rose above the booming cannon blasts as they swooped down on the *Ward*. There was a sudden outcry as one dropped a projectile from its underbelly. Thatch watched with horror as the finned cylinder splashed into the water and shot toward the ship propelled by spinning blades mounted on the rear. What turned those blades he couldn't fathom, but his heart was leaping from his chest as the rest of the crew pointed and made ready for devastation. He knew without being told it was a bomb of some sort racing toward the hull of the ship.

The ship lurched under his feet and Thatch gripped the railing with his knuckles turning white as the *Ward* executed a hard turn attempting to avoid the oncoming projectile hunting them like a shark smelling blood. Rounds spit out from a winged craft flying low on a lethal run, first hitting the water thirty yards off the port side, then marching closer until finally clanging and ripping into the side and deck of the *Ward*.

Sailors ran and dived for cover, mercifully avoiding the deadly shells. Thatch leaned over the rail as he watched the water-bound missile narrowly miss the stern of the vessel he was conscripted to. His eyes locked on a flying craft dropping low for an attack run at the ship. He heard the calling of orders and directions from the gun manned by Stanton, Kent and the other sailors known to him. He didn't need to look back at them to realize they saw this incoming threat. He watched as the craft pointed its blunt black nose at the *Ward*. Time seemed to slow for him as the roar of its engines increased and his view narrowed in on the cylinder-shaped bomb hanging beneath its belly.

KAPOW! The cannon behind him sounded and he felt the atmosphere reverberate as its charge blasted out and flew, seeking its target. Thatch instinctively flinched as the cannon-shot and the body of the flying craft met in an explosion of hot metal, glass, and flesh. The largest pieces of the beast skipped across the sea; several bits clanged against the iron skin of the *Ward*.

A cheer went up from the sailors on deck and Thatch watched as the remaining flying ships tipped their wings toward the island and abandoned their attack on the *Ward* as well as the *Queen Anne's Revenge* as if an order had been communicated throughout the entire flock. They moved swiftly toward the distant harbor that was now dotted with smoke, flame, and explosions. The entire fleet of craft dove toward the moored ships and created a zone of destruction and mayhem the scale of which Thatch had never seen.

He turned to see the *Queen Anne's Revenge* seeking out a path to a nearby cove while a waft of smoke swirled from the port side. It didn't look devastating from his vantage point, but fire could quickly become uncontrollable on a wooden vessel. He said a prayer for Roberts and the crew to put out the fire and find refuge in shallow water so as to lick their wounds.

He breathed deeply, knowing he was now on a path leading into a battle that wasn't his own.

He found himself in a war between two enemies, with no stance to take. What side did he find himself on? The oppressors or the oppressed? The *Ward* sailed with all haste to reach the battle. He understood that there would be no attempt made to drop him on board the *Queen Anne's Revenge*. He could jump ship and swim for it, but the distance was too great with Roberts already sailing toward the cove and the *Ward* moving in the opposite direction. Thatch was resigned to be happy the *Revenge* survived, and he would need to do the same if he was to be reunited with his ship, crew, and Colette.

He strode back to the bow and watched the battle unfold before him, peppered by warm, salty spray as the hull aggressively chopped through the sea. Even with the incredible speed at which this vessel traveled, the distance was too great for its captain to make an impact on the devastating fight ahead. He could see the enemy delivering blow after blow to the ships crowding the harbor.

It reminded him of the saying *"like shooting fish in a barrel."* There was nowhere for the ships to go. They could stand and fight, but he imagined they were lightly crewed, moored and docked as they were. This would be a catastrophic blow to the fleet.

It dawned on him that for the past week and more he had assumed these ships encased in metal would be impervious to cannon fire and attacks, but of course there would arise the ability to overcome those defenses. The armor of knights was once thought to be impenetrable until the design of the long bow, which had the ability to send an arrow at such a velocity as to pierce the metal even at great distances. The fortified stone of a fort also fell to the onslaught of cannon fire. War will always find a way to equalize the odds. He would need time to learn the new ways of war but then, as he always did, he would seek out power and treasure to rule the seas.

CHAPTER 5 – SURGEON

Philip frantically worked to clean out Sam Bellamy's wound as dark blood poured from his belly. Colette knelt beside him holding Sam's head as the poor man moaned with pain, eyes bloodshot and intense.

"Hold on, Sammy. It's going to be alright, mate," Roberts said as he looked down desperately at his friend. He knew little about surgery but had seen enough wounds to know that only a miracle could save Sam.

"Are there surgical instruments on board?" Philip called out.

Roberts nodded his head. "Caesar has gone to retrieve them."

The deck of the ship was a flurry of erratic activity as fires were battled and wounded were tended to. There were several bodies of fallen sailors that created obstacles for the crew as they rushed to save the damaged ship. The men and women moved about with caution and respect while in close quarters to their fallen brethren.

Black Caesar arrived and placed a large wooden box next to the patient, the contents clanking inside. Philip opened the box and looked up at Black Caesar as he pulled out instruments that belonged more in a woodworking tool kit then a surgical one. He realized that these were authentic implements of the eighteenth century. They were large and clumsy compared to the delicate medical tools of 1873. How was he expected to operate with these blunt, tools he thought in a panic. He needed to make use of them the best he could though.

Bellamy had a piece of shrapnel the size of a screwdriver embedded in his abdomen. Blood flowed from the wound freely with each beat of the pirate's heart. Philip found a pair of clamps and looked them over. Rust, dirt, and God knows what else coated them. He had already been given a bowl of fresh water but that was now tinged red with Bellamy's blood as Colette made use of the water and cloth to staunch and clean other wounds.

Philip dipped the clamps into the water and wiped them on a cloth. He took the matches from his pocket and gave them to Colette.

"Please try to light one, dear."

Colette went through several damp sticks, striking them, but without success.

"I'm so sorry. They won't work."

"Get me some fire, hurry!" Philip told Caesar.

Caesar quickly made his way to the closest of the several burning spots of the ship. He used his boot to break a piece of burning wood that had one end not yet aflame. He picked up the heated plank and held it like a torch as he made his way back to Philip.

"Hold it underneath these clamps."

Philip heated the implements over the flames in hopes of purifying the metal.

Bellamy's breathing began to shallow, and Philip knew time was short. He used the heated clamps to dig out the shrapnel, prying and pulling the lodged material from Bellamy's insides. The man yelled out in pain and thrashed against the deck in an attempt to escape the surgery.

"Hold him down!"

Black Caesar, Roberts and Colette did their best to steady Sam as Philip worked to remove the shrapnel.

Philip found a good grip on it and slowly extracted the metal. It was longer than he had estimated, and as it came out so did a larger flood of blood and intestinal matter. Philip did his best to staunch the bleeding, but he realized Bellamy was lost.

Roberts grabbed Sam's shoulders and held him firm.

"Don't you go, Sammy, stay with me, brother."

"Maria, dear Maria…" Sam's voice was low and distant.

"Sammy, no," Roberts told him as he held his shoulders.

The loss of blood was too great, and the pirate's face rapidly gave up its color to a haunted shade of white. His wide eyes clouded over, and his breath stopped.

Roberts gently let go of Sam and sat back, staring up at the sky.

They all were silent for a moment. Colette gently closed Sam's eyes with her hand, saying a quiet prayer.

Roberts crossed his chest then rose to look around the deck. A fire near the aftcastle was still spreading even though men continued to fight it. He squeezed Black Caesar's shoulder, and the two men hurried to help save the ship.

Colette looked at the dejected Philip and set her hand on his. He looked up at her and she could see that losing the man was wreaking havoc on Philip's nerves.

"There are more that need aid, let's find somewhere we can be of service."

Philip nodded to her, and she helped him to his feet. They moved to find another wounded crew member to assist, Philip carrying his bloodied box of tools.

Charlotte De Berry was at the helm, young Tom standing beside her waiting for an order. She had the ship pointed toward a large cove and ordered the sails to be reefed. There were large rocks protruding from the starboard side fifty or so yards from shore.

She looked down at Tom to give him an order, the boy's narrow eyes focused on her with intensity.

"We'll need to drop anchor precisely when I say. Go make sure someone is ready and that I'm heard."

Tom nodded and left at the speed of a rabbit, finding Black Ceasar standing a head taller than the other men surrounded by swirling wood smoke.

"We need to drop anchor on Miss Charlotte's orders."

Ceasar looked up from his battle with the dwindling flames that were eating away at the fine woodwork of the aft deck. He dropped his now empty water bucket and made his way toward the aft anchor windlass. He grabbed the attention of Mary Read, Anne Bonny and the James brothers.

"Boy, go stand at the main mast and await Charlotte's order."

Ceasar watched as the cove drew closer while the tide and momentum propelled the frigate toward it.

"Mary, take Frank to the fore anchor. Anne and Jesse, we'll man the aft."

Ceasar felt uneasy as he watched several rocks and reefs come into view while he hurried toward the aft of the ship. The *Queen Anne's Revenge* had already rested on the bottom of the sea just days ago and he was loath to see that happen again. Charlotte De Berry, with her poor eyesight at the helm, was draining his confidence but there was little to be done about it now.

The cowboy and the feisty young red-headed pirate stood with him at the ready to drop the anchor.

Charlotte squinted as she watched the waves crash into the large rocks scattered throughout the cove. She judged the height of the reef and the rising sand the best she could. It was time to bring the ship to a halt.

"Aft anchor!"

Tom loudly repeated her order from his position at the main mast.

Ceasar and Anne released the half ton anchor to splash down into the clear blue water. In a few seconds the entire ship lurched as the anchor found the sea floor and dragged several feet before stopping the vessel.

Charlotte held her steady as the anchor caught then allowed the ship to rotate parallel to the shore. She then gave the order for the bow anchor to be released.

Frank and Mary immediately dropped the anchor, and the ship was secured safely, twenty yards from a large lava rock peeking out above the water's surface but whose hull-crushing form extended out underneath for ten yards. Mary shook her head at the closeness of the potentially devastating obstacle they narrowly missed.

"There be the best example of blind luck," Mary said, nodding toward Charlotte. Frank looked at the rock then at the dreadlocked lady pirate who was walking away from the wheel. Mary began to laugh at her own joke that Frank didn't understand as he was unaware of Charlotte's poor eyesight.

The last of the fires were extinguished and the battle-weary crew turned their attention to the fallen men. Bellamy and the bodies of the other unfortunate sailors were moved to the mid-deck and covered with cloth.

Roberts called the crew together and he stood at the railing with the burning harbor of Honolulu off in the distance. He was soaked with seawater as they all were from being sucked into the mouth of the whirlpool. He used his hands to smooth his wet hair away from his soot-stained face. Roberts wore his white cotton poet shirt, open low at his chest. The ornate cross made of a crystalline white-pink metal encrusted with diamonds lay against his tan, exposed skin. The man's clothes clung wet to his figure, and he was exhausted yet managed to remain one of the most dashing and dynamic captains ever to sail as he addressed the crowded deck.

"I fear we find ourselves moved in time, yet again." He glanced over to the gathering of nineteenth-century men from the mutinied *Lurline* he had captained only a few hours ago. That ship now rested at the bottom of the sea near San Francisco, now back somewhere in time. "Some of you will be experiencing this bit of magic for the first time. We now have landed in this place, caught in a battle, not of our own, but one that has claimed the lives of our trusted mates."

Roberts stared at the shrouded bodies, not knowing which blanket of canvas covered Sam Bellamy.

"The magic of this is unknown. The mechanism to deliver us home is not within our grasp and may never be attained. I stand with you, without answers to the sights, horrors… and marvels we have just witnessed. We are battered and burnt but we are not sunk."

Roberts gestured with his hand at the coastline and city that stretched behind him. He turned his head and watched as the attacking airships began to turn from the harbor and fly out to sea, their battle seemingly won.

"I have been to this island before, as have many of you standing here. It has changed greatly but we will be able to make repairs, find food, water, and shelter there. They will be in chaos after this battle and because of that, we should be able to move about largely unnoticed, if we are cautious. We have a hoard of treasure that we must protect and keep hidden until we are sure of our safety."

He looked at the faces of the eighteenth-century pirates and nineteenth-century seamen. They were a hardy bunch, used to life throwing them into peril and the unknown.

"We will form a party to go ashore and assess the town and its inhabitants. The rest will guard the ship and make repairs. We can bring back supplies and information before we vote on a route to take… to take us—"

Roberts wasn't sure how to finish. He searched for words.

"Out of hell," Vane said.

There were chuckles and an easing of minds with Vane's quip.

"Aye. Less troubled waters may we find," said Roberts.

He looked over at the covered bodies laid out on the deck again. He drew a heavy sigh as his eyes again searched for the body of Sam Bellamy. The lad had become a trusted friend. The two of them had been shanghaied aboard the steam ship *Lurline* after landing in the late 1800s. Poor Sam had been depressed beyond belief after learning he was never again likely to see his love Mary Hallett, *or was it, Maria?* He and Sam had succeeded in igniting a mutiny aboard that steam ship and ousting the captain. Roberts had taken over command and raided the town of Honolulu outside of which they were now anchored. That Honolulu had been much smaller than this one, but he was now understanding that time seemed to have that effect on the world.

"Let us find a spot to bury our brethren, then get on with the business at hand."

CHAPTER 6 – MAKE YOU FAMOUS

Edward Thatch stood beside Stanton, Kent, and Brockman as they lounged against the .50-caliber cannon, all of them smoking cigarettes in the hot, humid air. The men were battle-weary, their clothing dirty and faces smeared with smoke and sweat. Their ship idled near the entrance to the devastated Hawaiian harbor, guarding the bay while dozens of boats and thousands of men and women worked to rescue the injured and drowning. Fires still raged on many of the ships and buildings that lined the port. There was a desperate effort being made to save the sailors trapped aboard a massive sinking battleship named *Arizona*.

The air surrounding the shore and harbor was thick with smoke and the scent of burning oil. The unsettling sounds of alarm and calamity drifted out to sea, disrupting the tranquility of the calm and warm Pacific waters. They remained on high alert, vigilant for any sign of another potential threat. Thatch had learned to pick out the symbols of the United States planes and ships that the *Ward* was associated with. The Japs used a blood-red sun-like disk and the US incorporated a white star set against a blue circle. *Planes* were what the flying machines were called, he also learned. All his questions about the world he found himself in were answered with amusement and the shaking of heads. Stanton commented that Thatch must have hit his skull at some point, knocking his memory loose. He let the men have their fun as he was too curious about learning the details of this time to rebuke them.

Several small boats had ferried men aboard, carrying both information and equipment. However, he was denied permission to leave the ship. Outerbridge let him know he would need to wait until they were given orders to stand down.

Thatch tossed the remainder of his cigarette into the sea as a man with a small black box tethered around his neck by a strap stopped a few yards from him and his new mates.

"Hey boys, give a look over here for the *New York Times*."

Stanton, Kent, and Brockman moved closer together. Kent, leaning next to Thatch, put his arm around his shoulder and gestured for him to look at the man who then put the box up to his face, one eye looking through it, the other squinted closed. There was a squat porthole-shaped protrusion on the front. An audible click sounded, and the man moved on, repeating the process over and over as he looked through the device to view the other sailors as well as the scenes of destruction visible in the harbor.

"What be the point of that?"

"What, you don't want your picture in the paper, Blackbeard?" asked Brockman.

"Make you famous," Kent said without humor. He was staring off at the devastation brought on by the Japanese attack. The Honolulu shoreline lay in ruins. "Think they attacked the mainland too?"

"They would have been spotted before they got there," said Stanton.

"Maybe the Germans hit New York, or Washington," Brockman wondered out loud.

"You be at war with the Germans *and* the Japanese?" Thatch asked with interest.

"No, well, we weren't… before this. Germany invaded Poland in thirty-nine, then France. They're at war with England and, since a few weeks ago, Russia. They got the Italians on their side, and now the Japs," Kent explained.

"Thirty-nine, eh? An this be… nineteen…?"

Kent gave Thatch a queer look. "Forty-one. Nineteen forty-one. What date did you think it was?"

Thatch just looked off and shook his head slowly. Kent and the other sailors exchanged glances. Thatch turned back to Kent after processing the passage of time.

"England is at war with Germany?"

"Mhmm. France fell fast, Hitler's army has occupied Paris for a while now. England and Churchill are continuing to resist them. We've stayed out of it… until now. How can you not know this? Where have you been?"

Thatch looked out upon the massive port, then glanced around the fantastical ship he found himself aboard. "I've been living in the past, the distant past by all accounts."

Stanton looked oddly at the other sailors. Kent rolled his eyes.

"Half our Pacific fleet just got destroyed," Brockman said with a head shake.

"Ain't no carriers at Pearl so we still have those," Stanton remarked.

"We got our nose bloodied, that's true, but we won't be caught again with our pants down," Kent said with grit in his voice.

"I need to get back to me ship, me crew," Thatch grumbled as he looked out, away from the harbor and to the open sea.

"That was quite a sight to see all of them old cannons firing at once. What is the name of your ship?" asked Stanton.

"She be the *Queen Anne's Revenge*. I pray she still floats after the beating she took from those… Jap planes."

"So, the rest of your crew pirates like you?" asked Brockman.

"Some, others Bart Roberts conscripted during a mutiny. We picked up a few in 1873, two cowboy fellows, brothers, Jesse and Frank James and a lady, the most beautiful you've ever laid eyes on."

"Bart Roberts? As in Black Bart Roberts?" asked Stanton.

"Jesse James? Come on. Are you just playing with us, or do you seriously think you're Blackbeard? The one from the seventeen hundreds?" Kent asked.

Thatch sighed. "The story is best told sharing a bottle of rum between us, but another rolled stick of your tobacco will have to do." He held out his hand and received a fresh cigarette and a light. "I don't know the magic of it, boys, but it all started with me mate, Benjamin Hornigold. He called a meeting of the pirate captains upon my arrival to Nassau. I should have smelled the makings of treachery after hearing that Henry Jennings and Hornigold were together in presenting a deal for our new Pirate Republic. But I be too soft-hearted and trusting when it came to me old Captain Hornigold. It was almost my undoing. Unbeknownst to me, the pirate hunter Woodes Rogers was tethered to me ship, lying in wait while we all met in the hold to discuss the terms of the King's pardon…" Thatch went on, telling his story of the time-moving storm, Hornigold's betrayal, and his adventures in San Francisco while the three sailors listened in rapt silence. All the while, ships continued to burn and sink along the Honolulu harbor.

CHAPTER 7 – DEAD AND THE DAMNED

Jesse James glanced over at the fresh grave site of the young pirate, Sam Bellamy, that he had only known for mere hours. It rested, alongside other unmarked graves, on a short rise of grassland that butted up to the sandy shore of the wide cove where the wooden tall ship sat anchored. In all they had lost eleven members of the crew. Most had been lost at sea in one way or another, but a total of five bodies lay buried on this Hawaiian island. He had heard the name of the island chain before, as well as a few brief descriptions of the faraway Pacific paradise, but never dreamed of setting foot on it.

"You reckon we stay tied with these odd sticks or take our share 'n find us a tub to take us home?" asked his brother Frank James while he sat on a rock attempting to clean his Remington with the thick, eighteenth-century oil, iron rod and coarse cloth given to him by the big quartermaster named Caesar.

Jesse squinted his eyes against the bright sun as he glanced back at the activity taking place on the shoreline. The ship had been pulled closer to careen and fix the damage it had taken in the two battles it had just fought. Two battles with foes of infinitely more powerful firepower, all in less than a turn of the clock. The pirates and seamen worked to secure the ship with ropes and poles planted in the sandy beach that stretched to the *Queen Anne's Revenge*, holding it at an angle so that the hull was mostly out of the water.

They began the work to replace wood, metal and tar to make her seaworthy again. He picked out the small frame of Anne Bonny lending her skills to the repair work. She and Mary Read were dressed in men's clothing of their time, shapeless pants that only extended to their calves and loose-fitting, bland shirts stained with sweat and dirt. None of the pirates wore shoes for this labor, while the crew that had come aboard with Roberts wore the same uniforms and boots they arrived in.

Jesse turned away from the sight as his mood remained foul. He and his brother Frank were growing quickly tired of the toil that came from ship-life that the others were so accustomed to. What he wouldn't give for a horse and a trail to ride. The sea was not in the blood of the James family, his brother had said as much an hour ago.

He looked beyond the grassy paddock that rose into dense foliage mixed with palm trees, frangipani and other flowering trees and vines he didn't recognize. The air had weight and moisture to it that clung heavily to his skin and breath. His pores continued to sweat no matter whether he stood in the shade or the sun.

His brother took a plug of tobacco from a canister and lodged it in his cheek then tossed the can to Jesse. He momentarily considered refraining as his nerves seemed already wound tight as a noose, but then he joined his brother in the indulgence of the nicotine chew.

"I ain't ready to go through the mill again out on that damn sea."

Frank nodded his head in agreement, then a funny thought entered his mind: "How about we rustle up one of them flying things and wing our way back to Missouri? They looked a might faster than even a train could travel," he said with a raised brow. He and Jesse stared at one another before they both chuckled at the ridiculousness of the statement.

"You believing Miss Bonny now about them moving through time?" Jesse asked his brother with all seriousness.

Frank sat in silence for a moment. He looked through the cleaned barrel of his pistol, flipped the cylinder back into place and slid it into its holster. "Ain't never seen a storm like that. Like an Oklahoma tornado sinking into the sea. Drowning us to surface in another part of the world. I certainly ain't never believed in any whoo-hoo before this…" Frank's eyes became lost for a moment staring at the *Queen Anne's Revenge*. "I am afraid that when we make our way back home… it ain't gonna be there no more."

"That may very well be, but then neither will the Pinkertons or the Wells Fargo men. The law and them newspapers will have forgotten our names."

Frank looked up at his brother standing there with his crooked grin, and he turned up his own smile. "An we got ourselves a heap more gold 'n silver than a horse could carry in that ship."

"Aye matey, 'n I could use me a drink right now," Jesse said in a squint-eyed imitation of the pirates he'd come to know.

Philip Albert looked up from the crate of books, notes and maps that he and Colette had carried from Blackbeard's cabin in order to rescue them from the mold and rot that threatened to destroy the items after the ship was swallowed by the sea—for the third time since its arrival at Nassau harbor in 1718. He could see Jesse and Frank James talking on a hill above the beachhead. These brothers were two of the most wanted criminals in the United States and now, somehow, he was bound to them. To them and the pirates from another era. *How did you find yourself in this mess, Mr. Albert*, he thought to himself. A scientist, specializing in chemicals and engineering, schooled at the Royal Society in London, was now plundering and pillaging alongside pirates and outlaws. He scoffed at the thought. *At least I didn't become a lawyer like my father, now that would be a true hell.*

The musical tone of '*hmm*' breathed audibly from the owner of the saloon and brothel known as The Paris. He looked over at Colette's soot-stained cheeks and the dried blood marring the sleeves of her dress. Her hair was twisted and knotted, needing a good detangling and brushing after the last twelve hours of drenching and the experience she had endured.

Philip was curious as to whether the thought of her losing the home and business she had worked so hard to build had entered her mind. He had frequented the establishment so regularly that he had formed a friendship with Colette that was in part to blame for his current predicament. She was absorbed in her labor of working her way through the damp pages and parchment, drying each individually with cloth as he had instructed her to do.

"Did you find something of interest, dearie?"

Colette glanced up at him, pale blue eyes dancing. "Edward's logbook, I believe." She carefully turned the pages, skimming the entries and gazing at the swooping and distinguished penmanship on display. There were sketches of ships, drawings of faces belonging to natives and sailors encountered, as well as various creatures of the sea throughout the entries. She landed on a page whose date showed it to be several months before his arrival in Nassau. She saw a list of notes and names from a gathering of several ships. She recognized two of the names said to be captaining two of the other vessels: Sam Bellamy and Benjamin Hornigold. It seemed Blackbeard had sailed alongside them and one other ship. The third captain's name was unfamiliar to her.

Philip leaned over her shoulder and read the entry with curiosity.

"Seems what they call a *'parley'* took place near the Seychelles. A few days of drinking and merriment over some merchant vessel they plundered. Captain Hornigold, Bellamy and someone referred to as the buzzard."

Colette looked more closely at the entry. "Buzzard? I took it as a man's name, Bussard maybe?"

Philip was now sitting beside her, and he turned the pages. "This will make very interesting reading. I believe these logs and those like them from pirate ships have been lost to history."

Colette looked up as the sound of one of the flying machines droned in the distance. She watched as the sunlight glinted off the metal wings. "As are we I'm afraid, Mr. Albert. Lost to history that is."

"A wondrous time perhaps. Imagine what might be possible in this place if man can now fly. We may have found ourselves in the greatest time of all," Philip said, staring at the machine floating through the sky.

Colette's face soured. "You fail to remember the death and violence inflicted upon us by those... beasts? Everything I've built with my sweat, blood and money is now gone. If we have come far enough in the future to have something so horrific as those flying things then what would have become of The Paris, my home?" She stood and began to walk off but turned to face him, her face a storm of pain and melancholy. "Has it all been given over to someone else? Exchanged hands without my consent? Or has it all turned to dust, burnt to the ground, covered in dirt like that young man buried over there that drank in my saloon just a week ago? He too is lost to history, Mr. Albert. I fail to see the wonderment in our predicament."

Philip watched her stride purposefully away from the beach toward the tropical foliage in her saltwater-stained blue dress that only yesterday had turned the heads of every man on the crowded San Francisco streets. It seemed apparent that she had given quite a bit of thought to the reality of having now lost everything, as had they all. He too was left with just the clothes on his back. Did he jump a hundred years into the future, a thousand? He looked at the wedding band around his dainty finger. His not-so-beloved Eunice back home in London would have surely gotten along without him, spending her days gossiping with her mother and sisters as she stuffed her expansive face with cream pies and puddings. Yes, he had lost everything from his past, he felt sure of it. A hint of a smile crossed his lips, and he began to hum a lively tune as he continued to flip through the parchments salvaged from Blackbeard's ornate cabin.

A campsite was set up on the beach away from the threat of high tide. Several fire rings were burning, and fish were being cooked along with provisions of rice and beans that had been stored before their departure from San Francisco. The crew was much larger then when the *Queen Anne's Revenge* prepared to make its escape, but Roberts had assumed the city not so far away would provide the necessary essentials required before their next journey. His men from the doomed *Charolette's Fortune* were weary and confused but willing to continue following his orders and trusting their fate to him. He gave a squeeze to Charolette De Berry's hand as he rose to address the crew. He ruffled the hair of young Tom as he strode to the center of camp.

"In the morn we should send a party to the town and get the lay of the land. There is more work to be done on the *Queen Anne's Revenge* so I will choose several of you that are not essential to that work. Once she is seaworthy, we will all visit the town if it's deemed safe. We can then divide the plunder, and the choice will be yours to stay crewed or go your own way." Roberts watched their faces and listened for objections but thankfully there were none. He needed many strong backs to finish the work repairing the frigate. He also knew the work would take their minds off the unusualness of their predicament.

"Those making the trek are Francis, Mr. Albert, Frank and Jesse James, Miss Bonny and Miss Read, Miss Colette and Charlotte." Robert's eyes landed on Charlotte's raised brow at hearing her name. "Light walking provisions and leave at dawn." He walked back to sit next to Charlotte and finish his food and drink.

"So quick to be rid of me, dearest?" she asked with narrowed eyes.

"It pains me to part even for a moment's breath, but I need someone I can trust. I can't send Vane and don't think Caesar trusts me alone with Blackbeard's prize. Francis joining will satisfy the crew members brought along from the steam ship."

"The *Charlotte's Fortune*," she said with a knowing smirk.

"Mhmm, and the cowboys are near worthless as shipwrights."

"I see, and sending all the women off on this errand keeps the men's minds on their labor."

"Aye, that it does," Roberts said, locking his eyes with hers.

"Well, my captain, if we are to be separated once again, I believe a proper goodbye is needed."

Roberts smiled and gave her a lusty look. He set the remainder of their dinner on the sand and took her hand, pulling her to her feet. "Let me show you to my quarters, lass."

"Lead the way, my captain."

CHAPTER 8 – BIG WHEEL

Blackbeard ducked his head to avoid the low metal bulkhead as he entered the near-empty galley of the *Ward*. He had not yet been given leave from the ship but was promised a ride to the harbor in the morning. Stanton had found him near the starboard rail gazing at the ruined ships as the sun gave up its hold on the sky and disappeared to brighten another hemisphere unseen beyond the horizon. He had stood marveling at the enormous vessels and buildings lining the devastated docks. The trade winds had blown the smoke past the island to dissipate into the atmosphere, though the battle left evidence scattered everywhere with scorched decks and flotsam cluttering the bay.

He had followed Stanton back toward midship before climbing down a ladder leading to the below decks of this iron beast. He continued to wonder at the construction of this vessel. His desire for such a ship was becoming ever more heightened as he learned of its capabilities.

The 'big wheel' wanted a word with him, Stanton had offhandedly told him on his way to the galley. Also, there was some BTO, 'big time operator', aboard ship taking notes, 'some army puke', Stanton had commented en route to the galley.

Outerbridge looked up from a pile of paperwork surrounding his late dinner and cup of black coffee. A man of medium height in a sharp white uniform paced behind him. He had his light brown hair plastered to his head, severely parted on one side. He turned as Thatch entered revealing a thin mustache stretched over pale lips and blue-gray eyes. Thatch guessed him to be about his age, mid-thirties, and felt an air of authority in his gaze. *A serious man*, thought Thatch, and one of rank to be sure.

"Good evening, Mr. Thatch, please have a seat," said Outerbridge indicating the seat across the table from him. "That will be all, Mr. Stanton, you're dismissed."

Thatch turned to watch Stanton scurry away and saw that an armed man stood watch to the left of the doorway. He looked back at Outerbridge who wore a humorless face and saw the other man had ceased his pacing and was looking Thatch over from feet to head then focused on his eyes, unblinking, in an attempt to bore into his soul. He decided to mask his discomfort.

"Happy to dine with you, Captain, though I had me fill alongside the crew just a time ago. Could use a spot of rum if ye have some to offer," he said jovially and pulled the chair out from the table as he sat and stretched his long legs to rest on another seat beside him.

Outerbridge gave a dark look at Thatch's inappropriate and casual manner. He adjusted his glasses, opening a file with several sheets of paper inside. "Sadly, no rum in our stores. I'm sure you will be able to find your fill on the island in due course."

"Ah, yes. When shall I have leave to go portside? I find meself anxious to reunite with me crew and me own ship. Not that I don't harbor good feelings to you and your men for fishing me out of the sea."

Outerbridge picked up one of the papers in front of him and skimmed over its contents quickly. "Before we bid you farewell, why don't we revisit some of your story about how you arrived in our care?"

Thatch glanced at the papers with their neat, densely written letters, all perfectly sized and spaced in what must have taken many hours for a scribe to achieve. "What parts is ye looking for a refreshing of?"

The serious man pulled out the chair next to Outerbridge and sat down, his eyes never leaving Thatch's. "Why don't we start with the part about you being from the seventeen hundreds?"

Outerbridge also kept his focus on Thatch. "This is Lieutenant Harris Becker of Army Intelligence."

Thatch stared back at Becker. The man reminded him of the pirate hunter, Woodes Rogers. The way he confidently moved, sure of himself and his position of power. Inside, Thatch wanted to strike him down and put him in his place, defy his authority and see him snivel while he pressed his neck under his boot. But he held himself in check. He needed to get off this ship. He wanted no part in whatever conflict they were involved in. His only desire was to reunite with Colette and his crew. The *Queen Anne* still held a bellyful of wealth in her that should take a lifetime of drink and merriment to deplete.

He twisted a lock of his beard in his finger as he decided the best course of action. He could tell the truth or brush off his stories as just that, stories, meant to entertain and thrill an audience. It seemed unlikely that these serious men would believe his tale—he himself wouldn't have a few weeks ago—but maybe in this time, which he found himself trapped in, such travel was commonplace; this ship in whose impressive galley he was now sitting and the flying machines that crossed the sky were no more fantastical than he and his crew moving through time. Maybe they could supply answers for him. Maybe they could provide a mechanism for him and his fellow pirates to travel back home, to his own time. He set his booted feet back on the floor and leaned his frame forward, toward the two stern men, and began his tale from the beginning.

Thatch moved from fore to aft of the thirty-six-foot launch, eyes full of curiosity as he took in all the aspects of the boat. Its skin was constructed of a strange material that was called fiberglass yet seemed quite different from any glass he'd ever touched. It was powered by fuel called diesel, able to propel the vessel at a speed of ten knots. The open deck was crowded with more than thirty men from the *Ward*. He knew only one of them, that man being the one that had questioned him last night along with Outerbridge, Lieutenant Becker.

Dawn had broken an hour ago and he had been served strong coffee and heated porridge along with buttered toast perfectly sliced. His acquired suit from 1873 San Francico had been returned to him cleaned and fresh smelling. He had transferred his small, concealed Derringer from his borrowed navy uniform as he dressed this morning. It wasn't the powerful set of Colt .45 pistols that he had a newfound affinity for, but it was better than the vulnerability of being completely unarmed.

It was a short trip from where the *Ward* was anchored to the busy wharf. The low dock that they moored against was highly trafficked with sailors and workmen busy clearing away debris from yesterday's attack. Grim, tired faces were worn everywhere he looked. This harbor had taken a beating. There were many enormous vessels floating alongside the wide docks that rivaled the castles and keeps of Europe.

He followed the crowd of sailors as he disembarked, making his way toward the buildings lining the harbor. The early morning air had just a touch of chill as a moistness clung tight, revealing dew glistening on all the surfaces. The familiar feel of the tropics steadied his nerves. He stopped short as he came to a roadway along the wharf. Carriages moved along noisily with nothing pulling or pushing them. The oddness of these vehicles left him slack-jawed and rooted where he stood. Several sailors bumped him as they passed, with looks of bewilderment as to why he stood in awe.

Thatch's eyes took in the wonderment of the scene. These weren't the trains he had marveled at in San Francisco, they were smaller and more agile, not relying on tracks to move. They didn't have the smokestacks breathing out the dark clouds that powered them; he likened them more to the boat that delivered him here from the *Ward*.

He pulled a man to a stop next to him. "Aye mate, where can a man get a drink?"

"It's a bit of a walk but if you head down that way and follow that road until you exit the gate, then go maybe about a mile and you'll find some shops and eateries. It's early for a bar to open. Maybe try a grocery store. Honestly, after that attack not sure what you're gonna find open. The world changed overnight."

Thatch continued to look at his surroundings. "Aye mate, that it has."

"Damn them Jap bastards," the man said, and walked on.

Thatch moved through the roads, mind in a fog from all the oddities it was trying to understand.

"Mr. Thatch."

He turned to see Lieutenant Becker approaching him.

"Can I give you a ride off the base?"

Thatch looked around the man, wondering what sort of ride he was offering.

"We can take this jeep over here." Becker approached an open-air wagon and stepped into the seat, motioning for Thatch to go around the other side and sit next to him.

He looked around the wagon and then bent to look underneath to see more metal and tubes. He climbed onto the seat, the vehicle bouncing under his weight. There was a short pane of glass in front of him and a wheel hitched to the cabinet in front of Becker, who was looking at him with curiosity.

"You act like a man who's never been in a car."

"Been in one? Never seen one b'fore this morn," Thatch scoffed.

"My apologies, of course you wouldn't have… being from the seventeen hundreds." Becker watched his face for deception.

"Do we need to say something for it to go?"

Becker snuffed at Thatch, thinking that he must be jesting. *No, he* thought, *the man is thoroughly confused by the operation of the jeep.* He placed his hand on the keys that were hanging from the ignition and twisted, foot holding in the clutch and giving it gas. The engine started on the first try. Thatch nearly jumped out of his seat from the vibration of the engine.

"Heavens!" Thatch exclaimed and braced his hands on the dashboard while Becker chuckled and placed the car in gear, accelerating down the roadway. In a moment, once he had realized Lieutenant Becker had actual control over the vehicle, Thatch's fear evaporated and his eyes danced along with the wind whipping his hair and beard. A smile formed on his lips as buildings, equipment, people and other vehicles whizzed by.

In a matter of minutes they had crossed the base and arrived at a gate guarded by three men with long rifles. There was a short line of varying transports waiting to enter.

Becker stopped the jeep in front of the guards who saluted after seeing his stripes. He put the car in neutral and turned to Thatch. "Well, Captain Blackbeard, this is where we part ways. It was a pleasure to make your acquaintance. I hope you are reunited with your ship and crew. You'll find the town center that way." He pointed down the road past the gate then held out his hand for Thatch to shake.

Thatch shook his hand with a calloused grip then carefully exited the jeep. He did one turn, taking in the gate, the buildings and the now distant ships, then began his walk, following the direction he had been pointed in.

Becker watched the tall, trim man walk away, eyes narrowed and probing. He placed the gear in first and started his drive back to his temporary office back on base. He waved his hand at Clair, his newly assigned secretary with a head of curly blonde hair, as he moved through the bustling operations center. She stood from her typing and snatched up a notebook and pen about to follow Becker into his office.

"I need a few moments, I'll let you know when you're required," he said curtly as he glided into his office and closed the door behind him. He paced the room several times before lifting the phone from its cradle. He hesitated momentarily then dialed a number. The line rang several times before it was answered.

"Roger's plumbing," a man said on the line.

"Yes, good day. I believe I have a leak that needs looking at."

There was a pause on the opposite end of the call. "There is a lot of service work that needs doing today, can it wait?"

"No. This is important."

A hesitation, then a sigh. "I see. Please describe the leak."

After collecting his thoughts Becker said, "I would like the leak to be found and watched, not necessary to fix right away. The… pipe is a little over six feet long, a mass of let us say black hair clogging all around it, rather hard to miss. Honestly, looks like it's from the Wild West… eighteen hundreds."

"What, are we talking about a Halloween costume? It's a little late for trick or treating."

"Just keep an eye on it and report back later." Becker hung up the phone.

CHAPTER 9 — METAL HORSES

Francis kept a cautious eye on Frank James, the infamous outlaw trekking through the dense Hawaiian vegetation just behind him. They were barely ten minutes into their walk from the secluded cove, where the eighteenth-century wooden ship lay anchored, still carrying the scent of salt water and ancient history. Their goal was to find a trail or road that would lead them to the harbor town that was attacked by the flying beasts yesterday. Francis had attempted some small talk with the stone-faced outlaw, but all he'd received in return were a few curt grunts.

As he glanced back, he noticed how quickly their group had splintered into smaller clusters. Colette, Blackbeard's enigmatic woman, strode alongside the little man everyone called 'the scientist', while Jesse James and that fiery red-haired pirate, Anne Bonny, were deep in a lesson on the art of pistol-spinning and the finesse of a quick draw.

Bringing up the rear were two women who, Francis suspected, were more dangerous than any man he'd ever known: the notorious Read woman and his captain's fierce sweetheart, Charlotte. Both were as strong as any man, and from what Francis had gathered, they might've spilled more blood than even the James brothers. There was an unspoken danger about them, something that told him they'd be more than capable of holding their own in any fight—and perhaps they'd killed more than their fair share already.

Francis was a brawler with an ample amount of broken noses and black eyes, but until a few days ago he'd never been a part of a war or seen violent death. He wasn't squeamish, he just hadn't experienced those things firsthand… until now.

They were ascending a gradual rise when the dense vegetation abruptly gave way to a winding road, its black surface unfamiliar beneath Francis' feet. The thick foliage of towering palms and broad-leafed trees clung to the rocky cliffs, their roots gripping the earth as if to keep it from slipping away. Vines tangled through the underbrush, bursting with vibrant blooms, and the scent of damp earth hung heavy in the humid air.

He stood at the edge of the road, squinting to the left, but the sharp curves of the terrain blocked his view beyond forty yards. The hills rolled into each other, shrouded in greenery that seemed to devour the landscape. To the right, the cliffs loomed, their jagged edges softened only by the relentless growth of plants clinging to every crevice.

Suddenly, the rumble of an engine shattered the quiet, the sound magnified as it echoed off the cliffs. Before Francis could react, a flash of red streaked into his peripheral vision, a blur that seemed out of place against the wild, untamed backdrop.

Frank James, with a quick hand on Francis' shoulder yanked him back as a speeding horseless vehicle narrowly missed him with the sounding of a loud horn momentarily frightening him to his core.

Frank pulled him to crouch behind a large tree trunk as another vehicle sped around the bend in the road, driver and passengers now visible through open windows. Francis could swear he saw kids in the windows of the vehicle. He looked over at Frank and saw him squatting next to him with his revolver at the ready.

The rest of the group arrived in a huff to see what the commotion was about, armed, and ready for action.

"Get down!" Frank ordered, and they all crouched watching for trouble.

"What is it? What did you see?" Jesse asked his brother.

Frank and Francis looked at one another, neither having the words to describe the speeding vehicles.

"I don't see anything," Anne said standing, pistol leading her movement forward.

Just then the quick, throaty roar of an engine emerged from a two-wheeled contraption with a helmeted rider as it rode past at an alarming rate of speed. Anne's hand was quick to raise her gun at the man riding by, but she held her finger from pulling the trigger, mouth open in awe.

She turned quickly, looking at the scientist as he began to stand from his crouched position. "What the devil was that?"

Philip was wide-eyed but curious as well.

"Like some sort of metal horse," Jesse mused.

Another vehicle rounded the corner from the other direction causing the group to flinch in surprise. This one was going slower than the last, so they were able to get a good look at it. It was a dull shade of yellow in color. They were able to make out the details of doors and glass windows surrounding the passenger compartment. Long fore and aft portions of the vehicle extended out past the wheels. For a few of them, the oddest part of the vision was that the driver and passenger were both young, attractive women operating the carriage-like vessel.

Colette slipped on the damp vegetation clinging to the ground as she approached closer to the roadway. Philip lent his arm to steady her, which she took with gratitude as she felt less sure-footed in this climate and this heat, that made her face flush and pores glisten with perspiration. She was also overwhelmed by the entire experience that had overtaken them all.

"What kind of magic is this place?" asked Mary of no one in particular.

"Not magic, dearie, inventions, innovations. Made by man," Philip said, then saw a hard glare from the woman pirate dressed more like a male. "Or a woman possibly." He pulled a compass from his shirt pocket and noted the direction. He stored it away and produced a notebook and scribbled quickly in it as they all watched another vehicle pass them by.

"That way—we'll find the harbor town," Philip announced, pointing ahead. Without a word, the group followed his lead, keeping as much distance from the road as possible while still moving alongside it. As they walked, Philip couldn't help but notice the sharp contrast between the jagged rock formations and the jungle-like vegetation that had clearly been cut back to carve out the road.

Less than half an hour later, they reached a stretch where the road straightened, allowing them to see more than a quarter-mile ahead. The dense trees gradually gave way to tall grasslands, their golden waves rippling over the rolling hills. In the distance, cattle grazed lazily, dotting the landscape like slow-moving shadows. The azure sea lay just beyond.

They had been overtaken by dozens of horseless carriages, some visibly worn from use, others built to haul goods in enclosed compartments or open-topped cargo beds. Many of the passengers peered curiously from their vehicles as they passed, their eyes lingering on the ragtag group walking along this unfamiliar path.

Then, after passing the group by, one such vehicle with an empty open cargo bay slowed to a stop by the side of the road. They paused their trek and instinctively several placed their hands on the butts of their weapons in readiness.

The lone driver leaned his balding head out the window. The man looked old and weathered, as did his carriage. His skin was dark, but not African, more like a native to the Caribbean Islands. They could easily see from the thickness of the arm that leaned out the window that he was quite heavyset.

"You headed into Honolulu?" he asked.

"Is that the name of the harbor town?" Philip asked.

"That it is."

"Then yes."

The man moved his eyes, roving from pirate to cowboy and back again.

"If you ain't planning on robb'n me you can all hop in the back, and I'll give you a lift."

The group all exchanged looks with Colette leading the decision to take the man up on his offer, as she was not fond of walking in this heat the rest of the day.

"Alright, mister," Jesse muttered, stepping toward the back of the vehicle. His hands gripped the metal frame of the cargo bed, eyes skimming over the rusted floor. A rubber tire, strapped down in case of one becoming damaged, rattled slightly as he leaned in. He entwined his fingers and crouched, offering Anne a step up. She accepted the boost, vaulting into the back with practiced ease. Colette followed, moving with a surprising grace despite the heavy, ornate dress that should have hindered her.

Mary Read and Charlotte, without a word, climbed in on their own, ignoring any offers of help. The men followed suit, finding spots on the metal floor, and soon Frank gave the side of the truck a firm pat, signaling they were ready to go.

The driver cast a wary glance over his shoulder, taking in their peculiar attire and the arsenal they carried. He thought better of questioning them, though a flicker of worry gnawed at him—what if they decided to steal his truck before they reached town? But it was too late to back out now. They were probably armed in case the Japanese invaded the island now that war had begun. Just this morning he had wished he too owned a firearm. With a resigned sigh, he shifted the old Dodge into gear, pulling back onto the road. The truck rumbled along at a steady forty miles per hour, while the strange, armed passengers jostled in the back.

The pirates and cowboys were eagerly watching each passing car, all seemingly different from each other in construction, paint color and usefulness. Their eyes were entranced by the lush scenery that was dotted with houses and small shops before they rode into the town of Honolulu amid wide travel lanes with countless vehicles and pedestrians crisscrossing.

Their driver pulled to the side of the road, coming to a stop in front of several blocks of shops and buildings of businesses and several food stalls opening for the day.

He leaned out the window to talk with them. "This an okay place to drop you off? I need to head into work a little ways further."

"Thank you, dear sir. Can you tell us the day and time?" asked Colette as Philip lent her a helping hand down from the cargo bay of the carriage.

"Monday," the man glanced at his timepiece attached to his wrist. "Eight thirty."

"Mhmm, what year might it be?" Colette inquired.

The man narrowed his eyes wondering if this was a joke or some sort of ploy to distract him while the armed men attempted to accost him. He glanced to see the entire group standing off to the side making no aggressive movements, weapons stowed in their holsters.

"You truly don't know the year, miss?"

"I'm sorry to ask, sir, but we have been traveling for some time on the sea."

They did look to be a weary and disheveled group. "Nineteen forty-one."

They all gave looks of horror at that number. Each one turned to see each other's reaction.

Colette turned to the man. "I see. And we are on the island of Hawaii?"

"O'ahu," the man nodded. "Paradise, at least it was until yesterday and them damned Japanese. There are a few hotels down the way." He looked back at the armed men. "You should probably stow those firearms. Police are probably pretty jumpy after the attack and the declaration of war by the President. The Japs could invade any day so watch your back." With that the man gave a wave and drove off down the street, turning at the next roadway crossing.

"Maybe we all should place our weapons in less conspicuous locations, like our rucksacks or something," mused Francis.

"I think I'll be keeping mine within easy reach, friend," said Jesse.

"I find folks to be more polite when they see me armed," put in Anne Bonny as she adjusted her Western holster.

"Very well then, let us find lodging before we search for news and provisions," said Philip and led the way down the smooth, cement-surfaced walkway.

The city before them was pristine and well constructed, though smaller and more charming than the sprawling streets of San Francisco or the grandeur of London. It had indeed an air of paradise about it, just as their driver had said. Tropical flowers and lush greenery lined the streets, their vibrant colors and sweet fragrances mixing with the warmth of the air. The sound of horseless carriages had become a familiar hum, their speed and noise no longer startling.

As they passed through the city, they noticed a steady flow of pedestrians, all dressed in a curious variety of clothing. Some wore short pants and light fabrics suited to the heat, while others were in neatly pressed military uniforms. It was a strange mix of casual and formal, and the group drew more than a few puzzled stares from the locals.

Anne noticed two young women in shorts that barely reached mid-thigh openly gawking at them, whispering as they passed. Her sneer deepened at their brazen stares, and she clenched her fists, resisting the urge to provoke them. But when she caught Jesse's wandering eyes trailing after the women, she felt a familiar flash of jealousy and annoyance. She was half-tempted to shove the barrel of her revolver into their pert little noses, just to watch them wet their small garments.

Philip and Colette, who were leading their little band of pirates and outlaws, stopped in front of a road leading toward the sprawling entrance way to a beautiful pink building, six stories high, that stretched out majestically on either side of its welcoming main structure. The grand building was sitting adjacent to the sandy beach and the ocean just beyond.

"I believe that is an inn," Philip remarked.

"For robber barons by the looks of it," Frank said.

"We seem to have the coins of several barons and lords," Charlotte said as she cheekily hefted her sack of coins; they had each been given one before embarking on this expedition.

"I could use a bath in water that isn't from the sea," Colette said, smiling at the entrance way. "Shall we?" She offered her arm to Philip, and he escorted her inside with the rest following them.

The interior was crafted from massive beams of rounded, polished wood, their white paint gleaming in the sunlight streaming in from window that stretched from the floor to the ceiling. Towering wooden archways lent the space the grandeur of a Spanish palace, their smooth curves catching the eye. The lobby was vast, adorned with plush lounging furniture where patrons reclined, sipping coffee and idly smoking cigarettes. Live tropical plants decorated the interior adding to the beauty of the teak and hardwood furnishings. The air was filled with the gentle strains of tropical music, its source hidden but seemingly emanating from every corner, weaving a soothing ambiance.

At the center of the room stood a grand Koa wood counter, its rich and striking grain patterns gleaming warmly under the light. Behind it, two radiantly beautiful native Hawaiian women attended with an effortless grace, their floral dresses adding a splash of vibrant color to the scene. As Philip approached, their warm smiles greeted him, and in unison, they welcomed the group with a melodic, 'Aloha'.

"Good morning, sir, are you checking in today?"

"Ideally, yes. Would you have rooms available?"

"I believe so, many of our guests have checked out today on account of the attack. How many rooms would you require?"

Philip looked back at his diverse crew.

Anne grabbed Jesse's hand. "We'll share."

Mary elbowed her. "I bet you will."

Anne thrust an elbow into Mary's side in return.

Philip looked at the rest of their faces and turned to the attendant. "One room for the ah… couple and separate rooms for the remaining."

"One night or will you all be staying longer?"

"One night should suffice, but we may opt for additional."

"Our rate is eight dollars per night…"

"Eight dollars?!" exclaimed Frank.

The young woman looked over at the rugged cowboy with a startled expression. She than swallowed hard and forced a smile.

"Well, since you are, ah… needing several rooms we could offer a group rate of seven dollars per room, maybe an upgrade for the couple."

Philip nodded at the cowboys and glanced at Colette who nodded back at him. "We might need an exchange for our foreign currency or coins." Philip opened his bag, removing silver and gold coins along with paper money from the Hawaiian Islands of 1873. This created a problem that required the manager of the hotel to assist with the transaction ending with the hotel holding gold coins on the condition of them returning with current money from a bank to settle the bill. The manager also insisted that weapons were stowed while they were on the property. Philip promised that their guns would not be on display while in public areas, which the pirates and cowboys reluctantly agreed to.

Keys to their rooms at the Royal Hawaiian Hotel were pressed into their hands, the elegance of the place a stark contrast to their travel-worn attire and unkempt appearances. Strangers to luxury—and in dire need of soap and water—they agreed to gather in the lobby in two hours, once they had the chance to wash away the grit of their adventures and reclaim a semblance of civility.

Jesse James closed the door of the hotel room and raised his brows as he glanced around the large bedroom with floor-to-ceiling windows facing the tranquil blue sea and golden sand beach visible between the half-open drapes. The décor was tropical wood furniture with paintings of beaches and native Hawaiians paddling canoes, and others with woman dressed in grass skirts performing dances. An open door gave a glimpse of a large bathroom with built-in sinks with faucets protruding from the cabinetry.

Anne excitedly ran from each piece of furniture and decorative accessory to the expansive windows then to the bathroom.

"Jesse!" she called to him with alarm from the ocean blue-tiled room. "What is this? Come quick."

Jesse approached the doorway and leaned against the frame as Anne examined each fixture and amenity. She leaned over the wash basin inspecting the brass plumbing that extended out of the tiled counter. She ran her hands over the handle and twisted it. Water came flowing out of the spicket and she jumped back in shock.

"Great Poseidon!" she remarked with glee. She twisted the handle in the opposite direction and the water ceased to flow. Anne reached her hand to the second handle and twisted it smoothly, sending a stream into the basin, and watched as it swirled down a drain in the center.

"Why would there be the need for two handles?" she asked, turning toward Jesse in curiosity.

He gave it a moment's thought. "Might be for right-handed or left-handed folks?"

Anne nodded and turned back to the flowing water. She cupped her hand and let the water splash down upon it, quickly pulling it back with a squeal of pain. Jesse ran toward her in alarm, and she held out her reddened palm to him. He took her hand in his and felt the heat upon her skin.

"It's hot! The water flows hot." Anne's eyes were wide, and a broad smile crept over her face. "It's… wondrous."

"How…?" Jesse stood over the basin as the water ran, a small amount of steam forming around the bowl. He tentatively put his rough hand in the water, feeling its heat run over his skin. He turned the opposite handle, and the water was then mixed with the cold and heated streams combining to become a comfortable warm temperature. "Incredible."

Anne moved on to push back a curtain made of a strange material that was white and decorated with paintings of seashells to find a large bathing tub. There was the same style of brass fixtures on one tiled wall. Two spouts were used to deliver the water, one just above the rim of the tub and the other just under the ceiling.

Jesse focused his attention on the commode that contained a pool of water with a handle on its side. He bent down to look at the small handle and give it a gentle twist. He sat back in surprise as the water noisily rushed out the bottom to be replaced by new water pouring from the inside rim. Anne looked down at him with wonder on her face.

"Is that a privy?"

"I reckon."

Anne turned to the tub and after a few moments of trial and error she had hot water raining down into the tub from the high mounted spicket. She noticed small bottles and a paper-wrapped bar that sat on a shelf next to the privy and opened each to find floral smelling soap and thick liquids meant for washing.

She turned and smiled coyly at Jesse. She removed her San Francisco-acquired pointed boots while standing. Then, in a quick maneuver, she swept off her buttoned shirt, not bothering with the unfastening of the wooden buttons.

Jesse drank in the sudden half-nakedness of Anne Bonny. The porcelain-white skin bordered by the suntanned areas that had been exposed to years of sailing only further accented the delicate feminine curves of her breasts.

Without a hint of shame, she slid her hands down to the waist of her britches, pushing them over her hips with a slow, sensual motion, stepping out of them as if shedding her last restraint. Her body, strong and supple, was now completely bare, but it was the look in her eyes—dangerous, playful—that held him captive. She licked her lips, biting the bottom one seductively as she turned her back to him, her hips swaying ever so slightly.

Stepping into the tub, she let the cascading hot water drench her body and wet her long strawberry hair to cling to her shoulders and back. She kept the curtain open, her gaze never leaving his as she let the water pour over her breasts and slide down her skin, deliberately inviting him into her private moment.

"Get out of those clothes, Jesse James," she purred, her voice thick with desire, "before I tear them from you myself."

CHAPTER 10 – RUM

Blackbeard wandered the streets of Honolulu, his boots clicking against the black paved roads slick from a brief rain. The shops and businesses lining the street were a stark contrast to the world he once knew. He marveled at the motorized carriages, each one more puzzling than the last. Some gleamed with a metallic sheen, polished and pristine, while others rattled by, rusted and worn, their exteriors coated in the dust and salt of the island. The colors were vibrant—brilliant reds, deep blues, and bright yellows—and the shapes varied from sleek and narrow to wide, hulking machines. He couldn't understand why anyone would choose such unnecessary flourishes for something as simple as transportation.

As he moved past the storefronts, the salty ocean breeze mixed with the rich aromas of grilled meats and sweet, tropical fruits. The air was thick with humidity, sticking to his skin, but he was more drawn to the strange mix of scents. He found himself entering a shop crammed with goods—tools stacked high on dusty shelves, sacks of rice and flour, and rows of brightly colored sweet treats wrapped in waxy paper that crinkled at his touch. In the corner, a glass cabinet filled with bottles glowed faintly. The chill that emanated from it was like nothing he had ever felt before. He paused, pulling open the door, and let the cool air wash over him. The island's oppressive warmth momentarily melted away as he basked in the strange relief.

A dark-skinned woman behind the counter watched him with a welcoming smile. Her eyes sparkled with curiosity at the out-of-place long-haired bearded man dressed in nineteenth-century Western garb as he gestured to the bottles encased in the cabinet. "Which of these hold liquor?" he asked, his voice rough with thirst. She pointed to several glass bottles adorned with delicate, painted labels. Blackbeard's fingers traced the edge of one, a white-labeled bottle filled with Caribbean rum. It felt like a relic from home. He licked his dry lips, his mind already savoring the taste of it.

But when the time came to pay, a heavy silence fell between them. His relic coins were worthless here, and the woman shook her head, sympathy in her eyes. He considered, just for a moment, the possibility of taking it. His fingers tightened around the bottle, but he could feel the weight of every set of eyes in the shop, every passerby outside. He wasn't just Blackbeard here— he was a stranger, a ghost from another time. With a sigh, he set the bottle back on the shelf. Today, he thought, he would keep his hands clean. There was always tomorrow.

The shopkeeper was helpful in directing him to the nearest pawn shop, where he could trade in his gold and silver coin and jewelry for the local paper money.

He wandered the next few blocks keeping his head as forward as possible while his eyes roamed the colorful and lightly dressed pedestrians. The heat of the day was beginning to cause him to sweat in his long trousers, shirt, and dress jacket. There was a heavy navy presence on the roadways and several men and women in uniform had passed purposefully by. Loud, wailing sounds accompanied a few large enclosed vehicles as they rushed through the streets with other carriages giving way as they passed. Tension and apprehension was thick in the air.

He needed to head along the coast and find a high vantage point where he could scan the waters for any sign of the *Queen Anne's Revenge*. The last he'd seen of her, she had taken damage but was still afloat, her sails straining against the wind. He hoped Roberts had been able to steer her into a hidden cove or sheltered inlet where she could anchor safely, giving Thatch the chance to rejoin the crew. They doubtless had no idea that he had survived the chaos and, like them, been swept forward through time.

A dull knot of heartache and guilt tightened in his chest as his thoughts shifted to Colette. The spirited woman, once so full of life and fire, had now been unwillingly thrust into the same twisted fate that had befallen him and his crew. Her life—her business, her home—everything she had known, left seventy years in the past. He wondered if there was anything left for her back there, in the world she'd been ripped from. The thought gnawed at him. It was his fault she'd been caught up in this. His fault that she had fallen into the hands of that ruthless pirate hunter, Woodes Rogers.

He clenched his jaw, his teeth grinding as the determination surged through him. He would find her, no matter what it took. And somehow, he would make it right.

Thatch stopped in front of a shop window that showcased a large, odd-sized musical lute, several oil paintings, lamps, jewelry, timepieces and various bric-a-brac. The writing above the door declared 'Aloha Pawn'. He reached into his pocket and fingered the coins that still remained from San Francisco. He looked at the remaining rings ornamenting his fingers and discreetly pocketed several that he wished to safeguard. He also adjusted his concealed Derringer pistol tucked inside his shirt sleeve. He then entered the establishment with a bell above the doorframe alerting his arrival.

A middle-aged man wearing a hat that featured a brim that only protruded in the front raised his eyes from a newspaper he was reading on the front counter. He wore a bright flowered print shirt that seemed to be the fashion on the Honolulu streets. It was short-sleeved and showcased arms that were heavily muscled with protruding veins roping his forearms and biceps. He had a dark mustache and dense black hair coated his chest that was visible between the unbuttoned sides of his festive blouse.

The man's dark eyes quickly took Thatch's measure and he folded his paper and set it aside.

"What can I do you for, friend?"

Thatch looked around at the wares. He searched the shelves for weapons and armaments for purchase, but alas there was none visible. "A shopkeeper a few blocks down the way suggested I pay you a visit to trade my coin for local currency."

This piqued the man's interest and he stood up from leaning on the counter. "That right? You sound like a Brit. Did I get that right?"

"Aye," Thatch said as he approached the counter.

"A Brit in a vintage Western suit. Tourist?"

Thatch was unfamiliar with the term and instead of responding he took a small handful of silver and gold coins from his pocket and placed them on the counter. "Would we be able to arrive at an equitable exchange for these?"

The man let out a low whistle as he looked at them, which inadvertently alerted Thatch that he was impressed.

"This Spanish?" asked the man as he picked up one of the gold coins and studied it. "The condition is… well, it looks newly minted." He sorted through several other coins, turning them in his hand, hefting their weight. He picked up a few that Thatch had acquired in San Francisco, silver dollars, the ones from Miss Colette's saloon, The Paris. "I've got a couple of these myself, though not in this condition."

"I trust that there is a deal to be had," Thatch suggested.

"We should be able to come to an arrangement, friend," the man said with nod.

"Would you happen to have any weapons for sale?"

That raised the man's brows, then he nodded again with a smile. "I get ya. Feel flat-footed after the Japs attacking. Not sure anything I got is going to do much good against a full-on invasion from those bastards, but I might have something to give you some peace of mind."

When Thatch stepped out of the pawn shop, his spirits were noticeably lifted. He wasn't entirely sure how much the shopkeeper had swindled him, but in his possession now were several denominations of the local paper currency, a revolving pistol with six bullets—though smaller than his cherished Colts—and a five-inch hunting knife, its sheath securely tucked into his boot. The weight of these new acquisitions brought a sense of comfort, despite the uncertainty surrounding him.

He paused at the edge of the street, gazing down the bustling road toward the coastline just a few blocks away. The flat terrain stretched before him, with hills and jagged mountains rising behind, further inland. His attention was drawn to a massive, imposing building that dominated the shoreline, its pale pink façade standing out against the blue sky. It was grand, almost regal, and it towered over the other structures around it.

Curiosity tugged at him. If he could find a way inside, perhaps the uppermost windows might offer a vantage point to search the sea for the *Queen Anne's Revenge*. The thought of spotting his ship—tattered but still sailing—filled him with a sudden rush of hope.

As his eyes scanned the streets, they briefly locked with those of a man standing across the road. The stranger, tall and alert, made fleeting eye contact before disappearing into a shop, a newspaper tightly rolled in one hand. Thatch hesitated, his instincts warning him of the man's intent. He lingered for a moment, watching the door, half-expecting the man to reemerge. But nothing happened.

Shaking off the feeling of unease, Thatch turned his attention back to the grand pink building. He started toward it, his mind set on reaching its highest point. Whatever awaited him inside, he was determined to find his ship—and perhaps answers to the questions still plaguing him. He stopped. *But first I'd like to try me some of that Caribbean rum chilled in that storage locker back down the street.*

CHAPTER 11 – LADY-LIKE

Mary Read leaned against a polished wood column surveying the expansive lobby of the hotel. The casually dressed patrons in floral and earthy tones moved about in comfort and ease. Many wore long necklaces constructed of cut tropical flowers and wielded decadent brightly colored drinks in glass tumblers decorated with tiny parasols paired with tubes they used for sipping the drinks.

Her skin and hair had been washed cleaner than she could ever recall after using the sweet fragrant soaps that were accommodated within her private bathing chamber. She tilted her head toward her shoulder to sniff the pleasant smell wafting from her long unruly hair and realized it was being spoiled by the salty sweat embedded into her clothing. She would need to wash her blouse and trousers or find new clothing to wear.

Her eyes roamed over the seated crew members who looked freshly bathed as well. Colette, Charlotte, Francis, and Frank listened as Philip outlined their plan of splitting into smaller groups to complete their tasks and meet back here at dusk. They were all waiting on the arrival of Anne and Jesse. A smirk hit her lips as she knew what was keeping those two captive in their room.

She had been stunned after Anne had set off alone to avenge the death of Calico Jack Rackham only to have her return, riding side by side with the very bloke that killed Rackham, Jesse James.

Mary and Jack Rackham had had a rather antagonistic relationship. She had joined Anne and Jack's merry band after the merchant ship she had been crewing aboard was taken by the pirates. Mary had been given the choice to join the pirate crew or be marooned on a tiny spit of land along with the captain and officers of the ship. She enthusiastically joined the pirates as life as a sailor on a merchant ship offered little reward for your labors and harsh treatment by the officers of the ship's hierarchy.

Rackham, Anne and the rest of the crew took Mary for a man as she had hidden her form under male clothes like she had done since childhood. Her mother had chosen to pass her off as her dead stepbrother so that she could continue receiving the stipend from the deceased boy's grandmother.

Mary had made fast friends with Anne who had been unaware of Mary's sex until she was forced to reveal herself to Rackham after he became enraged by his misperception that Anne was engaged in an affair with Mary. He had thought she was another young man with a fancy for Bonny. She and Rackham had almost come to swords before Anne had told him that she was a woman.

She didn't shed a tear when Jesse James had put a bullet in Jack's chest but she did feel a sadness for Anne's loss. She stifled a snort at the thought of Anne most likely bedding Jack's killer while she stood waiting in this ornate lobby. Life did have its twists and turns.

Moments later her suspicions were confirmed as she saw the cat-that-ate-the-canary grins on both Anne's and Jesse's faces as they strode into the immense hall. Anne made eye contact with her and in that brief moment Mary knew that their desires had been sated. She would be seeking all the fiendish details when they were alone.

Jesse sat down next to his brother who also gave a revealing look to his younger sibling, which was ignored by Jesse, almost. Anne sidled up to stand next to Mary and Mary used her hip to bump her. Anne returned the gesture with a backhanded slap to Mary's arm.

"Right, well, now that we are all here, we can get down to the business at hand," Philip said, bringing the group's focus to their current mission. "Information and provisions are our goals. Careful to not spend our funds on unnecessary and redundant items. We can discuss the wares this town has available and the best route for us to acquire our needful things once we reunite. It would also be best if we were to keep ourselves from attracting attention and keeping out of troublesome situations."

"I would think that task would be easier served if we left some of our weapons stored in our rooms as the staff had asked of us," Colette remarked, glancing at the pirates' and outlaws' blatant display of armaments. Mary and Anne still wore their cutlasses strapped to their waists, the James brothers each had their revolvers holstered on their belts and Charlotte kept her kukri and half a dozen other blades sheathed to her person.

"This time seems a lot more violent than the one we arrived from. I will be keeping me blades at the ready," Charlotte said, rising to her feet and adjusting her sword.

"I'm aligned with her," Frank said, standing across from her. "After the beating we took from them flying things, I'd even like to get our hands on the biggest caliber rifles our coin will buy."

"Yes, yes, well, armaments will be important but today is a scouting mission. The James brothers and Charlotte can find out more about this island, its city and inhabitants. Anne, Mary and Francis can use their knowledge of ships to find out information about the port and navy vessels. Colette and I will work on finding an equitable exchange for our currency and markets for us to buy provisions."

Jesse moved to hover menacingly over Philip. "An who made you the decision-maker for all of us?"

Philip stepped cautiously back from the looming cowboy but found himself against a high-backed chair with nowhere to go. "No one has elected me, I'm merely offering suggestions on how we should proceed. If you'd like to put forth a different tactic, by all means," he stuttered out.

Jesse continued his harsh look, but then broke out a wide grin, laying a calloused hand on Philips shoulder that had Philip teetering with its weight. "I think your plan is fine, scientist. Just making sure I don't need to start addressing you as sir," Jesse said with a chuckle.

Philip wiped the perspiration from his brow with the sleeve of his shirt. "No need for such formalities, Mr. James. I'm certainly not in the leadership position here, just lending my voice to spur us in the right direction."

Francis stood up and looked uncomfortably at Mary and Anne. "Shall we make our way to the docks, ladies?"

Mary scowled at him. "Ladies? Do we appear ladylike to you, swab?"

"You do smell a mite cleaner then I can ever remember," Anne said to Mary. "But that in no way makes you a lady." She walked past Francis and winked at Jesse.

"An you should talk," Mary said following Anne. She locked her arm in Francis' and pulled him along with her as they headed for the exit. "Come on, bucko, let's go see what trouble we can find."

Francis looked back at Philip with a mix of fear and trepidation as Anne played along with Mary and locked her arm with Francis' spare and the two woman sandwiched him, leading him out of the hotel.

Charlotte's eyes narrowed as she watched the two women depart, remembering exactly why she'd never warmed to those two harpies. She cast a glance at the James brothers, who, despite their inexperience with ships and sailing, had proven themselves capable enough.

"Alright then," she said to Jesse and Frank. "Let's do a little exploring. I'm eager to see what this city has to offer."

"I am as well," Frank replied, and without a backward glance at Philip and Colette, the three of them set off into the unknown city.

"Nothing good will come of this, will it, Mr. Albert?" Colette murmured.

"No, dearie. I keep hoping this is but a dream—that I'll wake up in a room above your saloon, nursing a devil of a headache and cursing myself for indulging too freely in your Kentucky bourbon."

"Since neither of us truly believes we're dreaming," she replied with a wry smile, "we might as well accept our fate and make the most of it. If I'm to find my way in this world, we should at least see what our treasure can buy." She looked around at the grand hotel, her eyes gleaming with ambition. "Who knows—perhaps this city could use a proper saloon and brothel."

CHAPTER 12 – SMALL VICTORIES

Woodes Rogers stood on the deck of the *Comanche* scanning the distant craggy shoreline of the island. He could still spot the cove that the *Queen Anne's Revenge* had hidden herself in. She wasn't visible but he could feel her presence deep in his bones. The rest of those rotten, scum of the earth pirates remained on that ship. Mercifully, he was finally rid of that demon, Edward Thatch. The Crown would grant him a knighthood for sending that man down into Davy Jones' locker. His job was almost complete.

In a testament to the savvy shipbuilders of this iron beast the *Comanche* was still afloat. It took hours to pump the water from its belly by hand, but they had succeeded in salvaging the ship from a watery fate. He had ordered the dead and drowned to be buried at sea since their soon-decaying bodies would be a detriment to the well-being of his crew. The original crew members who had intricate knowledge of the ship's machinery were now toiling to bring the engines back to life. The great cannons mounted in the turret could still be fired but the track that rotated the barrels was beyond repair.

He had watched the harbor battle that had taken place from the low deck of the ironclad along with most of his crew. The destructive power of the sky ships was both frightening and exhilarating. If England could have such ships, they would be able to rule the seas and the land throughout the modern world. He decided he would make intricate drawings of the craft to bring back to the Royal Society along with any other details of their engineering he could glean before finding a ship to bring him home. Perhaps he would claim the *Queen Anne's Revenge* for his own and sail that beautiful ship into London's harbor. First, he must have his captain's quarters thoroughly scoured of all the wretched filth of Edward Thatch's presence.

Rogers couldn't help but smile at the thought of Thatch's bloated body sinking into the depths of the sea. *Yes, finally the demon was vanquished.* He could feel the deep, wide scars on his cheek and jaw stretching the ruined skin as his smile grew. He gazed excitedly at the distant cove, feeling like the conquering hero once again, his mission close to reaching its end.

He heard the sound of boots on metal approaching him from behind. It was the gait of Henry Jennings and the stocky Wells Fargo man Bill Cooper.

"Sir," Jennings interrupted his musings. "The chief engineer is working to bring the engines back to working order."

"Most unfortunate this beast has no sails, we wouldn't be tarrying with our thumbs lodged in our arse if they had thought to rig one."

"The men seem short on wits and high afeared in our predicament. I know you're hot to tackle them pirates, but we may be well served in putting to shore and getting the lay of the land before pick'n another fight," said Cooper.

At this Rogers turned to the two men and gave a scowl. "What the men need is a chance to further bloody the enemy whilst they are still tired and weakened. A good victory will liven their spirits."

Bill Cooper turned and stared at the smoke hanging over the distant harbor. The enormity of the ships, buildings, and the sight of flying machines buzzing around unleashing hell upon all lingered like a waking nightmare in his mind.

"We don't even know where we are. Shouldn't we go to shore and—"

"We are in the Pacific," Woodes cut off Cooper's question. "The stars last night showed us that. If you were any kind of seaman, you would have known that. You are in my world now, Mr. Cooper. Please just follow orders and all will be righted. Oversee the repairs and keep the crew focused, both of you. Then we will sail to that cove and dispense with the pirates, claim back their stolen wares, and then we can all travel home."

Cooper and Jennings both had a skeptical look as Woodes stared at them like they were dimwitted whelps. The sound of several false starts to the engine below deck rumbled beneath their feet. The three men silently waited while the engines were tested several times, then with an echoing roar, the machinery came to life, a steady vibration reverberating through the metal hull as the engines idled. A cheer from below deck rose up from the open hatch as the men beneath celebrated the revival of the twin boilers and 320-horsepower steam engine.

Woodes looked kindly at the two men and his marred face distorted in a half-smile. "Small victories pave the way to great triumphs, gentlemen. You'll see."

Tom narrowed his eyes against the bright sun as he watched another flying machine cross his view. He could hear the distant, deep growling noise that came from its engine. The thrill of seeing them skirting through the sky still kept the boy's imagination thundering along at the speed of a locomotive. He was keeping track of how many different machines he was able to see.

Tom was leaning against the rope braces atop the ship's crow's nest while men labored below making repairs to the *Queen Anne's Revenge*. He had quickly become comfortable navigating amongst the ratlines, spars and sails as his quick, light body aided his balance and dexterity making him a natural for the jobs high above the deck.

His index finger tapped lightly against the handle of one of Captain Blackbeard's heavy pistols that he had stowed in his waistband. The tapping was a practiced habit that he was working on picking up from watching the famous gunslinger, Jesse James, do it. Tom was overwhelmed by his good fortune to be part of this adventurous pirate crew. In less than a week's time he had gone from a homeless, motherless street rat to a feared and wealthy pirate of the *Queen Anne's Revenge*. These new friends—no, he would now consider them pirate brothers and sisters—were teaching him everything about their way of life. It was like he was living a dream.

He squinted at the water beyond the cove, searching for any sign of trouble. So far, no ship, boat, or strange flying thing had come sniffing around while they hid in the tropical cove. Still, his heart thudded every time a shadow moved across the waves. He also kept an eye out for any clue that Captain Blackbeard might still be alive. He couldn't stop thinking about the ironclad the captain had been on. It had been swallowed whole by that monstrous whirlpool, the same one that had dragged them all into its roaring, frothy jaws. Did the ironclad arrive in these waters, surfacing to breathe the air of a new place in time like they had? Was there a chance the captain had escaped? He didn't know, but Tom wasn't giving up hope. Blackbeard was a man that no bullet, sword or cannon could kill.

"Tom!" Captain Roberts yelled from below.

He looked down from his lofty height to see the handsome, dashing pirate calling up to him.

"Aye?" the boy called back, now comfortable with his new ship-life terms.

"Any sign of trouble, lad?"

"No, sir."

"Well then, come down. I have another task for you."

Tom deftly climbed, slid and swung his way down from the crow's nest under the watchful eyes of an impressed Bart Roberts. The boy landed squarely on his feet after the last drop in front of Roberts as Black Caesar arrived carrying a box of tools.

"Come with me, boy," Black Caesar told him and started toward the stairway leading into the hold of the ship.

Tom took a step to follow the man, but Roberts laid a hand on his shoulder. "Here, you might need this."

Roberts held out a crimson scarf with a sheepish look on his face. Tom looked quizzically at the item before taking it and hurried to follow the quartermaster down the wooden stairs.

It took a moment for Tom's eyes to adjust to the dim light below deck. He hadn't had a chance to explore the depths of the three-masted frigate other than the gun deck and the captain's quarters. Most of the crew, himself included, has spent the night on shore in tents while the ship sat empty apart from the two men on watch.

Black Caesar led him down past the gun deck, crew's quarters, through the storage hold that held their treasure and supplies to the stern of the ship. The big quartermaster lit a lantern as the lower decks had no portholes. He was forced to stoop lower and lower the deeper they went until he was crab-walking underneath the wooden structure to a final hatch in the floor where he stopped and set down the overflowing toolbox.

The foulest odor that Tom had ever smelled assaulted his senses when Caesar opened the hatch to the ship's bilge. He stifled a gag, as nausea struck his belly and throat. The putrid fragrance of rot and mold, human and animal waste, combined with the stagnate briny seawater and mildew created a combination that he knew would be the subject of nightmares for years to come. The crimson scarf in his hand reflexively shot up to cover his nose and mouth.

He looked at Black Caesar, who he swore wore a slight grin of amusement on his face, about to plead mercy and ask to be released from the horrors of whatever task he was about to be assigned.

"It is a job only you can do," the man said encouragingly.

Tom shook his head, but Black Caesar only nodded. He set down the lantern and leaned toward Tom to take the scarf from his face. He took a metal box from his pocket and slid the top open. Dipping one of his thick fingers into the container he removed a waxy glob then smeared it underneath and around Tom's nose. Then he tied the scarf securely over the boy's face.

The goop had a strong smell of eucalyptus that helped mask the rotten smell of the bilge but only by a small margin.

"There is a leak that needs patching. It is four or five paces that way." Black Caesar pointed toward the left side of the hull. "I'll hold the light from the hatch so that you can repair it."

"I have to go down there?" the boy said with trepidation.

"I can't fit. Only a boy. An we only have one boy on the crew."

Tom let out a slow, heavy breath and started toward the opening but Caesar stopped him with a hand on his skinny arm. "Leave your shoes, breeches and shirt. Just smallclothes. The scent will never leave them."

Tom stripped out of his clothes while Caesar made ready with the tools. He couldn't understand how Caesar was able to suffer the stench without a face covering. *Maybe an adult's sense of smell faded the older they got?*

Tom sat with his feet hanging into the bilge hold wrangling the courage to drop down into the hellish dark void when he was startled by soft splashing and scampering underneath him. He quickly pulled up his legs and looked wide-eyed at Caesar.

"Just our four-legged crew members. They claim this deck as their quarters."

Tom nodded and started to drop down into the bilge. Caesar put his hand on his shoulder. "But don't let them get too close. You don't want a bite."

Tom knew full well that a rat bite could lead to sickness. He dropped down, landing with his feet and legs submerged in water almost to his knee. The foul liquid felt slimy and oily on his skin. He pushed the knowledge of its contents from his mind. He could see nothing in the murky darkness of his surroundings. He was surprised when Black Caesar's head appeared in the hatchway lighted by his lantern. He had stuffed wads of fabric into his nostrils to combat the smell.

"That way," Black Caesar pointed.

Tom turned and looked around the shadowy, cramped space that was now dimly lit by the oil lantern and his eyes took in the dark, wet wooden skeleton of the ship. The 'V' shape of the hull was pronounced at his current vantage point and after following Caesar's direction he found a plank that was pried loose with water flowing through its opening. He looked back toward Caesar, becoming aware of the beady eyeshine of several rats perched on beams while keeping a watchful eye on their unwelcome visitor.

"Found it."

"Aye, is it a hole or a crack?"

"Loose board. Separated from wall. Lost nails," Tom replied as he inspected the ship's wound.

"Mhmm. Take care to shuffle your feet then when moving. Bad luck to find one of the lost nails with your foot."

Tom hadn't thought of that, but he made a mental note to move his feet carefully through the sludge from now on.

"Grab some nails. You'll hammer the planks into place, then seal the seams with tar," came the order.

He nodded and set to work, moving as quickly as he dared. The stifling stink of rot and salt pressed down on him, the filth clinging to his skin like a second layer. Each breath dragged the foul, heavy air deeper into his lungs, and he fought not to think about the slimy bilge water seeping through his smallclothes leaving no patch of skin untouched.

Despite his misery, the ship had already claimed a place in his heart long before he'd ever set foot aboard her. Captain Blackbeard's stories and vivid descriptions had cast a spell on him, painting her as more than just wood and sails—she was a living thing, worthy of devotion. Now, as he worked to mend the leaking seam, he resolved to see her sail on forever, proud and unbroken. Perhaps one day he'd even stand at her helm, guiding her through open seas.

Tom worked diligently; his small hands steady despite the hot dampness of the bilge. Black Caesar stood nearby, holding the lantern aloft, its dull glow casting shifting shadows across the cramped space. Every so often, the pirate's deep voice rumbled with words of encouragement, a rare kindness that lit a spark of determination in Tom. Bolstered by the praise, he pushed himself harder, eager to prove he was up to the task.

He finished the tarring and examined the plank's seams for any sign of water seeping through, a quiet smile tugging at his lips beneath the damp scarf.

"How's she looking, boy?" Black Caesar asked.

Before Tom could answer, a deep, muffled rumble reverberated through the hull, like a distant thunderclap swallowed by the crushing depths. The very grain of the wood seemed to shiver with the sound. He whipped his head around to see Black Caesar's face, ghostly shadowed in the flickering lantern light. The man froze, his head snapping toward the noise, then lunged from the hatchway, hoisting the lantern high.

The bilge was plunged into suffocating darkness.

A mere heartbeat passed before the world erupted with unseen violence. A shattering roar ripped through the ship, a sound so immense that it felt alive, crashing over Tom like a tidal wave. The hull groaned in protest as the force slammed the ship sideways, its timbers vibrating like a struck bell. Tom was hurled into a beam with bone-jarring force, pain lancing through his skull just as darkness swallowed him whole.

CHAPTER 13 – REUNION

Charlotte was captivated by the lively scene unfolding in front of the grand hotel. Uniformed staff bustled about, unloading vehicles with practiced efficiency. Their crisp white pants and shirts, patterned with blue hibiscus flowers, contrasted sharply with the military uniforms worn by many of the arriving patrons. These newcomers carried large duffel bags slung over their shoulders, their movements purposeful and precise.

Taking the lead, Charlotte set off with the James brothers, Anne, Mary, and Francis in tow. The smooth roadway meandered through a palm-lined field, curving just enough to obscure the main road from view. The landscaped grounds felt almost park-like, dotted with pathways and inviting benches that seemed to whisper promises of quiet reprieve.

For a fleeting moment, Charlotte imagined Bart Roberts leading her to one of those benches, hand in hand, to share sweet words and stolen glances. She quickly dismissed the thought, scolding herself for indulging in such girlish fantasies. To mask her embarrassment, she casually spun one of her dirks through her fingers, a silent reassurance to herself—and a reminder to her companions—that her mind was firmly on more practical matters.

A glance behind her proved her mates were just as taken in by their surroundings as she was. Her eyes followed a large vehicle similar to the one that drove them into town round the bend in the road to approach the hotel. The sight was unremarkable now but once it passed, a tall man emerged, walking in its wake. Charlotte strongly squinted her eyes, not trusting her poor sight at this distance.

"Blimey! Ain't no way!" Anne Bonny remarked with excitement and ran toward the man.

"By the fires of hell…" started Jesse before hurrying along with the rest of the group to catch Anne.

A grinning Blackbeard stood with his hands on his hips as Anne reached him. She stopped in front of his tall, broad frame and pushed him with affection.

"Ain't no way it's really you! I thought the sea had swallowed ye whole."

"Aye, that it did. And belched me out here, aboard that damned ironclad."

"We thought you's was a goner for sure," said Frank.

They all arrived to greet Blackbeard and stare dumbfounded at him.

"No kraken, nor pirate hunter has bested me yet. Me ship and miss Colette came through this ordeal?"

"She's in that hotel with the little scientist," Jesse said with a nod to the enormous pink building at the end of the drive.

Blackbeard's white teeth shone through his smile as he looked at them. His eyes stopped on the unfamiliar face of Francis. "You one of Roberts' crew?"

"Yes. Name's Francis."

"The *Queen Anne's Revenge* still afloat? I trusted that rogue with her well-being."

"She is, took a few licks but he stayed behind to make repairs," Charlotte answered for him.

"I'm heartened to hear that." Blackbeard raised his head to look at his surroundings and the hotel in front of him. "Many marvels we've found ourselves in the midst of. Wonders and horrors."

"I'm guessing you've got a tale to tell, hmm?" asked Mary.

His face turned dark and looked them over, nodding his head. "I have a tale indeed," he said before lightening the mood as he pulled a bottle of rum from his coat. "Is there a saloon in that monstrosity?"

"Aye," answered Mary. "A grand one at that."

"Well then, mates, direct me to the apple of me eye and let's celebrate our good fortune to be reunited!"

Philip stood near the propped-open twelve-foot-tall wooden front doors while waiting for Colette to finish using the privy. He watched new patrons enter the establishment to be greeted and accommodated with their rooms. More than half of the new arrivals were in uniforms of the military, both men and women dressed smartly in blues, tans, and whites. Short, brimmed, matching hats adorned hair braided, tied in buns, or in the case of the men, cut brutally short.

He pulled his cigarette case from his breast pocket and opened it up. The paper rolls had dried out from the seawater and were crinkly to the touch. With a bit of trouble, he was finally able to get one lit and slowly inhaled a slightly stale-tasting breath of the smoke along with a tinge of the salt still clinging to his lips. He casually watched virtually everyone indulging in the habit of smoking, eyeing jealously their perfectly proportioned and milk- white-colored cigarettes.

A flourish of black fabric and wild matching hair caught his eye at the entrance and his smoke slipped from his lips to fall to the floor after bouncing off the toe of his boot. His mouth remained agape like a cod fish as the striking figure of Blackbeard the pirate stood in the entranceway drinking up the interior with his sparkling ocean-blue eyes framed under those thick ebony brows. Philip's pulse raced as that gaze found him and those eyes narrowed. He straightened his spine as the pirate strode quickly toward him followed by the rest of the motley crew which had set off on their mission only minutes ago.

"Well, well, well, Mr. Albert as I live and breathe." His long strides brought him quickly across the room to Philip. He bent down, picked up the cigarette and examined it thoroughly to find it still lit and functioning. He placed it between his lips and drew in a long drag, holding it for a moment, then exhaling with a cloud of smoke to match the size of his dark beard.

Philip was still gobsmacked when Thatch handed him back his cigarette. "Blackbeard—Mr. Thatch. You're alive," he stuttered.

"Aye. Quick and observant as ever," he said, laying a heavy hand affectionately on Philip's shoulder. He placed his other hand under Philip's chin and closed his open mouth.

Philip blinked his eyes several times as his mind and senses caught up with the reality of the figure in front of him. "It is good to see you, Captain, and in fine health it would seem."

"Fine health and on a fine adventure it would appear. Did you imagine joining us for a sail into the future? You being the first to understand our predicament, now you find yourself standing beside us in the year of our lord 1941." Blackbeard smiled briefly at the man then looked around the large room.

"I'm still trying to work out the science of how we—" Philip began, but Blackbeard's attention was suddenly pulled elsewhere.

Colette Dallaire appeared in the doorway, pausing as she stepped into the room. Her eyes widened with disbelief, and for a heartbeat, time seemed to stand still. Thatch's eyes locked onto hers, the intensity of the moment unspoken. Colette felt a rush of emotion swell in her chest, the threat of tears prickling at the corners of her eyes. With a quick tug of her heavy dress, she rushed toward him, her heart pounding in her chest.

Thatch nearly leapt to meet her. His large hands gripped her waist and swept her off the ground, spinning them both in a whirl of joy and relief. He kissed her deeply, his lips pressing against hers with a passion that seemed to make the whole world fade away. Slowly, their motion came to a halt, and Colette's shoes found solid ground again, though her feet barely seemed to touch the earth.

Without breaking the embrace, she wrapped her arms around his neck, pulling him closer. Thatch held her tighter, as though he could melt into her, their bodies pressed together in a way that felt both desperate and tender.

The others in the room, sensing the raw intimacy of the moment, gradually turned their attention away, realizing this was a reunion that needed no audience. Even the lobby patrons, for a moment captivated by the spectacle, felt the unspoken need for privacy and respectfully shifted their gaze.

Colette held his bearded face in her hands as their lips parted and eyes opened to look at one another. She smiled. "I thought I might never see you again."

He shook his head briefly, his voice low and resolute. "I'd have turned the very Earth upside down—rock, tree, blade of grass—if it meant finding you again."

She wasn't entirely sure that she believed this wild-tempered pirate, but she was certain that she saw sincerity in his fiery gaze. "What happened? How did you escape?"

His look became purposeful and with his arm around her he turned back toward his awaiting crew mates. "I wish to have a drink and celebrate with me love and mates while I tell you a tale of me exploits. Where is this bar you mentioned, Mary Read? Lead us to our salvation."

"It's through here," Mary said and set forth toward a hallway on the beach side of the lobby.

The group followed her with Philip vocalizing that they did have obligations for the day. He was shushed by a stern look and swat against the back of his head from Anne. In a short time, they reached a long, wide room with one wall that was dominated by windows displaying the sandy beach and lapping waves of the Pacific Ocean beyond their frames. A dozen stools sat empty in front of the bamboo-adorned bar. A tuxedoed man with dark skin poured drinks from behind the counter while a young Hawaiian woman waited with a tray for him to complete an order of drinks decorated with miniature umbrellas.

Thatch took in the richness of the interior, spending seconds sizing up the four groups of patrons lounging at low tables set near the floor-to-ceiling windows. Large doors made of glass stood open to welcome the warm tropical breezes. To a man and woman, they all gaped at him and his crew upon entering. As he, the James brothers and the three pirate women returned their stares they quickly averted their eyes.

Thatch made his way to the barstools and pulled one just left of the center for Colette to sit, parking himself in the center seat. As the rest found their spots, he motioned to the barkeep who quickly arrived.

"I have this rum, but no glasses, mate." He produced his store-bought Caribbean rum and looked over to the James brothers. "And those cowboys will be want'n your finest whiskey."

The barkeep stared from one unique character to the next, wondering if this group was a theater troupe or some sort of entertainment that had been lined up for a show before the world had decided to go to war yesterday.

Blackbeard became quickly impatient by the lack of response. "While we're young, knave. We have gold aplenty to pay our way." He turned his head from left to right at his friends and the pirates and cowboys reached into their pockets and slapped gold and silver coins onto the bar.

The curious look of the barkeep became all business as he produced glasses and a bottle for them. "What brings you to our fine hotel on this—?" he started in with everyday small talk.

"That will be all for now," Blackbeard said with a wave of his hand. He poured the rum into Colette's glass then filled his own and passed the bottle around. Once everyone had a full cup, he raised his in a toast. "To the Pirate Republic."

Only the three pirate women repeated his toast, but they all drank with him. He poured a second helping for all and raised his glass again. "To the winds of change that brought us all together once again in blood, fortune and love."

"In blood, fortune and love," was repeated by all and they clinked glasses and drank their drinks with merriment that lasted several rounds while Thatch told his story of survival and they in turn recounted their own violent emergence from the sea concluding at the death of Samuel Bellamy.

"That boy was an exemplary pirate, sailor, and leader. He sailed for a time with meself and Hornigold. He and that Paulsgrave Williams fellow were quite a pair. Hornigold had given Black Sam a captured ship of his own and he became a storied captain in quick order."

"I'd scarcely known the man a week," said Francis, "but that was long enough to know the steel in his spine and the kindness in his heart. The world's the lesser for his passing."

"Roberts thought of him as a brother," Charlotte noted with a misty eye.

"To Black Sam. May he rule the underworld as the right hand of Poseidon." Thatch raised his glass, and everyone took a muted drink. A somber moment passed as they all gave weight to the loss of Bellamy.

Colette placed her hand on Thatch's, watching his eyes mist over.

"Hornigold loved the lad's pirate codes. He incorporated them into the ideals of his pirate republic. Dreamers, those two." Blackbeard's face turned dark as he was brought back to Benjamin Hornigold's betrayal of him and the rest of the pirate captains. He held his tongue from telling that tale. Let the rest of them retain their rosy picture of the architect of the pirate republic. He caught the eyes of Colette and Philip, the only two in the room who knew the truth of Hornigold's fate. His own hands had held the sword that had run him through in front of a cheering crowd hosted by the pirate hunter Woodes Rogers.

He turned from the angelic face beside him and poured another glass of the smooth, caramel-colored rum. The store-bought liquor was spent now, the last drops in his glass. His grip tightened around the empty bottle until it threatened to shatter, his knuckles white as bone. Woodes was still alive, floating in that iron pot from San Francisco Bay alongside Jennings. There would be no peace, not a moment's rest, until that scar-faced bastard was dead and rotting.

Woodes blamed him for this mystical movement in time, this nightmare with only fleeting moments of reprieve. It felt like madness—a fever dream—but the storm of time had swept him up, tossing him body and soul, and dragging anyone near him a hundred years into the future in a heartbeat. What if he was to blame? What if he *was* the devil?

He had known men who had done worse deeds to achieve their goals: Jennings, Vane—they had taken ears, eyes, and lives for trinkets and baubles. That was never his way. He had learned long ago that fear was the sharper blade. The *appearance* of the devil could scare the heavens from a man's heart without spilling a drop of blood. He had perfected the theatrics of a madman that would have the colors of any ship lowered, and then they would raise the white with nary a broadside.

But now, everything he held dear was entangled in this game of storms and bloodied steel.

He nearly jumped when Colette squeezed his hand and whispered in his ear, "It will be okay, Edward. Let it go. You're not responsible."

"Reading minds one of your many talents, lass?"

"Plenty of men sat across my card table with that same 'weight of the world' look on their faces."

He turned to face her, gently lifting her chin to meet his gaze. Her sapphire eyes, steely and hardened by life, held a determination that struck him. She was remarkable—possessing the courage and wit to rival any pirate man or woman yet tempered with a grace and savvy as rare as it was captivating.

"Ahh, well dear, I'm merely out of rum. 'Tis the cause of any pirate's forlorn face."

Colette cracked a smile and raised her hand to the barkeep. "Another bottle of rum for Captain Blackbeard!"

The well-dressed man behind the counter gave a curious look but nodded his head and pulled a fresh bottle of Jamaica-Martinica-Guyana from the shelf with a label displaying a map of the Caribbean Ocean and its isles. He poured the honey-colored liquid to fill Blackbeard's and Colette's tumblers.

"Miss Charlotte, tell me your dear Bart Roberts has refrained from spending all our treasure on those gems encircling your neck."

Charlotte pointed her stiletto that she'd been using to preen her nails, as was her habit, at Blackbeard. "He's given me no gifts to date. These came willingly from a Mughal princess I happened upon near Sri Lanka."

"And what brought you to Sri Lanka?" asked Philip with interest.

"Why, it's where I prefer to summer, little man," she said with a sarcastic laugh.

"I bet she willingly parted with those jewels," snorted Mary. "Willingly with a blade at her throat." At that she laughed hard, joined by Anne and Blackbeard.

"Aye. She may have wet her pretty smallclothes before handing them over."

Anne raised her brows accusingly. "An how would you know her smallclothes were pretty?"

Charlotte brandished her blade at Anne, her narrowed eyes flashing with warning. "Don't lump me in with your bawdy and wicked ways, wench."

Anne, already half-drunk, burst into laughter, with Mary joining in on the merriment.

"I just question your eyesight. Could you see well enough to tell the difference between a bulge or a breast? One is in the pants, the other a blouse. Though one's more useful to my taste… at least some days."

Jesse watched Anne closely, his curiosity piqued, uncertain if the jab had been playful or something more.

Frank James, shaking his head, muttered under his breath, "These women are gonna be the death of me."

"So, the *Queen Anne's Revenge* remains afloat with a hold full of treasure for all. I must say that is a might better than the last time we were spit up from the mouth of a kraken," Blackbeard said before throwing back his glass of rum.

"I'll drink to that," said Anne clinking Jesse's glass.

"Not much that keeps you from drinking," remarked Charlotte crossly.

Anne let out an exaggerated breath of annoyance. "Was your time with Black Bart so unsatisfying to you that it has affected your mood? I couldn't tell from the noises you made in his tent last night." She turned to Mary. "What did you say it sounded like? A wild boar rolling in the muck?"

Charlotte abruptly flew off her stool sending it clattering backward to the floor, and swift as a jaguar leapt at Anne with her blade in hand. Anne ducked under the swipe, launching from her chair using one hand to push Charlotte away as she brought her own blade to bear.

Jesse and Frank were quickly to their feet, both holding their hands on the grips of their pistols, but they didn't remove them from their holsters, unsure of what to do as the two women started to circle each other. The patrons at their low tables jumped in horror upon seeing the wild women openly brandishing their weapons at each other. The barkeep kept his distance and motioned for the waitress to go get help.

Philip slowly moved behind the James brothers to arrive next to Colette and Blackbeard, who both remained seated while Charlotte and Anne took testing swipes at each other. Anne's face was masked with a sadistic smile while Charlotte's remained clouded with fury.

"Come on, Africa, show me what you got," Anne egged her on, dragging out the term *Africa* for effect.

Charlotte stabbed at Anne who then moved in close to the taller woman, blocking the blow and grabbing the wrist wielding the knife. Anne twisted underneath Charlotte's arm and slammed it onto the empty table next to them, sending the knife flying away. Before Anne could move with her blade to gain the upper hand, Charlotte had a second blade slashing toward Anne's chest. She rolled backwards over the top of the table, landing on her feet with the round table now serving as a barrier between them.

Charlotte aggressively tossed the table aside and moved toward Anne as she backed up, arriving close to four seated elderly patrons watching in horror. They scrambled away from the warring women before the two became locked together, each holding the other's arm over their head.

Francis slowly made his way to the open glass door to the beach side of the lounge along with several hotel guests wishing to escape the violence.

Philip nudged Blackbeard's arm. "Shouldn't you put a stop to this?"

"Me? How would you expect me to do that? Haven't I been bloodied enough these past couple of days?"

"Those two were bound to fight sooner or later. I've seen it happen in native tribes many times. They will either end as best friends… or kill each other," said Colette recalling her time spent in captivity with the Choctaw Indians as a young girl.

Philip took a long look at the odd couple before turning his attention back to the ongoing battle. The two women displayed contrasting fighting styles: while Charlotte's movements were as graceful as a dancer's, Anne's slashes and strikes were born out of the quick and dirty fighting style learned from the violent mêlée of the chaotic, close-quarter battle while boarding an enemy's ship.

Anne used her elbow to smack Charlotte in the jaw, loosening the warrior woman's grip on her arm. She then threw a knee, landing a blow to her thigh which sent a spasm of pain up the woman's leg. Charlotte quickly let go of Anne's arm and slammed her fist into her cheek.

Anne stumbled back, stars spinning around her eyes from the blow but kept her knife up and open hand ready to parry Charlotte's attack. The two women danced their knives at each other until Charlotte scored a slash near the bottom of Anne's cheek, drawing a line of blood. This sent a surge of rage through Anne, and she flipped the grip on her knife's hilt to send numerous backhanded strikes toward Charlotte's face. Charlotte in turn defended well but was being pursued and on the retreat. She moved to make a strike of her own to regain the upper hand, but Anne's foot snapped up to kick the knife from her fingers with a crack. The dislodged knife sailed through the air to lodge in the wall inches from Francis' head. He had been standing next to a bald man in a flowered shirt whose eyes widened like saucers as the blade vibrated beside him.

A new smile crossed Anne's lips as she faced Charlotte. The two women stared hard at each other, daring the other to make a move. Charlotte promptly unsheathed her twelve-inch kukri and flipped it skillfully around the back of her hand with violent intent. Anne eyed the long blade, its reach much longer than her dirk. She slipped the blade into her waistband and spun her revolver from its holster to aim it casually at Charlotte from her hip, her smile growing broader.

The retort of a loud bang from a pistol made everyone jump and turn toward the bar. Frank James held his smoking pistol above his head while he glared at the women.

"Would you two wildcats muster up a bit of civility so that a man could get drunk in peace?"

They all stared at Frank for a moment before a dozen armed soldiers burst into the room shouting in alarm, warning them not to move and to drop their weapons. A moment of indecision passed with thick tension hanging in the air. Charlotte was just steps from the open glass doors leading outside and she threw caution to the wind and bolted out, causing one of the soldiers to fire a round at her. In the blink of an eye Jesse and Frank James were firing rounds at the soldiers sending them scrambling for cover.

Anne tipped a table over on its side and fired her pistol at several of them, scoring a shoulder hit to one. She glanced at Jesse as he used one of his hands to rapidly stroke his pistol's hammer to fire his rounds. Through all the mayhem erupting around her she locked this new method away in her memory for later use as she opened her pistol's chamber, spilling the empty shells to the floor and calmly reloading her weapon.

Blackbeard felt more of a desire to protect Colette from the raining gunfire than sending a barrage of his own. He huddled his body against her as they knelt on the floor with their backs to the bar, Philip was also shielded beside them both. From the corner of his eye, Blackbeard saw Robert's sailor, Francis, sprint outside past the glass windows as they shattered from the gunfire that attempted to chase him down.

Mary Read darted from the bar and skidded to a halt beside Anne, taking cover behind the table that was being shredded by searing bullets. As Anne reloaded, Mary returned fire without hesitation.

"We need to get the bloody hell out of here!" bellowed Mary over the booming.

"Aye, not without Jesse," Anne answered seeing Frank and Jesse pinned down behind overturned tables of their own near the back corner. She eyed the large window that stretched to the ceiling nearest to them both. It was still intact even though several bullets had punched holes into its thick glass. She made eye contact with Jesse and glanced at the window. If it shattered away, they may be able to make an escape through it as the open door was too much in the soldiers' line of fire. Jesse immediately understood. He turned and took several shots at the window but frustratingly it held its form. Anne and Mary both spent several rounds attempting to burst the glass away from the frame but when their revolvers clicked empty it still stood intact.

"Blimey!" Mary exclaimed, turning back to reload and face the soldiers.

Frank fired his pistol until it was empty, then snatched a heavy metal-legged chair. With a brutal swing, he hurled it in a wide arc, sending it crashing through the stubborn window in a thunderous explosion of glass. Jesse gave his brother a quick grin along with a slap on the shoulder before sprinting toward the opening.

Mary and Anne exchanged a sharp nod, then unleashed a bombardment of covering fire. Anne seamlessly integrated the new move of using the palm of her hand to slap the pistol's hammer, triggering a rapid, heated onslaught of bullets. The two women hurried in a crouched run following the two cowboys out toward the lush hotel grounds.

The roaring noise of pistols and rifles ceased to an echoing buzz as several soldiers rushed out the glass doors to give chase and those remaining approached the squatting Thatch, Colette and Philip with their guns drawn. Thatch held his hands above his head as he eyed the stern faces surrounding them.

"Don't move! Drop your weapons!" was shouted at them again.

"Which is it, mate? Don't move or drop me weapon?" Thatch answered back.

"Don't play games, 'less you want your head blown off!" One of the men forced Thatch to the ground with a boot on his back and gun pointed at his head. Another soldier searched him, and upon finding his newly acquired pistol removed it and shoved it in his waistband. Thatch noted that they didn't find the Derringer in his shirt sleeve.

Philip and Colette were both found to be unarmed having left their own weapons in their rooms earlier in the day.

Two men in police uniforms came forward to pull Thatch and Philip to their feet and cuff their hands. Colette was left unshackled.

The heavier-set of the two policemen searched Thatch's pockets.

"You have ID on ya?"

Thatch looked at the man questioningly.

"Identification? Driver's license?"

Thatch looked at Philip for enlightenment. Philip just cocked his head, unsure himself of what they were asking for.

"We're just hotel guests. We've done nothing wrong," claimed Colette.

The barkeep came forward, unsteady on his feet. "They were with them! All of them, menaces! I thought they were from some theater group or actors of some sort, but they shot up the place!"

"*They* shot up the place! Not us!" exclaimed Philip, pointing at the soldiers. The nearest uniformed man aggressively pointed his pistol at Philip's nose, causing him to clam up, his face flinching from the still-smoldering barrel which was so close he could feel the heat radiating off the iron.

"Let's get them all in a cell down at the station while we sort out who's responsible for all this," said the overweight policeman.

"We'll be taking it from here, officer," said a man just entering the room with an air of authority.

Thatch recognized the voice—and the face that accompanied it. It was the Army Intelligence officer who had interrogated him aboard the *Ward*. The one with the pale blue eyes. *Becker, that was his name*, Thatch recalled.

"The army doesn't have jurisdiction here. This is a police matter," the heavyset officer said, his tone firm.

"Not anymore," Becker replied, stepping closer to the three prisoners. "We're at war. The President declared it this morning. They could be Japanese spies—or German."

His gaze swept the room, noting the heavy destruction, the scene resembling the aftermath of a hurricane ripping through the Pacific islands. Finally, his attention settled on the petite man and the striking woman beside Thatch. Their nineteenth-century attire was tattered, bearing the scars of some unknown journey. Thatch's wild story of time traveling from past eras filtered through his thoughts as he considered the three in front of him.

Becker stopped before Thatch, his expression unreadable. "Why don't we pick up your story where we left off, Mr. Blackbeard?"

CHAPTER 14 – BILGE RATS

Black Caesar shook his head, trying to shake off the disorientation from the deafening blast that had rocked the ship. Dust choked the air, and darkness enveloped him; the extinguished lantern at his feet no longer provided even the faintest flicker of light.

Grimacing, he pushed himself up, his legs unsteady beneath him, and stumbled toward the bilge hatch. Panic clawed at his chest as he bellowed, "Boy! Boy! You alive down there?" He dropped to his knees, straining to hear a reply from the cramped, suffocating space below.

Silence.

"Tom?" he called again, louder this time, his voice rough with urgency. Still nothing. The oppressive quiet was broken by the sudden staccato crack of gunfire from above, the sharp sounds cutting through the chaos like a blade.

Black Caesar's jaw clenched. Time was slipping away. His fists gripped the edges of the hatch as he hesitated for one final moment. He called down once more, desperation thick in his voice, "Tom! Answer me!" But the void offered no reply.

Heart heavy with the weight of his choice, Caesar surged to his feet and bolted for the stairs leading topside.

He reached the gun deck just as a shirtless Charles Vane stormed past, a band of sailors on his heels, each gripping long rifles with grim determination. Black Caesar barely sidestepped in time to avoid colliding with him.

"What the devil's happening?" Caesar barked, his voice cutting through the din.

"It's Woodes and his damn ironclad!" Vane shot back, shoving a pistol from his waistband into Caesar's hands. "They're trying to board us!"

Caesar glanced at the weapon, then at Vane, his lips curled into a snarl. "Let 'em try."

He followed Vane up the next flight of steps, the harsh sunlight spilling down from above like a pitiless eye. The deep-throated song of war filled the air—a symphony of booming cannon fire, the crack of rifles, and the agonized cries of men locked in battle. The drumbeat of munitions, the high-pitched screams of battle, all of this assaulted his ears and drove his heartbeat to match the crescendo.

Most men, unaccustomed to the raw violence of war, would have faltered at the sight beyond the looming open hatchway. But not Caesar and Vane. They charged forward, their strides unwavering, even as a bloodied body tumbled through the doorway and landed in a grotesque sprawl at their feet. The smell of gunpowder overwhelmed all other tropical scents as the two men burst from below and into the fray.

The ironclad sat twenty yards away currently with its long cannon swaying away from the *Queen Anne's Revenge*. Its navy soldiers had already swarmed their deck somehow and several others stood upon the iron ship firing long rifles at the pirates. Black Caesar searched the ship for fires or signs of destruction, but he could find none in the mêlée.

The loud crack of Vane's rifle sounded near his ear as the man shot an oncoming soldier brandishing a rifle of his own. Vane's shot hit home, the soldier's arms splaying out as he fell backwards. Black Caesar picked a target and fired his weapon, landing a killing blow on the third round. Vane bolted for the aftcastle in hopes of achieving the high ground advantage. Caesar spotted Henry Jennings locked in a pistol duel with Bart Roberts near midship and quickly made his way toward them.

Dead and dying men littered the crowded deck and many combatants were engaged in hand-to-hand fighting after emptying their firearms. Caesar downed another soldier with two shots to the chest and once he realized the gun was empty, he used it to club another to the floor with a swift strike to his forehead. Two men attacked him, grabbing him by his arms and attempting to pin them behind his back, but they were no match for his strength. He flung the first into the mast with the crunching sound of bones breaking against the thick wood and the second was hurled a moment later over the side of the ship.

Henry Jennings fired, the bullet aimed true at Roberts' heart—until Roberts spun at the last moment, the shot piercing only his shirt where his heart had been a fraction of a second before. The near miss sent him reeling, but he recovered quickly, raising his opposite hand to return fire. His shot missed, and as his pistol clicked empty, it was clear his luck had run out.

Jennings wasted no time, realigning his aim at Roberts' chest. His finger tightened on the trigger—

CLASH!

Black Caesar barreled into Jennings with the force of a breaching whale crashing back into the sea. The impact drove every ounce of air from Jennings' lungs as his body slammed against the unforgiving deck. Caesar's immense weight bore down on him, leaving Jennings sprawled and gasping beneath the pirate's crushing bulk.

Black Caesar looked up at Roberts in hopes that he was in time to save the man from a bullet in the chest but was surprised to see Roberts standing with his hands held high in surrender. He then felt the hot metal of a recently fired gun on the back of his head.

"Why don't you ease your bulk off that man, and we'll see what kind of flapjack you might have made of him," Bill Cooper said in his slow drawl.

Black Caesar turn his head to see the squinted eyes of the bearded Wells Fargo man holding a big .44 caliber Remington 1858. Beyond him was Woodes Rogers surrounded by his own British Navy men and some US soldiers as well. He was smiling, if such a thing was possible through those scars.

Black Caesar slowly pushed himself off Jennings, using the man's back as leverage to rise from the deck. He paused, hoping the weight of his massive frame had done its job—but a low groan escaped Jennings, shattering the satisfaction. Caesar scowled. He had hoped to crush the life out of him.

"Well, well, seems all is well in hand," Woodes said as several men began to tie up Roberts and Black Caesar.

There was a commotion on the aftcastle, and several shots were still being fired, then there was a loud splash of something or someone hitting the water. A moment later several men from that end of the ship approached.

"One man got away. A few went after him in pursuit, sir."

Woodes looked proudly around the ship, seeing that the day was won and the ship was his. "Very well. Keep at it. Make sure none of this scourge slip away."

"What did he look like, the one that escaped?" asked Jennings as he slowly made it to his feet feeling sprained and sore.

"Shirtless, long hair, big and strong," the soldier answered.

"Vane. It must be," sighed Jennings.

"No matter. They will all be rounded up in due course. We have their ship, their treasure, they have nothing left," Woodes said dismissively.

He strolled to stand in front of Bart Roberts. His eyes took the measure of the pirate then he slowly shook his head.

"The invincible Bartholomew Roberts. Dashing and handsome. The man no bullet nor sword could ever touch." Woodes took the cloth of Roberts' shirt in his hand and eyed the bullet hole just port side of his heart. "You seem to be living up to your reputation, Black Bart."

"As do you, king's man." Roberts said it as if it were a slur.

Woodes leaned maliciously close to Roberts' face. "I *am* a king's man, you pathetic, Godless scum. That king will surely knight me for bringing your lot to an end."

Roberts laughed in his face. "I didn't believe what Charlotte told me about you. That you couldn't wrap your mangled head around the fact we are no longer in 1718. Look around, simpleton! We are not even harbored in *1873* as we were only a day ago. Men fly through the sky and build ships the size of cities! Knight you? Your king is dust. Rot. They will have you banished to the basement of an abbey as a feebleminded dullard, feeding pigs and sleeping in their shit."

Roberts continued to laugh until Woodes slammed his big, calloused fist into his jaw sending the trussed pirate to fall unconscious to the wooden deck. He used his boot to roll Roberts over and watched the large ornate cross tethered around his neck fall from inside his shirt. Woods knelt and removed the necklace, studying the strange iridescent metal that made up the cross. It was almost crystal-like as it picked up glimmers from the light. He couldn't remember seeing such strange white material before. The cross was inlaid with diamonds and as he turned it, he noticed a pinkish hue. A groan from the pirate stole his eyes away from the prize and he tucked it in his shirt as he looked down with revulsion while Roberts started to recover from the blow.

Woodes turned back to his crew. "Get this scabrous, mawkish filth imprisoned below."

Woodes Rogers moved cautiously through the dimly lit interior of Blackbeard's quarters, his boots clicking softly on the freshly scrubbed planks. The air hung heavily with the lingering scent of mildew, a reminder of the ship's recent time beneath the waves, though efforts to air it out had begun to make headway. A faint trace of brine clung to every surface, an unwelcome testament to its watery grave.

The quarters, audaciously sized for a pirate's frigate, exuded a dark opulence befitting a man of Blackbeard's fearsome reputation. Heavy wooden beams framed the space, their edges carved with subtle, almost menacing details—coiled octopus and jagged waves. The walls were paneled in dark oak, polished to a dull sheen, with patches showing signs of repair where water damage had crept in.

At the far end of the cabin stood a massive desk, its surface scattered with maps, compasses, and what looked like hastily scrawled notes. A brass sextant gleamed in the muted light filtering through the recently replaced panes of the stern windows. A sturdy chair sat behind the desk, its arms and seat featuring stitched cushions of crimson fabric.

Above the desk, a wall-mounted rack held an assortment of weapons— a pair of flintlock pistols, a cutlass, and a dagger, all polished and arranged with care. A thick woolen rug, damp in places from the ongoing repairs, covered the center of the cabin, its intricate pattern just barely visible under a thin layer of grime that resisted the crew's efforts.

Despite the repairs, the quarters carried an undeniable air of foreboding, as if Blackbeard's presence lingered here, watching. Rogers felt it in the slight chill that brushed the back of his neck and the way the shadows seemed to dance against the wood. The room wasn't in disarray, but it bore the marks of its tumultuous history—like a beast brought back from the brink, snarling and defiant.

Woodes made his way back to the desk, his gaze fixed on the ivory-handled drawer adorned with serpents' heads. Their split tongues jutted outward, as if daring him to touch them. He hesitated, narrowing his eyes, before pulling the drawer open to reveal a set of revolving pistols.

He picked up one of the weapons, its weight balanced and precise. The design was impressively intricate, its engineering far beyond anything he had encountered before being spit out of the Nassau storm. These were no ordinary firearms. Likely purchased—or stolen—in that Pacific Coast city, San Francisco, he mused. His fingers traced the smooth cylinder as a nagging thought began to form, unbidden and unwelcome.

The vexing laughter of Bart Roberts echoed in his mind, fueling the maddening notion that perhaps, impossibly, he had traveled through time, not once but now twice. He shook his head sharply. No. There had to be a reasonable explanation. But even Jennings, a man as rooted in practicality as himself, had muttered about the oddities of this world and continued to push that they were indeed far in time from 1718.

With a frustrated growl, he dropped the pistol back into the drawer and slammed it shut, the force jarring the desk and rattling its contents. A cascade of coins and banknotes that had been neatly stacked spilled across the surface, drawing his attention. Among them, several map pages fluttered slightly in the breeze from the open window.

He picked up one of the coins and flipped it in his palm, examining the details of its minting. One side bore the engraving of an eagle, the words

United States of America, One Dol. encircling it. When he turned the coin over, his breath hitched—a seated woman holding what appeared to be a flag stared back at him. He rubbed his thumb over the date etched below: 1871.

A low hum rumbled in the distance. Woodes froze; the sound was still foreign and unnerving. He turned toward the cabin window just in time to see a winged craft gliding over the ocean, its sleek form cutting through the air with ease. His skin prickled as sweat broke out on his forehead.

Clammy and cold, he rushed to the open window, watching the craft disappear in the direction of the sprawling harbor that had been the scene of battle just a day before. His pulse thundered in his ears as his eyes dropped again to the coin in his hand. The date mocked him.

With a furious roar, he hurled the coin at a mirror mounted on the wall. It struck with a sharp ping but left no mark, its defiance only deepening his rage. The mirror reflected his own disheveled image, a man fighting the creeping suspicion that the world around him was not what it seemed.

He stormed out of the cabin, his boots pounding against the deck as he ascended to the upper level. Henry Jennings stood at the center of the activity, barking orders to the crew as they prepared the ship for sailing.

The *Queen Anne's Revenge* had fared surprisingly well in the attack, the lone shot from the ironclad having struck high above the waterline. Repairs were already underway, and Woodes knew it wouldn't take long to make the ship seaworthy again.

Yet none of that mattered now. The gnawing realization clawed at his mind: this was no longer the world he knew.

"Jennings!" he bellowed. "Jennings, I wish to see the king, or governor, or chieftain that runs this island."

"I don't know if that is wise," Jennings replied slowly. "We should finish the repairs and sail to England forthwith."

Woodes shook his head. "We need information. I'll sail to that harbor in the ironclad accompanied by my men and a small crew from the *Comanche*. You make ready for sail and finish your inventory of the ship's hold."

Jennings made a grim face and looked out toward the open sea. "This is an unnecessary risk. We have what we need. Pirates as prisoners and their treasure in the hold. We can sail Cooper back to San Francisco with Wells Fargo's stolen silver then make our way back home… whatever that might look like now."

Woodes put a fatherly hand on his shoulder even though Jennings was half a score older than himself. "I must find the truth of this," he said gesturing toward their surroundings. "I must. And I will. Then we will make sail to home." Woodes looked into Jennings' eyes, imploring his understanding.

Jennings nodded then turned and walked away. Woodes' mood lightened with purpose, and he shouted out orders for the men who would sail with him in the ironclad for their grand entrance to the island's harbor.

CHAPTER 15 – POLITICS & PLUNDER

"You two fillies planning to kill each other, or are we going to work together and make it back to that boat without getting caught?" Frank hissed, his frustration barely contained as the group hid behind a building at the edge of the town.

"Ship," Anne and Charlotte snapped in unison, their sharp tones cutting through the tension. They exchanged glares, but the violent energy between them had drained during their frantic flight from the soldiers.

"I don't give two shits what you call it," Frank shot back, voice low but firm. "I just want to get to it without you two getting me killed—or worse, locked up."

Frank glanced at his brother, crouched a few feet behind. Jesse had his pistol drawn, peeking around the corner of the building. His curt nod told Frank they had a momentary reprieve from their pursuers.

The group had been weaving through the coastal town's back alleys and narrow lanes, avoiding the main roads in a desperate game of cat and mouse. Francis had taken the lead, claiming that he could find the way back to the cove where their ship was moored. Anne and Jesse, however, had nearly derailed their escape at every turn by firing at their pursuers, each shot betraying their position. Frank had finally barked at the two hotheads to stop shooting if they wanted any chance of getting away alive.

Mary Read, ever the voice of reason, had worked to keep Anne and Charlotte from rekindling their quarrel. Meanwhile, Frank's thoughts were far from any notion of heroics. Going back for that insane bearded pirate, the saloon woman, and the scientist was not even a consideration. None of the others had brought it up, either. His focus was solely on survival—getting himself and Jesse off this island alive.

This place was madness: horseless wagons racing through the streets and flying Gatling guns raining death from above. Whatever Blackbeard's fate, Frank figured the bastard would find a way to defy it. He always did.

Jesse let out a low bird-like whistle, drawing Francis' attention. Francis turned back and gestured for them to move—the coast was clear.

Without hesitation, the five of them sprang from their cover, sprinting across the field of jagged pineapple plants. The sharp, waxy leaves scraped at their legs as they zigzagged between rows, their breath coming fast and heavy in the humid air. The sun beat down relentlessly, its heat intensifying the sticky, sweet scent of ripe fruit that practically begged to be eaten.

Reaching the edge of the field, they plunged into the cool, dappled shadows of a dense grove. Towering palms and thick underbrush swallowed them whole, muffling the chaos of the town behind them. They moved with swift deliberation, ducking low to avoid snagging branches and scanning their surroundings for any sign of pursuit.

The road they had traveled into town ran parallel to their path, visible in glimpses through the gaps in the foliage. The strange, horseless vehicles zipped back and forth, their metallic hums and growling engines an ever-present reminder of this unfamiliar, hostile world. Frank's grip tightened on his pistol as his eyes darted between the road and their path ahead, his mind racing with worst-case scenarios.

Over the next hour they trudged through various landscapes and obstacles and their demeanor relaxed into a state of calm determination. Francis still led the group even though there was just one road to follow. Mary and Charlotte walked behind him, discussing the politics of the pirate republic dreamed up by the recently lost pirate captain, Benjamin Hornigold. Frank brought up the rear in the steps of his brother and Anne Bonny.

"…and with the whole world searching for Henry Every and his treasure, the Pirate King up and vanishes. One moment he's getting drunk in New Providence; the next, he and his crew are lost to the winds," Anne recounted animatedly, her eyes gleaming as she spun the tale of the legendary pirate who was one of the few that retired a wealthy man.

"And they never caught him?" Jesse asked, intrigued.

"Never," Anne replied with a sly grin. "Rumor is he and his crew lived out their days in Madagascar." As she spoke, she twirled her revolver with practiced ease, perfecting her quick draw and holstering technique. She strolled beside Jesse, the swagger in her step matching the confidence in her voice. "So, tell me, Jesse James—who's the most successful outlaw? The one who got away with their fortune?"

Jesse scratched his chin, considering the question.

"John Wesley Hardin," Frank interjected from behind them, his tone matter-of-fact. "Killed more men than Ulysses S. Grant. Still at large, least he was last I heard." He shook his head, remembering it wasn't 1873 anymore. "Can't imagine he still is now though."

A quiet moment passed, the group walking in a rhythm set by the soft crunch of their boots on the mossy trail.

"Well?" Frank prompted, glancing at his brother. "Who do *you* reckon holds that reputation?"

Jesse's lips curved into one of his signature crooked smiles. "Me."

Anne tilted her head to study Jesse's face, a mix of pride and amusement lighting her expression. Suddenly, she let out a burst of laughter. "And that makes us the most successful pirates ever to live! Right, Mary? None have traveled as far or taken more booty—and lived to spend it!"

Mary glanced back with a wide grin that matched Anne's energy. "That's right, lass. Let the rest rot in their graves while we sail on with a hold full of treasure!"

With a playful nudge to Charlotte, Mary's enthusiasm was contagious. A faint smile flickered on Charlotte's face, threatening to break through her stern demeanor. For a fleeting moment, the tension of their earlier animosity melted into shared camaraderie.

Mary and Charlotte came close to colliding with Francis as he stopped dead in his tracks.

"Oy!" Mary exclaimed.

"Shhh." Francis hushed her and raised his hand, stopping everyone where they were. They all struggled to hear or see what caught Francis' attention, peering into the dense foliage of the trail but spotting nothing. Then they heard racing footfalls coming toward them, though not from a would-be pursuer behind but from ahead.

Without a word they all took cover and drew their weapons.

The flash of a shirtless man racing through the brush drew their eyes and suddenly the panting, cutlass-wielding Charles Vane was stumbling toward them along the path.

"Hold up, mate!" Mary said, rising to her feet. Wide-eyed, Vane brandished the sword in surprise but came to a halt, breathing heavily with his hands going to his knees as he bent over out of breath. He looked behind him quickly but could not bring words to his lips. He did not need to say anything, the crew knew he was being chased.

There were more approaching sounds behind him and Mary pulled the exhausted man into cover near Francis and Charlotte. Jesse, Frank, and Anne knelt behind concealing foliage with their pistols at the ready. Charlotte shook her head and held her finger to her lips for silence. She drew her kukri and shielded her form behind the thick trunk of a tree.

Two navy sailors from the ironclad appeared on the trail, rifles held at the ready as they kept a running pace watching for Vane further up the trail. As the first man came into striking distance Charlotte moved as swiftly as a cat, slicing open the man's belly and spinning to impale the second man with a thrust into his sternum. She followed up both blows with swift killing strokes to both men's necks, ending the conflict in mere seconds.

The rest of the group stood and watched as she wiped her blade on one of the soldier's shirts leaving a long smear of blood on the blue material. Charlotte locked eyes with Anne as if to say, 'that could have been you.'

Anne rolled her eyes. "Easy when your opponent's hobbled with fatigue."

The two women stared daggers at each other.

"Let's not rekindle old grievances," mumbled Frank walking over to Vane as the man started to catch his breath.

"Woodes has the ship," Vane huffed out.

"Bloody hell!" Mary exclaimed. "How does that rat bastard keep show'n up?"

"Snuck up on us as we's were finishing the repairs. Blasted a hole in the side and boarded before we could make a stand."

"Roberts?" Charlotte demanded with intensity.

"Woodes has him last I saw. He was alive, others too, but Jennings, the bank men and navy scum cut through most of the crew."

"But you got away clean, eh?" Anne said with a hint of accusation.

"Aye. Just. An if I stayed I'd be worm's meat. Is that what you'd rather?"

Anne shrugged her shoulders at Vane. "Just wondering how long you stayed. I know how easy it is for you to turn tail from a fight."

"Shut it, you poxing whore!" Vane shouted with venom at her.

Jesse's hackles rose and he stepped toward Vane to strike him, but his brother intervened, grabbing him to stop the blow.

"Damn! Do any of you pirates get along with each other? We need to figure out a plan to take that boat—ship—back. Instead of all you fighting each other, can we recover all our damn money?"

Anne made a taunting face at Vane who turned his head with disgust.

"They got the numbers now. Must have lost more than thirty men when they attacked." Charles Vane picked up one of the rifles from the fallen sailors and searched him for extra ammo. Francis picked up the other.

"Well, we can't go back to town, so we've got no choice," he said.

Vane looked around at the group. "Where's the scientist and that woman?"

Jesse spit tobacco juice on the ground near Vane's feet. "Locked up alongside Blackbeard I'd say."

Vane looked at them confused. "Blackbeard? Thatch is here? On the island?"

"He survived the storm on the ironclad just like Woodes. But these two," Mary indicated Anne and Charlotte, "they decided to raise a ruckus in a bar making the soldiers come a-running. Most likely Thatch is in irons, along with the scientist and Miss Colette."

"We can't worry 'bout them now. Let's make our way back to that ship, real quiet mind you, before they sail away with our loot," said Frank.

Woodes watched the cove disappear out of sight as the *Comanche* lumbered her way along the coastline toward the harbor. He stood on the deck of the ship, sea legs providing the balance to absorb the rise and fall of the flat-bottomed hull as they navigated the small ocean swells. He longed for his twenty-four gun sixth-rate frigate he'd left back in Nassau's harbor. It would have been a quicker, more suitable sail then this beast built for river fighting. His thoughts went back to that night when he and forty men had taken long boats out to Thatch's ship under the cover of night. Jennings and Hornigold had all the pirate captains in the hold for a meeting. They had cut the anchor to float the ship away from the town with the tides, but that sudden wind and storm was unlike anything he'd ever encountered. Within moments they had been swept out to the open sea. His long boat alone had been able to secure a tether to the *Queen Anne's Revenge*. The others became lost or sunk before they had a chance to row back to the harbor. Only he and a few of his men had survived the storm and whirlpool that swallowed him down to this hell.

Now, he had left Jennings in charge of the quick repair of Blackbeard's ship. They had secured the surviving pirates below deck and buried the many that had been cut down in a pit just past the beach head. He took just enough crew with him to run this contraption and some of Blackbeard's gold to buy something with sails to bring him back to the cove in the morn.

He felt the weight of Bart Roberts' necklace under his shirt. The cool metal never seemed to warm against his skin. Reaching into his pocket he removed the coin he'd found in Blackbeard's cabin. His mind clouded as he read the date again. Mocking him that more than a century had passed with this journey. He shook the foolish thoughts from his head. Soon enough, he would have confirmation that the date of the world was 1718. He rolled the coin in his fingers, gripped it tightly, then threw it far out into the sea.

Woodes was momentarily pleased, and his mind settled somewhat. He paced around the deck as the engines churned underneath his feet, pushing him closer and closer to the devastating scene of yesterday's attack. He harbored no desire to go down the ladder to submerse himself in the stale, oily-stinking air that clung to every inch of space inside the ironclad. He wanted a bit of solitude as well on this short journey.

He watched as the coastline became densely inhabited. Homes, buildings and roadways began to fill the landscape. Two more of those damn flying things roared through the sky near the beach in the opposite direction that Woodes traveled. They steadily sailed closer to the harbor as one of the wings started to circle them in a wide arc. The sight of the mighty ships and enormous buildings caused his heart to pound. Dread began to creep into his bones. The humidity, while no different from the Caribbean, gave weight to his breath causing sweat to bead his forehead.

He looked up at the white flag he had ordered a sailor to attach to the top of the turret—a signal to the local navy that they meant no harm. The flag puffed gently in the light breeze, offering him some small comfort that they would not be fired upon at first sight.

As they approached the harbor entrance, more boats and ships came into view than he could count. Smoke still poured from some burning wreckage, and many vessels lay incapacitated, ravaged by yesterday's bombardment. Men, women, sailors, and workers moved about with purpose, undertaking countless tasks on the decks of ships, along the docks, and aboard vehicles that buzzed like mice in a hold. Yet, despite all the activity, the area was barren of animals. No horses, cattle, or goats were anywhere in sight—only men and machinery as far as the eye could see.

Astonished, he choked back a stifled laugh. The only familiar sight was the birds. Gulls, cranes, and pelicans were everywhere, flocking and squawking, eager to pick at bones or steal remnants of meals.

"Halt! Stop!" an amplified voice blared from the bow of a gunboat. Woodes had been so mesmerized by the close-up view of this strange, mechanized world that he hadn't noticed two motorized metal boats approaching. Each was armed with large cannons to rival the two on the

Comanche. And now, a nearly three-hundred-foot metal warship loomed, moments from arrival. Woodes realized several ships were patrolling the harbor.

Of course, they would be, he chastised himself. They'd be bloody daft not to be watchful for enemies after that beating.

"Stop the engines!" Woodes called down the open hatch. He felt the *Comanche* lurch as the engines powered down to idle, momentum carrying the ship forward. The pilot briefly reversed the engines to bring the vessel to a halt.

The two gunboats circled the ironclad, their weapons trained on it the entire time. Each boat had two turrets, manned by operators seated in attached chairs, while half a dozen armed crewmen pointed rifles directly at Woodes.

Then a larger ship arrived, its wake rocking the ironclad so violently that Woodes had to grip the barrel of a cannon to stay upright. The massive vessel's two immense guns were trained on the *Comanche,* but at this range and given the ironclad's low draft, Woodes was confident they would struggle to land a hit.

Woodes remained standing there staring at the marvels while dozens of sailors lined the gunwales of the ship to get a look at him. One of the gunboats stopped their circling and expertly rode to the portside of the ironclad, with two armed men hopping down to his deck. The two sailors moved aside to cover him with their rifles as one more man came aboard. This man held a pistol to his side as he approached Woodes.

"You American?" the man asked, stopping several feet away.

Woodes slowly shook his head. "I am from Great Britian."

The man looked around at the deck of the ironclad. "That right? What are you doing so far from home, old chap? And where did you find this relic?"

Several men started to come up from below decks and the riflemen made ready for battle even though the *Comanche* sailors arrived from below with their hands in the air.

"We come in peace," Woodes called to the men and raised his own hands as he turned toward the crewmen lining the ship and the smaller gunboats. "We are not your enemy.

"Alright. Get everyone up from below. Slowly," the sailor ordered.

Two more armed men dropped down aboard the *Comanche* from the second gunboat and added to the task of guarding Woodes and the ironclad sailors. Woodes counted ten men in total that had accompanied him.

"That all of you?"

Woodes nodded that it was. The sailor looked him over then took in the navy crew members of the ironclad. He knew what kind of vessel he was now standing upon. He had seen them in books on navy history. A Civil War-era ironclad, or a replica of one. He eyed the uniforms of the sailors, noting the old style of dress and insignias that adorned them. *What the hell was going on here?*

"Bet you boys have a story to tell."

"That we do, lad, but I'd prefer to tell it to your captain."

The man smirked. "I'm sure the old man would prefer that too."

CHAPTER 16 – POX ON YOU

Blackbeard fumed as he paced the locked room where he, Colette and Philip had been imprisoned. There was a rectangular table in the middle of the room and four chairs had been placed around it. Colette sat in the one furthest from the door and Philip sat in another, staring at the light-emitting globe attached to the ceiling. His eyes darted to the wall-mounted switch near the door.

"Damn those troublesome wenches! Have I not had me fill of cells and capture?" Thatch slammed the door with the back of his fist in frustration.

Colette shook her head. "Edward, please sit down. Behaving this way will only worsen our situation."

He ignored her and continued his restless striding, bellowing, "Release us, you sons of Puritan bitches!"

Philip stood up from his chair and moved to the door, minding his steps so as not to interfere with Blackbeard's own movements. He cocked his head as he peered closely at the beige-colored switch on the wall. He flipped it into the downward position plunging the room into darkness, then back up, switching the light back on. It was the fourth time he had tested the mechanism and now he nodded his head in understanding. He turned back to the center of the room to suddenly find Blackbeard looming over him, face darkened with annoyance.

"Touch that again and I will tear your fingers from your hand with my teeth."

Philip shrank and moved back to his chair. "I merely wanted to conclude my study of the device. I have deduced that it operates by opening and closing an electrical circuit adding a most welcome convenience to lighting a lamp that is well out of reach."

"Pox on you, Mr. Albert!"

"Edward! Enough! You're acting like a child. We have done nothing wrong here and once we have had a chance to explain to whatever sheriff runs this town, we will be free to go," Colette told him firmly.

Blackbeard looked to the ceiling then hung his head, letting go of a deeply held breath. "Aye. Of course, you see the right of it." He turned toward Philip. "My apologies, good scientist. I value your observations."

Philip nodded his head at the dark-bearded pirate.

"Do be a true mate and share a smoke from your jacket pocket."

Philip pulled out his cigarette case and box of matches and slid them across the table toward where Blackbeard stood. "My matches are ruined I'm afraid, but you're welcome to try."

Blackbeard picked up the metal case, flipping the lid open with a flick of his wrist. He pulled out a cigarette, its paper tattered and worn. "No matter," he muttered, retrieving a metal lighter from his pocket. With a practiced motion, he struck his thumb over the tumbler, producing a sharp, fuel-rich flame that licked at the end of the cigarette.

The door burst open.

Everyone jolted as a weary-looking Woodes Rogers was shoved into the room, escorted by several armed navy sailors.

"You," Blackbeard growled.

The lead sailor smirked. "Seems you're all acquainted." He stepped out, locking the four travelers inside.

Woodes' eyes went wide as he took in his cellmates. The cigarette tumbled from Blackbeard's lips, forgotten as he lunged. He seized Woodes by the collar, spun him, and slammed him against the wall. Without hesitation, he pulled his fist back—long arm stretching as far as it would go—then drove it into the side of Woodes' scarred face.

Woodes barely managed to lift his arms before the next blow came. And the next. Each strike landed with the force of a storm, rattling through the small cell. He could do little more than shield his head as Blackbeard continued the assault, fists hammering down, fueled with hatred and vengeance that unleashed in every strike.

Colette and Philip shouted for him to stop; their voices drowned beneath Blackbeard's ragged breaths and the sickening crack of knuckles meeting flesh. They grabbed at his arms, struggling to pull him away, but his strength was overwhelming.

Woodes' arms weakened. His defenses crumbled. With a final gasp, he slid to the floor.

Blackbeard loomed over him, chest heaving, knuckles bloodied. Slowly, Colette's voice cut through the haze of his fury. He could finally hear her.

"Edward, stop! The man has had enough."

He didn't take his eyes off Woodes' bloodied face. "He would have killed you and meself given the chance." With a quick flip of his wrist the Derringer .41-caliber pistol was gripped in his large hand aimed at Woodes' forehead.

Woodes stared at the two-and-a-half-inch barrel, one eye beginning to swell badly, the other bloodshot but focused.

"Do it. Do it and may hell and the devil confound you," he muttered from his bleeding lips.

Blackbeard stared at him, sighting the pistol behind a squinted eye even though the adjacent proximity of the target made the odds of missing the mark close to nil.

"Edward. Please... don't kill him. If you do, then we will be charged with a crime and done for," pleaded Colette.

Woodes sat with his legs splayed, lowering his hands to rest on the floor. He felt more lost and defeated than ever before. After being taken aboard the metal warship, he had been interrogated by its captain, Outerbridge. The man had informed him that the world now stood on December 8th, 1941—a date that seemed utterly impossible. How could time have leapt so far from 1718? Yet the evidence surrounded him, undeniable and overwhelming.

At first, he had argued—albeit briefly—that his king and country still existed as they had just a week ago by his reckoning. But it was a futile defense against what was now painfully clear: the world he knew was gone. For hours, he had trudged solemnly from one ship to another, separated from his crew, each step exposing him to marvels he could never have imagined.

Every sight chipped away at his resolve, dragging his spirits lower and lower until he reached this wretched moment. Before him loomed the villainous pirate of his darkest nightmares, gloating with cruel satisfaction. Woodes wished only for death, yearning for an end to this unbearable torment.

Thatch watched Woodes' eyes and knew that defeat nestled behind them. He had seen it many times from those unfortunates confronted by his aggression and prowess. He smiled darkly and slid the pistol to rest once again in his shirt sleeve, hidden from view. He strolled to where his cigarette lay on the floor and picked it up. Blackbeard pulled a chair from the table and relaxed his lanky frame in the seat, propping his boots on the surface of the table.

"I find meself heartened by your predicament, Woodes. Seeing you flapping like a fish without water pleases me more than putting a round shot into your skull." Blackbeard let out a hearty laugh. "Woodes... surely you saw the enormity of the vessels and armament these future blokes have?

Pirates would have no place in this world. You have followed me around the globe and hurled yourself two hundred and twenty years forward in time to see me retire from the profession of plundering the Crown's ships. The *Queen Anne's Revenge* contains a king's fortune in its hold for me and me crew. I shall buy me a richly estate and spend my days getting fat and drunk while you wallow in your self-pity."

He watched as Woodes wiped the blood from his lip with his sleeve and pushed himself into a more comfortable sitting position against the wall.

Blackbeard shook his head slowly. "Maybe you can write a book about your adventures again. I had heard you had made more money as a scribe than any of your sailing ventures, which by all accounts left you bankrupt."

Woodes' mouth stretched in what could only be called an attempt at a smile as he looked up at Blackbeard's smug face with his one unswollen eye.

"You'll never see that treasure, friend. Jennings and the Wells Fargo man had seized your ship, killed your crew and started their journey back to England. That dream of yours is now lost, you villainous demon."

Woodes' words sank in slowly, and a murderous darkness shadowed Blackbeard's face. His fingers clenched the edge of his chair so tightly that his knuckles cracked like breaking twigs. Every muscle in his body coiled, ready to lunge—ready to wrap his hands around the pirate hunter's throat and squeeze the life from him.

The door clanged open.

Two soldiers strode in, positioning themselves on either side of the doorway. A moment later, Lieutenant Harris Becker entered, his pale eyes sweeping over the room. If he had any thoughts about Woodes—beaten, bloodied, and slumped on the floor—he gave no sign. Expression unreadable, he stepped forward and placed a handheld case on the table.

"Good evening, gentlemen. Lady," he said smoothly before turning to the guards. "Wait outside."

The soldiers nodded and exited, shutting the door behind them with a heavy click.

Blackbeard studied the intelligence officer, noting he was unarmed. Of course, there could be a hidden weapon, just as Blackbeard himself carried, but if Becker had come without a weapon, it meant one thing—he didn't want to risk a fight where he could be overpowered and end up arming his prisoners instead.

Colette took a measured breath, her voice calm but firm. "Sir, you must understand—we've done nothing wrong. The two women who were fighting may be known to us, but we were innocent bystanders. Please, release us. Or at least tell us what crime you believe we've committed."

"Please sit." Becker looked over at Woodes. "At the table, Captain Rogers." He glanced around the room at the others and Colette and Philip took seats across from him.

Woodes groaned as he gathered himself off the floor and made a show of dragging a chair to the opposite corner from Blackbeard before sitting heavily down.

"I have just a few questions before you all will be allowed out of this room. Please be truthful with me so that we can end this little affair as quickly as possible." He didn't wait for their affirmation but instead began to flip latches on the case to open the lid. He withdrew several papers and laid them on the table along with a small metal box that had a keyhole. He read from one of the papers. "Philip Edward Albert, born 1837 in Liverpool, attended Oxford University, married, no children, immigrated to America 1869, worked for several mining companies in Boston and later in San Francisco. Last known place of work was Comstock in 1873, no further entries. Is that you, Mr. Albert?"

Philip nodded, face etched with curiosity.

"Colette Dallaire, born in Louisiana 1847, proprietor of The Paris, brothel and gambling hall sold to Adolph Sutro after the business was seized due to bankruptcy."

"Bankruptcy!" Colette exclaimed. "How can they do that?"

Becker looked up from his report. "I take it you claim to be the same Colette Dallaire?"

"Of course I am!" She looked over at Thatch then back to Becker. "I must return to San Francisco at once. This needs to be resolved!"

Becker looked at her blankly then back to his report. "Woodes Rogers, born in Bristol, England, 1679, married to Sarah Whetstone, one son, two daughters. Accomplished sailor who circumnavigated the globe, twice. Rescued the stranded sailor Alexander Selkirk who would later be the inspiration for the novel *Robinson Crusoe*. Written by your friend, Daniel Defoe." He looked at Woodes who gave a curt nod.

Blackbeard's brow rose when he heard the name 'Crusoe', now understanding the reference the sailor on the *Ward* was using when referring to him as that stranded sailor.

"You were sent by King George the First to become governor of the Bahamas but shortly after your arrival you were lost at sea during a hurricane."

Blackbeard chuckled, drawing Becker's attention. He shuffled some papers until he found the one he needed.

"Edward Thatch or Teach as some have written it, though better known as Blackbeard... for reasons that are obvious," he said, glancing from the paper to the long, braided beard attached to the face of the mid-thirties pirate seated in front of him. "Wanted throughout the Caribbean and the Americas for piracy. Last seen in Nassau 1718, disappearing during the same hurricane aboard the *Queen Anne's Revenge*, a ship that was carrying many of the pirate captains of that time. All lost and never seen or heard of again. Until now.

Two hundred and twenty-four years later to be exact. With a short rest stop in 1873 to pick up these two," Becker pointed to Colette and Philip. "And for Captain Rogers to commandeer a Civil War-era ironclad."

Becker set the paperwork on the table and placed his palms on the surface, leaning in toward Blackbeard. "So, how does an illiterate pirate time-travel entire ships and their crews into the future? Twice?"

Blackbeard sat quietly, all the eyes in the room watching him. "Illiterate? Aye. Time travel you say? Wouldn't that be a real trick now? Quite a yarn you be spinning, Mr. Becker. Next you will have us all believing in mermaids."

Becker stared stone-faced at him. Blackbeard offered nothing more.

"You now deny the story you told me on the *Ward*?"

Blackbeard shrugged his shoulders. Becker shook his head. "You sailed with Benjamin Hornigold, right?"

"Aye."

"Was he with you on this journey?"

"Aye, for a time."

"Where is he now?"

"Dead," Woodes piped up.

Becker looked at Woodes, then turned back to Blackbeard. "Sam Bellamy?"

"He's dead now too," answered Colette.

Becker nodded. "Out of the pirates that time traveled with you, who survives?"

"Can't be sure but Mary Read, Charlotte De Berry, Anne Bonny. Only Woodes would know the rest."

Becker turned to Woodes for information.

He rubbed at his swollen jaw and moved it around, causing an audible clicking sound. "Bart Roberts lives, Black Caesar… possibly Vane, Charles Vane."

Blackbeard looked hard at Woodes. "What about me cabin boy? Did you or your scurvy-bellied men harm a young China boy named Tom?"

Woodes looked at him with knitted brows, annoyed by the question. It was lunacy to think this devil cared for the well-being of another soul. He shook his head. "I don't remember seeing a boy, fallen or standing, aboard the ship."

Blackbeard stared daggers with those blue eyes full of cold fire. Woodes just narrowed his own at him. The two men exuded hatred toward one another in silence.

"Did you sail with a pirate named Olivier Levasseur?" Becker asked, breaking the standoff.

Blackbeard looked at the lieutenant with sudden curiosity.

"The Buzzard? Aye."

Becker took a pad from his case along with a pen to take notes. "And when would that be, and where?"

Blackbeard leaned back in his chair and let his eyes search the ceiling, giving himself a moment to collect his thoughts. Colette and Philip watched him with interest, both remembering that name, the Buzzard, from Blackbeard's logbook.

"Levasseur wasn't in Nassau for our… *rendezvous*," Blackbeard said, his voice edged with suspicion. "Last I heard, he was in the Seychelles. Did he move forward in time as we did?" He still wasn't certain whether time travel was a common occurrence now.

Becker shook his head and pulled a small key from his pocket, unlocking the metal box on the table. Inside, nestled among dark velvet, were gold coins—worn smooth by time and trade. He plucked one out and slid it across the table.

Blackbeard leaned forward, his long, calloused fingers closing around the coin. He turned it over, studying the engravings. One side bore the outline of a three-masted ship, surrounded by weathered script that read: *WE LIVE BY THE CODE.* The reverse depicted a Jolly Roger, set above the date—1718.

Colette leaned in, curiosity lighting her eyes. Blackbeard flipped the coin toward her, and with a fluid motion, she caught it, rolled it across her knuckles before resting it in her palm. She looked up at Becker. "Is it rare?"

Becker shrugged. "You can find them in antique markets. A few hundred are known to exist, though most have been clipped or melted down for their gold. This one's among the best examples."

Colette passed the coin to Philip. Becker retrieved another from the box and slid it to Woodes, who studied the inscription.

"The pirate code," Woodes muttered with disdain.

"Something you'd know nothing about, *king's man,*" Blackbeard growled.

Becker ignored the tension and scanned their faces. "Have any of you seen this coin before?"

They exchanged glances before shaking their heads.

"Who minted it?" Woodes asked.

"The pirate king."

Silence fell over the table as they waited for Becker to elaborate.

"And who might that be?" Woodes pressed.

"Levasseur."

Blackbeard let out a sharp, booming laugh. "The Buzzard? That rot bastard claimed to be *pirate king?*"

Becker's expression remained steady. "By all accounts, he was. He lorded it over Nassau until 1721, amassing an armada for over three years.

No trade moved between the Old World and the New without Levasseur taking his share. His fortune was said to rival the coffers of King George and Louis XV."

He leaned forward from his standing position and placed his palms on the table. "It wasn't until the governors of the Americas allied with England, Spain, and France that his reign came to an end. They waged what became known as the War of the Bahamas. It lasted barely more than a year but shattered the Pirate Republic. Seeing the downfall of his island fiefdom, Levasseur spent weeks ferrying his treasure away from Nassau to places unknown. He struck a deal with the European crowns and was exiled to Madagascar—where he stayed quiet... for a time."

Becker let the weight of his words settle before continuing. "Then he and a handful of banished captains took to the sea again, raiding the Indian Ocean trading lanes. He was eventually captured in 1730 and sentenced to hang. His last words were a taunting puzzle to find his hidden treasure. He tossed a necklace into the waiting crowd from the gallows that held a rolled parchment stored inside a charm. Before he was hung, he reportedly called out 'Find my treasure, ye who understand it.'" He watched their eyes, seeing their rapt attention. "The content of the parchment was a cryptogram which would supposedly lead to where his treasure was kept secret. A seventeen-line cryptogram."

"I imagine that no one has yet found this treasure," said Philip.

"That is correct. It's estimated that he stored tens of thousands of these pirate republic coins but also much of the treasure he had plundered over the years as well. The cryptogram is a pigpen cipher, the brackets and dots representing letters like the layout of a pigpen."

"Pigpen ciphers were widely used by the Templars and Freemasons. Was Levasseur a member of either?" Philip looked at Blackbeard, who was deep in thought ignoring him. "Has anyone cracked it?" asked Philip.

"A French historian in 1937 was able to decipher it." Becker paused to search each of their faces. "It was a recipe."

Woodes scoffed at that news. "Recipe? These pirates are all foppish dog apes."

A smile broke out on Blackbeard's face. He let out a chuckle. "La Buse always fancied himself an excellent cook."

They all turned his attention to him.

"La Buse?" asked Colette

"Levasseur had more names than a Spanish prince at his christening." He stood from his chair and paced to the door with the group watching him. "So, the Buzzard, with all rivals gone, including our dear downtrodden Woodes Rogers, seizes the opportunity to declare himself king and rule the seas for a few years." Blackbeard turned back to face the table, leaning his tall frame against the door. "What is it you want from us?"

"You, specifically. The treasure has remained hidden for hundreds of years, and now by some unknown science, you arrive. A man that knew and sailed with Levasseur. Someone with intimate knowledge of how the man thinks. With your help we can locate this treasure and possibly discover how you and your friends were able to travel through time," Becker said with a trace of awe.

Blackbeard gave a counterfeit smile. "Ah, that sounds like a grand adventure, mate, but we are a bit weary. I'd like to sail Miss Colette and Mr. Albert home, recover from me wounds with several weeks of good food and drink before embarking on another journey. If you'd kindly allow us to go back to our ship, we can revisit your treasure hunt in a few months' time. Besides, it seems you have a war to fight."

Becker's face soured. "Your help could be voluntary or involuntary. It matters not to me."

"You mean to hold us all captive unless we help you in some sort of treasure hunt?" Colette asked with exasperation.

Becker's face was a mask as he packed up the coins and reports and locked them away in the case. "That is exactly what I'm saying, Fräulein. Guards!"

Blackbeard was pushed aside by the door opening and two armed guards burst into the room.

Colette stood haughtily. "You have no right to keep us here!"

"*You* are the one without rights. All of you," Becker said, taking his case under his arm and briskly walking toward the door. Blackbeard made a sudden move at the man but was stopped short by a pistol pointed at his head by one of the guards.

Blackbeard stood fuming with rage as the guards waited for Becker to exit then left the room as well, locking the door behind them. He looked at Woodes sitting in the chair with narrowed eyes. He considered momentarily how good it would feel to take his frustrations out on his scarred and beaten face. He could sense the weight of Colette's stare on him though, and he made his way to her. He took her in his arms and felt her resist momentarily, but she relented and held him in return. He breathed in the floral fragrance of her perfumed skin and hair. He longed for time alone with her to explore every inch of her petite frame.

"I will get you home, lass. It is my one true goal."

"I believe my home is gone now."

Blackbeard nodded his head, holding her shoulders and looking into her eyes. "I am your home, and you are mine from this moment forward. We will take what we will and damned be the world that stands in our way."

She smiled coyly at him. "You do know the way to my heart, Mr. Thatch." She stood on her toes as he leaned down to kiss her lips.

A groan of annoyance from Woodes brought them out of their intimate moment. Blackbeard stared hard at the man, then glanced to see Philip studying several reports.

"What have you there, Mr. Albert?"

"I was able to remove a few items before the lieutenant packed up his case, namely those pertaining to Levasseur's history and treasure."

"You little scamp," Colette said, smirking.

Blackbeard grinned. "I'm impressed."

A noise outside the door cut the conversation short. Philip hurriedly folded the papers and stuffed them into his coat just as the lock clicked.

The door creaked open. A metal canister tumbled across the floor, clattering to a stop.

Then, a hiss.

A sickly amber smoke began to billow from the device. The door slammed shut.

They scrambled backward, pressing against the wall, expecting an explosion. But the canister only spewed its choking fumes, thickening the air with every second.

Blackbeard tried to shield Colette, but it was useless. The gas burned their throats, making their eyes water. Their limbs grew heavy, knees buckling. One by one, they collapsed, a tangle of bodies sinking into darkness.

CHAPTER 17 – TOP SECRET

Outerbridge oversaw the refueling and reprovisioning of the *Ward* from the mid-deck railing. They were due to leave on patrol this evening and he watched proudly as his crew members performed their duties in a timely manner. He gazed out at the ruined Pacific fleet and heavily damaged harbor and the burning in his gut intensified. He was long overdue for a midday meal to quelch the acidic coffee he had continued to drink throughout the long morning.

He spotted a hurrying young ensign approaching the gangway with a folder held tightly in his hand. His head was on a swivel, eyes searching for someone as he was stopped before boarding the ship. Outerbridge sighed as he knew whatever was held in that folder was for him and it must be important by the haste of the delivery man. His meal would have to wait.

He approached the stairs leading down to the main deck as the messenger trotted toward him.

"Commander Outerbridge," the ensign said breathlessly.

"Yes."

The ensign practically skidded to a stop, saluting smartly before handing the document over.

Outerbridge took the folder and noticed the stamp designating it 'Top Secret' and unwound the string keeping it closed. He began to take out the documents to examine them when he realized the winded and sweating man was still standing at attention breathing hard.

"At ease, sailor. You can get yourself a drink of water in the galley if you need."

"Thank you, sir, but I'm to remain until you've finished reading it then take you to the nearest secure phone."

Outerbridge threw a curious glance at the ensign then turned his attention to the documents. He read them over twice to make sure their entirety was clear in his mind. He packed the sheets back in the folder and rewound the string into place. He did a quick scan of the men on his deck and spotted ensign Stanton. He called the man over.

"Sir?"

"Stanton, I need you to get our previous guest, Mr. Thatch, from the brig on base. Take Brockman along with you since you both will recognize him."

"I don't think anyone could mistake him, sir."

"Right, well, you two might seem like friendly faces to him so there won't be any trouble."

"Yes, sir," Stanton replied and set off to find ensign Brockman.

Outerbridge turned to the waiting man. "Alright, lad, lead the way to that phone."

Becker waited impatiently while four navy corpsmen loaded up the four unconscious travelers onto gurneys and wheeled them into the hallway. He looked behind him to see the curious desk clerk watching the process.

"Let's get them out of the building and into the truck."

The corpsmen followed Becker's orders as he led the way through the halls displaying his ID and rank as they went. No one questioned the parade of patients as they wheeled them out of the structure that made up the Pearl Harbor naval brig.

A large military truck with a canvas-covered back was waiting in front of the building.

Becker greeted a heavyset man dressed in navy fatigues that were ill-fitting for his size. He had greased-back, blond hair and a ruddy complexion. Sweat beaded his face like he was unaccustomed to the humid Hawaiian air. The two shook hands.

The corpsmen began lifting the gurneys, one by one, into the rear of the truck.

"Did you secure us the provisions I asked for?"

"In the back."

"Good, good. We'll be quite the heroes then," Becker said glancing back as the gurneys were being stowed.

Fifty yards away a jeep came to a stop and Stanton, along with Brockman, exited and approached the entrance to the building.

"You're crazy, the Sox were only nine games down from the Yankees and if they were in the World Series they'd have beaten the Cards in five," Stanton ranted in his Boston accent as the two men walked. "Next year they're going all the way."

"If there *is* a season next year. Everyone going to be fight'n Germans and Japs. You think baseball is going to continue while we're at war?" Brockman said, damping the mood.

Stanton held the door for Brockman to enter and something caught his eye. He stared over at the truck in the parking lot as the last gurney was loaded. He caught a glimpse of long black hair and a bearded face as the canvas was pulled closed and the corpsman hollered that they were done. He watched as the man he recognized as an Army Intelligence officer—Becker was his name, he recalled—nodded his head and climbed into the passenger seat, shutting the door with a clank. The idling truck ground into first gear and pulled away as Stanton let the door close without entering the building and slowly walked toward the moving vehicle.

Brockman pushed the door back open to see what caught his crewmate's attention. "Hey, you going on French leave or what?"

Stanton ignored his mate's quip and stopped one of the corpsmen that had loaded the gurneys into the back of the truck. "Hey, who did you guys put into that truck?"

The man shrugged. "Four civvies. A dame and three men. Spies maybe. Some Army Intelligence puke carted them off."

"Did one of them have a long black beard and hair? Beard with braids in it like a girl's hair? Real tall fellow?"

The corpsman nodded his head and walked off to join his companions.

"What's going on?" asked Brockman as he approached. "What was that bedpan commando saying?"

Stanton was just watching the truck make its way toward the exit gate of the base. His face turned white as the blood drained from it; a feeling of dread overtook him. He bolted for the jeep. "Come on! We need to follow that truck!" he yelled back at Brockman.

"Who are you, Bulldog Drummond?" Brockman shook his head but ran to catch up with Stanton. "What is going on?"

Stanton had already started the jeep and punched it into first gear when Brockman slid into the passenger seat. The jeep lurched forward and raced toward the end of the street to hang a right turn onto the main road of the base.

"They have Thatch in that truck. Something fishy is going on!" Stanton said as he took the right turn fast enough for Brockman to be thrown toward the driver's side.

"Who's *they*? And how do you know?"

"It was that guy from Army Intelligence. I saw him get into the truck as we arrived. They shoved Thatch, strapped to a stretcher, in the back." Stanton pressed down on the accelerator and passed several vehicles as he navigated along the busy road.

Brockman held on to the door frame and the glass windshield of the jeep. "Well, what of it? That guy is a strange sort, and we don't have the rank to be questioning an intelligence officer."

Stanton hit the brakes as they came to a line of three cars waiting to exit the gate. "There! There!" he pointed at the canvas-backed truck heading left on the street past the gate.

Brockman stood up in the jeep to get a good view as the truck drove off into the distance.

Stanton laid on the horn to hurry the guardsmen. One of them glanced at him with a look of irritation. He waved the car that was first in line through and beckoned the next one forward. He made a show of looking closely at the occupants and Stanton honked his horn again.

"Easy, Stanton. He's never gonna let us through if you keep that up."

"Come on, come on." Stanton fidgeted.

When their turn came, the guardsman looked darkly at the two ensigns. "Where's the fire?"

"Damn it, man…" Stanton started, but Brockman put his arm on his shoulder and leaned over.

"My friend here is about to be a father. He just got a call from the hospital," he said smoothly.

The guardsman's tone changed, and he nodded his head. "Congratulations, sailor. Hope it's a boy," and he waved them past.

Stanton stepped on the gas and the jeep shot forward, skidding around the left turn, merging into traffic.

With the wind blowing through their close-cropped hair, Stanton gave a snorted laugh. "Good one, Brockman."

"Well, I had a feeling anything that was going to come out of your mouth was going to put us both in the brig."

"Can you see where they are?"

Brockman leaned up over the windshield to get a higher view. "I see them. About five or six blocks up." He watched as Stanton navigated around several cars that were slowing him down. "They're making a right up ahead."

Stanton wound around an old wreck of a car only to be slowed down by another merging into his lane.

"What is your plan when we catch up with them?"

"Don't have one, but the skipper is going to want to know what happened. He said the navy wanted to bring Thatch back in for questioning and he obviously didn't know the army was going to grab him."

Stanton steered the jeep onto the next street, and they could see the truck driving six cars in front of them.

"Alright, maybe we just keep our distance. Follow them to see where they go." Brockman looked at Stanton to see what he thought of the idea. Stanton considered it for a moment then nodded his head. He stopped trying to race to catch the truck and stayed with the flow of traffic to keep some distance.

The two sailors drove in silence for some minutes until they spotted the truck turning onto the road leading to a small airport. Brockman looked questioningly at Stanton.

"What do we do?"

Stanton pulled to the side of the road before the airport entrance and leaped out of the jeep. He trotted up to the fence with Brockman right behind him. They watched as the truck drove out onto the tarmac and parked next to a squat, top-winged blue and white seaplane. The fuselage door was open and a tall man with curly blond hair and a mustache shielded his eyes from the sun as Becker stepped out of the truck. The driver came around and the three men opened the canvas flaps of the truck bed. They carried the four loaded stretchers one by one into the plane. From this distance, Stanton was able to see what looked like Thatch, two men and one woman unwittingly stowed aboard.

The three men unloaded two other crates from the truck to take aboard the seaplane, and the engines started up with a roar. Brockman looked at Stanton helplessly. Stanton just took a big intake of air and slowly breathed it out as the plane taxied to the end of the runway.

The engine revved loudly, and the pilot disengaged the brake allowing the hefty craft to lurch forward and race down the runway, building up enough speed to leave the ground and climb into the sky. The two sailors stayed long enough to see which direction the plane took before they walked back to their waiting jeep. Neither said a word on the whole ride back to the base.

Outerbridge sat alone in the cramped office, nursing a bitter cup of coffee he knew he'd regret later. The hot brew did little to settle his churning stomach as he leafed through the same classified documents he'd been handed over an hour ago. They read like the plot of some pulpy mystery novel—one with a heavy dose of science fiction.

The navy brass was on edge. Japanese and Nazi spies were rumored to have infiltrated the military, and whispers persisted that Hitler had agents scouring the globe for lost artifacts—items that could cement his grip on the entire world. One US operative had even gathered evidence of the Reich's fixation on the occult, its belief that mystical relics and experimental rockets might hold the key to their supremacy.

But none of that compared to what was in his own report. A pirate from 1718 had allegedly appeared in the waters near Pearl Harbor, along with a wooden tall ship that he claimed to be the captain of, all the while insisting he was the legendary swashbuckling Blackbeard. This was followed by the arrival of a Civil War ironclad in Pearl Habor that had vanished without a trace in 1873. If that weren't enough, it had all coincided with the Japanese launching their devastating sneak attack on the Pacific Fleet.

He was half-expecting Errol Flynn to arrive through the door dressed as Captain Blood, cutlass strapped to a sash around his waist. The absurdity of it should have made him laugh. Instead, his stomach twisted itself into knots.

Ring! Ring!

The red phone on the desk jolted him from his thoughts. He picked up the receiver.

"Outerbridge."

"Lieutenant Commander, this is Henry Stimson," came the voice of the Secretary of War.

Outerbridge straightened. "Hello, Mr. Secretary."

"Have you located this…" A pause. Paper rustled on the other end of the phone line. "Thatch fellow?"

"Not yet, sir. I sent a couple of men to retrieve him from the brig. I expect them back shortly. There was an altercation at the Royal Hawaiian involving several of these so-called pirates. Local authorities managed to detain a few, including Thatch. Fortunately, we had navy personnel on site, including Lieutenant Becker from Army Intelligence. However, four, possibly five, of their group escaped. Patrols are out searching for them now."

Silence.

Outerbridge checked the line, wondering if they'd been cut off.

Then—

"Lieutenant Becker from Army Intelligence is dead, William."

It took a moment for the words to register. Stimson had called him by his first name which also gave him pause.

"Dead, sir?" His grip on the receiver tightened. "When? How?"

"Becker was found murdered in his home four days ago in Atlanta."

A cold weight settled on Outerbridge's chest. "Atlanta? I don't understand. He was with me on the *Ward* just hours ago."

"My team reviewed your report. You stated that Harris Becker was in Honolulu within the past two days, but the only Harris Becker in service to the US army was killed—his throat slit, along with his wife and child. They were found Friday when he didn't show up for duty. His identification was missing." A beat passed in silence. "The man you met on your ship was not Harris Becker."

Outerbridge felt the acid rise in his throat. His mind raced. If Becker was already dead… then who the hell had he been speaking to?

Before he could respond, a quiet knock at the door made him look up. The door cracked open, revealing a grim-faced ensign Stanton and Brockman.

CHAPTER 18 – CHARLOTTE'S SWIM

Jesse, Frank, Anne, and Vane crouched behind the thick jungle foliage, their bodies tense as they peered through gaps in the dense greenery. The afternoon sun bore down, turning the secluded Hawaiian cove into a shimmering canvas of gold and turquoise. The scent of salt and damp earth filled the humid air, mixing with the distant sweetness of hibiscus. The rhythmic lapping of waves against the sandy shore below nearly masked the occasional creak of rigging from the *Queen Anne's Revenge*, which remained moored in the cove's sheltered waters.

From their vantage point above the beach, they watched the hijackers move about the deck. The captured ship, its brown hull dark against the sunlit waves, bustled with activity. Armed men patrolled the weathered planks, their rifles slung over their shoulders, their wary gazes flicking toward the beach. A few of them worked on the rigging, others moved supplies, preparing for departure.

"Where's that tin bucket they showed up in?" Jesse asked, shading his eyes against the glare.

"It may be sitting just outside the inlet, standing guard," Vane replied, squinting toward the open sea. The sunlight made it difficult to make out details beyond the cove, but he had a feeling the ironclad lurked just out of sight, its heavy guns at the ready.

"I haven't seen the pirate hunter," Anne muttered, scanning the deck.

Vane's gaze hardened as a man emerged from below. "Aye, but there's Jennings, the idle shifter," he said to Anne with a sneer.

Anne followed his stare, watching as Jennings strolled across the deck with his usual self-important swagger. He moved to the gunwale, propping an elbow on the rail as he gazed out at the horizon.

"That's a lot of guns on deck," Frank observed, his sharp eyes taking in the rifles stacked near the main mast and the pistols holstered at the men's belts. Even in the heat, they stood alert, scanning the beach as if expecting trouble.

"If we're gonna make a play at them, it'd be best to wait for later," Jesse murmured, glancing up at the sun. "Give it a few hours till the heat drives 'em lazy."

Anne frowned. "How do we know they're going to sit and wait for us? They could pull anchor and shove off at any moment."

Frank watched Jennings closely, noting the tension in his stance. Then he pointed toward the man at the rail. "That feller is waiting for something."

"Aye. I think Woodes took the ironclad, and Jennings is waiting for the bastard to return," Vane muttered, gripping the hilt of his cutlass.

Jesse clapped his brother on the shoulder. "You keep watch for a bit. The rest of us will scout around and see if we can spot the other boat out there. I'd like to know where those big guns are before we go hijacking Blackbeard's ship back."

They crept back through the dense underbrush, dodging low-hanging palm fronds as the afternoon heat pressed down on them. The sun reflected off the broad leaves, sending bright flashes of light through gaps in the canopy. Insects hummed in the thick air, and the occasional call of a myna bird echoed through the jungle.

When they reached the clearing where Mary and Francis were waiting, they found the two in a familiar argument.

"I'm telling you," Mary said, exasperated, "a well-manned sailing ship has the advantage in endurance. No need for coal, no reliance on mechanical failure—"

Francis scoffed. "And a steam-powered ship can run circles around it without a lick of wind! You really think Blackbeard wouldn't have taken an ironclad if he'd had the chance?"

Neither looked ready to back down.

Anne cut in, her voice sharp. "Where's the sea witch?"

Mary and Francis exchanged puzzled glances before glancing around for the missing Charlotte De Berry.

"She was sitting right there a minute ago," Francis said, frowning at the empty spot beneath a twisted banyan tree.

The jungle, which moments ago had been filled with the sounds of the island, now felt unnervingly quiet. The wind stirred the palms, but there was no sign of Charlotte.

They stepped forward cautiously, scanning the area. The warm breeze carried the scent of the ocean and the faint sweetness of tropical flowers. Jesse searched the ground for the impressions of footsteps that might show where the woman pirate had gone to. He found the tracks he was looking for, the boot size a bit larger than Anne's or Mary's. He followed them to where they faded into the foliage, heading down toward the cove where the pirate ship floated in the calm water. The woman was making her way closer toward the prize on her own. He turned back to the group with a shake of his head.

Charlotte was gone.

Black Caesar, Bart Roberts, and a dozen other men remained locked in the cramped storeroom below the gun deck. The space reeked of sweat, salt, and the sour stench of unwashed bodies, thickening the already stifling air. Every breath felt like inhaling warm, stagnant water, and the oppressive humidity clung to their skin like a second layer. The faint sway of the ship did little to cool them—this deep in the hold, the heat only compounded, baking them like bread in a hardwood oven.

The men from the mutinied steamer ship fared the worst. They were used to the bracing, fog-chilled air of San Francisco, not the suffocating embrace of the tropics. They sagged against the bulkheads, sweat rolling down their faces in glistening rivulets. Meanwhile, Black Caesar and Roberts, seasoned by years in the sweltering waters of the Caribbean, endured with a grim patience.

"We've made a fine mess of this," Roberts muttered, his voice a dry rasp in the dim light.

Black Caesar only grunted in response, his arms folded across his chest.

Roberts let out a humorless chuckle. "I've lost two ships in a week. A bard will one day write a true tragedy about my life. From storied pirate to beaten dog, sent to hang from a noose in London—captured by the great pirate hunter, Woodes Rogers."

The ship groaned around them, the slow rise and fall of the tide making the timbers creak. The low thud of boots above signaled movement on deck, while a steady drip of water somewhere in the hold marked the slow march of time.

"I've failed me captain," Caesar muttered, his deep voice thick with frustration.

Roberts patted him on the back with a wry grin. "Ah, I do not put the blame on you, mate."

Caesar stiffened. "You are not me captain," then, catching the tease in Roberts' tone, he exhaled and rolled his broad shoulders, loosening the tension.

"I hope Charlotte and the others don't stumble unaware onto the beach and get caught in Woodes' net."

Black Caesar pushed to his feet, doing his best to stretch his long legs in the cramped space. The low deckhead forced him into a stooped position, making his powerful frame seem almost caged. He strode to the heavy wooden door and pressed his palm against it before giving it a firm shove.

A fist slammed against the other side, followed by a barked order. "Settle down in there!"

Caesar scowled but stepped back, flexing his fingers as if imagining wrapping them around the guard's throat.

Roberts stood, brushing dust from his torn shirt and sleeves. Dried blood still crusted his knuckles, and bruises darkened his jaw and ribs, souvenirs of their capture. He scanned the dimly lit storeroom, his sharp eyes taking in their meager surroundings. Jennings had their men clear most of the supplies, leaving only a few empty crates, several short lengths of rope, and a piss pot.

"Well, mates, we've done enough lamenting our fate," Roberts announced, cracking his knuckles. "I say we start planning our escape."

A weary Chester leaned against the bulkhead; arms crossed. "And how are we supposed to do that?"

"Our landing crew is due back from their scouting trip to town," Roberts explained. "And when they return, they won't leave us to rot in here."

"Their odds aren't favorable," Black Caesar rumbled. "Only six of them against this lot."

"Aye," Roberts conceded, "but they'll try. I know my Charlotte. And when they do, we'd best be ready to help."

He surveyed the room again, this time with a fighter's eye. He pointed to the crates. "Break those apart. We can use the planks as clubs." Then he gestured at two of the stronger sailors. "You two, make some noise."

The men leapt into action. The two sailors slammed their fists against the wooden door, shouting to be let out, their voices bouncing off the tight walls. Roberts raised his boot and drove it against the nearest crate. The first kick merely rocked it, but the second splintered one of its planks.

Caesar took a different approach. He turned a crate upright and brought his heavy boot down in a crushing stomp, shattering the wood in a single blow. The men worked quickly, prying apart the splintered remains and divvying up the planks. Some had jagged nails still jutting from the ends—crude, but effective weapons.

Black Caesar swung his makeshift club through the air, testing its weight. His broad face twisted into a violent grin as he met Roberts' gaze.

Roberts nodded.

They would be ready for battle when the time came.

Charlotte knelt in the damp earth, her fingers curled around the hilt of her kukri, steady despite the wild drumming of her heart. The jungle around her buzzed with the sounds of unseen insects and rodents, while the scent of brine and damp foliage hung in the air. She squinted, cursing her weak distance vision, forcing herself to track the movement of the figures aboard the *Queen Anne's Revenge*. The ship loomed in the late afternoon sun, swaying with the tide and hulking against the silver-dappled waters. Somewhere within its bowels, Bart Roberts was held prisoner.

Bart Roberts—the man they called Black Bart, she mused, the scourge of the Atlantic. She thought back on her knowledge of the man. Even before they had all been torn from their own time and cast into this strange, distant future, his legend had loomed larger than life. A Welshman with fire in his veins and steel in his spine, a man who had taken to piracy not out of desperation, but out of a fierce, unbreakable will. He had loathed the cruelty of merchant captains and vowed he would never again take orders from a man who did not earn his respect. Within a year of raising the black flag, he had commanded one of the most fearsome fleets the seas had ever known.

And yet, for all his swagger, for all his iron discipline and relentless ambition, it had taken so little time for Charlotte to slip beneath his defenses.

She had never known a man like him. Never allowed herself to. She had lovers, certainly, fleeting passions in the dark corners of taverns or stolen moments aboard stolen ships. But love? Love was something she had always considered a weakness, a shackle that would slow her down, leave her vulnerable.

And yet here she was, pressed into the dirt like a hunter stalking prey, ready to spill blood for the man who had unraveled her resolve in mere weeks.

How had it happened? Was it his mind that had drawn her in first? That keen, calculating brilliance, the way he could read the wind, the sea, and the hearts of men with the same effortless skill? Or had it been something softer—the rare, fleeting moments when he let the weight of his burdens slip and met her gaze not as the indomitable Bartholomew Roberts, but simply as Bart?

She had told herself it was foolishness. That she was simply caught in the heat of shared battles, that this bond between them was forged from circumstance and the ever-present nearness of death. But she knew better.

She loved him.

And she would not leave him to die in chains.

Her knuckles whitened on the hilt of her blade as she scanned the deck once more. He was below. He had to be. But even if she made it to the ship, she couldn't slip aboard unnoticed without something to draw the guards' attention elsewhere. She needed a distraction.

Her mind worked quickly, weighing options, assessing risks. The James brothers would spot her absence soon enough, and they'd know her well enough to understand what she intended. Mary and Francis would follow. And Anne—well, Anne would either help or get in her damn way.

Charlotte exhaled slowly, pushing aside the thought of that insufferable woman. That was a problem for another moment. Right now, she needed to set her plan in motion.

Her gaze flickered to the jagged lava rocks lining the shore. Twenty yards to the water. A deep enough drop to plunge beneath the surface unseen. One or two breaths, and she'd be at the hull. From there, she could find a way inside.

She just needed the right moment.

She watched and waited. There was no sign of movement across the cove where she had left the others. Surely, they were concocting their own plan. That was fine, as long as they remained still. If they acted too soon, if gunfire erupted before she reached the ship, the risk would be too great. She had to be aboard *before* chaos broke loose.

A low, distant hum drifted through the thick afternoon air. Charlotte stilled.

One of those flying ships.

She pressed herself deeper into the shadows, heart hammering as the sound swelled. It was still beyond her how such things could exist, let alone function. They were designed like massive birds of metal, yet their wings did not flap. How did they stay aloft? What force kept them from plummeting like a cannonball into the sea?

She shook the thought away. That was a question for later. Right now, she had to focus.

The drone deepened to a growl, then the craft burst into view—skimming low over the hills, following the curve of the coastline. It hugged the tree line, its unnatural silhouette stark against the bright blue sky. A heartbeat later it cleared the cove, covering half the bay in an instant before banking wide, tilting its unnatural wings as it made a slow, deliberate circle over the moored tall ship.

Charlotte flicked her gaze to the *Queen Anne's Revenge*. Every sailor on deck had turned their head skyward, necks craned, eyes locked on the flying intruder.

Her distraction had arrived.

She launched herself forward. Soft boots skimming the jagged shore, she raced the final rocky stretch and leaped, slicing into the water like a diving pelican, her body a compact blur against the sun-sparkled water. The sea wrapped around her, warm and familiar, and she let the momentum of her dive carry her deep before she began her strokes, silent and strong.

Slowly, carefully, she released her breath in a stream of bubbles, controlling the air's escape so it wouldn't draw attention. She counted each pulse of her strokes, each second that ticked by in agonizing slowness as she cut through the water, aiming for the looming stern.

Her lungs burned, the need for air tearing at her chest. She fought the desperate urge to surface, pushing herself forward with dwindling strength. When she could endure no more, she broke through the water, drawing in a deep, quiet breath before slipping beneath the waves once again.

Her arms ached; each stroke became slower than the last as she clawed her way toward the ship. Just as exhaustion threatened to overtake her, a vast shadow swallowed the sunlight above.

The *Queen Anne's Revenge* loomed before her, its massive hull rising like a dark, impenetrable wall against the sky.

For a moment, she hovered in the water, treading silently beneath the ornate aftcastle. Sunlight glinted off the decorated windows, their glass catching the midday glow. The captain's cabin jutted out over her, so close yet still out of reach.

The sky ship was still circling overhead, its engine's steady drone blending with the shouts of alarm from the deck. Charlotte's pulse quickened. If they pulled anchor and set sail, she'd lose her chance. Desperation surged through her as she scanned the hull for a way up. She ran a hand over the smooth planking, searching for handholds, but deep down, she already knew—there would be none. Ships of this make were built to be sleek, their hulls meant to repel the sea, and anyone trying to climb them.

Biting back frustration, she turned her gaze toward the port side. She swam around the aft of the ship to the side facing the open sea. Relief flooded through her at the sight of the aft anchor line still running taut into the water. Silently, she swam toward it, and grasped the thick, water-slick rope. Its coarse fibers bit into her fingers as she coiled her legs around it, wrapping her ankles tight for purchase. With straining muscles, she inched her way upward, moving slowly and steadily, her damp clothes clinging heavily to her skin. Every few feet, she stole glances toward the railing, praying that the crew remained too distracted to notice her ascent.

Halfway up, a crack of gunfire split the air, followed by another, then several more in rapid succession. The boom of pistols and rifles echoed over the cove. Jennings' furious voice bellowed above the chaos, cursing his men for wasting ammunition. Charlotte risked a glance. The flying craft veered away, banking sharply as it abandoned its circling path. The men were shooting at it not her, she realized with relief. Unlike the metal warbirds she had seen before, this one bore no obvious weapons.

Men rushed toward the rail, dark silhouettes moving against the bright afternoon sky. The rope was no longer safe. Heart pounding, Charlotte released her grip and lunged for the nearest window ledge along the captain's quarters. Her fingers scraped against the wood, catching hold—but only barely. Her right hand slipped, and for a terrifying moment, she dangled by one arm, her body swinging away from the ship. The weight of her wet clothes and boots threatened to pull her down.

Gritting her teeth, she scrambled with her free hand, nails clawing at the wood. Her boots searched desperately for a foothold. At last, the toe of her boot wedged into a narrow gap where one plank stood out further from the one above, halting her swing. Her muscles burned, but she steadied herself, taking a deep breath to slow the wild pounding of her heart. With renewed determination, she adjusted her grip and hauled herself higher, both hands finally securing the ledge.

The window was small, meant for ventilation rather than passage, but it was her only way in. Pressing her shoulder against the frame, she tested it. The wood creaked, but the latch gave way. Bracing herself, she twisted sideways, exhaling to make herself smaller as she wriggled through the narrow opening. The moment her boots cleared the sill, she dropped silently onto the thick, musty rug that covered the wooden floor.

The cabin was cool and dark compared to the glaring afternoon light outside. Heavy drapes softened the daylight to a murky glow, and the air was thick with the scent of pipe smoke, aged wood and the undernotes of encroaching mold. The room thankfully was empty of men.

Charlotte exhaled in relief, pressing her back to the wall to listen. For now, she was unseen. Now, she had a chance.

Anne shook her head as she watched Charlotte dive into the bay, cutting through the water toward the *Queen Anne's Revenge*. The men aboard the ship shouted and pointed at the circling airplane—*airplane*, a term Anne had only recently learned while they'd been holed up at that grand hotel on the beach. She sneered. Half of her hoped one of the sailors would spot the woman and gun her down like a seal. *No*, she thought darkly. *I'd rather be the one to send that hag to Davy Jones' locker.*

Hidden in the trees along the sandy shoreline, Anne and her crew crouched low, eyes fixed on the unfolding chaos.

"I don't fancy a swim," Mary muttered, peering out over the water. She turned to the James brothers. "You blokes reckon you could pick off a few of those bastards from here?"

Jesse squinted, sizing up the distance. "Might manage with a long rifle," he said, thumbing the grip of his pistol. "But with these, we'd need the devil's own luck."

Francis ran a hand through his sweat-damped hair, eyes narrowed in thought. "We'll need to board her if we've any chance of getting her back."

Anne's gaze flicked to the shoreline, where the *Queen Anne's Revenge*'s longboat had once rested. Now it was gone—hauled back aboard the ship.

Frank let out a low growl. "If we swim for it like that woman, we'll have to keep our powder dry and pray we're not picked off like sitting ducks."

The group fell silent, watching as Charlotte inched closer to the looming hull. The airplane wheeled overhead, the men on deck still distracted. Anne's jaw clenched. If they were going to act, it had to be soon.

Francis flinched as shots began to ring out from the deck of the ship. His tension quickly eased as he realized the sailors were targeting the flying craft circling overhead. They watched as it dipped its wings in a tight banking turn and increased its speed to escape the small arms fire. Climbing higher, with the engine roaring loudly, it flew off in the direction of the harbor. "I imagine that is going to cause them to come back with a lot more of those things and a lot more firepower."

Mary caught site of Charlotte scaling the anchor line where it stretched into view as she climbed the rope on the opposite side of the ship from them. Their sight of her was then obstructed by the rear aftcastle as she climbed higher. "We can follow her up that way if we must."

"If she can do it, I can do it," grunted Anne.

Frank shook his head, but didn't comment. *Them women'll have me six feet under 'fore the next full moon.* He had no desire to leap into the water, take that long swim to the boat, then shimmy up a rope to reach the deck while dozens of men guarded the railing with rifles just looking for the chance to put a bullet in his head.

Jesse's keen eye watched the movement on the ship. After a few moments they all realized Charlotte must have made it on board without being discovered. "Alright. We follow that African. Let's quietly make our way to those rocks she jumped from and wait for an opportunity to do the same."

CHAPTER 19 – GHOST SHIP

The radio operator aboard the *Ward* pressed his headset tighter against his ears, straining to hear the crackling transmission over the hum of the ship's engines. His pencil scratched across the notepad as he jotted down the message, each word sending a jolt through his veins. Heart racing, he shot up from his chair—only to be yanked back with a sharp jerk as his headset cord snapped taut, nearly pulling him off his feet. Cursing under his breath, he fumbled to unplug the line from the CR-100's panel and shoved the cans down around his neck.

"Here! Get this to the skipper!" he handed the paper to a waiting crewmate with the last name of Kelley.

Dodging past two ensigns in the narrow passageway, Kelley barreled into the pilot house, breathless.

Lieutenant Commander Outerbridge stood at the forward windows, his hands clasped behind his back, eyes locked on the horizon. The *Ward* cut through the choppy waters, leaving the safety of the harbor behind. The humidity hung thick in the air, mixing with the distant splashing of waves breaking against the hull as the ship increased speed.

"Sir!" Kirkman's voice cracked with urgency as he thrust the message forward. "A JSR-1 on shore patrol just spotted that wooden tall ship. It's holed up in a cove, six miles from Pearl."

Outerbridge turned, his eyes narrowing behind his glasses as he scanned the paper. The coordinates stared back at him, a pinprick of ink marking the cove's location. Without hesitation, he handed the message to his navigator. "Plot a course. Full steam ahead, let's make hay." His gaze swept across the bridge. "Prepare a fast boat and a boarding party. Everyone stay sharp."

The bridge snapped into action, the crew moving with practiced precision. Outerbridge's jaw tightened. Orders from the Secretary of War had been clear—pursue the origin of these so-called pirates with all haste. The top brass was on edge after the bold kidnapping of four prisoners right under their noses. And since it was the *Ward* that had ferried Edward Thatch and Woodes Rogers only yesterday, the task had fallen squarely into Outerbridge's lap.

He glanced back out the window, where the waves were glittering under the afternoon sun. Somewhere out there a squadron of planes was scouring the skies, searching for the seaplane that had spirited away Thatch, Rogers, and that couple from the Royal Hawaiian's bar fight. While the navy combed through the ironclad relic that Rogers had sailed into the harbor, Outerbridge and his crew would confront the ghost ship itself.

A ghost ship. The thought made his stomach tighten. His father once told him a tale about the *Jenny*, a schooner found drifting near the Arctic in the 1840s. She'd been lost for seventeen years, her crew frozen solid where they stood—one man still gripping the wheel, the captain seated at his desk, logbook open, pen frozen mid-word. The story haunted him as a boy. Now, it seemed almost quaint compared to the absurdity of time-traveling pirates. Yet here they were, chasing shadows across the Pacific, and the evidence was piling up that the Nazis believed the impossible. Perhaps they shouldn't discount it either.

His eyes flicked to Stanton and Brockman, his two ensigns standing rigid at their stations. They'd missed their chance to stop the abduction at Pearl, but Outerbridge didn't fault them. Becker—or, at least, the imposter who had adopted the real Becker's name—had fooled everyone. He had posed as

Army Intelligence, smooth as you please, and now it seemed he might be a Nazi agent who'd slipped through their fingers not once, but twice.

Outerbridge clenched his fists. The weight of failure sat heavy on his shoulders. Still, there'd be no time for regrets once they reached the cove. First, they'd lock down Blackbeard's ship. Then, if fortune smiled on them, they'd get another crack at Becker. And this time, there would be no escape.

The *Ward* surged forward, slicing through the waves. Outerbridge's eyes narrowed on the horizon.

"Let's see what kind of ghosts we're dealing with."

Charlotte moved through Blackbeard's quarters with feline deftness, the kukri blade held ready in her hand. The cabin was dim, the only light spilling through the salt-streaked windows casting long shadows over the dark oak furniture. Her eyes scanned the room, alert to any movement, each step silent as a whisper on the worn floorboards.

The room held the weight of its infamous captain. An ornate set of cutlasses hung on the wall near a framed painting of Queen Anne, the ship's namesake. The English queen's fair skin seemed to glow against the oil painting's darkened varnished frame, her regal expression softened by curls cascading over her silk-clad shoulders, the fabric rich with lace and opulent embellishments. Even in portrait, she seemed to watch Charlotte with a quiet judgment.

Charlotte ran her thumb along the edges of the wall-mounted cutlasses, frowning at their dullness. Yard-long blades like these weren't suited to her style. She fought close, quick, slipping through an enemy's guard and cutting deep before they could react. Let them hang as the showpieces they were.

A faint scratching noise drifted from beneath a small, round rug. Charlotte froze. Slowly, she stepped toward the sound, the floorboards creaking beneath her boots. The scratching stopped. The silence pressed down on her. Kneeling, she peeled back the edge of the rug, revealing a split in the floorboards. She ran her fingers over the gap, feeling the faintest breeze against her skin.

Whump.

The cabin door swung open behind her.

"Well, what have we here?" The voice slithered through the dimness.

Charlotte spun to her feet, blade at the ready. Bill Cooper stood in the doorway, his bulk filling the frame, eyes glinting with predatory amusement. "Where've you been hidin', little daisy?"

She said nothing, her grip tightening on the kukri. Cooper stepped inside, unsheathing his Bowie knife with a slow, deliberate whisper of steel against leather. He held it high, the blade catching the light, and beckoned her with his free hand, grin curling beneath his close-cropped beard.

"You wanna play, darlin'?" He circled her, black pointed boots thudding softly against the wooden planks. "Let's play."

Charlotte struck first, a blur of motion. Her blade sliced through the air, aiming for his head. Cooper jerked back, the kukri missing him by a hair. He countered with a wide slash, the Bowie knife singing past her cheek as she ducked low and pivoted to his flank.

They danced, testing each other. Charlotte glided across the floor, light as a whisper, while Cooper moved with surprising speed for a man of his size. He wasn't much taller than she, but he was stout with muscles rippling beneath his shirt, each step heavy with power. He lunged, trying to snare her with his free hand, but she twisted away, feeling the air stir as his fingers grazed her sleeve.

He grunted, eyes narrowing. "Slippery little thing."

She darted in close, kukri flashing, and scored a shallow cut across his forearm. Cooper hissed, yanking back. Blood welled in the wound, dark and glistening. Undeterred, he pressed forward, swinging his knife in a brutal arc. Charlotte sidestepped, but not fast enough—the blade nicked her side, slicing through her shirt and into flesh.

Pain flared hot and sharp, but she swallowed it down, gripping her kukri tighter. Cooper grinned, emboldened by the hit.

"Come on, girl," he taunted. "Let's see if you got more bite than bark."

They circled each other, breath ragged, muscles coiled, and ready to strike. The cabin felt smaller with every passing second, the shadows watching silently as steel clashed against steel, each move bringing them closer to the edge of life and death.

Charlotte made for a lunging swipe and Cooper surged in tight to block her blade and run her through with his own, but Charlotte's move was a fake and she twisted her body to avoid Cooper's knife hand. She leapt upon the heavy desk and used its height to launch herself over the top of the off-balance brute, stopping her decent by sinking three inches of her kukri's blade into the soft meat of Cooper's shoulder.

He bellowed in pain but wasn't done fighting. His elbow shot back, catching Charlotte's temple with a crack that sent stars bursting across her vision. He swung his weight back against her and she stumbled toward the wall. Cooper pivoted around to face her, causing Charlotte to lose her grip on the hilt of her blade. He pushed her back against the wall, kukri still implanted high in his own back. She was slammed against the wall and the room shook with the impact, shelves rattling as trinkets and maps clattered to the floor.

Cooper's hand closed around her throat, his grip like an iron shackle. The edges of her vision darkened, lungs burning for air as she clawed at his wrist. Her free hand fumbled at her belt for another weapon, but Cooper drove his knee into her gut, stealing the last of her strength. The room spun. Her legs buckled.

He loomed over her, blood streaming from his wounds, a sick grin curling his lips. Slowly, he raised his Bowie knife in a backhanded grip, its tip glinting in the dim cabin light, poised to split her skull.

BOOM!

The Wells Fargo man was ripped from her view. She slid to the floor gasping for air. Charlotte's ears rang loudly, and the acrid scent of cordite swirled through the room. She rolled over on her hands and knees to catch her breath, and looked over at the wrecked skull of Bill Cooper lying several feet away, blood pooling around the gore-spattered floor. She sat back again, resting against the wall, and looked over to see who had fired the killing shot.

Young Tom stood frozen, Blackbeard's massive Colt .45 revolver trembling in his grip. Smoke still curled from the barrel as the cabin boy squinted down the sights, his narrow eyes locked on the corpse. He took a shaky step forward, the open trapdoor behind him revealing his hidden entrance.

Charlotte forced her battered body to move, staggering upright. The shouts of men and pounding of boots echoed from above; the ship was alive with chaos. She stumbled toward Cooper's corpse and planted a boot firmly on his back. With a wet, sickening squelch, she wrenched her kukri free, blood slicking the blade.

"Watch the door, boy," she hissed, her voice raw. Tom nodded, eyes wide, as Charlotte steadied herself, gripping her weapon tight. The battle wasn't over yet, in fact it had only just begun.

She moved quicker after a few seconds of recovery, blood now pumping to all her extremities. She made her way to stand ready at the door. She pointed to Blackbeard's oak desk. "Behind there! Use the desk to steady your aim at anyone who comes through that door."

Charlotte listened intently for the footfalls of the men coming toward the cabin. She glanced at Tom and found the boy was nervously pointing the pistol at her. "Ay, boy!" She motioned for him to aim at the door and edged herself further away from his field of fire. She shook her head. If she didn't die at the hands of Woodes' men, she'd catch a bullet from the lad's panic.

THUD!

Three men stormed in, rifles at the ready, eyes wild and searching. Tom squeezed the trigger before they could take aim. The Colt roared, each shot slamming through the cramped quarters like cannon fire. The boy kept pulling the trigger long after the cylinder ran dry, the hammer clicking uselessly as his face twisted in terrified determination.

One sailor dropped like a sack of stones, a bullet clean through his heart. Another stumbled, clutching his side, crimson staining his shirt. The third spun toward Tom, raising his rifle.

Charlotte moved.

Her kukri flashed in the dim light, slicing through the air with lethal grace. She darted low, slicing across the wounded man's thigh. He howled, crumpling to one knee. Before he could raise his weapon again, Charlotte's blade found his throat, silencing him with a wet gurgle.

The last sailor swung his rifle toward her, but she twisted aside, the muzzle flashing past her cheek. The shot punched a hole through the wall, wood splinters biting her skin. She drove her shoulder into him, knocking him off balance. He swung the butt of his rifle, catching her ribs with a sickening crack. Pain flared through her side, but she gritted her teeth and drove the kukri into his gut, twisting the blade before yanking it free. He slumped to the floor, dead.

Breathing hard, Charlotte wiped the blade against the man's trousers and looked at Tom. The boy was frantically searching his pockets for more bullets, hands shaking. She placed a steadying hand on his arm.

"No time," she said, voice low and urgent. The sounds of distant shouting and pounding boots echoed through the ship. "If we stay here, we're dead."

He looked up at her and nodded his head. It was then the putrid scent from the boy hit her nose. She gasped and turned her face from him.

"Ugh, why do you stink like a bilge rat?"

"Because that's where I was. Black Caesar had me…"

She strode toward the door ignoring the rest of the boy's story. Stopping in the doorway to look for trouble, she motioned him to stay quiet. She glanced back at Tom, the kukri in her hand glinting red in the hallway's flickering lamplight. "Follow me, boy."

Bart Roberts, Black Caesar, and the rest of the captive men were on their feet the moment the first gunshots echoed through the ship's wooden bones. The creaking timbers groaned underfoot, and the air was stale from the confined space. Distant shouting carried through the dim corridor, muffled by the heavy planks, but the reasons for the commotion were clear enough: a battle was taking place.

"Stay where you are!" the guard behind the door barked, his voice strained with fear.

Black Caesar gripped his makeshift club, the massive weapon dark and blunt in the lantern's flickering glow. Without hesitation, he hurled his bulk against the door, each impact reverberating through the confined space. The wood splintered beneath his relentless assault.

"Stop that! Stay back, or I'll shoot!" the guard warned, rifle trembling in his hands.

Caesar ignored him, driving his shoulder harder into the door, feeling the frame groan beneath his weight.

BLAM! BLAM!

Two shots exploded in the narrow space, deafening in the tight quarters. Wood splintered, and a bullet sizzled past Caesar's chest, the heat grazing his skin. One of the men behind him cried out, clutching his arm where a fragment of lead had torn flesh. The others scrambled for cover, pressing themselves against the rough-hewn walls.

Then—silence.

Bart Roberts exchanged a wary glance with Caesar, both men holding their breath. The only sounds were the ship's mournful creaks and the distant chaos above. Slowly, Caesar stepped back from the door, his chest heaving.

The lock turned with a metallic click, and the handle began to shift.

Weapons at the ready, the prisoners tensed, prepared to fight tooth and nail for their freedom.

The door swung open, the lantern's dim light spilling into the corridor. There, standing with a grin wider than the Devil's own, was young Tom. The boy cradled a pistol in his small hands, his chest puffed with pride.

"Black Caesar!" Tom cried, racing into the room. He flung his arms around the giant's waist, burying his face in the man's side. Caesar patted the boy's head, his broad hand gentle against Tom's mop of hair.

"Good lad," Caesar rumbled, his voice low and proud.

Bart Roberts was the first to step into the corridor, his long legs swiftly closing the distance to where Charlotte knelt over a fallen guard. The bodies of two sailors lay crumpled nearby, their blood pooling across the worn planks. Charlotte was rummaging through their belongings with practiced efficiency, scooping up spare bullets and a discarded rifle.

Roberts fell to his knees beside her, his chest tightening at the sight of her battered face. She looked up, her eyes meeting his. Relief washed over him as he pulled her into his arms, the scent of gunpowder and blood lingering between them.

He kissed her, slow and deep, but she winced at the pressure against her bruises. Roberts pulled back, his dark eyes scanning her face, taking in every cut and contusion. His hand cupped her cheek, thumb brushing over the darkening bruise beneath her eye.

"Looks like you've had a time of it," he murmured.

Charlotte let out a breathless chuckle, though it came out more like a rasp. "Thought I might've lost you."

He nodded, resting his forehead against hers. "No sword nor storm shall keep me from you, lass."

She snorted softly, the corner of her lips twitching. The man had a flair for dramatics, but she saw the truth in his gaze. He meant every word. She kissed him again, quick and fierce, before the moment could slip away.

Gunshots rang out above deck, the ship shuddering beneath them as the fight raged on. The timbers groaned, and somewhere aboard ship, a cannon fired, the blast rattling the very air.

Black Caesar stepped past the couple, peering up the nearest ladder. Several bodies littered the floor, their blood seeping into the cracks of the aged planks. Charlotte's kukri work, no doubt.

"The fight is up there. We need to take back the ship," Caesar said, his deep voice rumbling through the narrow corridor.

Roberts stood, rifle slung across his shoulder. "Aye. Split the party. Half of us go up from here. The other half takes the far ladder, up to the bow. We box them in."

Charlotte nodded. "Bonny and the cowboys. Read. Francis. They'll be up there."

Roberts chambered a round with a decisive snap. "Time to send these bastards to hell." And with that, they surged forward, the promise of blood and freedom guiding their every step.

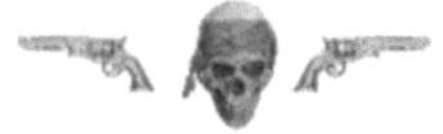

Vane struggled to swim with one arm holding a pistol above the seawater as he made his way toward the ship. The bastards were reloading the aft swivel gun to blast another round shot at him and his mates as they swam toward the anchor line. He knew this plan was doomed to fail as soon as they were spotted entering the water where Charlotte had, but their choice was decided when they heard the gunshots and shouts from aboard the ship signaling the beginning of a battle.

Bonny, the James brothers and Francis were faring better then he by closing the distance to the ship while choosing their shots carefully and one at a time shooting to keep the defenders at bay. Mary was the only one who loathed swimming more than he. The woman looked close to drowning as she moved through the water like a barn animal, spitting the sea out of her mouth every couple of strokes.

The splash of a bullet entering the water just inches from his head brought his mind back to focusing on his efforts. If they could make it to the safety of the protruding aftcastle the enemy would not be able to get a bead on them. He dunked his head down into the water with the pistol still precariously held in the air above him and swam like a frog with everything he had to reach the safety of the tapered hull.

Anne, Frank and Jesse reached the cover of the aftcastle and trod water, catching their breath. Francis was seconds from joining them when a rain of bullets from above caused him to abandon his rifle and dive beneath the surface. Jesse swam to the edge of the protecting ledge and fired at the sailors above deck, forcing them to take cover. Reloading, Jesse moved back while Frank, then after him, Anne, fired up to the railing as the rest of their ragtag crew arrived at the ship's hull.

Jesse was still winded from the awkward swim, but they needed to move to the next phase of the boarding. He looked out at the anchor rope just a few yards away that Charlotte had used to gain entry to the ship. "Cover me," he told them all.

He started to swim for the rope and was assaulted by a hail of bullets as well as several twelve-pound cannon balls dropped from above, which caused him to duck dive and spin back around. The group was unable to even get off one shot at the defenders.

"Maybe swim under the water until you reach the line?" Francis mused nervously.

"You first," Jesse growled.

They all waited for someone to come up with a plan. The creak and straining sounds of the anchor windlass turning began to sound and the group watched in horror as the line began to ascend from the bay.

"Damn it all to hell."

More gunfire and battle shouts thundered down from the unseen deck, the echoes rattling through the ship's hull like the pounding of war drums. Jesse sucked in a deep breath, with the warm seawater feeling like a heavy blanket as he plunged beneath the surface. His boots felt like anchors, but he kicked hard, arms driving him forward in a desperate sprint through the clear water. The anchor line shimmered in the dim light, the iron wedge rising steadily. He lunged for it, boots scraping against the slick metal as he clung to the neck of the anchor, gripping the drenched rope with one hand.

The anchor surged upwards, dragging him from the depths, saltwater streaming from his hair and clothes as he broke the surface. Perched on the rising iron, Jesse's waterlogged revolver was steady in his grip. One of the riflemen spotted him, eyes wide with disbelief as he swung his rifle to take aim. Jesse pulled the trigger—click. Misfire.

The rifle's crack split the air, and Jesse flinched as the bullet ricocheted off the anchor with a metallic shriek, sending sparks into the spray. He pulled the trigger again—click. Panic surged through him. The sailor followed his spinning form through the rifle's sites, finger on the trigger ready to blast him when his aim was true. The third time, the revolver finally barked, the shot punching into the sailor's chest and sending him sprawling backwards.

The anchor jerked to a halt, swinging Jesse wildly against the hull. He clung tight as the rope twisted, turning him into a spinning target. Another rifleman leveled his weapon, struggling for a clear shot as Jesse dangled helplessly. He squeezed the trigger on his Peacemaker once more—another misfire. His heart pounded, each breath ragged.

From the deck above him came a blood-curdling scream. Jesse craned his neck to see Black Caesar, a hulking shadow against the sunsetting sky, swinging a hardwood plank into a sailor's skull with a sickening crunch. The man shrieked, arms pinwheeling as he pitched over the railing and vanished into the bay with a splash. A mêlée ensued between the startled riflemen and Caesar's men. Several of the ironclad's sailors were lifted like dolls to be tossed overboard.

Tom appeared at the rail, face grim but determined, tossing a rope ladder over the side. Jesse swung the anchor closer, leaping to grab the ladder just as the anchor began to sway back. His boots slipped on the wooden rungs, seawater pouring from his sleeves and pants legs, but he climbed, muscles burning, until his hands gripped the deck's edge.

The scene that met him was chaos. Pistols roared. Blades flashed in the late afternoon sun. Blood slicked the boards beneath his boots. He dumped the empty casings from his Peacemaker, fumbling fresh rounds into the cylinder with wet fingers. The gun was soaked, the powder likely useless as water most probably seeped through the seals of the casings, but he loaded it anyway, stowed it in his holster then drew his hunting knife with a grim set to his jaw.

Vane hauled himself aboard behind Jesse, eyes burning with fury. His eyes searched the mayhem until he spotted Jennings amidships and bared his teeth. "Jennings," he growled, charging into the fray. Anne followed close behind, a wicked grin on her face, blade flashing as she carved through the enemy.

Tom yanked the ladder back up once everyone was aboard, kicking it aside. "No comin' back for the bastards!" he shouted, face flushed with battle. Mary grabbed him in a fierce hug, then wrinkled her nose. "You stink, boy."

Frank reloaded with swift, practiced hands, his eyes scanning the carnage. The deck had become a slaughterhouse—bodies sprawled across the planks, the air thick with the stench of gunpowder and blood. Black Caesar waded into the fight like a force of nature, each swing of his makeshift weapon breaking bones and sending men screaming to the floor with cracked limbs and skulls.

Jesse wiped the salt from his eyes and squared his shoulders. The *Queen Anne's Revenge* was alive with the clash of steel and the roar of gunfire. They'd come for their ship, and they weren't leaving without her.

The ship swayed from the beach with the anchors raised and the tide pulled the frigate out to the mouth of the cove. The wind was picking up but with the sails furled and no one manning the tiller she drifted of her own accord.

Vane leaped over several bodies as he ran toward the bow where now Jennings and his men were battling Bart Roberts, Charlotte De Berry and several members of the steamer crew. A man was emerging from a ladder leading below deck wielding a pistol in front of Vane and without stopping his momentum he stomped on the man's head, using it as a step stool to reach the top of the forecastle. He fired the last round from his gun at a sailor sending a scorching bullet into the man's side, then clobbered him with a swing of the empty weapon, ending any fight the man might have left.

He scooped up a cutlass from a fallen man and continued on his mission to reach Henry Jennings.

Jennings finished off a sailor that was brandishing a wooden plank studded with rusted nails as his eyes took notice of the oncoming menace and violent intent of Charles Vane. The flicker of a smirk slid from one side of Jennings' mouth as the man rushed toward him. *Good, we shall finish this at the last*, he thought.

Vane roared as he reached Jennings, swinging his cutlass in a wide arc. His old captain was ready for the wild slash though and maneuvered his own sword to intercept and deflect the swing. Vane's momentum carried him past his enemy to skid to a stop and switch to a defensive stance but not before the practiced swordsmanship of Jennings scored a glancing slice on the back of Vane's shoulder.

The drawing of first blood sent a laugh up from Jenning's throat.

"You were always so impulsively naïve, and it shall be your undoing."

Vane paid no heed to the wound as the pain didn't register in his violent state of fury. The years of being under Jennings' thumb—and his boot—

fueled his rage. He chopped at the man using his brute strength to drive him back on the defensive. Jennings was already fatigued from the battle, but he was no stranger to the brutality of war and found the energy within his core to move his tired legs and arms to avoid Vane's onslaught. He defended and watched for an opening, taunting the man in hopes he would make a mistake.

"No worse captain has ever sailed these seas, Charles. How many times had your men turned against you over your idiotic or cowardly decisions?"

Vane growled and increased his brutal hacking slashes with Jennings blocking each with the clanging of metal against metal.

"You even lost command to that curly-haired low-birthed whelp, Bellamy. I gave you a ship to run and you shrank from battle. Yellow blood flows from your twisted heart. You are a craven, foul, calf-lolly."

Enraged, Vane swung with a two-handed grip, attempting to break Jennings' sword underneath his mighty blows. He overextended his swing at that moment and left himself open for Jennings to counter. Vane strongly felt the pain this time as he was slashed across his bare chest, opening a shallow but foot-long gash that stretched across his darkly tanned skin. He stumbled to the side and hastily brought up his cutlass to defend against a killing blow from Jennings. Their swords rang out in the clash and Jennings' sword hilt caught against Vane's. Jennings twisted it quickly and flung Vane's sword from his grasp. Vane stared up at the matched hatred beaming from Jennings' eyes as the man made ready to swing his blade and remove Vane's head.

A sickening crunch sounded as the tip of a wide, curved blade emerged from Jenning's middle. Vane used the last of his strength to shoot up to his feet and plunged a dagger from his waistband deep into Jennings' belly. His lips were mere inches from his former captain's face. "May you never have a day's rest in hell," he said in a hoarse whisper.

He twisted the knife as he abruptly removed it from Jennings' gut. Standing behind Jennings, Charlotte removed her blade, and the dead man fell between the two exhausted pirates. Vane nodded his head in thanks to her but felt bitterness at not besting the man. That feeling faded fast as the pain of his wounds grew stronger and the fuel of the battle faded from his muscles. Blood flowed freely down his chest as he surveyed the battleground.

He glanced over to Anne Bonny as she shot a sailor repeatedly in the chest, the impact backing the man toward an opening in the rail. The man stood with several holes leaking blood, still alive but too stunned or too shocked to move. Anne's revolver was empty, but she casually approached the bleeding man and pulled a second gun from in the dying man's waistband. She brought it up to his head and pulled the trigger. It was the last gunshot of the battle, and the man fell backwards, over the side, to splash dead into the sea.

Bart Roberts, in his blood-soaked fancy-shirt, leaped majestically to stand on the gunwale, one hand holding a line, the other raising a cutlass in the air. "Huzzah! The ship is ours!"

"Huzzah!" chorused back Anne, Mary, Black Caesar and Tom.

"Huzzah!" shouted Roberts again, and the rest of the crew joined in, chanting the hearty exclamation.

Chester stood near him and glanced toward the beach. He moved closer to the railing to get a better view. "Captain…" He pointed at the dozens of soldiers amassing on the sand from the foliage around the cove.

Roberts turned his attention to the beach and his eyes narrowed. "Make way! Unfurl the sails! We need to catch the wind and make haste, men!"

The crew snapped to their tasks and Roberts strode back to the wheel. He rotated the tiller to bring the *Queen Anne's Revenge* out the mouth of the cove and into the open sea. They ignored the shouts and sounds of activity that carried across the water from the sand. The ship had already drifted a good distance from the beach, and they were safe from being boarded by the newly arrived soldiers.

The sail first dropped from the forward mast and began to catch the wind. The short-handed crew was making their way through the sheets as best they could, and the ship started to lurch forward, gaining speed as the canvas pulled taut with the wind. The breeze was swift and decidedly in their favor as they emerged onto open water leaving the small Hawaiian cove behind. Roberts gazed toward starboard, undecided in his direction, and noticed numerous ships milling nearby, several sailing from the distant harbor. On further examination he felt a chill run up his spine—one of the large ships-of-battle seemed on a route directly toward them and several smaller gunboats were aligned on their path as well. He watched as two of them seemed to correct their course after, it seemed, they spotted the *Queen Anne* emerging into the open.

"Make full sail, Mr. Caesar!"

"Aye, full sail—!" Black Caesar called, the word *captain* catching in his throat, not giving up his reluctance to address Roberts as the ship's captain. He wove throughout the deck of the ship making sure every yard of cloth was unfurled and trapping the wind.

Mary looked back from her position near the stern and watched the powerful ship that was now giving chase. The wind was brisk, and their small crew made short work of bringing the ship to full sail, but would Blackbeard's frigate be able to outrun these engine-powered beasts? The storied pirate had boasted she would cut through the sea at fourteen knots but, that would be in the most advantageous conditions. She guessed they would now see whether she or Francis would win the argument over sails versus steam.

CHAPTER 20 – FLIGHT

Blackbeard's eyes strained to open, fighting against the hazy darkness that threatened to drag him back under. The air around him thrummed with a deafening roar, vibrating through the hard surface beneath him. His body, numb and inert, jolted with each unpredictable movement, the sensation foreign, yet vaguely reminiscent of being tossed on a stormy sea. He forced his eyes open, but his vision blurred, the dim glow of fading daylight casting flickering shadows against the metal walls surrounding him. He was below deck—at least, that's what he told himself. The enclosed space, the unnatural din of machinery, the way his stomach twisted with each sudden drop and rise—it had to be a ship, though something felt profoundly wrong.

A fractured memory teased his mind. A sky filled with smoke and roaring beasts, their wings spread impossibly wide. He had seen them yesterday—metal birds soaring high above, faster than anything he had ever known. Was this one of those? No, it couldn't be. Such things belonged to the sky, not the sea. And yet, the sensation beneath him—was it the rolling of waves, or something else entirely?

His thoughts scattered as his body lurched forward, the relentless roar around him dying into a strained whine then abrupt bouncing of the entire vessel. The motion beneath him changed—gone was the unsteady pitching, replaced by a rhythmic rise and fall that he recognized all too well. The sea. He was certain of it now. The ship had settled on water. His muscles ached as unseen hands unfastened the straps binding him. His head lolled forward, the weight of his own skull too much for his neck to bear.

Blurred faces swam before him, their voices distant, speaking a language familiar but distorted so that he barely understood. Rough hands gripped him, hauling him toward an open hatchway where golden light poured in. Squinting against the glare, he glimpsed the vast ocean stretching to the horizon, its surface rippling in the dying glow of the setting sun. The air was thick with salt and fuel, the mingling scents assaulting his dulled senses.

Ahead, men strained against a rope, pulling them toward a strange metal craft—a vessel unlike any ship he had ever seen. It sat low in the water, its rounded hull glinting in the amber light. At first, it looked as if the ship had capsized, but then he spotted the narrow tower rising off center, a large deck-gun mounted between the tower and the bow. A warship of some kind. Not like the great wooden beasts he knew, but something new, something more menacing.

The pontoon beneath him rocked as the two vessels met. He looked above him and saw the underneath of a metal wing. His eyes widened, roaming the sky vessel he was being carried from. His mind swam at the thought of being flown through the sky in its belly. His head spun in a dizzying fog. A gangplank clattered down, bridging the gap between the ship and the flying wing. The men holding him hesitated for only a moment before dragging him forward, his boots scraping against the metal surface. He tried to protest, but his tongue felt thick, his words slurring into nonsense.

Behind him, Colette, Woodes and Philip were being handled in the same manner, their bodies as limp as his own. He wanted to call out to Colette, to see if she was still breathing, but the effort was too much. His head reeled, the world tipping as he was hauled across the gangplank onto the waiting warship.

As soon as his feet touched the cold steel, he knew this was no ordinary ship. The deck was too smooth, the space too confined. The sailors in dark uniforms moved with machine-like precision, their expressions unreadable. Before he could make sense of it, he was lowered through an open hatchway into a suffocating metal hole dropping down into a crowded, low-deckheaded room filled with machinery.

The interior differed significantly from any vessel he had previously encountered. Pipes lined the narrow corridors, hissing softly as men moved with careful efficiency. The air was thick, heavy with oil and metal, the scent clinging to his skin. He was carried past compartments where men worked over strange instruments, their voices low and tense. The small spaces were filled with piping, valves and red painted wheels, their purpose unknown to him.

Finally, he was deposited onto a narrow cot, the thin cushion barely softening the hard metal beneath it. His long frame stretched awkwardly over the too-small bed. Turning his head, he caught sight of Philip, Woodes and Colette being stuffed into similar hanging cots, their bodies unmoving. A guard remained by the doorway, his hand resting near a holstered pistol, his stance rigid.

Blackbeard tried to fight against the weight dragging him down, but the drug still coursed through his veins. His eyelids drooped, and the swirling confusion swallowing him once more as he slipped into darkness.

Lieutenant Dirk 'Dutch' Van Buren squinted his eyes at the unusual site twelve thousand feet below him and due west of his Douglas SBD-3 Dauntless. He looked to find his wingman off the port side of his aircraft. It was positioned at an even altitude and angled five degrees away from his own reconnaissance dive bomber.

"Contact," he announced in his calm manner.

"I see it," his rear gunner, Stanley, said just seconds later.

Dutch maneuvered the plane, banking to start a flyby over what appeared to be a seaplane floating next to a submarine. *What the blazes?* At first glance he thought, *It must be ours.* He began a gradual descent on his approach to get a better look. This afternoon's preflight briefing had focused on hunting Japanese aircraft and ships, but secondarily they were to be on the lookout for a hijacked Grumman G-21 Goose. His keen eyes could tell immediately the flying boat below him was that very same plane.

His Dauntless was equipped with a sixteen-hundred-pound center mounted bomb and two six-hundred-fifty pounders under each wing. He, and every other flyboy combing this side of the Pacific, was itching for some payback. The *Enterprise* aircraft carrier that he called home had been just two hundred-fifty miles from Pearl when the attack happened. They had been coming back from Wake Island, due in on the sixth, but had been delayed by bad weather. The entire crew wished that they had been there, but the reality was that the *Enterprise* would have been just another sitting duck for all those Jap bombers on the seventh if they were.

He had hastily written a letter to his dad and little brother vowing to sink every Japanese carrier and battleship in an act of revenge for the Pearl Harbor attack. Hopefully this mission would start that road to payback.

The orders weren't clear on the rules for engagement if they found the Goose but if that was a Japanese sub it was squatting next to, that bastard was going to the bottom with a giant hole in its hold after he dropped one of his eggs on it.

"That looks like a U-boat, Dutch!" his gunner announced with excitement.

Dutch craned his head to look out the cockpit window and concurred— a Type XB by the looks of it. "What the hell is that doing in the Pacific?"

"I'm copying the *Enterprise*," Stanley said as he began entering a Morse coded message to the carrier.

At this altitude he could see activity on the deck of the U-boat and unless that crew were entirely made up of ninety-day wonders, they knew that they had been spotted. Those IXs were equipped with two anti-aircraft guns, each able to fire thirty rounds per minute. Dutch knew he needed to decide right now whether this was a recon or direct-action mission. The US wasn't technically at war with Germany, but everyone knew it would be coming any day now.

He was at eight thousand feet when the 3.7 cm SK C/30 Flak behind the con tower targeted him and his wingman. Within seconds he was leaning heavily on his flight stick to avoid dozens of rounds seeking to tear through the thick skin of his aircraft. Dutch needed to adjust his trajectory to get himself in position to start a dive-bomb run and pound these Krauts to the bottom of the ocean.

After banking hard Dutch climbed five hundred feet in altitude, trusting that his wingman was following his lead. He watched below for the telltale signs of the diesel engines kicking into high gear—and there it was. Brown smoke puffed out of the U-boat's exhaust pipes just as the two four-hundred-fifty horsepower Pratt & Whitney R-985 wing-mounted engines powering the G-21 Goose also came to life. Dutch narrowed his eyes in determination, vowing that these two bastards were not going to escape his wrath.

The U-boat and the seaplane started to slowly move in opposite directions. Dutch continued to work hard dodging incoming munitions while setting up his position to go vertical from his lofty altitude. He signaled his wingman to target the Goose, and the two Dauntlesses separated into a coordinated attack.

The onslaught of rounds suddenly stopped and Dutch knew that meant the U-boat was about to dive below the surface. He needed to act now; he opened the targeting window in the floor of the plane, aiming at the sub.

When he was in position he pressed hard on the stick, his stomach lurching into his throat as the plane's nose quickly dove to point directly at the sea. The thrill of rushing headfirst in a seventy-degree dive at 275 miles per hour was something you couldn't experience anywhere else on Earth. Only a rare breed of pilots had what it took to execute a maneuver that brought you and your gunner a mere second from certain death as you plummeted from the sky to pull out of the devastating dive seven hundred feet above your target, to drop your payload and decimate your enemy in a fiery explosion just beneath your wings.

Dutch gritted his teeth as the force of gravity pressed his entire being into the back of his seat. The sub had started to dive; the sea began closing over the hull just as he was finishing his run. He was going to be late. He stretched his descent until the last split second to release the center-mounted bomb and pulled back on his stick with all he had. With the bomb dropped, the sea was rushing toward Dutch's cockpit window at a velocity that seemed impossible. The engine noise was so loud he could feel the plane's skeleton vibrating down into his own bones. His heart pounded against his ribs so hard that he thought they would break from the pressure of each thundering beat.

His gunner's scream split the air a second before the sixteen-hundred-pound bomb exploded beneath them. The ocean erupted into a towering pillar of fire and water, and the blast punched their plane upward like a toy in a storm. Dutch's hands locked on the controls as the craft bucked and twisted, gravity and chaos tearing at every seam. Sweat poured into his eyes. He wrestled the yoke with brute force, the stick trembling like a live thing, until he finally forced the nose level, dragging them back from the edge of death.

Gasping for breath, he scanned the boiling sea below. No oil slick. No shattered wreckage. Just angry, broken waves swallowing the evidence.

A blur caught his eye—the G-21 Goose, engines roaring as it tried to claw free of the water. Dutch's wingman swept in low, his strafing run timed with surgical precision. A line of fire erupted from the machine guns, ripping into the Goose's fuselage. The seaplane staggered under the assault, smoking and hemorrhaging metal.

Then it broke apart, pitching into a savage spin, wings folding like paper. It hit the water in a shrieking, cartwheeling mess, disintegrating on impact. Shards of twisted metal and scraps of human flesh rained down, vanishing into the churning sea.

The sky was quiet again. But Dutch knew better. War had only just begun.

Colette emerged from unconsciousness with a flood of nausea that threatened to empty her stomach. Wrapping her arms around her waist, she lay curled in a fetal position for a minute, letting her eyes adjust to the dim light and her ears to the constant hum of engines.

She found herself in a narrow bed that resembled a shelf mounted against the wall. There were only six inches between her face and the bunk above. Rolling over, she spotted an open hatchway leading into a cramped corridor lit by cage-protected lamps that were mounted securely to the wall so that they would not swing with the vessel's motion. A man stood just outside the hatch, only half visible.

Gingerly, she swung her legs down, one hand gripping the metal frame for support. Her knees wobbled under her, but she managed to steady herself. The man glanced in and she caught sight of a stern face, thinning blond hair combed forward to disguise a retreating hairline, before he turned away and called something guttural down the corridor.

German. She was sure of it.

Next to her, bunked close together, Philip, Woodes, and Edward still lay slumped, sleeping, dead to the world—or so she hoped. Heart hammering, Colette crossed unsteadily to Philip and shook his shoulder.

Then Edward. More urgently.

He stirred, groaning, then blinked up at her. Relief flooded her chest as she grasped his face in both hands.

"Are you well, lass?" he rasped.

"Dizzy, but it's fading."

He glanced past her to see Philip rising from his cot, head cradled in his hands like he nursed a splitting headache.

"Mr. Albert?"

Philip gave a small, pained nod.

Holding Colette with one arm, Blackbeard planted a hand on his bunk and pushed himself upright, stooping under the low, curving deckhead. Once steady, he turned and kicked Woodes' bunk, hard enough to jar the sleeping man awake.

At that moment, a shadow filled the hatchway—Lieutenant Becker stood in front of them but now flanked by a taller man: the curly-haired, mustachioed stranger Blackbeard remembered from the streets of Honolulu.

"Becker," Blackbeard growled.

The man shook his head.

"Hildebrandt. Otto Hildebrandt," he corrected, his American accent evaporating into clipped, precise German tones.

"A spy, then?" Philip muttered.

Hildebrandt only smiled and shrugged.

"Where are we?" Blackbeard demanded, his eyes sweeping the strange metal interior.

Hildebrandt smiled wider. "You are aboard one of the most advanced submarines in the Reich. The pride of the German Navy: U-122, Type XB."

He stepped aside as a man in his mid-thirties entered, upright, commanding, with an air of authority that filled the cramped space. His blue-gray eyes scanned the prisoners sharply.

"This is your host, Commander Hans-Günther Looff," Hildebrandt said, then switched to German. "Commander, may I present Miss Colette Dallaire, Philip Albert, Captain Woodes Rogers, and Edward Thatch, better known as Blackbeard."

Looff looked them over, lingering too long on Colette. Blackbeard stepped in front of her, his glare sharp as a blade.

The commander smirked but moved on, studying Woodes with clinical detachment, taking in his battered appearance.

"They will be of value, Commander, I am sure of it," Hildebrandt offered smoothly.

Looff turned to him and replied in German, his voice low but not so low that Blackbeard couldn't catch the meaning. "The Führer trusts you, Otto. Who am I to question that? We have a long voyage to the Seychelles— you'll have time to explain what kind of 'magic' these four command, and how it can win the war now that the Japanese have brought the Americans in."

He clapped Hildebrandt on the shoulder. "No brig on a U-boat. Let them move about—but they work. The woman can serve the crew. The men can clean. No free rides, Lieutenant Colonel."

With a final glance at Colette, he moved on.

Hildebrandt stood rigid, his jaw clenching. Here on the sub, Looff held power, regardless of rank. Outside these steel walls, it would be Hildebrandt in charge—a full Oberstleutnant of the Abwehr. Looff was just a Korvettenkapitän.

Coincidentally, it was the same rank structure Hildebrandt had stolen when he killed the American intelligence officer Harris Becker in Atlanta.

This sub, known as U-122 had a reputation—one born of legend. A ghost ship. Presumed sunk in the North Atlantic, she had miraculously resurfaced months later, battered but functional. Admiral Canaris, head of the German Navy, had seen the opportunity: a phantom vessel that could now operate unseen across the Atlantic, raiding and spying without a whisper of suspicion.

Now, after surviving Pearl Harbor disguised as a Yankee officer, Hildebrandt's reward was greater than he had ever imagined. Not espionage. Not sabotage.

Time travel.

The mythos Hitler was obsessed with—relics, artifacts, keys to unearthly power—might finally be real. And it stood right in front of him, in the form of four battered travelers, plucked from history itself.

And among them... Blackbeard. Pirate. Legend. The only man alive who had sailed with Olivier Levasseur, the infamous pirate king rumored to have hidden a fortune in gold—and the key to something far more dangerous: the Fiery Cross of Goa.

Hildebrandt could almost feel the hand of destiny guiding his every step.

Blackbeard, meanwhile, narrowed his eyes. "Seychelles? That's where you're taking us?"

Hildebrandt nodded. "Levasseur made his home there in his final days. It is the most likely location of his hidden treasure."

Blackbeard exchanged a glance with Colette, then Woodes and Philip. A slow, bitter smile curled his lips.

"So," he said, voice low and grim, "we are pressed into service... for a treasure hunt."

"Call it what you like," Hildebrandt said, his voice full of triumph. "But make no mistake—you will find it for us. Or you will die trying."

Colette swallowed the rising lump in her throat. The air inside the U-boat felt heavier now, as if Hildebrandt's words had stolen the last of the oxygen. She touched the edge of the bunk to steady herself, but Blackbeard caught the small motion and shifted instinctively closer to her—a silent promise that no harm would come without a fight.

Philip straightened his rumpled jacket, his mouth a grim line. "And if we refuse?" he asked, his voice low and razor-edged.

Hildebrandt's smile thinned even further. His gaze flicked toward Looff's retreating back. "Commander Looff has little patience for useless cargo. He's been known to fire more than just torpedoes from the tubes."

Blackbeard gave a low, humorless laugh. "Best pray no harm comes to the lass, German, else this voyage will end with your lifeblood staining your own decks."

For a heartbeat, the two men locked eyes—pirate and spy—each measuring the other, each aware that when the time came, only one would walk away.

Woodes finally found his voice, raspy and cold. "Treasure or no, we'll find a way off this coffin."

"Afloat or at the bottom?" Hildebrandt said lightly. Then, to the guard: "Get them fed, Müller. Then put them to work. They start immediately."

Without another word, Hildebrandt vanished down the corridor, his boots clicking against the iron deck plates.

Müller lingered a moment longer, his pale eyes unreadable. Then he jerked his head sharply toward the hatch.

"Move."

Blackbeard rested a hand briefly on Colette's back, steadying her as they filed out into the low-lit passage. The hum of the engines vibrated through the soles of their feet, a constant, ghostly heartbeat.

As they shuffled after their captors, Colette caught Philip's eye. In that fleeting glance, she saw it: not fear, not surrender—but the first spark of defiance.

They would find the treasure, but they would not allow these heathens to keep it.

CHAPTER 21 – BIG GUNS

Jesse James did his damnedest to keep pace with the seasoned sailors working the rigging and following orders barked by their current captain, Bart Roberts. The orders echoed down the chain of command, starting with Black Caesar, the hulking quartermaster—or first mate. Jesse wasn't sure which, or if there was a difference.

"Look alive, blue eyes!" Anne shouted from her station, where she wrestled ropes, cogs, and winches. She winked at him as her arms strained with effort.

Jesse refocused on his task, winding some sort of contraption with uncertain purpose.

"You're gonna be takin' orders from that filly the rest of your days, brother," Frank teased, laying out rope and line to assist the rigging crew.

The wind was strong, the ship rising and falling with heavy spray as it cut through the chop and swells. All around, the crew shouted and moved with urgency, determined to outrun the pursuing warship. Jesse stood upright and glanced back—stern, aft, whatever it was called. The metallic beast was gaining, belching the diesel smoke of a Mason Bogie locomotive devouring track like a starved goat let loose in a preacher's garden. Worse were the enormous cannons now aimed directly at their wooden hull.

"She's gonna catch us," Charlotte said as she strode to Roberts, who gripped the big mahogany wheel.

Roberts turned, jaw tightening as he looked back at the warship. Then he met Charlotte's gaze.

"Aye, lass. We need to slow them down." He scanned the deck for Charles Vane and Black Caesar, who were moving among the crew, helping where they could. "Take the wheel. I'll see if we can put them off the chase."

Charlotte took the wheel without hesitation while Roberts moved swiftly toward Vane.

"Charles, Caesar, find some able hands. Let us give that devil ship something to think twice about!"

Vane looked aft, nodded, and ordered several men to follow. They met Roberts on the quarterdeck, with Black Caesar arriving close behind.

"Old Blackbeard have any fire barrels in the hold?"

"Aye."

"Then let us get as many as we can. Time to give that beast a reason to turn tail."

Boots thundered down the stairs into the hold. Roberts surveyed the deck, searching for crew members not essential to sailing. He spotted the James brothers handling rigging with all the finesse of men more accustomed to cattle.

"Jesse, you and your brother would be more useful manning the aft deck-guns than here." He looked for the women who had brought these cowboys aboard. "Bonny! Read! Take the James boys aft and start convincing that captain to reconsider his pursuit."

Mary whistled for them and led the group up to the aftcastle.

Roberts turned his narrowed eyes on the horizon. The sun would soon set—perhaps they could escape under cover of darkness. He prayed for a moonless night and favorable wind. Looking up, he spotted Blackbeard's cabin boy, Tom, high in the main mast, watching the pursuing ship.

"Mr. Tom!" he called. "Are they readying to fire?"

Tom cupped his hands to his mouth. "They just stand by the big guns!"

"That may change. Tell me when it does."

Black Caesar emerged from below carrying a barrel wrapped in rope. Roberts placed a hand on his shoulder.

"Light them and start tossing them overboard once the sun dips below the horizon."

Roberts then sprinted up the stairs to the aftcastle where Anne and Mary were loading a rail-mounted cannon and explaining its operation to the cowboys.

"Think you four can move a twelve-pounder here?"

Anne glanced at a nearby cannon secured for a broadside ten yards to starboard. "Aye. With these two strapping men, we'll make short work of it." She smacked Jesse's rear and led the way.

Roberts shook his head at the same time as Frank James did. *God help these men, as these two pirate wenches will drag them down to hell itself before they are done with them.*

He hurried toward the stairwell and slid down the railing rather than using his feet. Roberts had always had a flare for the dramatic. He knew his crew without fail responded positively to his theatrics. Before taking to the sea, he had considered becoming an actor. For a time, he had been consumed with love of Shakespeare, fancying himself a modern-day Hamlet. He saw himself leading a theatre troupe at the Theatre Royal Drury Lane in London. Alas, the tides of fortune had brought him to sea. He could not resist a self-satisfied smile as he arrived at Charlotte's side. His half-African beauty with skin the color of sweetened coffee and the spirit of a tigress kept a steady hand on the wheel.

"You have a plan, my love?" she asked without taking her eye off the rolling sea.

"That I do. We shall slow them down and lead them astray with a trail of fire and smoke. With luck, we will lose them under the cover of night while they mistakenly follow the path of the fire barrels."

"And if we don't lose them?"

Charlotte watched his eyes staring at the massive ship pursuing them while she waited for an answer.

Roberts calculated in his head the distance between the ships and how much light was left in the day with a slight shake to his head. The odds were not favorable.

"She hasn't fired, so sinking us is not her goal," Charlotte suggested while she maintained her hold on the ship's wheel, making small adjustments to their path through the rolling swells.

"Aye," Roberts agreed. "But desiring to join us for a cup of tea is not her goal neither. They are at war and, as you said, tensions are high on that island and poor Sammy and I had made off, just days ago, with a hefty haul of their silver and gold." He shook his head, realizing that was in 1873 and now he'd been told it was 1941. "I would suppose that crime has been forgotten."

"They may have a long memory but that was a different ship, the drowned steamer you christened *Charlotte's Fortune*, and you didn't stay long enough for someone to paint your picture, did you, love?"

"No, dear heart. That I did not. Still, we shall not raise the white so easily. Blackbeard would have my head for giving up his prize without a fight."

"And what a handsome head it is," Charlotte deadpanned.

Outerbridge stood outside the pilot house, watching the fleeing *Queen Anne's Revenge* through his US Navy-issue Mark 45 7x50 binoculars. The lenses brought the eighteenth-century, three-masted frigate to life as he trained his view from the ship's hull to the ornate aftcastle, then up to the top of the mainmast. She was a rare beauty.

He was able to discern activity on the rear deck as they continued to gain on the pirate ship in the fading daylight. Four crew members were exerting effort to move a cannon to the aft gunwale.

He pursed his lips as he watched. It was being maneuvered by two men dressed as cowboys and two women, each with long, reddish-colored hair. He considered the fanciful notion that these sailors were going to attempt to engage his Wickes-class destroyer with a twelve-pound round shot iron cannonball. The odds that such ancient munitions would damage his ship were too low to measure, but it was possible it could harm a crew member— so he would be forced to return fire. One blast from the .50-calibers and that relic would be reduced to kindling, scattered on the surface of the Pacific.

He looked out with unaided eyes at the horizon and counted three decent-sized squalls, then pressed the binoculars to his face to decide which direction the wind would blow them. This area of the Pacific was continually active with small, short-lived storms that moved across the island chain, dropping rain for fifteen to twenty minutes at a time before moving on. The skies would darken, and a deluge of rain would burst from the low clouds, intensifying the cascading waterfalls scattered around the islands.

The sky was darkening quickly now that the sun had set below the horizon. He scanned the deck of the pirate ship again—the swarthy men working diligently to keep the frigate at its top speed. He could see a dark-skinned mountain of a man leading others to move wooden barrels to the starboard railing amidships. He lost track of them in his vision as the *Ward* crested, then descended, a large swell. When he was able to bring them back into view, he let out an audible gasp. The barrels were lit aflame, then lowered into the sea, dark smoke pouring out the top like a pot boiling over. He was witnessing the eighteenth-century version of naval mines.

Outerbridge couldn't stifle the harrumph that came to his throat. He let the binoculars hang against his chest by the straps and positioned his glasses back on his head, twisting the earpieces to fit snugly and securely.

He stepped back into the pilot house and gave an order to the first mate. "Ready a fire team, and I want four sets of eyes on that ship. We will not lose her in the night."

"Yes, sir," came the reply.

Brockman, Kent, and Stanton were staffing their .50-caliber while sharing the pair of binoculars between them to scan the wooden tall ship as they continued to gain ground.

Kent whistled as he peered at the rigging and masts. "She's a real-life pirate ship. Goddamn, I hope we don't have to sink her."

"Be a real shame," echoed Stanton.

"Whoa! Look at that. They just dropped a fire barrel over the side," said Brockman. "Shit. You think the big wheel is going to order us to fire at her?"

It was getting dark, and the ship was becoming a silhouette against the horizon. One by one, smoking and flaming barrels were lowered over the side to bob on the surface behind the *Queen Anne's Revenge*. A half mile to port, the first of several squalls was approaching the two ships. The sheets of falling rain added to the thickening inky blackness of night. The earlier blue-green of the Pacific now appeared a dark shade of coal, with glistening sparkles from the fire barrels as the destroyer roared toward them.

Smoke billowed in a thickening curtain as the vision of the pirate ship was obscured—just a quarter mile from the *Ward*. The first drops of rain began to fall.

Several searchlights lit up the water and moved across the surface, illuminating the burning barrels, but they couldn't penetrate the smoke and sheets of rain.

"Don't lose sight of her!" came a shouted call from near the pilot house.

"Too late," Kent said.

"Just follow those barrels," Brockman offered.

"I think that was her plan," Stanton said as he searched with the binoculars. The squall had overtaken the pirate ship, and even with the rain, the fire barrels still burned and bobbed in the *Ward*'s path. *They must be coated with oil. Must be such a dire threat to a wooden ship but harmless to us*, he thought.

KAA-BLAM!

The flash of cannon fire and the boom of the concussion rang out in the night.

KLANG!

The twelve-pound round shot shattered into many pieces as it collided with the *Ward*'s steel hull.

"Damn, that was a lucky shot!" Kent said, flinching along with his two crewmates at the sound of shot hitting their ship.

"I want two shots a hundred feet above their heads, boys."

The men turned to see Outerbridge standing behind them, pointing to where the cannon flash had appeared.

"Don't hit the hull or the deck. I don't want to sink them—just give them a chance to surrender. Maybe you knock out one of the masts."

"Aye, aye, sir."

The three men targeted the position where the ship had been seconds ago, with Stanton in the firing seat.

"Locked!"

"Ready!"

"Fire!"

"Hard to port! Now!" Roberts called out.

The order was echoed and carried out by the crew; all were in position for the abrupt change in direction. The keel of the *Queen Anne's Revenge* groaned in protest as the rigging, sails, and rudder fought the sea and the wind to turn the ship with such force it threatened to tear her in half.

The sound of two rounds being fired at them from the warship's enormous guns thundered above the storm and sea.

Tom, for the second time in just days, was hanging from atop the mast—rope wrapped so tightly around his wrists it cut off the bloodflow to his fingers. He opened his clenched eyelids to see the rolling Pacific just thirty yards below him, the deck no longer beneath him but far off to the side. The ship creaked like an earthquake as the sails shifted from taut, wind-filled sheets to loose and flowing curtains of oiled canvas.

His feet suddenly slipped off the spar he was standing on, the drenched surface now slick from the rain that assaulted them. His scream was lost in the roar of the wind and sea. The ship ceased its tilting with a frightful pause—then, without warning, began to right itself. Tom felt like a pebble in a slingshot. He quickly twisted the rope once more around his arm as the mast reached its peak. His small body was hurled forward, swinging around the top of the mast in a full circle before landing with his feet on the spar with barely a wobble.

His heart thundered in his chest. He looked around, then down toward the deck to see if anyone had witnessed his amazing acrobatic feat.

Alas, his crewmates were too busy filling the sails with wind, desperate to escape the metal warship.

Jesse James felt the ship lurch forward, pushed hard by the wind. He had been pinned against the railing by the inertia of the snap turn these pirates had forced the wooden sailing vessel into. He longed for the day he'd be back on solid ground, galloping on a horse instead of being tossed around on the endless sea.

He looked back to where the warship had been and couldn't spot it through the blackness and smoke.

He had counted two shots that rang out before their desperate maneuver. He looked over at Anne—her hair was damp and wild around her pretty face. Her excited eyes danced as they shifted from the sea back up to the sails, taut with wind.

"We're headed straight into the heart of the storm!" Frank called out.

"That's Roberts' plan, prairie man," said Mary.

"It's just a squall, and we'll lose them in the night," Anne said.

Black Caesar's face emerged from the night like a wraith. "Hush. Voices travel far on the water. No more talking," he warned, then moved silently toward midship.

The ship and its crew fell quiet. Only the creaking of the wood and the snap of lines and canvas remained beyond the steady drumming of rain drops. Orders were whispered, and Black Caesar motioned up to Tom that he should descend the ratlines and meet him on deck.

"Boy," he whispered when Tom softly set his feet down, "can you make a bird sound?"

Tom readied himself to caw like a crow, but Black Caesar placed a large palm over his mouth.

"I'll trust you can," he said quietly. "That sound will be the signal, should you spot the enemy. Keep silent until then."

Tom nodded and made to climb back up, but Black Caesar stopped him with a hand on his shoulder. He handed the boy a heel of bread, knowing that he hadn't eaten in many hours.

Tom nodded his thanks, stuffed it in his pocket, and started to climb back to his perch, high above the deck.

By the time Black Caesar made his way to the wheel, the rain was already dissipating. They had steered through the short-lived storm in less than ten minutes. The deck was dark, with no lanterns lit, but he was able to see Charles Vane approaching from the bow. The two men arrived at the same time, coming to stand near Roberts and Charlotte, who still manned the wheel.

"Any sign of 'em?" came the whispered question from Roberts.

Vane and Caesar both shook their heads.

Roberts nodded and looked at the brass-and-bone, German-made gunpowder flask-sundial-compass he held in his hand. The flask was currently empty of powder, and he silently wondered whether he'd ever need to use that feature again now that he had acquired new weapons. He held it for Charlotte to see the compass' direction. With a quick nod, Charlotte made a course adjustment to keep a heading that would hopefully put more distance between them and the pursuing warship.

The three men kept watchful eyes behind them as the ship continued to cut a path through the calming sea. The swells were dying down as the storm moved further away, and stars began to appear in the night sky.

From the crow's nest high above them came the high-pitched tone of a mimicked caw. As one, they all looked up to spy Tom pointing due east. Emerging into view through the breaking fog and mist of the storm were the lights of a ship, now a mile or two away. The warship was traveling forty-five degrees south by southeast of them, its searchlights combing the sea—but the *Queen Anne's Revenge* remained unspotted.

"Captain," Charlotte said in a hushed voice, and nodded toward the bow.

He looked out to the inky horizon and saw many lights far out to sea. This location was thick with shipping activity. He reasoned that his ship might be the only one sailing tonight with no illumination.

"Weave between them, love. Let's stay out of their line of sight and put other vessels between us and that warship."

They continued to speak in low voices as the crew readied the rigging for each course change Charlotte made, as well as every shift in the wind. The warship stubbornly adjusted its path to stay within sight of the pirate ship.

The captain is a seasoned sailor. He understands what path I must take to stay ahead of them and keep the sails full, Roberts thought. He had no map for this part of the world, but the time he'd spent studying the charts aboard that steamer he briefly commanded remained etched in his memory. His current heading would take him on a long journey to Asia—five thousand miles of ocean before arriving near Japan and China, with only a handful of island chains in between. He would need to change course and head south once free of pursuit. From there, he could sail east and reach the Americas within a week or two.

Blackbeard and the other two crew members I had briefly met will have to fend for themselves. There is now no hope of sailing back to that Hawaiian island to rescue them.

It may be that we never see them again. Which meant the *Queen Anne's Revenge* and all the treasure in her hold would be his alone to distribute.

He looked over at Black Caesar, who was scanning the horizon for threats and keeping a close watch on the crew. *He'll be the difficult one*, Roberts thought. *Fiercely loyal to Blackbeard—for reasons I don't understand. The rest of the pirates will leap at the chance to claim their share of Blackbeard's plunder. I'll have to keep a close eye on Caesar if we manage to slip away from that metal warship.*

Caesar looked over at him, eyes narrowing. Roberts felt pinpricks of cold sweat form on the back of his neck, as he worried the man was reading his mind. A loose line flapped and a winch squealed loudly stealing the quartermaster's attention. He strode off to lend aid to Francis, Chester and several crew members making adjustments to the sheets. Roberts' eyes followed him and then he turned back to see Vane studying him.

"This ship ain't yours. It's ours. All of us that's left now. We ain't going back for Thatch or that scientist and wench. We'll have ourselves a proper vote in the morn who should captain this ship."

Roberts stood next to Charlotte as Vane turned his back and strode away to find a task.

"Mutiny in that man's eyes," said Charlotte.

"Aye. In his heart as well. We shall be ever watchful to crush down such talk before it spreads."

"Say the word, love, and he won't live to see the morn."

Roberts held Charlotte's gaze while he considered her offer.

Above them, Tom watched the pair with narrowed eyes.

CHAPTER 22 – PIGPEN CIPHER

Outerbridge looked over the transcript of the latest decoded message just arrived from Pearl. The contents informed him that two scout planes had intercepted the flying Goose that abducted Edward Thatch and the three other persons of interest. It was believed that they were now aboard a German U-boat. The last known coordinates were attached; coordinates now burnt into Outerbridge's mind. According to Naval Intelligence, the submarine was likely headed west, toward the Sea of Japan.

And his orders? Pursue the pirate vessel.

Apprehend the occupants.

Use of deadly force: not approved.

Outerbridge exhaled and leaned back in his chair, letting the message flutter down onto the chart table. That last line brought a measure of relief. He had no appetite for blowing that tall ship out of the water. For all he knew, the vessel was English-built, and the Union Jack had been a partner to the Stars and Stripes since the Great War. Even now, Britain stood as a bulwark against the Axis.

But do those pirates know that?

He shook his head, jaw tightening. The absurdity of the situation gnawed at the edges of his rational mind. Pirates. Real pirates. An eighteenth-century galleon somehow sailing through the Pacific in 1941. Every instinct told him to reject the idea, to find the trick, the illusion. Yet his own eyes had seen it:

wooden hull, canvas sails, iron cannons. Not a museum piece. Not a Hollywood mock-up. A living ship with a living crew.

They had been chasing shadows for more than an hour after losing the ship in the smoke and storm. He folded the report and put it in his shirt pocket. The latitude and longitude of the U-boat's last location may come in handy at a later date.

"See if you can get us some air support in finding that damn relic. She's moving swift in these conditions and silent without an engine," he told the waiting radio operator.

"Yes, sir."

It was impossible that they could have sailed that far, and a couple of scout planes should be able to spot them before they escaped the net. It was a game of cat and mouse, but the cat had a flock of hawks on her side. Outerbridge nodded to himself, agreeing with his own thoughts that the pirates would be caught before dawn would break.

He stepped outside into the cooling night air. The single-digit wind speed was bringing the fresh smell of clean ocean air. It was one of his favorite times to be out at sea. Once the sun had set and the star shine was at its peak the temperature dropped several degrees, and the heat and humidity of the day was merely a memory. His crew was now rotating watch with a third of the men racked in their bunks. He wondered if the pirates would run their crews on a similar schedule.

His thoughts wandered toward the details of his mission, his firsthand accounts of the men involved in this mystery. Woodes Rogers, the man claiming to be the Governor of the Bahamas, seemed more unhinged than Edward Thatch. God, king, and country had been the intensified rhetoric Outerbridge had had trouble following when the spy posing as Harris Becker had interviewed the 'Governor'. He had mostly sat silently, listening to the statements Rogers was giving. The man was obsessed with bringing Thatch to justice, which would have been fine if he had credible evidence of his crimes. They were all events that took place two hundred years ago. He ended up only sounding crazier than Thatch as he ranted about purgatory and duty to the king of England in eliminating the world of Blackbeard and the other pirates sailing with him.

Both Thatch and Rogers recounted experiencing hurricane-force storms and a massive whirlpool capable of swallowing a ship. However, neither could explain how such an event might transport them into the future.

Becker had suggested that he would take Woodes Rogers in for a psychic evaluation. His department would contact the Brits and see if they could track down the man's true identity. Outerbridge had so many more important things to deal with, namely a war with Japan, that he had been glad to get rid of the man and close the book on both Rogers and Thatch. Now he had been thrust back into this comic book-like story by the God damn Secretary of War. He had been told that Roosevelt himself was interested in the outcome of this narrative.

He stared out to sea, searching the horizon for the masts of a 200-ton tall ship that started out as a slaver in the early 1700s. The ship was last recorded to have been seen in the harbor of Nassau in 1718. History had it fated to have been wrecked by a hurricane. *So, was there a partial truth to the entire lie?* It was possible that the ship had survived somewhere in a foreign harbor, well cared for and maintained. What was impossible was that its original captain and crew continued to walk the Earth. He found it hard to believe that his superiors would go through these efforts if they hadn't known the Nazis were risking so much by kidnapping these men along with the couple whose part in the puzzle he was unclear about.

He picked up his thermos of coffee where he had left it on the deck and took a sip. He watched the horizon; gone were the lights of ocean traffic this far out to sea. The *Enterprise* wasn't far off from them now, and every able-bodied ship and plane was out there searching and watching for the Japanese. He wondered what would happen if the Japs found the pirate ship first. He didn't think they would *aim high* as he had done. They'd sink her faster than an iron anchor. It would be best for everyone if the *Ward* were first to the prize.

The Queen Anne's Revenge. Where are you, old girl?

Thatch and Philip had been cleaning water-damaged valves and pipes for hours in a tight compartment toward the bow of the strange vessel. The sailor tasked with keeping tabs on them quickly tired of his duty and was relaxing above them reading a German magazine titled *Signal*. They were able to converse freely with each other as the man didn't seem to speak a word of English.

"Half these bolts are loose and in need of a good tightening," Thatch grumbled.

"They don't trust us to wield a wrench I imagine."

"Aye, rightfully so as I would bash their crowns to pulp if I had one."

Philip didn't respond, wondering if someone above would understand their language and lock them away or bind them for the remainder of the journey due to Thatch's violent threats. So far, they had relative freedom of movement but were told not to touch anything unless instructed. Colette and the battered Rogers had been put to work preparing food and cleaning up after meals were finished. For a while he and Thatch were intrigued with the construction of the ship, but by now each pipe and valve was beginning to look much like another.

Philip continued to move his bucket of solvents to the next rusting metal part in the cramped space under the main deck.

"Oy, let me see the Buzzard's old recipe."

Philip glanced up at the opening where the sailor sat absorbed in his reading material. He reached into his shirt where he'd hidden the documents that he had secretly taken from Hildebrandt before their kidnapping.

"Keep at your toils," Thatch told him after taking the recently printed papyrus. Philip had deduced that it was a reproduction of the original document that the Germans had made. He sat down to stretch his long legs in front of him as he examined the text.

"It's in German."

"Aye."

Philip watched Thatch's eyes as they played over the script.

"Can you read German?"

"Aye."

"Levasseur was French, was he not?"

"Aye."

"So, he would have written the cipher from the standpoint of French text. The first page is the cipher, obviously, and the second is the decoded message in German. The subtleties of his words and ideas could be lost when translated into German," Philip mused. "I wonder if they had taken that into account? In addition, there may be meanings of words and phrases that have been changed or lost in time from when Levasseur had inked it." He looked down at Thatch who was ignoring him.

"How is your French? Do you speak any of it? Mine is more than passable if you run across anything—"

"Mr. Albert," Thatch growled, fixing Philip with a glare. "If you don't stop your jabbering, I will stuff that cloth in your yapping maw."

Philip looked down at the rag full of solvents and rust he was holding in his hand then back to Thatch's furrowed brows. He nodded his head and went back to cleaning, glancing every so often at the seated pirate on the floor then toward the open hatch where their watcher lounged.

"Pigpen ciphers," Thatch ruminated. "The Freemasons used those as I recall."

"The Rosicrucian brotherhood as well."

Thatch looked up at Philip. "Rosicrucian…?"

Philip nodded his head. "Several fellow classmates of mine who were studying the sciences alongside me were members. The Rosicrucian Brotherhood, Edward, is a secretive society, part mystics, part alchemists. They fancy themselves keepers of ancient wisdom, blending Christian mysticism, esoteric philosophy, and the occasional dabbling in alchemy. Their aims, they claim, are enlightenment, the betterment of mankind… though in truth, I believe they mostly enjoy the allure of secrets and the illusion of power. I was invited to join but mixing the spiritual realm with our growing insights of the physical world seemed, well, a misguided attempt to weave esotericism into the fabric of reason. Besides, I've always found secret handshakes to be a poor substitute for proper research."

"How fructuous for me that such a learned man as yourself is now pressed into the same crew." Thatch handed back the parchment. "Can you translate the original cipher?"

Philip looked over the cipher's symbols and dots, all replacements for letters. He nodded his head to Thatch. "I've already started to decode it into French. There are a few possible misspelled words and turns of phrase from the German version."

Thatch shook his head with a slight smile. "Not French. The Buzzard was from Calais. His first language was Flemish."

Philip absorbed this insight with widened eyes.

"A bloody hard man to understand. He was like a bastard born of Dutch and French heritage growing up in that region."

"Flemish... that may give us the upper hand. Edward, I'll need your help in the translation. Do you speak it well?"

"Not well, but I can speak a passable Buzzard," said Thatch with a smile.

"*Zurück zur Arbeit!*" came a call from above paired with a slap on the metal frame of the hatch.

Philip stowed the document back in his shirt. Thatch pushed himself up from the floor and the two men restarted their task of cleaning rust from almost every joint of the metal ship.

The U-boat's galley was a cramped, metallic box. Every surface gleamed with the dull polish of grease and rust stains. Pots clattered as Colette tried to keep her footing on the swaying floor, balancing a heavy ladle of thin, greasy soup that smelled faintly of boiled cabbage and diesel fuel. She understood that the vessel sailed above the water the majority of the time and submerged when other ships were sighted. The ship riding on top of the waves did little to allow good ventilation inside the metallic hull. The air was close—thick with the sharp bite of metal, sweat, and the lingering tang of unwashed bodies. The low hum of the engines, the occasional creak of the hull, and the distant crash of waves were a constant, inescapable backdrop.

Beside her, Woodes Rogers wiped at a grimy table with a rag that was likely dirtier than the surface itself. His face was tight, his movements precise and controlled. Colette could see the flicker of tension in his scarred jaw, the subtle tightness in his shoulders and soreness of his muscles.

Two German sailors sat eating nearby. They watched them with idle curiosity, their words a blur of clipped, sharp sounds. They didn't speak English, or at least pretended not to. Colette could feel their eyes drifting to her, lingering longer than they should have. She kept her head down, focusing on ladling the soup into the battered tin bowls to be distributed to crew members, her breath catching in her throat when one of them let out a low chuckle and muttered something that made the other bark a laugh.

Then *he* entered.

Hans-Günther Looff.

The commander of U-122 moved through the small galley like a man who owned it, which, in a way, he did. His uniform was crisp despite the oppressive heat, the gold braid on his cap gleaming as if it had just been polished. Brown hair, neatly combed, caught the low light of the fixed wall-lamp. His blue eyes were sharp, pale, unblinking as he scanned the room, landing on Colette with a casual intensity that made her skin crawl.

She stiffened, keeping her gaze on the soup, but she could feel him watching her. The weight of it settled on the back of her neck like a hand. His boots clicked against the metal deck as he stepped closer. The two sailors fell silent, glancing at each other but saying nothing.

Looff's voice, when he spoke, was low and measured. His German words slid into the room like a blade through silk. She couldn't understand them, but the tone needed no translation. There was a lilt of amusement, a thread of command, a quiet confidence that suggested she was now the most interesting object in the room. A long, unsettling pause followed.

Colette risked a glance upward and immediately regretted it. His eyes were fixed on her, unblinking, a faint, amused curl at the corner of his mouth. He nodded once, slowly, as if confirming something to himself.

Then, without a word, he reached out.

He brushed a stray wave of hair from her face, tucking it behind her ear. The touch was light, almost gentle, but it sent a cold shiver through her spine.

His fingers lingered for a moment too long, a subtle reminder of the power he held in this steel coffin of a ship.

Colette jerked her head away, pretending to adjust the pot on the stove, her hands trembling slightly.

Looff's expression didn't change. If anything, the faint curl of his lips deepened. He stepped back, his gaze never leaving her as she stood in her now well-worn blue dress. Another string of German, directed at the sailors. The words low, soft, like the murmur of a threat disguised as a joke. The two men laughed, though one of them did so uneasily.

Rogers straightened, his hand gripping the rag in a white-knuckled fist. He fixed Looff with a hard stare, but the commander didn't even glance his way. To Looff, Rogers was nothing, a piece of furniture, a prop in the scene he was playing out.

After a long, uncomfortable moment, Looff finally turned away, moving back toward the hatch with the same deliberate confidence. His boots echoed down the narrow corridor, leaving behind only the oppressive silence and the sharp scent of fear.

Colette exhaled, a shudder slipping through her shoulders. She caught Rogers' eye. His face was grim, jaw clenched so tight it looked as if it might crack.

"Bloody bastard," he muttered under his breath.

Colette didn't reply. She didn't trust her voice not to shake.

She turned back to the soup, but the ladle felt heavier in her hand, and the tight, confined walls of the U-boat seemed to close in a little more.

A deep unease coiled in her chest as she realized how far she was from the life she had built for herself. Now, she was the only woman aboard a ship full of men at war. Her only protectors were Edward and Philip, and she sensibly harbored doubts about Rogers.

They were all captives here, surrounded by an overwhelming force of enemy soldiers. And Colette understood too well the dangers for a woman in such a situation. Owning a brothel had taught her how dark and ugly men's desires could become. Yet, she had always been the one in control, the one holding the power, the leverage, the final say.

Her heart sank as she considered what the coming days, weeks even, might bring aboard this ship.

If Edward saw or even sensed a threat to her, she knew he would react without hesitation. It was his nature. And she also knew it could very well be the end of him if he pushed too far. Hildebrandt needed Edward alive, at least for now, to find the treasure they sought and the secret to traveling through time they believed he possessed. But Colette wasn't so sure this Looff bastard placed the same value on either prize.

She needed to find an edge, some way to regain the upper hand. She'd done it before, first as a terrified teenager taken in by the Choctaw, later as a woman who bent San Francisco society to her will as a landowner and business operator.

She would find a way to claw her way out of this, too. She opened a drawer, looking for a towel, and in it she saw several interesting items. Scissors, a bottle opener, ice pick, pencils, paper and something that gave her an idea. She glanced at the two men sitting at the table and reached into the drawer.

The two sailors looked up as she approached them with a smile on her face. They watched her with curiosity as she neared.

"Do you boys want to play a game?"

Colette pulled out a chair for her to sit with them, Woodes watching her with interest. "Ever played twenty-one?" Colette set a deck of cards on the table and began to shuffle them expertly.

CHAPTER 23 – CRAVEN

Remembering to disconnect the cable from the radio panel, the operator sprang to his feet.

"Kelley!" he handed the message to the waiting ensign so he could keep his post while the message was delivered.

Kelley's boots thudding against the steel deck as he moved briskly through the narrow corridor. He clenched the handwritten coordinates tightly. Sweat dotted his brow, not from exertion, but from the electric pulse of urgency that always followed a confirmed sighting.

Reaching the captain's quarters, he rapped twice with his knuckles on the metal door.

Inside, Commander Outerbridge stirred. The knock had pierced his light sleep like a siren. "Hang on," he mumbled groggily, swinging his legs over the side of his narrow cot. His joints ached faintly from too many nights spent awkwardly half sleeping in uniform. He rubbed his eyes and reached blindly for his eyeglasses on the metal side table. He checked his wristwatch in the dim glow of a yellowed bulb above the door—quarter after five. He held it to his ear. Still ticking. So was the mission.

When he opened the door, his expression had already sharpened into command presence. The wiry young man stood stiffly, holding out a slip of paper like a war medal.

"We got them, sir," Kelley said. "Scout plane off the *Enterprise* picked up visual confirmation. *Queen Anne's Revenge*, matching rig and heading. Less than twenty minutes ago."

Outerbridge scanned the coordinates, nodding once. "Well, don't just stand there grinnin' like a lark on Sunday—get this to the helmsman, set a new course, and wake the bridge crew."

Kelley turned to go but paused when Outerbridge added, "And tell someone to fetch me a fresh cup of coffee. Real strong. I've a feeling I'll need it."

"Yes, sir."

Outerbridge shut the door and exhaled through his nose. He stripped off his shirt and undershirt and splashed cold water onto his face from the tiny sink bolted to the wall. He caught his own reflection in the mirror—eyelids puffy, streak of silver invading the remaining brown hair at his temples, and a jaw clenched tighter than usual.

As he dressed in a neatly pressed uniform, the ship began to hum with renewed motion. Footsteps clanged on the steel catwalks, doors opened and slammed shut, and the distant chug of the engine room increased tempo as the helmsman adjusted course. The *Ward* was alive again.

Ten minutes later, Outerbridge stepped onto the bridge, buttoning the last of his tunic. Lieutenant Clarke handed him a steaming enamel mug and the updated heading.

"Scouts are holding a visual lock, sir. They'll keep circling until we're in range or they run low on fuel."

"Let's make sure it's the former," Outerbridge said, sipping the bitter coffee. "Keep our speed steady, but if the seas stay calm, I want flank speed ready on my word."

The officers and crew were at full readiness now. Men buckled gear, checked instruments, and manned their posts with a silent precision born of discipline. The grey metal bones of the *Ward* vibrated with purpose as it cut toward its quarry.

Outerbridge stood near the observation station, binoculars in hand, staring into the dark horizon. Somewhere ahead, a ghost ship from the 1700s sailed under canvas and cunning, haunted not just by time, but by the men chasing it.

He muttered quietly to himself, "This morning might just make history—or break it."

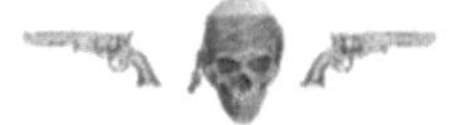

The crew aboard the *Queen Anne's Revenge* kept wary eyes on the airplanes circling high overhead. In the crow's nest, two hundred feet above the deck, Tom scolded himself for having dozed off more than once during the long night watch. At least he'd been the first to spot the planes, noticing their dark silhouettes trailing red and amber blinking lights across the pre-dawn sky.

None of the pirates, cowboys, or sailors had left their posts since nightfall. Most had nodded off where they sat, slumped against barrels or railings, still recovering from the day's battle and their narrow escape from the Hawaiian island.

Anne stirred awake, her head having rested on Jesse's shoulder as they sat together against the railing of the midcastle. She rubbed the sleep film from her lips with the back of her hand, then stretched her arms high in a slow, feline motion. Jesse blinked himself fully awake as he watched her rise, twisting her body to loosen stiff muscles. Her copper-red hair spilled freely over her shoulders and back. Bare feet flexed as she stood on tiptoe, her calves tightening with the stretch.

Jesse rose to stand behind her, slipping his arms around her waist and pressing his face into the warmth of her neck. She reached back with one hand, fingers sliding through his hair to hold him close.

"Those buzzards still circlin'?" he murmured, eyeing the blinking lights overhead.

"Aye. I can still hear their moans." She turned in his embrace, teasing. "Or be those yours in my ear?"

"Mmmm. You'd know mine, sweet cherry."

Mary Read made a dramatic retching sound as she adjusted a windlass just a few feet away.

"I haven't had me breakfast yet, and you two are temptin' me to empty my guts over the side."

Anne shot her a rude gesture before breaking free of Jesse's arms with a grin.

Chester and Francis were making their way toward the aftcastle when Mary called out to them.

"Oy! You boys know these waters well. How close are we to dawn?"

"Soon, I say," Chester replied. "Thirty minutes, maybe."

"Why haven't those birds attacked?" Jesse asked, helping Frank up from where he'd been slouched beside a coiled rope.

"They're watchin'. Waitin'," said Francis, dusting off his coat.

"I've got a sinking feelin' they're waiting for the posse to arrive," Frank remarked as he put a plug of morning tobacco in his cheek.

Mary smacked him on the back of the head.

"Ow! What was that for?"

"You don't talk about sinkin' on a ship, landlubber."

"Damn you, schoolmarm! I almost swallowed my chaw."

Anne studied the interaction between the two. Was there something developing there? The girlish side of her she always sought to squash bubbled over at the thought of she and Mary finding mates in the James brothers. What exciting adventures the four of them could have.

Chester and Francis walked on toward the wheel. They saw that Roberts and Charlotte still maintained their positions at the helm. The couple were talking in hushed whispers when they arrived. Roberts made a motion with his head for the two to approach.

With a serious glance around the deck, he spoke in a quiet tone. "Charlotte tells me there have been conspiratorial murmurs among the crew. Have either of you been approached or heard such talk?"

"We both had heard a call to vote at dawn for captain. It's why we're coming to talk to you," Francis said with eyes that roamed the deck.

"It's Vane and Black Caesar," Charlotte said knowingly and with her head motioned up to the main mast. The three men looked up at the silhouette of the cabin boy high above. They all knew that voices carried further on the water than on land.

"Aye. It was well and good that they followed Blackbeard's orders when he made me captain, but now that they know he's still alive, Caesar's going to want the ship back for that bearded rogue."

"And Vane is just looking for an opportunity to pounce," added Charlotte.

"We still outnumber them even with our losses yesterday," said Chester.

"We and the rest of the *Charlotte's Fortune* crew remain loyal to you."

Roberts clasped his hand on Francis' shoulder in thanks.

"Those two are nowhere to be found topside," Charlotte said. "I'm going to see where they are lying about."

Roberts nodded at his two trusted crewmen. "You two accompany her."

Charlotte shook her head. "Nay. It may require stealth. I will go alone."

Roberts looked hard at her, then nodded his head. He knew what a dangerous creature she was, but he was zealous in desiring her to be safe. He also had quickly learned that she would do as she pleased. "Be cautious."

Charlotte slipped away and soon blended with the shadows of the night as she left the main deck to explore the interior of the ship.

Black Caesar and Vane were shirtless and sweaty as they stowed heavy gold- and silver-laden crates into a hidden compartment just outside the main storage hold. The heat and humidity, constant this far beneath the ship and thickened by the warm air above, caused sweat to bead on their foreheads. Vane's long, dirty blond hair clung to his face like seaweed plastered to a tide-washed rock.

They spoke in hushed voices as they began sealing the false wall made up of cleverly disguised planks that served as the compartment's doorway.

"I feel better that our shares are hidden away from Roberts and his lot," said Vane.

"Aye. Blackbeard would not be pleased to find an empty hold if we're boarded by that warship and they seize our plunder."

Vane was just about to lock the last plank in place when Caesar set a heavy hand on his arm. Vane turned, brow furrowed. The quartermaster took the ornate, fiery cross from around his neck. Somehow, despite the dimness, the amulet glittered, casting pinpoints of light across their faces.

"Roberts wore one of these. I heard Woodes took it from him after the battle," Vane said, turning the cross over in his hands. "How much would you take for it?"

"I shall not part with it."

Vane looked up at him, confused for a moment by the tone. Then he gave a slight shrug and placed the necklace carefully into the secret hold before sealing it shut.

The two men rose and returned to the main storage area, pushing the remaining crates and boxes together to obscure the missing goods. Vane picked up a cutlass with a bejeweled hilt and guard. He gave it a few swings, testing its balance.

"Pretty to look at but almost useless in a fight," he said, running a calloused finger along the edge. "Dull as a debutante's virtue."

He twirled the blade with a smirk and tossed it back into the pile with a clatter.

As they turned to head topside, they froze. Charlotte De Berry stood in the entrance, hand on the hilt of her kukri. The low light behind her outlined her silhouette, casting her in shadow and gleam.

"And what are you two cravens plotting?" she asked coolly. "Filling your pockets with the spoils?"

Vane didn't flinch. "We're going to need to be well armed if we're boarded by that warship sniffing around out there."

"That right?"

"Aye. We were searching the stores for more armaments that could be of use. Alas, most sturdy blades have already been plundered. The rest is just finery and fluff," Vane added, gesturing at the pile of discarded weapons.

Charlotte studied them for a long moment. Neither man offered anything further.

"Dawn is breaking. We should be above deck," said Black Caesar, stepping past her.

"Is that when mutiny will arise as well?" she asked, her eyes narrowing.

Vane shook his head. "No need for mutiny. We'll have a vote. Follow the code, as we've every right to do."

"Aye. Follow the code. Or does Roberts rule as a king?" Caesar added.

Charlotte tapped her finger on the kukri's hilt. A pale wash of daylight began creeping into the hold.

CLANG, CLANG, CLANG.

The sharp ringing of the ship's bell shattered the standoff.

"Ship spotted!"

Caesar brushed past Charlotte and bolted for the ladder. Vane and Charlotte exchanged one last look before following.

The main deck was buzzing with activity.

The sun was just rising on the horizon, and the warship was just off the port side a mere mile or two away. Caesar glanced up the canvas, searching for advantageous winds. The sea was calm and so was the air this morning. He hurried port to the midship rail, grabbing the wood with both hands tightly. That beast was moving briskly toward them propelled by engines that cared little for a gust of a wind. Four aircraft now flocked around the ship many hundreds of feet above. He wasn't sure if they were the type to carry munitions, but it wouldn't matter as that warship had a grand arsenal of its own.

Caesar stared back at the *Queen Anne*'s wake and estimated that they were only doing five knots fully rigged. He turned away and hollered up to Tom. "Oy! Boy!" He waited for Tom to look down from his nest and acknowledge him. "Make your way down!"

He bounded up the steps to find Vane in discussion with Roberts. Charlotte and several others were gathered around.

"The winds have damned us. They'll be on us in minutes," said Roberts as he turned the wheel to keep the oncoming ship facing the port side of the hull.

Vane stared as the ship raced toward them. He turned with wide eyes to confront Roberts. "Do you have a mind to give them a broadside? Have you gone mad?"

"Your vote will have to wait, Charles. The code does not allow a change in leadership during battle."

"You wish to make war with that beast just to keep your rank?" asked Vane incredulously.

"You'd have me raise the white?"

The warship adjusted its course—moving to come at them from astern. Its captain had guessed Roberts' next move. Turning to port would close the gap. Turning starboard would lose the wind entirely.

He turned to Charlotte in frustration. Her look told him Vane was right. They would be taken or sunk should they choose to attack. He looked back at the disturbingly close ship bearing enormous cannons on its deck. The sound of the airships above droned in his ears. His heart was sinking as his crew waited for him to make a decision: stand or fight. He cast one more long look at the warship now behind them, the stark gray mass with its guns trained on their hull.

"Mr. Caesar, raise the white."

"Blackbeard tossed it overboard when we took her. He would never possess such a flag."

"Of course he won't," Roberts sighed heavily. "Reef the sails. We shall parley with these Hawaiians and see what they have to offer. Disperse arms. We shall not be lambs when we treat with them."

Outerbridge barked orders to his officers and sailors as the USS *Ward* held steady, maintaining a fifty-yard distance off the stern of the wooden frigate. Once the pirates reefed their sails, he knew the chase had ended. He allowed himself a measured breath of relief. They had reconsidered. Smart move, he thought. Picking a fight today with his destroyer would have been suicide.

From the command deck, he watched as three of the four LCVP Higgins boats were lowered into the water. Each of the thirty-six-foot craft, dubbed "Papa boats" by the crew, was designed for speed and versatility. They could ferry three dozen armed men or haul equipment and vehicles, even a jeep. Today, they would carry boarding teams.

Through his binoculars, Outerbridge scanned the *Queen Anne's Revenge*. The pirates milled about in plain view, roughly forty of them visible topside. There might be more hidden below, but they looked lightly armed. The cutlasses and antique pistols they carried posed little threat to automatic rifles.

He kept one Papa boat in reserve. It was standard protocol, but also a quiet insurance policy.

Outerbridge lowered the binoculars and gave a brisk nod to his XO.

"Tell the boarding teams to fan out. Take the deck fast, no unnecessary roughness. We're here for answers, not a bloodbath."

"Yes, sir."

As the boats churned across the water, the morning light gleamed off the surface like a thousand shards of broken glass. The warship's engines idled as the men readied themselves to meet ghosts from another age.

Stanton's dark brown eyes squinted against the glare of the rising sun as the Higgins boat motored quickly across the narrow stretch of sea toward the pirate ship.

Pirate ship.

He rolled the word around in his mind again, still not quite believing it. Even now, with the *Queen Anne's Revenge* looming larger by the second, it felt like something out of a fever dream or a boyhood fantasy.

The towering masts creaked gently under their own weight, rigging taut like webbing spun by a giant spider. Sails lay neatly furled along the yards, patched in places, stained by salt and smoke. The ship was a relic, ornate, battle-worn, and magnificent. Not a museum reconstruction, not a set piece from some Hollywood backlot. She was real. She had survived.

The men around him tightened grips on rifles and sidearms. The tension in the landing craft thickened as the shadow of the pirate vessel fell over them. Stanton kept his weapon ready but low, eyes fixed on the rails above. He half-expected cannon fire. Or cutlasses flashing down from the rigging.

Instead, only silence. Watchful eyes peered over the edge. Men, some shirtless, hair worn long and unkempt, stood looking menacingly down on them. A dashing figure in crimson standing near two men in cowboy hats. Women with pistols and swords on their hips. One of them, the red-haired one, wore a devilish grin.

Stanton kept his rifle pointed down but ready. The others around him did the same, the tension coiled tight inside the Higgins boat.

He didn't know what kind of reception they were about to get.

But this much he did know: whatever happened next, history would remember this moment.

Stanton held tight to the gunwale as the skipper throttled back and the Papa boat came alongside the wooden hull.

"Stand back," the senior officer called out.

Several sailors readied rope ladders and long iron hooks, the kind used to pull a boarding line taut or grab a rail. The *Queen Anne's Revenge* loomed above the Higgins boat, its hull high and unwelcoming. With practiced ease, the men began securing their makeshift paths upward—no cannon fire, no shouting, just the quiet, tense shuffle of boots and rope.

The three groups of US sailors climbed the ladders in steady silence, their boots thudding softly against the wooden hull as they ascended. At the rail, the pirates made no move to resist. They gave the Americans space to board but stood their ground, a rough and ready line of rogues armed with an eclectic array of weapons held loose, but not lowered.

Stanton stepped forward alone, the humid morning clinging to his uniform. His fellow sailors held position behind him, weapons at the ready but unraised. The brass back on the *Ward* had picked Stanton to break the ice. He was the only one among them who had any rapport, however thin, with the pirate captain they called Blackbeard.

Stanton glanced among the faces. They looked tired, sun-worn, and watchful. He cleared his throat and stepped closer, doing his best to project calm over unease.

"Morning," he said, voice level but firm. "Who did Blackbeard leave in charge?"

The question stunned the crew. How did this man know Blackbeard's name?

Bart Roberts stepped forward, pistol in his hand pointed at the deck, the other firmly gripping the pommel of his sheathed cutlass. "Bartholomew Roberts, and who might you be?"

Stanton found the name familiar but wasn't sure if it was from a pirate story or a name Edward Thatch had mentioned while he was onboard. "Ensign Stanton of the USS *Ward*, United States Navy," he answered crisply.

Roberts looked around at all the armed men that had come aboard the *Queen Anne's Revenge*. Not a one was beyond thirty years of age, most were still too young for a full growth of facial hair. They all wore strange blue trousers, not of linen or wool, but some coarse-looking fabric. Their shirts, pale blue and buttoned to the collar, clung to their frames, damp with nerves and sweat from the humid morning air. Around their waists, sturdy leather belts held pouches of metal cartridges and odd implements he couldn't name.

Their hats were the oddest of all—soft, white things shaped like overturned pie dishes. Not a feather or braid among them. These men bore no showy colors, no plumes, no polished buckles. Their boots were scuffed, their weapons brutal and efficient, lacking any ornament.

Roberts glanced from the sailors to the hulking ship lurking just sixty or so yards away before returning his attention to the young man addressing him. "Am I right in remembering your ship lending aid when we were attacked by those metal birds days ago?"

Stanton nodded. "Blackbeard, Edward Thatch, was on board our ship. We had fished him out of the water before the attack. He convinced my captain to lend a hand and save your asses from those Zeros."

Roberts cocked his head as he tried to decipher the sailor's words.

"Where is Captain Blackbeard now?" Black Caesar asked with an edge of malice to his voice.

"Don't know for sure but we are looking for him."

"Why?" Jesse James growled. "Why are you looking for him, and why are you chasing us?"

Stanton looked at the motley crew before him trying to guess what brought them all together. "That's above my pay grade. Right now, we just want to talk. Get information."

"Talk, is that all? No need for all those rifles if we're just going to parley."

"Well, you did fire your cannons at us," stated Stanton.

Roberts put on a wide smile. "A misunderstanding then. Why don't you go back to your captain with an invitation for tea? We are happy to receive him, perhaps noon."

Stanton's eyes roamed the group, seeing the tension rising and fingers becoming twitchy. There was a rising tide toward violence in the air. He slowly shook his head. "Commander Outerbridge would like you to come aboard the *Ward*, as our guests." He motioned with his M1 carbine at the pirates. "All of you."

Vane and several others erupted with obscenities and in seconds everyone was heatedly pointing their pistols, rifles and weapons at each other.

Stanton looked down the barrel of his rifle at Roberts who had a dark-skinned woman next to him wielding a wicked-looking machete and a flintlock pistol. His eyes then locked on an Asian boy of about twelve pointing a Civil War-era Colt .45 at him. "Everyone settle down! We have ten times as many men and four .50-caliber guns pointed at you. Those heavies will cut you to ribbons in seconds and there is not a speck of cover on this ship that would save you."

Stanton's heart pounded in his chest. In a rush, his whole life in Boston flashed before his eyes—his mom, dad, three brothers, high school, baseball, sweethearts, and the grueling basic training that had brought him here. He had to deescalate the situation fast, or the deck of this beautiful old ship would be awash with blood—possibly his own. He glanced down at the dark stains embedded in the oak planks. Were those bloodstains already?

"Look, all we want is to find your captain, Blackbeard. We're not here to take your ship. We can help you figure out how you got here. I don't know all the details, but I've spoken with Blackbeard. We rescued him. Now the Nazis or the Japs have him, along with your other friends. We're on the same side."

Roberts studied him for a moment. They were outmanned and outgunned. Caught, but not yet dead. His experience had taught him to play the hand he was dealt, and always keep a trick tucked away. A smile crept across his lips.

"Well, why didn't you say so when you boarded, mate?" He lowered his pistol and gestured for the others to do the same.

Stanton exhaled the long breath he'd been holding and signaled his crew to stand down.

"That's a fine vessel you've got there, Mr. Stanton," Roberts said, looking over at the *Ward*. "I think we'd all like a tour of it. I do hope it's well provisioned—my crew's a mite famished this morn."

CHAPTER 24 – PIRATES & OUTLAWS

Outerbridge stood at the stern of the *Ward*. A dozen armed crew members were stationed just behind him, standing at attention. It had taken three hours of negotiations for Stanton to convince the pirates to leave their weapons stowed aboard their ship. Their treasure, which seemed to be their greatest concern, would remain in the hold. Outerbridge knew he would have to keep offering reassurances that the navy had no interest in their "plunder." He only hoped command wouldn't reverse that position and force him to break his word.

Each time Stanton broke away to radio updates, the pirate ship erupted in murmurs and unrest—presumably because none aboard had ever seen or heard of a two-way radio. Outerbridge shook his head. If these people truly came from the distant past, what would that mean for the world? He wasn't sure he wanted to see *The Time Machine* by HG Wells play out in real life.

Once they were all aboard the *Ward*, he was to tow the pirate vessel and rendezvous with the *Enterprise*, which was en route to provide cover for Wake Island in case of a Japanese attack. With any luck, the *Enterprise* would take custody of the ship and its crew. Then Outerbridge and his destroyer could return to the mission of hunting the damn Japs. The *Ward* was fully staffed with two hundred and thirty men. Adding another forty-eight would stretch things past comfort, and possibly past efficiency. Forty-nine, he reminded himself, as Naval Command was sending a historian from Maui by seaplane to evaluate the authenticity of the ship and its inhabitants. A WAVES junior lieutenant—Women Accepted for Volunteer Emergency Service.

Outerbridge wasn't thrilled about having a woman aboard but considering there were three pirate women being ferried over as well, it might be helpful to have a female US Navy representative on hand to question them.

He straightened his back as the first Higgins boat arrived to deliver the first group. The first man up the ladder was a striking figure, handsome, with a thin mustache and an air of command. He looked like Errol Flynn, straight off a Hollywood film set. His flamboyant clothing added to the impression. Behind him came several sailors in drab uniforms that looked like they belonged to a merchant crew from a century ago.

Then came a towering Black man whose dingy white shirt hung open, fastened only by buttons made of bone. His massive chest was visibly scarred and streaked with sweat. His dark eyes narrowed as he took in the *Ward* with a silent, careful gaze.

One curious character after another stepped aboard, and with each unique boot on his deck, Outerbridge's trepidation grew.

Stanton finally climbed aboard and led the group forward. He stopped and saluted crisply. Outerbridge returned it with a casual nod.

"Sir, this is Captain Bartholomew Roberts," said Stanton introducing the two captains to each other.

"William Outerbridge, Lieutenant Commander of the USS *Ward*," he replied, offering his hand.

Roberts took it in a firm, calloused grip. "A fine ship you have here. Be it a first-rate ship of the line?"

Outerbridge recognized the term. The Royal Navy had once classified its warships from fourth-rate to first-rate depending on firepower and size. He offered a half-smile.

"We don't classify our ships that way, nor does England anymore. This is a Wickes-class destroyer. She was commissioned in eighteen—" he paused, "nineteen eighteen."

"Only six guns?" Roberts asked, scanning the deck.

Outerbridge nodded, then added with a touch of pride, "And twelve torpedo tubes."

Roberts turned to eye the strange midship machinery, four clusters of long tubes mounted in sets of three on either side of the ship.

"Torpedoes?" he echoed, testing the unfamiliar word.

Outerbridge decided not to elaborate. He gestured back toward the pirate vessel. "Tell me a little about your ship."

"Blackbeard's ship," Black Caesar corrected him.

Roberts sighed; Black Caesar was not going to let that go unsaid in any conversation. "The *Queen Anne's Revenge, formerly* under Blackbeard's command, was a French merchantman—"

"Slaver," Black Caesar cut in. "Blackbeard took her, the *La Concorde*, near Martinique. She's two hundred tons, forty cannon, and swift as a porpoise."

Roberts held back a response and gestured. "May I present our quartermaster, Black Caesar."

Outerbridge extended a hand. The massive man gripped it in a crushing shake that nearly pulled the lieutenant commander forward. He flexed his fingers to bring back circulation after the release.

One by one, Roberts made introductions. Outerbridge couldn't keep up with all the names, but two stood out. Dressed like cowboys from a John Wayne or Tyrone Power movie, the men were introduced as Frank and Jesse James.

He forced himself to ignore the avalanche of questions that threatened to surface. Legendary Wild West outlaws on the deck of his modern destroyer? He'd deal with that later.

Ensign Kelley approached, holding a pair of binoculars. "Sir, a PBY Catalina is on approach."

Outerbridge took the field glasses and spotted the floatplane a few miles out.

"Seems our historian is double-timing it," he muttered, handing back the glasses and adjusting his own spectacles.

He watched as the pirates on deck craned their necks, awestruck as the plane descended and skimmed the water's surface. It landed and taxied between the *Ward* and the *Queen Anne's Revenge*. One of the Higgins boats moved to retrieve their newest guest.

Hopefully, she could make heads or tails of the pirates' stories.

"Ensign Stanton mentioned breakfast in his last report. Seeing as we've reached midday, let's get your crew fed. You gave us quite the brilliant chase through the long night. We've got a couple of excellent cooks. Why don't you follow us down to the galley?" Outerbridge said, gesturing and leading the way.

"Why do I feel like a lamb headed to slaughter?" Mary whispered to Charlotte. "I hope your lover boy isn't delivering us to the gallows."

Charlotte said nothing, but her thoughts mirrored Mary's unease. As they followed the officers through the winding passages of the iron ship, she couldn't help but think, if it came to a fight, there was no defense they could mount that wouldn't end in death and defeat. This ship was a floating fortress, but as with any fortress it was most vulnerable from within, and now Roberts had brought them inside.

Once the pirates were all gathered in the galley dining on Salisbury steak and scalloped potatoes, Outerbridge excused himself to meet with the historian. He found her in the wardroom, setting up a tape recorder, legal pads, compact camera, and several books on naval history. She was an attractive woman with Russian features in her late twenties with wavy, mahogany-brown, shoulder-length hair and expressive brown eyes.

"I hope you have one on Old West outlaws," he said indicating the stack of books.

She smiled in greeting and approached with a soft handshake that he was grateful for after the show of force the pirates had displayed on his joints, though he frowned at her informal greeting.

"Doctor Miriam Katz, my friends call me Miri."

"I'd say 'at ease' but that usually means a junior lieutenant had saluted and was standing at attention."

Miriam's eyes widened in embarrassment. She quickly snapped to attention and saluted, leaving her hand at her forehead.

"I'm sorry, sir. This is still new to me. I'm still getting my bearings."

Outerbridge gave a fatherly smile. "At ease, Lieutenant. Have a seat and I'll get you up to speed."

They sat across from each other and Miriam was careful to not slouch or leave her elbows on the table; the latter was just formal manners her mother insisted on and that she thought it better to adopt in the present moment. She glanced at her stack of books. "I'm sorry, sir, you asked about Old West books?"

"Ah, yes. Well, we seem to have aboard a group of pirates that claim to be from the early seventeen hundreds." He paused and fidgeted a moment with the cuff of his shirt sleeve and watch band. "Along with two men claiming to be Jesse James and his brother Frank James."

Miriam nodded with a half-smile and when it wasn't returned, she turned serious and jotted down the two names on one of the pads. "And you're buying their story… sir, that they are really the people they claim to be? Jesse James?"

"That's why you're here, doctor."

They stared at one another for a moment, each wanting the other to verbalize a theory.

"How did the ah, pirates, say the James brothers came to be with them?" Miriam asked, preparing to take notes.

"We haven't questioned them. They just came aboard as you were arriving. Most of the story came from the fellow we fished out of the water near Pearl the day of the Japanese attack, Edward Thatch."

"Blackbeard," she nodded while writing.

Outerbridge was loath to use that name, as it might give too much credence to the story. "Yes, as you've undoubtably read in the report. Then when that Civil War ironclad sailed into the harbor with Captain Woodes Rogers aboard we had a chance to question him, and he told a similar tale."

"The *Comanche*. Yes, of course." She shuffled through the stack of books and opened one to a dog-eared page. She tapped her slender finger on a black and white image of the ironclad, a photograph that had been taken after it had been reassembled and commissioned at Mare Island naval shipyard near San Francisco in 1864. Outerbridge leaned forward, then nodded his confirmation.

"It's still sitting at Pearl. Did you get a chance to see it?"

"No. I was on Maui at an archeological dive when I got my orders."

"It was pretty banged up, so I don't think it's going anywhere for a while."

"I have to admit, I'm more interested in that eighteenth-century frigate sitting next to your destroyer. Have you been on her?"

He shook his head. "It's taking all my willpower to not row over there right now. Do you want to interview these pirates or explore the ship?"

"Like you, Commander, I feel that ship has a strong lure, but I was told the first order of business is deciding if their story is bullsh—, BS, or if they are the real McCoy."

"Alright then." Outerbridge stood up from the table. "Who would you like to see first?"

"What are my choices?"

"Ever hear of Bartholomew Roberts?"

Miriam raised an eyebrow. "Black Bart Roberts? Captain of the *Royal Fortune*? That Bartholomew Roberts?"

Outerbridge just gave her a coy smile. "I'll have him brought over."

The sun was behind Miriam's back as she stood at the stern of the *Ward* watching the *Queen Anne's Revenge* cut through the wake as it was towed behind the destroyer. The sailing ship had been attached to the chocks by thick steel cables. A contingent of eight sailors were stationed on the old frigate to keep manning the helm so that she kept center behind the *Ward*.

Miriam had only made it a third of the way through the interviews before needing to break for supper. Her head was truly spinning from the tales she had heard, and her fingers ached from taking furious and meticulous notes.

Tomorrow morning, she would resume the *interrogations*, though that was a strong word that still played well in her head since most of them were indeed pirates and outlaws. *Real pirates and outlaws*—what an adventure this was turning out to be. Once she had notes on them all Miriam would then be free to tour the pirate ship. Outerbridge arrived to interrupt her musing. They hadn't spoken since their morning meeting.

"It looks like we both missed the opportunity today to climb aboard and play pirate."

She turned and brushed her hair from her face as it was blowing in the warm Pacific air while the two ships pushed through the gentle waters at a brisk twelve knots.

"I left my tricorn in my apartment," she retorted. "Sir."

They both leaned against the gunwale and watched the wooden, three-masted ship rise and fall with the swells, canvas furled and stowed leaving the ship a picture of spiderweb-like ratlines and skeletal spars.

"So, are they playing pirate, or..." Outerbridge asked after a few moments of silence while they enjoyed the view of the sunset-lit water and the trailing ship.

Miriam turned to face him. "I haven't spoken with any of the women and I do have a bias that I will be able to read them quickly for authenticity. My perception is that I would spot unique peculiarities and idiosyncrasies that a woman born in the late sixteen-nineties would possess. I now understand that there are only a handful of pirates from that era in the crew, the rest were picked up in the late eighteen hundreds after their first jump in time."

Outerbridge listened with interest, unwilling to interrupt with the questions that were popping into his head.

"I'll start by saying that none of them so far have any idea how they traveled in time. There is no talk of a machine or device that is the catalyst.

Just the storms. And before I comment on the pirate men, let me jump to the cowboys, Jesse and Frank James. Neither could be described as chatty." She chuckled, remembering how difficult it was for her to get any information out of them. "But I happened to do several research papers in high school as well as one in college on Jesse James. My father is a huge fan of Westerns, and I think I wrote them all for his benefit and approval. He owned a tailor shop in Brooklyn and made a few Western-style vests for the Broadway play *Destry Rides Again*." Miriam became lost in the memory of her father for a moment. "Anyway, while there are no photographs of pirates who lived in 1718, there *are* pictures of cowboys in 1873." She raised her brow. "And there are many of Jesse and Frank James. Those images are burnt into my brain. Now, there could be look-alikes I suppose, but two look-alikes, brothers? The pictures were black and white, but those two men aboard your ship… they are the spitting image of them."

"Hmm," he muttered but waited for more.

"I paid particular attention to their clothing. Did you notice the buttons, seams and fabric?"

Outerbridge shook his head.

"Again, the daughter of a tailor, mind you. I spent many years learning the family trade, helping my parents in the shop, learning about textiles, fasteners and the origin of design. Commander, I am completely positive that not one of those men is wearing garments that were produced in this century. Not exactly proof of time travel but difficult to costume that entire crew in such a way. There is, of course, the story of how the James brothers just disappeared after a California train heist. They had gotten away with a fortune in silver, and it was commonly agreed upon that they retired after that enormous haul." She picked up her notes and tapped the top of the page titled *Pirates*. "The pirates, Roberts, Charles Vane, and Black Caesar, are harder to authenticate. There were of course no cameras to capture their images. The only reliable portraits painted in that age would have been of royalty and the upper classes so everything about them comes from secondhand accounts. The artworks depicting them were all created well after they were alive." She flipped through several of her handwritten notes. "Vane and Caesar were even less talkative than the James brothers if you could believe. But our dashing Bart Roberts was pleased as punch to recount his entire life story to me."

Miriam took what looked like a pocket watch from her pocket and held the item for Outerbridge to examine.

"What have we here?"

"He lent it to me. I promised I would give it back to him in the morning."

Outerbridge held it up to the fading light, examining the strange hybrid object. "Looks like a compass had a baby with a pocket watch and a canteen."

She offered a faint smile as he handed it back to her. "Not too far off. It's a multi-function timepiece, built in Germany, likely around 1590. What you're looking at is a combination of a powder flask, a sundial, a mechanical clock, and a magnetic compass… all in one compact device."

She rotated it carefully, pointing to each element. "The body is rosewood, with inlaid rosettes made of brass and bone—decorative, but also functional. Here," she tapped the outer ring, "is a twelve-hour clockface, twice-marked for the full day. Mechanical, albeit crude by our standards. And under this lid," she lifted the engraved brass cap with its transverse hinge, "is a horizontal sundial, usable from six in the morning to six in the evening. You stretch this thread here to create the gnomon, but it's fixed to a single latitude. Not exactly portable across oceans."

She turned it again. "The compass is simple, just north-south alignment, no correction for magnetic deviation. A soldier or sailor in the late sixteenth century wouldn't have had the means to calibrate it more precisely."

"And this?" Outerbridge asked, pointing to a small opening on the side.

"That's for gunpowder. The object's primary function was as a powder flask. The funnel is bone, capped with a spring-loaded brass lid. You'd fill it through this socket here."

She leaned back, letting him take it in. "A high-status piece, part tool, part timekeeper, part weaponry accessory. Likely made for someone educated or aristocratic. Roberts said he was gifted it by a duke's son, who happened to be aboard a ship he'd taken."

"Gifted," Outerbridge chuckled. "And, with this information are you leaning…"

Miriam held up her hand. "Sir, if you'll let me, I'd like to see the ship and talk with those women in the morning, plus the boy, and hear their stories before giving an opinion."

Outerbridge looked out at the darkening silhouette of the *Queen Anne's Revenge*. "My orders keep changing every hour. The Japanese fleet is being spotted all over the Pacific. We need to remain nimble. We'll be rendezvousing with the *Enterprise* in three days. Please finish your report by then. God willing, we'll be handing this saga over to them. Good evening, doctor."

Miriam held the compass watch open in her hand, gazing at the intricate device for a moment. She pocketed it then started back to the ship's wardroom to go over her notes once again. She decided to stop by the galley in hopes of a fresh cup of coffee. Her history books, notes and thoughts of time traveling pirates had her too excited to think about sleep.

CHAPTER 25 – RECIPE FOR CHICKEN

Rough hands roused Thatch, Philip, Rogers, and Colette out of the deep sleep they had fallen into. The day-night cycle had blurred to them over the past several days. A crowd of eight or so men began pulling them from their bunks and started to search through their clothing and bed rolls. Hildebrandt stood nearby barking orders in German with Looff by his side.

Thatch became enraged when they began to paw at Colette, searching her clothing, and she fought to be free from their grabbing hands. He used his strength and size to pick one sailor up, raising him to slam the top of his head into the metal bulkhead. The man crumpled unconscious at his feet and he struck one of the two men holding Colette with a clenched fist.

Philip was thrown against the wall and searched, while Rogers fought back against the sailor seizing his arms.

"Leave her be, you damn German scum!" Thatch roared as he fought with the men holding Colette. Several men grabbed at him from behind. He slammed one of their noses with an elbow and continued to wrestle with the others.

Looff removed his pistol from his holster and clubbed the back of Thatch's head with the metal grip.

Dazed and stunned, Thatch slid to the deck.

One of the men searching Philip spoke sharply in German, holding up a sheaf of papers he found in Philip's shirt.

Hildebrandt came forward and held them to the light. "I should have your fingers for that, little Englishman."

Looff strode over, pistol still in his hand, and brought it to bear on Philip's forehead. "We do not tolerate thievery on a vessel of the German Navy."

Philip's bowels threatened to loosen their hold on their contents when Looff cocked his Luger P08. He watched the man's icy-cold eyes narrow while his finger began to gently press on the trigger.

"*Aufhören!*" Hildebrandt exclaimed.

A smirk overtook Looff's lips as he kept the barrel of his gun pressed against Philip's head.

Hildebrandt approached Philip and pointed to the papers. "You've marked it. What did you find, Mr. Albert? These notations, I don't recognize the writings."

Philip kept quiet, eyes focused on the hand with the gun pointed at his head.

Hildebrandt set his hand on Looff's pistol and lowered it from Philip's forehead. He looked down at Thatch who was starting to rise, rubbing his bruised skull. "You two have discovered something in the codex, haven't you?"

"Just an excellent recipe for chicken boiled with conch shells. Find us a well-stocked tavern and we'll fix it for you bastards," Thatch said with a hearty chuckle.

Looff stalked toward Colette and grabbed her arm from the sailor that was holding her. She let out a screech when he forced her against the wall.

Thatch roared and started to lunge but stopped when Looff placed his gun to her cheek.

"Take another step and I'll blast this woman's head all over the wall!" he called out in German. Colette's eyes were wide with fear.

"Tell us what you found or that beautiful face will be nothing but gore that *you'll* be forced to clean from the walls," Hildebrandt said in an eerily calm voice.

Thatch looked only at Colette, wanting so badly to help her, to rip the man threatening her apart with his bare hands.

A sudden exclamation of awe sounded from one of the men holding Woodes Rogers. The sailor had reached into the pirate hunter's shirt and pulled out the unique diamond-encrusted cross that Rogers had taken from Bart Roberts. He had worn it hidden underneath his shirt.

"What have we here?" Hildebrandt whispered. He approached and took the necklace from Rogers and held it up to the light, examining the pink-hued metal. It was unlike anything he'd seen before.

"Did it not occur to you to search these vermin after you captured them?" Looff asked in German, his words dripping in irritation.

"They had already been prisoners; I imagined that the Americans had searched them."

Looff and Hildebrandt continued conversing in German.

"The Americans are infested with Afros, Jews and homosexuals, their decision-making abilities are compromised by inferior bloodlines." Looff turned to his sailors. "Search them from top to bottom, I shall stay here to make sure the job is done correctly." He stood and motioned with his pistol for the task to begin. "Start with the woman."

Colette had been given one of the smallest sailor's uniforms aboard the ship to replace the blue dress that Hildebrandt deemed too intoxicating for the male crew, including Looff, who had taken a noticeable interest in her. Hildebrandt wanted Thatch to remain cooperative as they made their way to the Seychelles. His knowledge of Levasseur could be the key to deciphering the clues left by the long-dead pirate.

He watched Colette as she finished washing the dishes and pots from the morning's meal of boiled oats. It was understandable why Looff was so taken with her, she was fetching, even in the ill-fitting men's attire. Hildebrandt was determined to keep her untouched by the ship's commander, using the threat to her safety as leverage to keep Thatch under control. He'd already had to argue with Looff not to kill the three male prisoners after a thorough search revealed an ancient single-shot pistol hidden in Thatch's sleeve. Hildebrandt endured a long lecture on proper prisoner handling after that.

Thatch, Rogers, and the English scientist were now under guard near the storage hold on the lower deck. Hildebrandt's argument for keeping them alive was growing weaker by the hour as Looff continued demanding their purpose.

He rolled his fingers over the crystalline, white-pink metal of the cross. He didn't know what it was made of or when it had been crafted, but it was truly exquisite. Woodes Rogers had claimed he took it from a pirate named Roberts, but knew nothing of its history. Seated at the mess table in the galley, Hildebrandt leaned back and rubbed his eyes. He opened his case and spread the contents out on the surface—notes, ciphers, reports, and Pirate Republic coins. He picked one up and tried to flip it through his knuckles, mimicking what Colette had done at their first meeting. It clattered to the table. With a smirk, he flicked it with his finger, sending it spinning upright next to the cross.

The light caught the gold coin's surface with each rotation, flashing rapidly like a pulse. He glanced at his notes, intending to review the coin's minting details from 1718.

Colette, drying a large pot, paused when she noticed the spinning coin. Ten seconds passed. Then fifteen. Twenty. The coin continued spinning. She stepped closer. Hildebrandt glanced at her, then back to the coin. It spun mere inches from the cross.

At thirty seconds, the coin still hadn't slowed.

Colette now stood before the table. She leaned down to check beneath the coin, looking for a mechanism or trick. She saw nothing. When she looked at Hildebrandt, he appeared just as bewildered.

Curious, he touched the cross and pulled it slightly toward him. The coin immediately wobbled, then slowed, traveling a few inches before clattering to a stop.

Colette touched the coin, then the cross. She slid the cross to the center of the table and picked up the coin again. With Hildebrandt watching silently, she spun it once more. The coin resumed its flawless spin. She picked up another coin and spun it on the other side of the cross, then did the same with two more. Within moments, four gold coins spun steadily around the cross, none losing speed.

Hildebrandt and Colette exchanged stunned looks, neither able to conceal their awe.

Down the corridor came Looff's voice, followed by the sharp rhythm of boots on the metal deck. Hildebrandt acted fast, sweeping the coins and cross into his case just before the commander entered. Colette turned and resumed scrubbing a pot as if nothing had happened.

Looff appeared with his first officer and glanced at the spread of papers in front of Hildebrandt. Speaking in German, he said, "The Japanese have begun their attack on Wake Island. We'll avoid the area and continue west until we find a depot to refuel. I suggest you uncover the cipher's secrets soon. The Führer expects progress from this risky endeavor."

Hildebrandt gave a tight nod and feigned interest in his notes.

"Have you?" Looff asked, more pointedly.

Hildebrandt looked up, irritated. "I'm working on a few theories that are beginning to bear fruit. We're weeks away from the Seychelles. With the pirates' help, we'll find the resting place of Levasseur's treasure."

Looff frowned, skeptical. "And the mystical time machine? Any progress there?"

"That also has a theory in the works," Hildebrandt replied, glancing at Colette.

Looff followed his gaze and smiled. "Well, these next few weeks may prove quite entertaining." He turned after a lecherous look at Colette and left with his officer.

Once they were gone, Hildebrandt collected his papers and leaned toward Colette.

"You'd do well to keep what happened to yourself. I'm in a position to protect you—protect all of you. Cross me, and I'll let Looff have his way with you. And I won't stop him next time he wants to eject Thatch and your friends out of a torpedo tube."

Colette said nothing, her mind racing. She was fairly sure Hildebrandt wanted to keep the discovery secret from Looff more than anyone else. Philip and Edward needed to hear about the cross. Did Edward or Woodes know about its strange properties?

She had never seen anything like it—outside of parlor tricks, that is. But those required preparation, and she'd seen most of them before during her time in saloons to spot the tricks. There had always been charlatans and snake oil salesmen with sleight-of-hand illusions to amaze the crowd. She was no stranger to such deceptions. She could make a coin appear or vanish in a blink.

That was why she'd tested the coins herself. If Hildebrandt hadn't scooped them up, would they have spun forever? Was it divine? The cross was a religious artifact, after all. Still, the effect was localized, just a few inches. When Hildebrandt moved the cross away, the coin slowed and fell. Could it be magnetism? But gold wasn't magnetic. Maybe the coin wasn't pure gold. That had to be it.

My stars, why did I get taken in so easily? she scolded herself. But she knew she had to tell Philip and Edward. They'd want to know. Especially about Hildebrandt's reaction.

Colette shared her findings with Edward and Philip in whispered words later that night. The men were tired after the crew had worked them hard throughout the day, if it was indeed day. Woodes lay in his bunk, back to the group. His body was still recovering from the beating he took from Edward and his mind was still coming to terms with the fact that he was forever lost in time, never to arrive back at London's harbor in 1718.

"I would have thought the Buzzard too proud to mint coins mixed with lead," Thatch said with a huff.

"We all did handle them, their weight would have fooled me into thinking they were pure gold. I'd consider myself a good judge after all the coin I've handled at The Paris."

"Even if it were magnetized, the coin would not have spun like you describe. It would have attached itself to the cross if it were magnetism that affected it," Philip said.

"It spun for almost a minute without stopping. I had four coins spinning without a hint of slowing before Hildebrandt swept them away. I'm sure a minute had passed or more."

"What does it matter? It brings us no closer to finding an escape from this Ub boat or whatever they call it," grumbled Thatch.

"Black Caesar had a similar cross, did he not?" asked Philip, remembering something he had seen.

"Aye. Found it in the hold. It was part of a plunder we'd taken."

"So, there are two, matching crosses. One Roberts wore when he boarded the *Queen Anne's Revenge* the night of the meeting, the parley between you all?" asked Philip.

"Aye."

"The same night of the storm."

It wasn't a question, but Thatch answered anyway. "Aye, that it was."

"Caesar's cross was in the hold. He found it when he was diving to raise the ship from the bottom of the San Francisco Bay. I remember when he found it, that he said it almost cost him his life."

Thatch sat up on his cot and looked at Philip with renewed interest.

"Where did Roberts get his?" Philip asked.

Thatch shook his head. He had no idea. He had never met Roberts nor heard too many stories of the man before meeting aboard his ship in the harbor of Nassau.

"Where did you acquire yours?"

Thatch's face clouded with a memory. "What does it matter? It's just some royal's trinket is it not?"

"It is always cold," came the voice of Woodes.

They turned to look at him in the darkened space. He still lay with his back to the group.

"What do mean, cold?" asked Colette.

Woodes sighed and rolled over to face them. "It never warmed to my skin, like any other metal would do. It always felt cold against my chest."

"That is because you are a cold-blooded bastard with an icy heart."

Woodes stared daggers at Thatch. "A pox on you, pirate." He flipped back over, turning his back to the group.

Philip turned toward Thatch. "You didn't see but when Roberts came aboard and shook hands with Black Caesar something odd happened. The storm was upon us and rain fell in large drops. I was standing there when the two men were close, the crosses on their necks were close. I thought it was a trick of light or something…"

Thatch and Colette watched the little man while he struggled with his thoughts.

"What? Spit it out, Mr. Albert."

"The rain stopped."

Thatch frowned. "What of it?"

"The rain stopped in midair but only that which was between the two men, between the crosses. The drops stopped falling and were suspended between them. As more rain fell it started to accumulate above the field the crosses created at their chests. I watched those raindrops, frozen in time, then when the two men—two crosses parted, the rain fell as normal."

Thatch rubbed his face and long beard with his hands. "Ah, magic crosses, are they? Able to spin coins and stop the rain?" He stood up and paced the small space aggressively. He needed to duck his head from the curved deckhead. "Mr. Albert, you betray me. I presumed you a true scientist. Now you would have me believing in mermaids and fairies."

"Edward," Colette said with a scolding tone.

Thatch stopped his pacing and sat down next to Colette.

"Not magic. Science. The fact that we don't know the nature of it doesn't mean there is not a scientific reason for it. Look around us. If I would have told you a few days ago that men could fly through the air, and travel beneath the waves for days at a time, would you have believed it?"

Thatch considered what Philip had said. "Ah, well, my science-minded friend, you have enlightened me once again." He turned to Colette. "You see, I did tell you the man would come in handy at some point. Aren't you glad I didn't toss him to the sea as you had suggested?"

Colette slapped his leg but offered a smile. "I said no such thing and you know that."

"What now?" asked Thatch.

"Let's start with how you acquired the cross that Black Caesar wears."

Thatch sighed and sat back against the bulkhead. "Well, that tale brings me back a year or so. I was sailing with me old mate, me old captain, Benjamin Hornigold. This was before that rot-bastard lying over there corrupted him," he pointed at Woodes. "An young Sam Bellamy was there too, just newly captaining his own ship, me being the first mate for Hornigold. We were a few days out from St. Thomas when we had run across a man you may have heard of…" He stopped, dramatically looking at Philip and Colette's eager faces. "Olivier Levasseur." Thatch chuckled. "The Buzzard had his feathers a-ruffled on account of Hornigold being unwilling to plunder one of England's precious merchants."

"At least the man was loyal," Rogers chipped in.

"Aye. To a king that had no loyalty himself," grumbled Thatch. "But that is not the whole story. Bellamy and Levasseur were enraged with Hornigold's stance as a fat merchant was left to pass unharassed. Then, while we treated, a new prize made her appearance on the horizon."

CHAPTER 26 – THE BUZZARD

1717 The Caribbean Sea, somewhere between St. Thomas and Anguilla

The salty wind snapped the colors overhead as three pirate ships floated just off the Leeward Islands. Aboard *La Louise*, tempers flared hotter than the Caribbean sun.

"Damn your rules, Hornigold!" Sam Bellamy's voice rang across the deck. His dark curly hair was soaked with sweat, and his pistol belt hung low, ready against his young trim waist. "You let another prize slip through our fingers. English or not, it carried silver and powder!"

Benjamin Hornigold, steady as always, kept his hands behind his back. "We are not at war with England, Bellamy. I will not plunder a ship flying the Union Jack."

"Then what in hell are we but pirates turned yellow?" Olivier Levasseur growled from the quarterdeck, arms folded across his chest. His accent twisted the words as if they'd been soaked in French wine. "You have loyalty to a crown that would see us hanged. Don't speak to me of flags. We've spent months robbing half-empty slave ships and rickets-filled merchants while fat English brigs sail by, stuffed with spice and wine, and we just stand there, holding our peckers, watching them pass."

"The Spanish come through these waters as well," Hornigold growled. "Those be the targets that will make our pockets brim with gold and silver, La Buse."

"Bah. The Spanish guard their treasures with hundred-gun fleets. I have twenty-two and you two between ye have twenty-four," Levasseur said dismissively. He poked a finger into Hornigold's chest. "I do not sit on my arse while a Frenchman sails by, I run up the colors, give'm a broadside and a sharp blade in the eye!"

Behind Hornigold, the tall spare frame of Edward Thatch—yet to earn the name Blackbeard—stood watchful and silent. His thick black hair was pulled into a sailor's tail, and he had the first hints of what his soot-and-oil black beard would become with his months-old beard. His blue eyes flicked between the men. He almost let out a chuckle, musing to himself that the Buzzard was the one that had gotten a sharp blade in his eye. The braggart only had partial use of his left eye after a knife had left a long brutal mark running from his forehead to his cheek, not bothering to stop at his now clouded eye.

Bellamy paced, frustrated. "This isn't the first prize you've turned away. And it won't be the last. You hold us back, Hornigold."

"Enough," Hornigold said coolly. "You've made your grievances known. You're free to sail without me if you've grown tired of my command."

Thatch noticed Levasseur's hand drift near the hilt of his cutlass. For a moment, it looked as though blood might be spilled between men meant to be brothers.

But then a shout rang down from the foremast.

"Sail, ho!"

They all turned. The lookout leaned out from the crow's nest, waving wildly.

"Portuguese rigging! She's heavy in the water!"

Levasseur's eyes lit like cannon fire. "Now there's a prize no one here will weep for."

Bellamy broke into a grin. "Finally, something we can all agree on."

Orders rang out. The pirates scattered back to their ships, grinning and shouting like wolves given a fresh scent. Bellamy returned to the *Marianne*, Hornigold to the *Ranger*, and Levasseur strode aft and took the wheel of *La Louise*.

Thatch quickly followed Hornigold up the rope ladder to the deck of the *Ranger*. "Think they'll try to claim it first?"

"Let them," Hornigold said. "We'll see whose cannon speak loudest. Ready the gun crews and make sure we board her first."

"Aye, provided the Buzzard doesn't go too far and sink her in his bloodlust."

Hornigold didn't respond but was reminded that that happened once before. The man was quick of tongue, quicker of temper, and quickest to strike when it came to violence.

Levasseur left the wheel to his helmsman and approached the bow of his ship with a dozen men eagerly following in his wake. He took from his belt a telescoping spyglass he had acquired from a pompous member of the Royal Academy of Science that happened to find himself hanging feet first from a yard arm while Levasseur questioned him about the location of the silk merchant that was thought to be sailing with him. The man gifted him several quality trinkets before bleeding out into the ocean, then he was dropped into the sea to satisfy the hungry, circling sharks. He pulled the brass interlocking cylinders to their full extent and brought the eyepiece to his good eye.

He spied the Portuguese ship and licked his lips as his view improved five-fold under the device's magnification. She was indeed heavily laden but with what treasures, he wondered. She was a three-masted, 1,000-ton galleon with two gun decks. He quickly surmised that she would face them with fifty-six to seventy guns along with hundreds of men occupying her decks. *What be the reason for you to be all alone in this part of the sea?*

"Does she look like a prize, Captain?" asked one of his crew members.

"She does indeed, matey, and if we are first to score her we'll be demanding the lion's share, so don't just stand there drooling and salivating. Let us catch the wind and beat Hornigold and Bellamy to the meal!"

Samuel Bellamy slapped the back of his first mate and friend Paulsgrave Williams. "The Buzzard is moving starboard so let's sail port and box that galleon in."

"We sail port, and we'll cut off the *Ranger*. She'll have to come about and lose some wind."

"Aye, Hornigold will sail in our wake, late to the party as ever," he said sharing a laugh with Paulsgrave. They had sailed for months with Hornigold and learned a great deal from the older and more experienced sailor, but youth and exuberance had pushed them to find their own ship and crew that thirsted for riches and adventure. The sloop they sailed was a prize they had plundered while sailing with Hornigold. Bellamy was voted captain and many of the younger crew had opted to join Bellamy and Paulsgrave on the newly christened *Marianne*. He regretted that Thatch stayed with Hornigold as he would have loved to have his intelligence and experience aboard, but the man was fiercely loyal to his captain.

They made haste in bringing their nimble ship to full sail alongside the *Ranger*. Bellamy shouted and encouraged his crew to squeeze every inch of wind into the canvas. They sailed so close to the *Ranger* that he could hear the voice of Thatch and Hornigold bellowing to their crew to work harder, faster, but the bigger ship began to lag behind.

Bellamy glanced back at Paulsgrave and matched his smile as they knew they were going to beat them to the fight. The *Marianne* steered very close to the *Ranger* causing Hornigold to turn port just a bit to avoid a collision, and then Bellamy had the upper hand as well as the wind.

"You little bastard," said Hornigold after maneuvering his ship to sail behind the *Marianne*.

"The boy doesn't know his place," Thatch growled as he approached a fuming Hornigold.

A moment passed then Hornigold shook his head and smiled. "No, never did, that clever pup."

"Aye. I hate him and like him all at once."

Hornigold nodded at Thatch then looked at the galleon now trying to make an escape. "She's big. If she's fully manned, then we do ourselves a favor by letting those two jackrabbits face the broadside first. Move men and guns to the bow. We'll attack from astern."

Thatch gazed at the floating fortress and measured her to be similar to a third-rate ship of the line. "What's she doing here all alone?" he wondered aloud, searching the empty sea.

"Perhaps she sailed with others, but that storm three days ago had caused her to separate from her fleet. If we hadn't hunkered down in that cove we'd have had a time of it as well."

Thatch nodded his head than grabbed several sailors to move a few guns to the bow and make ready for battle.

"Fire!" Levasseur called out from the gunwale at the port side of his ship. The order was shouted in turn to the gun deck, and the waiting fire crew lit the fuses of their eight-inch, ten-inch and twelve-inch cannons.

KABLAM!

A combination of round shot and chain shot exploded from the barrels of *La Louise*'s guns. Levasseur had waited to give the galleon a full broadside while it had fired the first shots attempting to ward off the pirate ships. Bellamy's *Marianne* was about to be in position to fire a broadside of their own from their starboard side. Levasseur timed his volley so that Bellamy's ship would not be directly across to mistakenly get hit from his attack.

It had taken four hours of nimble sailing to set up their position with two pirate ships on either side of the galleon and Hornigold's *Ranger* directly behind.

Levasseur stood defiantly while the galleon's crew fired rifles, railguns and pistols at him and his men. Smoke wafted and clouded the space between the two ships. He only ducked down when thirty cannons blasted at him from the galleon. His helmsman had brought *La Louise* abruptly to starboard after they had fired. This move helped in avoiding the brunt of the returned cannon fire. It also got them out of the line of sight of the *Marianne*'s onslaught that happened a moment later.

WOOMPH!

A store of gunpowder below the deck of the galleon must have been ignited by the *Marianne*'s blast. The galleon rocked to starboard from the explosion forcing Levasseur's ship to maneuver even further away from the bigger ship.

The *Ranger*, who was just astern of the ships, slipped in between the galleon and *La Louise*.

BLAM!

Six guns rocked the galleon from Hornigold's ship and the aft mast of the Portuguese ship splintered and cracked. It fell to the port side of the galleon's deck, crushing several sailors underneath as it crashed through the railing. The *Marianne* was so close to the ship that the mast now lay as a makeshift bridge linking the two.

Hornigold ordered his crew to send over grappling hooks and the men pulled the two hulls closer. Hundreds of sailors were firing small arms at each other as two pirate ships were now linked on either side of the galleon.

A large fire raged below deck and smoke choked the air while blood and bone littered the wooden planks of the galleon. Thatch was the first to lead dozens of men aboard the devastated ship. The crew was either too brave to surrender or too scared to be taken captive because they fought like tigers as the pirates began to swarm their deck.

The Portuguese sailors battled with honor but inside of twenty minutes of violent mayhem their captain was slain by Levasseur in a series of furious strikes from his rapier. With their captain's blood pooling on the deck they began to surrender in clumps and groups until they all had laid their weapons down and took a knee before the triumphant pirates.

The galleon's hold was heavy with coconuts, wine and whale oil. The commodity items would be a good haul, but the ship was in poor condition and listing heavily to port. Had the powder not exploded and burnt the gun deck, the ship itself would have brought a hefty price at any port, other than one ruled by the Portugal Crown.

It was decided that the ship would be sunk, and the surviving crew could join the pirates or float away in the skiffs that were stored aboard the galleon. After the ship was emptied of its cargo and with most of the crew rowing away in small boats, eager to put distance between themselves and the pirate ships, one of Levasseur's men brought forth the galleon's navigator who had refused to join *La Louise* and turn pirate.

"This muck was heard telling his mates that they would find the two other galleons they had sailed with but were lost in the storm."

Levasseur looked at the navigator with interest. "That so? An where be the heading of those ships?"

Hornigold, Thatch, Bellamy, and several other pirates came forward at that news.

The navigator refused to answer. He turned his head in defiance of the pirates.

"Shall we use this grouse to clean the barnacles from the *Ranger*'s hull, Captain?" asked Thatch as he strode up to the shackled man.

"Been a good while since we had a proper keelhauling," Hornigold said, sizing the man up.

Levasseur stepped forward and struck the man with the back of his hand with a crack.

Bellamy and Paulsgrave were quiet. The two young men were no strangers to violence, but both had a distaste for torture and brutality.

Levasseur took the man's chin in his hand and brought his face close to his. "Don't be keeping secrets from us, swab. I might be forced to keep something of yours." He stroked the man's cheek with a dagger stained with dried blood.

The man began to stoically speak in Portuguese a string of sentences.

Levasseur looked at the sailor that brought the man over. "Does he not speak English?"

"He did a few moments ago."

Levasseur smiled and with a quick flick of his blade he removed the lower half of the man's ear. The man screamed out and with his hands bound he went to his knees, cradling his head with his shoulder. Levasseur pick up the severed ear and knelt in front of the man. "I think you shall start talking in English, or French if you wish, for if you don't, I will feed this bit of ear to you. I'm a wonderful cook, I'll have you know. Many tasty recipes in my head." He tapped his skull with his knife. "Samuel, have I ever served you my fat Portugal fingers in honey sauce?"

Sam Bellamy's face blanched but he made no move nor said any words.

Levasseur took the navigator's nose between his thumb and forefinger, bringing his blade to slice it off. "Navigator nose and nettle soup might be bubbling in our pot tonight."

"He had said the other galleons are far off, on their way to Brazil, and that we would never catch them," said Thatch.

Levasseur looked at Hornigold's second in command sharply. "Were you going to hold your tongue that you spoke his language, Thatch? Keep the knowledge for ye self?" Levasseur stood up and moved toward Thatch aggressively. "I see how you and Hornigold plot—"

Thatch, quick as a snake, pointed one of his pistols at Levasseur's head. "You *see* horribly, Buzzard." He pointed the pistol an inch from Levasseur's good eye, his long arm putting the shorter man at a disadvantage. "Should you wish to not see at all, keep flapping your beak at me."

Levasseur grimaced and then his lips formed into a smile. He began to laugh and laugh loudly. Hornigold and Bellamy exchanged a worried look. He dropped his knife hand to his side and turned away from Thatch. "You see, Portuguese, I am but a softy compared to me mates. All I seek are answers. Answers that you can give freely, without harm. No one would condemn you. There are no officers to take your rank for spilling the information to the wind." Levasseur knelt in front of the crouched and wounded navigator. "Where!"

The man looked at him with contempt. Levasseur brutally sank his knife into the man's foot. The man let out a howl of pain.

"Where are they headed?" he stabbed again. "Where! Where!" He stabbed the other foot repeatedly.

The man was screaming in pain and then he began yelling in Portuguese a string of words but one that was shouted in English was the word 'treasure'. This brought a pause to Levasseur's torture.

"What's that, mate? What did you say?" He turned to Thatch. "What did he say?"

Thatch moved closer as the man was mumbling, whimpering and close to passing out from his wounds. "He's saying... he said, there's treasure aboard. Hidden in a secret hold." His eyes were lit with sparkles. He knelt next to the cowering man. "Where be this hoard?"

Thatch, Bellamy and Paulsgrave moved several crates of tools and ship parts to uncover a large hidden doorway under the lower decks. Hornigold and Levasseur held the broken navigator up by both arms. The poor man remained shackled, and a trail of blood had followed them down into the hold from his leaking feet and missing ear.

Thatch threw open the door and picked up a lighted lantern to shine it down into the dark space.

"Well?" asked Levasseur with impatience.

The light spilled against Thatch's face as a wolfish grin formed.

Levasseur dropped the left side of the injured man and hurried forward to have a look for himself. Hornigold almost lost his grip on the navigator but managed to set him down without dropping him completely.

Thatch stood his ground when Levasseur squeezed into the secret hold and dropped down into the space. He shook his head in annoyance and stared at Hornigold. Bellamy and Paulsgrave entered the hold, with Bellamy laying a friendly hand on Thatch's shoulder. They all joined Levasseur to see what awaited them.

There were a dozen chests and crates secured in the narrow room. The deckhead was low, causing the men to crouch as they moved around. Levasseur used an axe from his belt to break the clasp of the closest chest. The contents sparkled and shone in the lamplight. Silver and gold ingots packed the three-foot by two-foot container.

The pirates crowded around to see the contents. "First in, first claimed. There are twelve chests, four for each captain and their ship." Levasseur stood and used his axe to point at the two chests next to the one he opened, thinking they would probably contain the same riches. "These three are mine, I claim them for *La Louise*."

"We shall see what the others hold before we make any such deal, La Buse," Hornigold said as he moved to the corner of the room where three chests sat, one ornamented with a painted symbol of three crowns stacked above each other. He took his cutlass and swung it thrice before one of the locks broke away from its clasp. Bellamy and Paulsgrave began opening the remaining three while Thatch stood at the entrance, fingers twisting the ends of his beard, watching with interest.

There was an excited gasp from Paulsgrave once he saw the contents of their share. He grinned at Bellamy.

"We agree with the deal," Bellamy said.

Hornigold looked through each of the containers he'd chosen and was immensely satisfied as well. He picked up an object wrapped in an old, dirty cloth. He unfolded the covering and revealed an ornate Christian-looking cross. It was embedded with diamonds and the metal shimmered oddly with a pinkish hue. Thatch stepped over to look at the treasure. Hornigold held out the cross necklace and his first mate held the item up to the lamplight watching it glimmer.

"I think there might be a very angry king once news of this plunder reaches Lisbon," Thatch mused.

The navigator spoke weakly in Portuguese as he sat against the bulkhead watching the pirates admiring the riches. Thatch looked over at the man then back at the cross.

"What did he say?"

He looked at his captain then tossed the cross back in the chest. "The cross was meant for the Pope. Everything in that chest with the triple crown painted on it was on its way to Rome."

"Did each galleon have such treasure?" asked Bellamy.

Thatch repeated the question to the navigator and the man nodded his head.

"Ah, then we know which way they would be sailing. Are you with me, Samuel?" asked Levasseur.

"Aye! We be with you."

"Hornigold?"

Hornigold looked for a moment at Levasseur then at Thatch, giving it some consideration. He shut the lid on the chest. "I believe this is where we part ways. On a win. I wish you both luck, but we will sail to Nassau and enjoy the spoils."

Levasseur looked as though he was going to retort but held his tongue and just nodded his head. Within the hour the treasure was transferred to the three pirate ships and Thatch found himself one of the last to leave the galleon. Only Levasseur and Paulsgrave remained. Three rowboats floated while tethered to the port side. The deck of the ship was awash with pitch and oil.

"Well, we have ended with a hefty haul despite the yellowness of Hornigold," Levasseur said while Thatch lit a torch with his tinderbox. "I don't know why you continue to sail under him, Thatch. You should have your own command."

"It is always open for you to sail with us," Paulsgrave commented.

"Benjamin has his methods and principles. I shall have a ship of me own in due course."

Levasseur scratched his chin. "We should work together again one day. I set up a camp on a lovely island in the Seychelles. It is called Île de France, as Louis the Fourteenth claimed it for France a couple of years ago. But it's my money and trade that props its governor. One of me wives looks after me affairs. Me settlement is near the anchorage of pigeon rock."

"Pigeon rock?"

Levasseur nodded to Thatch. "On the northeastern tip there is a rock face that looks like a pigeon twisting its neck. At low tide you can see inside its beak, from there, there is a trail inland to the settlement. I'll go back in a few months to oversee its construction and growth."

"Seems you be preparing for a governorship," Thatch said with sarcasm in his tone.

Levasseur shrugged off the affront. "My father was a well-to-do merchant and gave me a proper education. Before setting sail I made my way as an architect."

"I was a jeweler," put in Paulsgrave.

"No one asked you, boy," hissed Levasseur.

Thatch grew tired of the conversation and stepped over to the main mast. He held the torch to the stout wood coated with oil and it quickly caught fire. The flames leaped high above and spread quickly. He turned and walked to an open entryway to the hold below and tossed the torch inside.

"Fair winds to you both," Thatch said and climbed down the rope ladder to one of the waiting row boats. The three men parted and sailed their separate ways as the Portuguese galleon burned.

CHAPTER 27 – INTERVIEW WITH A PIRATE

Anne Bonny stepped into the small wardroom to find a woman dressed in a dark blue uniform with large brass buttons up the front of the jacket with a white collared dress shirt underneath accented by a darker blue, almost black tie. Her hair was pulled back from her face and hidden inside a soft brimless hat that matched the color of her jacket. She was attractive in a plain sort of way, Anne mused, with an intelligence behind her deep brown eyes. She had red painted lips and other touches of feature-enhancing makeup. She sat straight in her chair, writing instrument, books and papers spread out before her on the table. She looked like an educator—Anne hated her instantly.

"Good morning, Mrs. Anne Bonny, is it?" she asked glancing at a list in front of her.

Anne just grunted something that sounded like a yes and made a show of wandering around the room in her leather boots and Western outfit inspecting the contents of the table, the chairs, walls, and bulkheads. She still wore her holster though it was empty of weapons. She knew she was being held captive, but she and the crew had been mostly free to wander most areas of the ship and were fed quite well.

"Can I get you something to drink before we begin?"

Anne glanced down her nose at the woman, then pulled the chair out with a loud scrape. She made a show of sitting, slowly pushing it closer to the table, the legs screeching with each inch. Propping her boots up on the surface, she crossed her ankles and inspected the dirt under her worn fingernails. "Whiskey or rum. No need for a glass," she said, tossing two coins onto the table.

"I meant coffee or tea."

Anne snorted. She pulled the two coins back and plopped them back into a pocket and stared at the deckhead.

"My name is Doctor Miriam Katz; I'm a lieutenant in the US Navy…"

"Wha? They have doctors for cats in this age?" Anne said, feigning seriousness.

"No. Sorry. My name is Katz. I'm not a physician but hold a doctorate in history and archaeology."

Anne let a smirk cross her lips.

"Oh, I see. You were making a joke. We actually do have doctors for animals. We call them veterinarians, they take care of cats, dogs, horses, et cetera."

Anne laughed hard, then became serious and gave Miriam a hard look. "You take me for a fool. You and your books and tomes. I'm learned as well. My father was a lawyer and a merchant. I studied before I was married, I'll have you know."

Miriam picked up her pencil and made a quick note. "I see. No disrespect intended. Please, tell me about your background."

"Why?"

"Well, we want to help you, to understand more of how you got here, in this time." She looked the wild woman across from her in the eye. "Your crewmates, I interviewed many of them yesterday and they contended that your ship and all the occupants were sent forward in time from 1718 and then from 1873. Is that also the truth as you know it?"

Anne's eyes had a far-off look for a moment. "Aye. That be the truth of it—as I *contend* it," she said, her tone dripping with mock emphasis.

Miriam watched her face for signs of deception but saw just a strong-willed woman who turned and met her eyes, daring her to not believe her. "Let's start with your name. Anne Bonny, right?"

Anne grunted in response.

"Married?"

"Widowed."

"What was your husband's name?"

"James."

"Can I ask how he died? When?"

Anne blew out a breath of air. "Drowned. Maybe a few weeks ago." She snorted as she continued, "Seventy years ago. Depends on your point of view."

"I see. The time issue."

"Aye. The time issue."

"What would your occupation be?"

Anne looked at her with confusion.

"Do you have a job, a career, a way you make a living?"

Anne smiled. "I'm a sailor."

Miriam looked at her then took a few notes.

"Your king allows women in the navy?"

"The United States doesn't have a king. It's a representative republic, more similar to what Rome had, but yes, women can perform many positions in the services."

Anne laughed a hearty laugh. "When have we not been allowed to perform many positions as services?"

Miriam tried but it was hard not to laugh at that.

The two women looked at one another and the ice seemed to melt a bit between them.

"I'm sorry to hear about your husband, James. It must have been awful."

Anne brushed her hair from her face and leaned back in the chair. "He was a fink and a coward. He was lucky Jack didn't bury his sword in his belly."

"Jack? Who is Jack?"

"He was me love," Anne said. Her eyes teared up at the memory of her dear Jack. "Jack Rackham. Captain of the *William*. He was the most handsome prince of pirates. Poor Jack." She shook her head.

"What happened to Jack?"

Anne sighed and wiped her eye with her sleeve. "He lost a pistol duel with Jesse."

Miriam stared at Anne, watching a smile creep across her lips. "Jesse James? The same Jesse that is traveling with your group."

"Aye." Anne leaned forward with her arms on the table. "He is the fastest with a pistol. Jack never had a chance. Have you ever seen a cobra strike, up close?" Miriam slowly shook her head. "Well, that is how fast Jesse is. No one could best him." She smiled. "No one. That I know."

"Jesse James, the real Jesse James," Miriam whispered to herself.

Anne narrowed her eyes at the woman. "He's *my* man now. Don't think you're going have him. I'll cut your pretty throat if you try," she said leaning forward with a finger pointed aggressively at her.

Miriam blushed, but didn't show the fear that ran through her heart. "I… I have a beau of my own already," she lied.

Anne settled back down in her seat but kept her eyes on Miriam.

"So, you arrived on the *Queen Anne's Revenge* with your husband James, along with Jack Rackham, James drowns, Jack is killed by Jesse and you… what? You fall for him, even though he killed Jack?"

Anne shrugged. "I planned on taking my revenge, but then I had a change of heart. Men have changes of heart at their whims. There are no rules with love, and even if there were, I never liked rules. I enjoy breaking them."

Miriam sat in the Higgins boat as it motored her and Outerbridge to the *Queen Anne's Revenge*. She had finished her interviews with the remaining crew members a short time ago. She had found Mary Read likable and the most talkative of the group. The story that she had told was fascinating and unless she was being entirely duped, it was also credible. Charlotte De Berry was less forthcoming, and Miriam felt that the woman might reach out at any moment and snap her neck.

The Chinese cabin boy was her last interview, and he held such a dichotomy of emotions for her. On the one hand, he was a cute, yet serious boy of twelve or so. He was orphaned and homeless on the streets of San Francsico as he told it. Along comes Blackbeard, the pirate, to save him from being beaten and left for dead. The man befriends him and offers him the chance to join his crew. The boy now has a family of sorts along with a share of the pirates' treasure—a treasure, she is told, sits in the hold of this tall ship.

Miriam is first up the rope ladder and her sensible shoes seem less sensible as her soles repeatedly slip on the thick rope, damp with sea spray. She makes it over the rail to the deck with the embarrassing help of Outerbridge as he climbs up after her.

She steps onto the ship and her eyes roam the masts, yards and furled canvas. She almost stumbles into Outerbridge but the truth is they are both staring in awe of the intricacies of the wooden frigate and not watching where they are going.

Outerbridge lets out a long whistle.

"She's a beauty, don't you think sir?" Stanton says.

"That she is, Ensign."

Miriam recovers from her moment of amazement and approaches the mast and its woodwork. She begins to examine the fittings and hardware that make up the construction of the vessel. Nothing is modern. The nails, ironwork and pullies appear ancient by today's standards.

"A replica?" asks Outerbridge.

Miriam immediately shakes her head. "It would be a difficult undertaking to construct a ship this size using eighteenth-century methods. Enormously expensive and time-consuming. It would be newsworthy."

Outerbridge nodded. She was smiling. It was difficult to keep a smile off his face as well, but he was a commander of a US Navy destroyer at a time of war. He looked toward Stanton. "Well, give us the tour."

"Yes, sir."

They followed Stanton from bow to stern, then went below decks. They moved through the galley, crew's quarters, gun deck, powder room and Blackbeard's private quarters. Outerbridge could have explored the pirate's cabin for hours, but they had yet to see the hold where their treasure was stored.

Miriam and Outerbridge entered the hold, and Stanton lit several sconces and illuminated the shadowy room with the help of his flashlight. There was a heady mix of several fragrances hanging in the air of the room: tobacco, wine, woodsmoke and salty mildew. The scene disappointed as they had both dreamed of a fantastical mound of overflowing chests of riches and coins. There were several piles of ornamental weapons that looked discarded outside of closed chests and crates.

Miriam approached several of the crates that were identical in size. They were stamped with the words 'Wells Fargo'. She attempted to open several of them before Stanton approached.

"These two are open, ma'am." He removed the lids of two crates and shined his light on the silver bars that were stacked inside.

Outerbridge whistled again as he stared down at the precious metal.

"Look at this one over here." Stanton excitedly ushered them to an ornate chest with three crowns painted on the lid. He opened it and used his flashlight to illuminate the contents, sending sparkles dancing along the edges and underside of the top. The container was only half full of jeweled wares and golden coins.

Miriam plucked a coin from the pile and held it up to the light. It was dated 1701. "Spanish." She flipped it over. "Flowers at Fleece." The men looked at her blankly. "The fleur-de-lis decoration on the back. These are Spanish escudos, early eighteenth-century. Pretty rare."

Outerbridge looked over her shoulder and she turned and handed him the coin. He pushed his glasses up so he could look at it unaided. "It doesn't look that old."

Miriam shook her head. "No. We are seeing it as it was in 1718." She motioned around the room. "All of it."

"Then, you're saying it's all true? Their stories, this ship, everything here… all of it, true?" he asked.

"Aye, matey," Miriam smiled.

Stanton's eyes were as wide as saucers. Outerbridge nodded. He let out a long sigh and turned to his ensign. "I want all of this moved to the *Ward*."

Stanton gave a confused look of concern.

"But I don't want the pirates to see it or know about it. Get it ready to transport then move it when they won't see. Do it while they are eating or sleeping but lock it down." He pointed his finger at Stanton. "Pick a couple of men you trust to keep their mouths shut and make sure not a word about this gets out."

"You're going to steal it from them?" Miriam said with hard accusation in her tone.

"That is not my intent, but this is way above my pay grade, and we are in uncharted waters with this damn time travel. Orders from the admiral came down this morning and he wants this treasure under lock and key. We'll rendezvous with the *Enterprise* and turn this mess over to them."

"You had me promise them that the treasure would stay in the hold of the *Queen Anne's!*" Stanton said with anger in his voice.

"I know what I said, Mr. Stanton. That was before I talked with fleet command and saw how much is sitting down here. The temptation could prove to be too much for my crew or theirs. I need everyone focused on the tasks at hand. Millions of dollars sitting in wooden crates and boxes unsecured and unguarded is a recipe for disaster. The top brass wants the damn treasure stateside before they release these characters back out into the world."

"Why not just assign guards for it on this ship? Are you going to tell them that you're moving it? You're asking for trouble!"

Outerbridge glared at the young rating. "You're out of line, Ensign! Damn it! Follow orders, sailor, or you'll find yourself in hot water. They are pirates for God's sakes, and those crates say Wells Fargo, burnt into the wood. I'm under orders and now, so are you."

Stanton swallowed hard and forced himself to cool his temper. "Yes, sir."

Outerbridge turned to Miriam. "A parcel is on its way to us for you. There is a team of researchers combing through records from eighteen seventies San Francisco and they are sending you copies of their findings. When we get back to the *Ward*, I want your report to send to the Secretary. I have a ship-to-shore call routing to Washington at oh-fourteen hundred."

Miriam nodded.

"Good work. Both of you." He turned to make his way back to the Higgins boat but turned back and looked hard at them both. "Understand— the old adage applies; loose lips sink ships."

Miriam was finishing her report detailing her findings and professional opinion of the authenticity of the pirate ship and her interviews with the pirates and sailors when an ensign arrived in the doorway of the wardroom and saluted.

"Pardon, Lieutenant. This was just dropped by a plane for you." He approached with a bundle wrapped in plastic.

"Thank you." She tore the package open as the ensign left the room. It was a bundle of files labeled 'Top Secret'. She broke the seal and quickly flipped through the notes and documents. She would study them in detail later but she wanted to see if any of the information would be important to include in her report.

There were documents pertaining to bank robberies, a train heist, and news reports of a sea battle that witnesses attested to in the Bay of San Francisco in 1873. She glanced through business documents for a saloon located in the Barbary Coast district named The Paris. Photos and files for the Civil War ironclad that was harbored at Mare Island were in another folder and she spent a few minutes glancing through them. She was looking forward to visiting that relic when she returned to Hawaii.

There was a facsimile of a newspaper article that contained a worn, black and white image of a group of men and women dressed as pirates in front of an opera house in San Francisco. She stared at the picture for a long moment, not believing what she was seeing. The date of the article was highlighted by the investigative team, 1873. She rummaged through her bag to locate a magnifying glass. She found the black-handled device and held it over the copied image to enlarge and enhance the figures. The photo was grainy and weathered but she was able to see their faces with enough detail to make her catch her breath with excitement.

The photograph depicted eight men and three women. She recognized the faces of Bart Roberts, Black Caesar, Charles Vane, and the three women she interviewed this morning, Charlotte De Berry, Mary Read and Anne Bonny. She studied the other men and thought she could discern their identities as well. Blackbeard was the easiest by his long dark beard. It was twisted and braided as his legend told it would be. What was surprising to her was that he appeared younger than he was imagined to be in films. He was taller than the rest of the men other than Black Caesar. He was wearing a long coat over his broad shoulders, and his frame was trim and lanky. His true self seemed very different from his portrayal in movies. She found him to be rather handsome, despite the prominent and wildly flowing beard.

She looked at the list of pirates that Bart Roberts had given her in his interview that were participants in their time travel journey. She then noted on the facsimile the identification of a dashing Jack Rackham, a boyish Sam Bellamy, a forty-ish looking Benjamin Hornigold, and a stern-looking man she presumed was Henry Jennings.

"Oh my," she breathed out. This was the proof that these men and women existed long ago in the late 1800s. Now, sixty-eight years later, six of them were alive on this ship, looking no older than they did in the photograph. She moved quickly through the other files and documents searching for more photographic evidence and found several images that had been taken of the two James brothers. Her school days memory of these photos had served her well as these further confirmed the identity of the two notorious outlaws.

She looked at her wristwatch and saw that she had still twenty minutes to get her report to Outerbridge before his call with the Secretary of War. She quickly arranged the images to the top of the files and stacked them all together. She held them close against her chest as she hurried through the corridor to find the commander at the pilot house or the radio room.

She was walking fast around a corner when she almost collided with Charles Vane and Black Caesar as they were crossing from a stairwell. She felt her cheeks flush as she quickly brushed past them. The two large men tucked against the bulkhead for her to get by.

"Where's the fire, lass?" Vane asked with a charming smile that made the darkly tanned skin at the sides of his eyes crinkle.

"Excuse me, gentlemen."

Vane laughed and slapped Black Caesar on his back. "That warm shower must have done us good, mate. When was the last time a lady called you a gentleman?"

"This be the first," Black Caesar said with a laugh.

Miriam gave a quick look back at them as they watched her hurry off. She climbed the stairs to the pilot house and found Outerbridge walking toward the radio room, a bundle of papers held in his arm.

"You have completed your report, Lieutenant?"

"Yes, sir," she said stopping in front of him. "If I may, sir, I want to show you something before your call with the Secretary."

"Quickly please."

Miriam pulled the facsimile of the newspaper clipping that had the group photograph of the pirates along with her notations. She had linked the names of each person in the image to their name.

Outerbridge examined the photo and pushed his glasses further up his nose as he looked closely at each face. His expression was unreadable to Miriam.

"Interesting," he said.

"Now look at these." She handed him the images of Jesse James and his brother Frank. There were four images of Jesse on his own and one solo of Frank.

"I see. Your conclusion is these… individuals are on my ship."

It wasn't a question, but she answered anyway. "They are, sir. They shouldn't be, but here they are, in the flesh."

Outerbridge nodded. "I'll keep these for the moment. Good work."

Miriam watched as he moved through the corridor and entered the radio room. Her hands were now empty, and she realized she was wringing them together unconsciously. She made an effort to keep them at her sides and walked down to the main deck of the ship. Clouds were casting shadows on the deck as they moved through the blue sky. The air was humid but comfortable and she inhaled deeply to savor the freshness that was denied in the cramped quarters below.

The crew of the *Ward* went about their business while dozens of men from the *Queen Anne's Revenge* mingled, watched and lent helping hands where they could. They seemed eager to be of use and right at home living on a ship. She was headed toward the stern to gaze out upon the pirate ship in tow but noticed that on the port side she would have to pass by the two

James brothers, Anne and Mary, who were conversing and watching the sea. Now that she was indeed sure that she was looking at the infamous outlaw Jesse James she decided to give them a wide berth, instead taking the starboard side path.

When she arrived at the aft railing she found Black Bart Roberts with his arm around the shoulder of Charlotte De Berry. The two pirates turned on her arrival. She gave them a nod as she stood to admire the great wooden ship trailing in their wake. It was majestic and imposing as the ornate bow rose and fell, cutting through the waves, chopping the water like a butcher's blade.

"What is in store for we humble sailors, doctor?" asked Roberts.

Miriam wasn't sure how to answer that question. She avoided his eyes and continued to gaze at the frigate.

"Cat got your tongue, lass?"

"I'm not sure. The commander hasn't told me anything about that. I do know we are rendezvousing with the *Enterprise* shortly and most likely you and your ship will be transferred to them."

"What is the *Enterprise*?" inquired Charlotte.

"Ah, it is a big ship. A very big ship that launches planes from its deck."

Roberts and Charlotte looked at one another, both trying to imagine such a vessel.

"Are we to be transferred as prisoners?"

She turned her head to look up at Roberts. "I don't know why they would do that. You've committed no crimes—at least in this century." She shook her head with a light chuckle. "Also, you're not German or Japanese and took no part in the attack on Pearl Harbor. I do think they may hold you in hopes of discovering how you were transported in time."

"But we have no knowledge of our plight. We didn't move through time because of want! It is not our doing," argued Charlotte.

"Aye," Roberts insisted. "It just happened. We do not know the way of it."

Miriam looked forlornly at the couple. "That may be, but it has never happened before. Can you imagine the power someone would possess if they could control it? The US government can't let such a thing fall into the hands of our enemies. Don't you want to find out the how of it? Maybe go back to your time?"

"Our only desire is to be free," Roberts said firmly.

Miriam nodded her head. "The US **is** a free country. You will be, after. I've been told your friend Blackbeard was captured by the Nazis. The Nazis, Germany, are the most feared nation that has ever existed. There are rumors that they are killing Jews, Poles and many others by the thousands. Not soldiers, just people, people they have deemed inferior to themselves. Don't you want him rescued?"

"We are not *friends* with Blackbeard, lass. We only knew him by reputation beyond several weeks ago," Roberts said.

"Our desire is to take our share of the treasure in there," Charlotte pointed at the ship in tow, "then go our own way in peace."

Miriam looked away from the pair then down to her feet. She nodded her head. "I'll do what I can." She walked away, trying not to hurry. She didn't trust herself not to let on that the treasure was no longer secured for them.

Charlotte stared after her with wary eyes.

"I do not feel our interests are in play," Roberts murmured.

"Aye," Charlotte agreed.

CHAPTER 28 – GREAT POSEIDON

Colette dealt cards to a group of German sailors who spoke no English, but the game of poker had a language of its own. There were six men playing in the round, with Thatch, Philip, and Woodes standing around the small galley table. Thatch translated between the groups, but Colette was beginning to pick up words and phrases after so many days in captivity aboard the U-boat. Most of the sailors were barely past their teenage years, doing their duty to their country, proud to be part of such a technological marvel. Looff and Hildebrandt, however, were another matter. Both men were driven by agendas and pride, often with opposing goals.

She tried her best not to think about how far from home each day took her. She had come to terms with the fact that everything and everyone she had left behind was gone. Her business, employees, and friends were likely dead, buried, and in the case of her beloved Paris Saloon—gone.

She looked up at Edward. His wounds were healing, and their captors were becoming less strict about working them to the bone. He was almost back to the magnificent, rugged figure who had walked through her door that drizzly night in 1873. They were able to rest and eat alongside the rest of the crew. The ship was well stocked from the provisions Hildebrandt had acquired for them in Hawaii. Philip and Edward had narrowed down the search area for Levasseur's location, holding a few details close to their vests. There was little else they could do, as their survival was at stake. She and Edward had stolen moments when possible and avoided Looff's eyes the best they could. The unusual cross was an enigma that Hildebrandt kept to himself. Colette knew he always kept it on his person and showed fierce aggression whenever Philip inquired about it. Woodes was the one person not adapting well. He was despondent, suffering from a fever. She feared his injuries, inflicted by Edward, were more serious than originally thought. Hildebrandt had only worsened his low spirits by continuing to boast that England would soon fall and that the German Führer would be living in Buckingham Palace by the year's end.

The U-boat spent most of its time on the surface, as its speed decreased when submerged. The crew had opportunities to get fresh air and sun above deck, but Looff was adamant about keeping the four captives below. Colette had asked that Woodes be given some time outside, but her request was rebuked. The commander instead put Woodes to work toiling amid the diesel-fumes of the engine room. She never imagined how much she would miss the sun after being locked away in small, suffocating spaces with only artificial lights. Her mood was dark, and the only moments that brought her hope were those spent with Edward and the distraction of the evening card games—if it was indeed evening.

She carefully hid a smirk as she watched two sailors poorly bluff while raising the pot, sure they were about to lose to the young, hound-dog-eyed man who she believed had a flush. After the last bet was laid and the cards turned, the two bluffers slapped their hands in disgust on the table and threw their cards at the smiling winner. Thatch chuckled and said something in German that the men found entertaining. As the winner began scooping up the Reichsmarks, an alarm rang out, drawing everyone's attention. The first mate called the crew to quarters, and the ship lurched to starboard.

Colette cleared the table of cups and debris while the rest quickly went to their stations. Thatch moved as close as he could to the pilot room, remaining pressed against the bulkhead out of the way of passing sailors.

Philip stood just behind him, anxious to glean information about what was going on. They watched as Looff and several men climbed down from topside, and he began giving clipped orders that were repeated down the line.

"What are they saying?" Philip asked in a hushed voice.

"We've been spotted. Looff is ordering a dive."

Looff shouted, pointing three men toward the ladder. He stood in the center of the room, utilizing the periscope, a spyglass-like device that Thatch had learned to use. More orders were given, and the focus of the sailors was sharp as a blade on their duties.

"There are several American ships about, airplanes headed in our direction," Thatch quietly told Philip.

"I don't imagine they'll stop to ask if there are innocent civilians aboard before they try to sink us."

"I think not."

"Then I wish the captain godspeed to whisk us out of danger."

"Aye, I wish him dead, but would rather not follow him to that fate," Thatch grumbled.

The thunderous sound of the deck-gun reverberated in their ears. The engines roared at full power, and the ship shook from an explosion off the port side. The crew was thrown from side to side, and if they weren't holding onto something secure, they were knocked off their feet. Thatch held fast to Philip's shoulder to keep the man from being tossed against the iron bulkhead. He looked back at Colette with concern, but she was savvy enough to have seated herself at the bolted table, holding fast to the edges.

Woodes moved cautiously toward them, his pale face twisted in a grimace. He stood behind Philip, holding tightly to a pipe running overhead as the ship maneuvered wildly.

Looff barked orders that were relayed to the men topside. They climbed down the ladder within a minute and secured the hatch tightly after a drenching of saltwater cascaded down while the order to dive spread throughout the vessel.

The crew began to quiet down as the U-boat submerged beneath the sea. Hildebrandt watched the action in the pilot house, his hand unconsciously touching the cross worn under his shirt. Looff moved through the space, ensuring each crew member remained vigilant at their posts.

He noticed the three "guests" standing and watching with curiosity. He pointed at them and gave orders to Thatch, which he translated to the others.

"We are to comb the decks and search for leaks."

They headed to the ladder that would take them down one deck, watching the pipes and seams for leaks along the way. None wanted to be in the iron coffin, and they felt it best to conform to the needs of the vessel. Thatch squeezed Colette's hand as they passed her.

They spent several minutes moving through the cramped spaces, twisting and stretching to see if anything was amiss. New orders were shouted throughout the crew. Thatch put his hand on Philip's shoulder, signaling him to stay put. He looked back at Woodes, who was holding his ribs while spot-checking seals. He raised his hand, signaling him to stop and stay put. Just six feet away, several men had swung into action. They were right outside the torpedo room, and Thatch had heard the order to arm the munitions. They had been kept from this area of the submarine, and now the crew was too busy with their tasks to pay attention to them. Either that or they had immersed themselves enough to blend in with the group.

"They're going to launch one of those tubes at a ship," Thatch whispered.

Each man watched as the torpedoes were pulled from their nests, the heavy munitions placed into the tubes, armed, and locked into the barrels. More shouting between decks took place, and the ship continued to sharply maneuver. Thatch kept one hand firmly on the seam of a hatchway. He saw

Woodes stumble as the ship lurched to one side, and before he could think better of it, he grabbed his arm to keep him from banging his head on the fall. Woodes steadied himself, and Thatch let go. The two men stared at each other, not knowing how to react.

Thatch broke first when the order to fire was called out in German. There was a hollow *thunk* but no loud cannon blast as they had expected. The men began the operation to load another torpedo, while Philip glanced back at Thatch. He shrugged his shoulders.

The ship made several more maneuvers before the order to fire was given again. Silence hung heavy for a moment, then a cheer erupted from above, carrying through the German crew like wolves calling to their pack. The torpedo men patted each other on the back and smiled. Philip's eyes studied the munitions and the contraption that fired them out of the submerged ship. Thatch nodded toward the other direction, and they made their way back to where Colette was waiting for them.

The crew was celebrating, and Looff strode through the ship like a peacock until he reached the galley. He puffed his chest and spoke in German. "The arrogant Americans continue to get their eyes blackened. The might of Nazi Germany will prove too much for them, and the world will soon bow to the Führer and bend to the will of the Reich. You four are lucky to witness it all from the belly of the pride of Germany."

Looff moved further through the ship, shaking hands with every sailor on his route.

"What did he say?" Woodes asked.

Thatch shook his head. "A boast only a man who hides his inadequacies beneath his belted pants would make."

Colette chuckled, but it was clear they were in for a dangerous voyage.

Jesse James couldn't take his eyes off the monstrosity that sailed close to half a mile from their ship. The deck was a vast, flat surface that stretched far beyond the sky-high hull of the carrier. The middle was dominated by an enormous tower that sat to one side of the 'runway,' as one of the *Ward's* crew members had called it, to allow airplanes to take off and land while the vessel sailed into the wind. They had watched several planes touch down after descending from the sky.

The guts it must take to operate those craft, he thought. *They could drop out of the sky at any moment.* Jesse took a last puff from the cigarette given to him by Brockman, the navy man with short blond hair, and flicked it into the sea.

"Great Poseidon," remarked Mary, stepping to the rail with Anne and Frank to gaze at the aircraft carrier they had heard about from the crew.

"The *Enterprise*, she's called," said Anne.

"How close we gonna get to that beast?"

Jesse glanced at his brother but didn't have an answer.

Brockman and Kent overheard, and Kent piped up, "Pretty close. I heard we're handing all of you and your ship off to them. They've got a lot more room and support than we do."

Brockman pointed out several smaller ships sailing alongside the carrier. "Those supply ships and destroyers were following it to Wake Island, but we got word last night that Wake fell to the Japanese. The *Enterprise* is heading back to Pearl. We're gonna keep chasing that U-boat that got old Blackbeard. It was spotted just about a hundred miles west from here."

"Yeah, we hook up the *Queen Anne's Revenge* to one of those support ships and they'll tow you back to Pearl, then see about getting back stateside," Kent added.

"Well, hot damn. I'm real sick of bobbin' up and down in the water. Be real glad to put my boots on dry land," Frank said, slapping his hand on the rail.

"They should just let us sail our own way back," Anne remarked.

"With our plunder intact, mind you," Mary added.

"That's above my pay grade," Brockman said.

Jesse looked hard at Brockman and shook his head. "If I had a nickel for every time I heard that phrase aboard this tub."

Kent nodded innocently. "That's navy life for ya."

An hour later, two Higgins boats were being prepared to transport the pirates to the carrier group. It was still a topic for discussion about how to deliver the pirate ship to one of the carrier support ships to take over the job of towing. Outerbridge was on deck, engaged in a heated discussion with Bart Roberts.

Roberts watched as thirty or so of his men were boarded onto one of the smaller boats. "And we be feelin' like prisoners with no say in our future."

"If that ship is sailing back to Hawaii, there's no need to tow the *Revenge*. Let us sail her back alongside," Vane griped.

"You technically are prisoners until the brass says otherwise," Outerbridge stated flatly. Roberts looked around, seeing many sailors armed with rifles. His pirate mates were defiantly against being transferred to such a large ship, potentially housing a thousand men.

"I need the rest of you on that boat in the next ten minutes so we can get a ship close enough to tie your frigate to it," Outerbridge said gruffly, pointing at the second Higgins boat as the first one began to motor away.

"I'm not leaving Blackbeard's ship."

Outerbridge looked up at the enormous Black Caesar looming over him with his arms crossed over his chest. Outerbridge knew he needed to get them off his ship so he could continue his mission unencumbered. He wanted them, their treasure, and the damn pirate ship in someone else's hands.

"Let's go, little lady," one of the navy sailors said to Charlotte, putting his hand on her arm to steer her toward the waiting boat. Charlotte whipped his hand away and swung her fist, landing a solid blow to his chin. The man hadn't expected it and fell flat on his back.

The aggression set everyone in motion. Vane elbowed the closest sailor in the nose and twisted the rifle from his grip. Black Caesar grabbed Outerbridge by his jacket and held him aloft. Tom kicked a man hard in the shin and wrestled his pistol from the man's holster. All around the deck, men drew their weapons and pointed them at the pirates. Jesse, Frank, Anne, and Mary were caught off guard near the railing but soon found several rifles pointed at them.

"Stop!" Stanton yelled, holding up his hands.

"Put me down, young man," Outerbridge said, his brow sweating profusely.

Black Caesar surveyed the dozens of rifles aimed at him. Vane spun with his rifle, unsure where to point it. Tom, however, didn't suffer from indecision. He pointed the pistol at Outerbridge, eyes narrowed, his focus fixed on his target, held in the air by Black Caesar.

Ensign Kelley hurried down the ladder and arrived on deck near the standoff. "Japanese fleet spotted! We've got orders to bug out!"

They all looked at the *Enterprise* as the roar of planes taking off reached their ears.

Outerbridge looked down at the big man holding him in the air like a small child. "Son, you need to put me down. We have bigger fish to fry."

"Look!" Stanton called out, pointing to more than a dozen planes flying high in the sky toward the carrier.

Black Caesar looked at Charles Vane for guidance. The man's tan face was a shade or two lighter in fear. They had all seen the devastation those planes could cause. He lowered his rifle, and three sailors were on him, taking away the weapon. Black Caesar gently lowered Outerbridge to the ground, then straightened the man's cap, which had become askew.

Stanton approached Tom slowly and held his hand up to steady the kid. "Let's not do anything hasty, Tom. This is just a misunderstanding. Why don't you lower that weapon and hand it over?"

Tom looked over at Black Caesar, who nodded his head. "Aye, lad. We pick our battles. This one is at an end."

Tom twirled the pistol once and handed it over to Stanton, butt first.

Kelley handed Outerbridge a message that had been in his hand. Outerbridge glanced over its contents, then looked up at the Japanese planes closing in.

"Damn."

"Should we recall the Papa boat?" Stanton asked.

Outerbridge looked over to see the boat closing in on the *Enterprise*. "Negative. That crew is now conscripted to the *Enterprise*. General quarters, Mr. Stanton. If any of those birds get close, blow them out of the sky. We're setting sail to the last known location of the U-boat. Seems they picked a fight with the USS *Tambor* and gave her a bloody nose. They're trying to follow the best they can, but they took some damage from a torpedo. By the looks of it, they're heading toward the South Pacific."

"Aye aye, sir. General quarters!" Stanton called out, sending the crew into motion.

Charlotte looked up at the sky, watching the incoming Japanese planes about to engage with those from the *Enterprise*.

Outerbridge turned to Roberts. "Are we going to have to keep you all under lock and key?"

Roberts was watching the airplanes as well. They came from several miles away and several miles above. Munitions spat out from the vessels, and smoke began to surround the battle. He looked at the captain. "Our quarrel is at an end for now."

"For now… hmm. Well, keep out of the way, Mr. Roberts. We are at war, and wartime rules apply. Are we clear?"

Roberts nodded, and Outerbridge made his way to the pilot house.

The pirates and outlaws congregated toward midship. The *Ward*'s crew were anxiously awaiting the opportunity to fire its guns. Planes continued to launch off the deck of the carrier as the first Japanese Zeros and bombers reached the range of its guns. The *Ward* was now well over a mile away, but the sound of those four quad .75-caliber and twenty-four .50-caliber guns rang out like they were standing on the gun deck of a ship of the line.

Anne looked around at the shrinking crew of the *Queen Anne's Revenge*. All that remained were the original pirates along with Jesse, Frank, Tom, Francis, and Chester. Barely enough crew to sail the ship if they were released.

Jesse, as if reading her thoughts, said, "Seems our numbers are dwindling."

Vane looked out at the distant carrier. The boat that had ferried the majority of their crew had already been stowed aboard the massive ship. Just eleven members left. "Aye, but our share of plunder just grew." He looked down at Tom. "I think you be the richest cabin boy that ever lived."

Tom looked around at the remaining crew, his heart swelling with pride. They were the fiercest men and women he'd ever known—pirates, outlaws, and legends all rolled into one. He didn't fully understand it all yet, but he knew this was where he belonged. These weren't just any people. They were the ones who took what they wanted, who laughed in the face of danger, who fought when they had to, and lived like no one else.

Tom felt a warmth spread through him as he realized he was part of this. He was one of them. He wasn't just some orphan boy from the streets of 1873 anymore. He was a pirate. And pirates didn't bow to anyone. He thought about the day he'd first boarded the *Queen Anne's Revenge*—so full of fear and wonder. Now, as he looked at the crew, he didn't just admire them; he was proud to stand beside them, to count himself among them.

Tom grinned to himself. He didn't need gold or riches to feel wealthy. He was already rich, rich in the greatest treasure of all—adventure.

CHAPTER 29 – TWINS OF GOA

January 1942

Charles Vane wrapped his fingers over the knuckles of ensign Kent's big hand as they sat facing each other across the galley table. There was a small crowd of sailors surrounding them discussing and making wagers upon the outcome of this bout. This arm wrestling was a popular game that the sailors aboard the *Ward* loved to participate in.

Vane eyed Black Caesar hovering over the crowd to watch his performance in the event. There were only a few challengers that had tried their luck with the mighty pirate but after several crunched joints and sore hands from being slammed into the hard surface of the table, no one rose to battle the man again.

The weeks spent aboard the American warship had brought the two crews close together. After a time, the commander of the vessel allowed them to participate in light duties aboard the ship. They were barred from certain areas and kept away from the *Queen Anne's Revenge* during the voyage, but they outwardly took it in stride. Inside, though, in their gut they felt something was being kept from them. Roberts had instructed them to learn the workings of the ship, gain the trust of the crew. While Vane and Black Caesar had their doubts about Charlotte, Roberts, and his remaining loyal crew members, their fates were now tied together.

They had all been fitted with crew uniforms—in Black Caesar's case, 'ill-fitting'—but free of any rank insignias the main crew had. The ship had multiple stops at ports on their route. The *Ward* would idle out at sea while a supply ship would refill their fuel and stores. They never went to shore, and several boats and air-ships dropped documents and messages for the captain and the crew. Some they knew were letters from home that many of the crew openly read to each other. Pictures of family and sweethearts would be displayed and enjoyed by them all. The pirates were amazed by how quickly news traveled in this century. What could take months or years in their world, here arrived in weeks or days. The most fascinating communication device was the radio. Through the air messages could travel instantly over great distances. A device called a telephone was installed in almost every home in their country that linked to every other home with a coded number. It was something they would have to see to believe.

Kent's young hand clinched in Vane's felt soft against the pirate's rough calloused skin. This was a rematch from several days ago. Kent had lost to Vane in an arm-wrestling duel that had lasted for the better part of three minutes. Kent had an inch or two in height over Vane along with a ten pound or so advantage. He was a big-boned kid who had played a game called football while in school. The savvy twenty-year-old from Boston harbor, Stanton, set his hand on their clinched fists to count down the start of the contest.

"Ready? Set. Go." Staton removed his hand and the they both grunted in effort as each man pressed hard to get the upper hand.

Vane narrowed his eyes, sun-weathered creases exaggerated, as he glared at Kent. The roping veins stood out along his muscled forearms as he strained to push the younger man's knuckles against the table. Kent strained as well, focused on Vane's fist he was grappling. There was a marked difference in skin tone between the two. Vane's skin was deeply tanned and stained in some areas either from dirt or pitch after a life at sea. Kent's face flushed a deeper shade of red with the passing seconds as he struggled to keep his arm in the power position. He leaned forward to get better leverage on his opponent's arm. The crowd cheered, exchanging wagers with each new twist of the contest. Anne, Mary, Jesse, Frank, and Tom watched eagerly, their bets riding on the outcome. Frank, in particular, had been the only one placing large bets against Vane after a public argument with him earlier that morning. Frank had even wagered in view of the *Ward's* men with Black Caesar, betting that the pirate would lose this time.

For more than a minute, the tide of the battle shifted back and forth. Sweat poured from Kent's face as Vane began to edge his opponent's arm closer to the table.

"Come on, Kent!" shouted Brockman from the crowd.

Kent's jaw clenched, and with a rallying cry, he leaned into the struggle. His muscles bulged as he pressed against Vane's strength. For a moment, the younger man was gaining ground. Vane grunted loudly, struggling to keep his hold as Kent's arm rose, pushing against the tide of their locked muscles.

With a final roar, Kent forced Vane's arm down, slamming his fist against the table with a resounding bang.

The crowd erupted in cheers as Kent leapt to his feet, raising his arms in victory. Some groaned, others cheered, and money exchanged hands as the pirates and sailors alike reacted to the wagered outcome. Vane slowly stood, rubbing his sore arm, then nodded his head in respect.

"Well, I'll be damned. That was a good match," said Kent holding out a hand to Vane who accommodated the gesture with a handshake.

"Aye. You're a stout fellow, mate."

As the two shook hands, both accepted pats on the back from the crew.

Stanton glanced at his wristwatch. "Alright, ya bunch of slackers, let's get back to it before the big wheel catches us loafin' around."

The crowd dispersed to their duties, while the pirates gathered at the stern of the ship, where Charlotte and Bart Roberts stood in conversation. There was laughter from the group as Frank distributed money to them all from a wad of bills he held in his hand.

"What's this about?" asked Roberts.

"Just a bit of good old-fashioned grifting," answered Frank.

"Aye, you missed that game of wrestling arms the sailors play," said Anne as she counted her bills.

"We all threw a little money on Vane to win while Frank bet heavily against him," added Jesse.

Charlotte looked at the battle- and sea-hardened Vane and understood. "You purposely lost."

Vane harrumphed. "The boy is as soft as a sow."

Roberts shook his head. "Take care to not get on their bad side."

"I am."

"We need to have the trust of the crew."

"I know," Vane growled at Roberts. The two men stared hard at one another. Roberts nodded and strode off toward midships.

"It's your man that needs to learn a thing or two about trust," Vane said to Charlotte.

She narrowed her eyes at Charles. "Earn it then. You all risk it with your petty games. If we are to get that ship back with the treasure in her hold, we need to stick to Roberts' plan and be ready to act."

"This is all part of the plan, building their trust. I let the whelp win, didn't I?" Vane remarked with a patronizing grin.

"We'll see." She turned and strode off.

"She wins no friends with that charm," Anne snarled behind Charlotte's back.

"I'd like to toss them both overboard, drown their smug smiles," said Jesse.

"For now, we need their numbers. Our destination must be drawing near," said Black Caesar.

"Aye, an we can almost keep this metal beast sailing if we had too," Mary said.

"An work those guns," Frank said with a gesture toward the .50-caliber cannons.

"We can divide the loot and give them the wooden boat. I'd rather commandeer this iron pot then have to work those damn riggings again," Jesse said looking back at the *Queen Anne's Revenge* in tow.

"Mr. Roberts."

Bart Roberts heard his name called by a woman's voice from above. He looked up to see Miriam, standing at the railing with her curly dark hair blowing in the breeze, looking down at him.

"Mr. Roberts, do you have a few minutes?"

Roberts shot her with a charming smile. "Of course, lass."

Curious, he climbed the ladder and followed her to the wardroom. The space was now completely cluttered with boxes, papers, and files that had accumulated during their journey. Every week, more folders seemed to appear, delivered by sea or air, keeping Miriam busy for hours as she reviewed their contents. She would privately debrief Commander Outerbridge once she had gone through all the documents. Although they had conducted numerous interviews over the course of the voyage, it had been over a week since they had spoken one-on-one.

Miriam closed the door behind him.

"Coffee?"

Roberts preferred tea, and the acidic brew favored by the Americans never agreed with him. He shook his head.

"Please, sit," she offered as she poured herself a cup from a metal carafe. She took a sip of the near-warm drink and sat across from Roberts. She was a bit disheveled, as though she'd had little sleep and few chances at grooming her hair or applying her usual painting of makeup to her face.

He, on the other hand, had cleaned up well over the past few weeks she noticed. His face was freshly shaved except for a thin mustache that matched his ink-black hair, which he wore neatly cut to just fall upon his collar. He was slightly taller than average, with a lanky build. His face was deeply suntanned, and his teeth were white and straight—unlike many of the others who had traveled through time.

"I'm going to tell you something I'd ask you to keep private," Miriam said, looking at him seriously, "but I'd be a fool to think it will do any good."

Roberts smiled, leaning forward. "I'm happy to keep the secrets of the realm, should you wish to knight me as protector of the American crown."

She smiled back, well aware that his jest was meant to lighten the mood. They had often discussed the structure of the United States government in their previous talks and its lack of a monarchy.

"My questions will force me to reveal to you some secrets we've uncovered," she said, her tone turning more serious. "Secrets that could help us understand the mechanism of your time travel, the destination of the Nazis holding Blackbeard, and what they hope to find."

Roberts leaned back, considering her directness. So far, they had only been told that the U-boat that had captured Blackbeard had been spotted several times by their allies, and their pursuit was based mostly on educated guesses as to their heading. Had they uncovered the science—or magic—that had brought them forward in time? "I see," he replied, his voice flat.

Miriam picked up a file, flipping through the pages before holding it up. The folder was labeled 'Top Secret'.

"Are you familiar with the Sacred Lotus Twins of Goa?" she asked.

Roberts smiled and shook his head. "Part of some harem the Bishop of Goa kept?"

Miriam raised an eyebrow. "You're partly right."

"Oh? Which part might that be?"

She handed him a photograph. Roberts took it, examining the image closely. It was a reproduction of a religious painting, depicting a Roman Catholic bishop seated with one hand raised, the other resting on the head of a man in robes kneeling before him. Roberts' attention was drawn to the cross necklace the bishop wore. He studied the details more carefully, then Miriam passed him a magnifying glass without a word. He glanced up at her briefly, then turned back to the image, zooming in on the cross. To his surprise, there were two identical crosses hanging from the man's neck, slightly offset from each other. The detail was subtle enough that one could easily miss it.

He placed the photograph down and set the magnifying glass atop it. "The Sacred Lotus Twins of Goa?"

She nodded. "You've seen one?"

"I owned one," he replied, his voice steady but tinged with a hint of nostalgia.

Miriam leaned forward. "Where is it?"

Roberts stood up and paced the room, his hands resting behind his back. "Woodes has it, I imagine."

"Woodes Rogers is held by the Nazis with Blackbeard," Miriam said, her voice tight. "The ironclad Woodes sailed upon was thoroughly searched and there was no cross found. It was also not aboard the *Queen Anne's Revenge*. They would have the cross now, the Nazis."

Roberts nodded. "Aye. I can't say for sure, but he took it from me when he and his men captured the *Revenge*. He was wearing it the last time I saw him."

Miriam took careful notes while they spoke, her handwriting neat and precise. Roberts observed her, accustomed to the sharp efficiency with which she conducted her interrogations.

"You had both, or just one?" she asked.

"One," Roberts replied, his tone unwavering.

"Had you ever seen the other one?"

He had anticipated this question and answered smoothly. "No. I assumed there was only one."

Miriam looked up from her notes, studying his face as if weighing the truth of his words. "Where did you acquire yours? Was it part of plunder from a ship you captured?"

Roberts hesitated for a moment, then replied, "Ah, it must have been from plunder, but not by my doing. I won it in a game of liar's dice."

"Liar's dice." She nodded her head. She was familiar with the popular historic dice game of the age of sail. "Who did you win it from?"

"A man named Olivier Levasseur, he was a loudmouthed Frenchman we traded with in Madagascar."

"The king of the Pirate Republic of Nassau, I've studied him," she said nodding again.

Roberts looked at her with a confused furrow to his brow. "King? The man was a pirate and a blowhard craven."

Miriam shuffled through her notes to find a list of timelines she had created. "Ah. Yes, this makes some sense," she mumbled to herself while Roberts waited for an explanation. "You left in mid-1718 and it wasn't until the following year that Levasseur began to gain power."

Roberts leaned forward as Miriam pushed a large tome toward him with a cover the color of tree bark and the texture of soft leather. The spine read 'Encyclopedia Britannica'. She opened the book to a page that had been dog-eared and spun the volume so that he could read its page. There was a drawn depiction of a man with the likeness of Levasseur. He read through the entry as it gave the history of how the man had ruled the Caribbean seas for many years from the republic of Nassau. He had escaped the noose after the combined efforts of the European nations finally brought an end to his rule and he went into exile before finally being executed.

"This happened?"

"Yes. I've given it a lot of thought over the past month. The supposed death of so many pirate captains along with Woodes, who was the appointed governor of the Bahamas and enforcer charged with bringing the pirates to justice, caused a power vacuum that left an opening for an opportunistic man such as Levasseur."

"Vacuum?"

"In this case it means an emptiness."

Roberts flipped through several pages of the book with growing interest.

"So, you have no idea where Levasseur got the necklace?" Miriam asked.

He shook his head.

"We've intercepted several messages the U-boat sent to Berlin. They believe time travel is real, as do we—yourself, your friends, and the *Queen Anne* are proof enough. The Nazis are focused on the Sacred Lotus Twins of Goa. They must believe those crosses hold the key. Levasseur was said to be one of the pirates who raided a Portuguese ship carrying the crosses across the Atlantic toward Rome. After further research, I think your Blackbeard was with Levasseur, along with Samuel Bellamy."

Roberts looked up at her when he heard his old friend Sam's name. "Aye. I knew Sammy well. He sailed with Levasseur for months. They had a successful run, but Sam grew tired of Levasseur's brutality and antics."

"If Blackbeard was with Levasseur when the crosses were taken, he might have one, or at least know where it is. That's probably why the Nazis are holding him. It could also be that Bellamy had the other cross. Do you think it could have been in his possession?"

"He never spoke of it."

"If he didn't have it on him when you all were brought through the vortex, then it's likely lost to history."

Roberts leaned back, contemplating the details. "If they have my cross—the one Woodes took—why do they still need Blackbeard and the others?"

"Here's how the original search started. Hitler is obsessed with treasure and relics. On one hand, he needs to fund his wars, but there's also speculation that he believes heavily in the occult, in magic. He's searching the world for divine artifacts, and once in his hands, he uses them to claim that his Nazi party is blessed by God in their pursuits. The Nazis have sent hundreds of teams to all corners of the globe hunting for undiscovered riches. Levasseur's treasure is one of legend. Before his hanging, he claimed to have a hidden trove, and he tossed a cryptogram into the crowd, challenging anyone who could decipher it to find his prize."

"What was in the cryptogram?"

"We have no idea. Most of my colleagues think it was just a fictional story and that no such document would have survived the years even if it was true."

"But the Nazis believe. This Hitler believes."

Miriam nodded. "They were searching for the treasure when one of their spies learned of the *Ward* fishing a man out of the Pacific claiming to be Blackbeard. I'm sure the appearance of a Civil War-era ironclad in Pearl Harbor, captained by Woodes Rogers, only made things more entangled. It makes you start believing that there might actually be treasure hidden by Levasseur, and who better to help find it than a man who sailed with him two and a half centuries ago?"

"And the secret to time travel?" Roberts inquired.

Miriam visibly shuddered. "Hitler and the Nazis must never be allowed to control such power."

Roberts had never thought of time travel as something that could be controlled. For him and his crew, it was simply something that happened to them, no choice in where or when they would end up. The thought that such a power could be manipulated, that one could choose a moment from a history book or a timepiece to visit, was foreign to him. It only took a moment to understand how easily such power could be corrupted. Black Caesar's cross must stay hidden until they knew the true mechanism. If it contained the power within it, waiting to be released, then it would be best that it remained a secret from these Americans. There was none that could be trusted. He would need to take Caesar's cross and hide it away until he discovered its secrets for himself.

CHAPTER 30 – SABOTAGE

Philip crept stealthily past a sleeping sailor that snored quietly as he lay in a nook between a bulkhead and rack of fans. The man's watch had started two hours ago and only half a dozen men would be awake on duty at this hour. The monotony of the late-night watch had bested sailors since time immemorial. Thatch followed just steps behind, bare feet moving soundlessly on the metal deck. Woodes lay a deck above in his rack feigning sleep with one eye open watching for crew members moving about. Colette stood in the galley slowly readying a pot of tea and tasked with engaging anyone who made their way past.

Philip edged closer to the torpedo room and his heart beat so loud against his chest, he worried that it could be heard in the furthest reaches of the ship. The sleeping sailor stirred with a groan that froze him and Thatch in their tracks. They glanced back as the man rolled on his side to settle into a cramped fetal position.

Philip looked up at Thatch's face and relaxed when the pirate gave him a nod to continue. The corridor was bathed in low light and once they crossed to the hatch that barred the torpedo room Philip stood aside so that Thatch could twist the handle to open it. They had oiled the latch a day earlier so that it would be mostly soundless but in the quiet of the night the groan of the metal caused Philip to close his eyes and pray that no one would hear. The two men stepped inside and gently shut the metal door behind them.

"Alright, Mr. Albert, time to prove your worth," Thatch whispered.

Philip nodded and crept over to where he had hidden a cache of tools and wire. They stood over the racks of torpedoes and Philip looked them over, his hand sliding over the smooth surface of the munitions.

"Let's take the last one in the line."

Thatch nodded and the two men hefted the torpedo from its bed. They set it on the floor, and it made a scratching-creaking noise that caused them to halt their actions and just listen quietly for a moment. They resumed their work once they were sure the sound did not travel past the closed hatch

Philip rolled the missile until he found the latches to release the casing that was covering the inner workings of the bomb. He deftly used his tools to remove the cover, and Thatch used a stolen flashlight to illuminate the guts of the device.

Philip studied the workings and carefully used the tip of a screwdriver to move wires and peer further inside. He poked around and rotated the torpedo to find another removable plate and opened it to see where more wires led.

"Can you do it?"

Philip waited to answer as he moved his hands over the propeller and around the casing. "Quite ingenious really. These fins are stabilizing, and this blast cap is pressure-sensitive but not too much so, as it allows the bomb to be launched safely from the tube. I imagine that its speed could be increased by a larger propeller or possibly having multiple to increase the thrust."

"Before I squeeze you into one of these myself, answer me if you **can** do it."

Philip smiled at the pirate. "You just take this wire and run it hidden behind those overhead pipes and leave it to me."

Thatch glared at Philip then took the coil of wire and began feeding it behind the piping that ran above his head toward the bulkhead. He used a hand-drill to start the time-consuming task of creating a hole for the wire to poke through the other side of the hatchway along the pipe-way.

Philip hummed to himself as he started disconnecting wires and attaching a device he had made to the inside of the torpedo.

Colette worked at a snail's pace in the galley. She had a plan in her head if anyone came to check on them or make rounds on their late-night watch, she could engage them and give Edward and Philip the time they needed. Woodes would do the same should they pass her by. They knew the routines of every man on the ship after nearly two months of sailing. They had made no trouble over the past week to keep the men off guard. It was not such an easy task for Edward. He was constantly at odds with Looff and Hildebrandt, testing their patience by spinning yarns and stories about plunder and treasure from long ago.

She heard Woodes cough from his bunk; it was a wet rasping sound that grew worse each week. She knew that the pirate hunter was a mortal enemy to Thatch but even he showed the sickly man kindness now and again. Philip said that if Woodes didn't receive a doctor's attention soon, he would be too far gone to survive. She bent down to search a cabinet for a tea strainer that she knew was somewhere in the small galley. The lights were dim to allow the crew to rest and the space under the stove where she rifled allowed little light to see by.

She finally found the metal handled mesh bowl and stood up.

Her eyes went wide, and her heart skipped a beat when she found Looff standing behind, looming above her.

"What are you doing up so late, Fräulein?" he asked her menacingly in his native tongue.

Her grasp of his language was almost conversational now and she masked her face with innocence. She spoke back to him in German.

"I wanted to make some tea for Rogers," she answered and almost smiled when Woodes let out a rasping cough.

He watched her assemble the pot and fill it with water.

"Why bother? The man is not long for this world."

"He could have a chance if you would get him to a doctor. You can just leave him at any port so that he could get help."

He shook his head. "We must stay with our mission. We are now nearing the island of Levasseur. If the pirate is correct and we discover the treasure, then you will be free to go. Take him to a doctor yourself if he still lives."

Colette held a glare in check as she lit the stove to heat the pot of water.

He turned to go, and her stomach clenched as he made his way toward their bunks and further to the back of the ship where the ladder leading to below-deck was located. She couldn't allow him to discover Edward and Philip were not in their bunks while they carried out their secret mission.

"Captain… how much further do we sail? You mentioned that we are close."

He turned to her with curiosity on his face. "A day at most."

"So soon? Nine thousand miles in just over a month. This vessel is so fast upon the water."

He stopped and moved back toward her. "More. Eighteen thousand kilometers. We've sailed at more than eighteen knots periodically but averaged fourteen most of the trip. Our engineers are the greatest the world has ever produced. Did you know our speed while submerged is a record at seven point three knots with a range of one hundred twelve kilometers?"

Colette shook her head. She knew the man couldn't resist bragging about his ship, Germany, and his Führer. She turned on a charming smile and added tea leaves to the strainer. She caught herself as she momentarily searched for the galley's cooking timer in a drawer. She closed it and looked up at Looff. "Would you like a cup, Captain?"

Sweat dripped from Thatch's brow as he labored with the hand-drill to finish the hole in the metal plate between the torpedo room and the outer corridor. He pressed harder to finish the job and when the bit finally broke through to the other side his weight sent the handle of the drill to clang against the metal plate.

Thatch turned his head to see Philip's wide eyes as he stared at the hatchway. He gently pulled the drill bit out of the hole and moved to the hatch to listen for movement on the other side. Philip finished his work and began closing up the torpedo covers and attached one end of the coiled wire to his mounted device.

Thatch placed one end of the wire through the hole he had made then quietly cracked open the hatch to peer out. His heart sank upon seeing the sailor on watch now awake and stretching from his cramped position. He closed the hatch and went to kneel next to Philip as the scientist finished his work.

"He's wakened," Thatch whispered.

"That'll be an issue. Guard the door. I'm almost done here."

Thatch rose and stood at the hatch ready to act if the sailor entered. He held a screwdriver ready to strike. Philip finished and stowed his stolen tools in a wrapping made from a torn shirt. He stood beside Thatch and listened intently while the pirate eased open the hatch just enough to see beyond. The watch had his back to them and started to do several deep knee bends to loosen his muscles and work the sleep from his tired body. Thatch silently shut the portal. He helped Philip stow the modified torpedo in its bay. He stood next to the hatch and glanced around the room. "We are trapped here."

Philip nodded in agreement. "What are we to do? If we're caught, Looff will not look on this too kindly. Most likely he will kill us both."

"Aye. Wait here." Thatch brandished the screwdriver, and his hand went to the handle of the hatchway door.

Philip grabbed his arm. "What are you planning to do?"

The pirate looked back at the scientist with fire blazing in his blue eyes. "What I must."

Colette slowly poured the seeped tea into a metal mug, the aromatic brew steaming the rim as it filled. She repeated the process into another cup and set it in front of Looff.

"*Danke.*"

Colette nodded and took the other mug and started to walk toward their sleeping quarters. Looff grabbed her arm, stopping her with a slight spilling of the tea she held.

"The man can wait. We haven't finished our conversation."

She cringed inwardly at his touch.

Woodes coughed loudly down the corridor.

"I should get this to him; besides I know you must have work to do in the pilot house."

Looff's gaze turned dark upon her. "My work is of no concern to you. It is I that give orders and dispense tasks upon others. Not the other way around. I'm certain that the whims and wants of a woman aboard my ship are of little consequence."

A thump and clang rang from beyond the corridor. Looff's eyes broke from Colette, and he stood, his body rigid.

"Your pirate is able to sleep through Rogers' hacking?" He let go of her arm and started toward the sound.

Colette's heart was beating fast as she thought quickly of what to do. She reached back and grasped the metal pot of near-boiling water and brought it around to strike Looff in the head.

"Is that fresh tea I smell?" came a voice from down the corridor.

Colette hesitated with the pot firmly gripped in her hand.

The man on watch from below was in mid-yawn as he entered the galley. He stiffened upon seeing Looff standing there. He snapped to attention and saluted. "Captain," he said nervously.

"Shouldn't you be at your post, sailor?"

"Yes, yes, sir. I just was feeling a bit tired, and I could smell the lady's tea from below. I didn't see the harm in coming to get a cup."

Looff loomed into the man's personal space, his nose inches from the frightened young sailor. "Didn't see the harm? We sail with the enemy within our midst. Now, you have left the torpedo room unattended." He pushed past the sailor and strode purposefully toward the far end of the ship and the ladder leading below decks.

Colette hurried after him, unsure how to distract the captain from discovering Philip and Thatch in the middle of their planned sabotage.

Looff was suddenly gasped by Woodes Rogers as he stumbled through the passageway. Woodes coughed loudly and held on to Looff's arm in an attempt to stay on his feet.

"What is the meaning of this?" he yelled and pushed Woodes away from him, to slide down the bulkhead in a fit of weakness.

"I, I was waiting for my tea," Rogers said breathlessly.

Colette was quick to his side and tried to raise him up. "Please, Captain, help me get this man back to his bunk."

Looff and the watchman each took an arm after a moment of hesitation. They half-carried, half-walked Woodes to the prisoners' little corner of the vessel.

"Where are your companions?" Looff asked as they were about to arrive at the sleeping berth.

"What the devil is going on?" Thatch demanded, annoyed, his eyes full of sleep.

Philip rolled over on his thin mattress as well and rubbed his eyes.

Colette's heartbeat eased in her chest seeing that they must have made it back after the watchman had left the torpedo room. "I was just making tea for Woodes, then he fell on his way to the galley."

Looff pushed Woodes onto his filthy, sweat-stained mattress. He glared at the four captives then turned his attention to the sailor standing next to him. "Leave your post again and you'll find yourself sent to one of the camps at our next port. You can spend the remainder of the war breathing the stench of Jews and gypsies. Understood?"

The young sailor gave his salute with fear in his eyes. "Yes, sir!"

"Then go!"

The watchman hurried away down the corridor.

Looff turned to Colette. "You do not have free rein to roam about the ship at night. It seems I have been far too kind and lax in my rules. That now changes. If I find you wandering about again, I will chain you all to the wall." He turned on his heels and left.

Colette peeked around the corner and saw that he had moved to another part of the ship. She turned back to Thatch and Philip. "Well?"

The two men nodded and smiled. She looked at Woodes; he too wore a grin on his pale disjointed face.

CHAPTER 31 – PIGEONS & TIDES

The Isle of France (now known as Mauritius)

The U-boat continued to stay submerged while it circled the island that sprawled in the ocean like a crooked teardrop, the coastline fringed by coral reefs. On its northeastern tip, a solitary cliff jutted out, its profile uncanny—the beak and bent neck of a pigeon turned skyward as if listening for the wind.

They had remained hidden earlier in the day while the ship's periscope monitored the small Port Louis royal naval base on the western side of the isle. There were no major warships sighted, and the worsening weather helped hide their arrival. Boat traffic was light as the sky darkened in the late afternoon.

Looff waited for lights to appear ashore that would indicate a local presence surrounding the craggy outcropping where they floated beneath the waters of the Indian Ocean. An hour after nightfall it was apparent from the lack of lights across the landscape that this tip of the island was uninhabited. He ordered the ship to ascend to the surface. A landing crew was to be assembled, armed and twenty-four sailors strong. He would stay aboard, leaving Hildebrandt in charge with Müller also accompanying the party. He also ordered the woman to remain along with Captain Rogers as he was too weak to leave the ship regardless. The pirate and the scientist would assist in the search for Levasseur's treasure with the knowledge that Miss Dallaire's life depended upon their success.

Thatch and Philip had changed out of the German uniforms and back into their personal clothes for the journey. Colette slipped her hand into Edward's. He squeezed it reassuringly.

"It will be alright, lass."

She looked him in the eyes and gave him a weak smile. She slid her arms around his back and pulled him close. He leaned his head down and her hair nuzzled his nose, he breathed her scent in. She whispered to him, "They won't let us live when this is done."

"Aye, but we will not go quietly," he said softly in her ear. "You know what you must do?"

"I know."

"Give yourself enough time."

"I will."

He pulled his face away to look deeply into her eyes. "You must. I will not live in this world without you."

She moved her hands to hold his bearded cheeks. "Nor I. Do what you must to survive, my love."

They kissed deeply then separated. Thatch looked at Woodes. "If you are to do anything worthwhile in your miserable life—keep this woman safe."

Woodes clung to the bulkhead as he unsteadily rose. "I will, but not because you ask it, I do it because she is kind, and it is right."

The two enemies stared hard at one another. Thatch just nodded.

He turned to walk away but Woodes reached out with a calloused grip to his arm that belied his frail state. "And you don't let these bastards win," Woodes growled.

Karl Müller arrived to stand in the corridor, his large frame filling the space. He commanded them in German. "It is time. Move." He indicated their direction with the rifle held in his hands.

"Be careful," Colette told both Philip and Edward, then the two men left with Müller herding them toward the ladder leading topside.

Philip took in a deep breath of the fresh, moist night air once he stood on the deck of the U-boat. The wind was brisk, and he looked up into the starless sky. Rain drizzled down upon him, but he paid it no mind. He hadn't breathed fresh air in weeks and just this small pleasure set a smile on his face.

He glanced over at Thatch, who had just emerged from the narrow hatch, taking deep pulls of the refreshing air. The pirate turned slowly, scanning the dark horizon and the jagged silhouette of the shore, eyes narrowing as though weighing the place.

Two rubber dinghies bobbed alongside the U-boat, their black skins slick with spray. Each could carry only four men, and the crew had already made several trips ferrying sailors to the rocks before the prisoners were ordered topside. Now the rafts waited, oars in hand, for Thatch, Philip, and Müller. They split them between the boats, three Germans for each captive.

Philip felt the raft dip as he climbed in, the saltwater seeping through the seams to lick at his ankles. Across the swells, Thatch sat in the other boat, watching the shadowed cliff that Levasseur had once described to him. Even in the dim light, the jutting stone resembled a pigeon craning its neck, its beak poised above the sea. The waves slammed into the base of the rock, surging into a dark cleft in the cliffside and vanishing into shadow. The hollow boom of water echoed faintly back, like a heartbeat deep within the stone.

The rafts scraped against the jagged shoreline, their rubber skins hissing against wet stone. Hands grabbed at Philip's arms, hauling him onto the slick rocks. Across the narrow inlet, Thatch was likewise dragged ashore, his boots finding purchase on the uneven ground.

A cluster of shadows detached from the cliffside, resolving into the lean form of Kapitänleutnant Hildebrandt. He stood in his officer's cap, the brim dripping with spray, flanked by two dozen armed sailors in dark U-boat leathers. Each man carried a rifle or submachine gun slung over his shoulder, their belts heavy with extra magazines. A few cradled the stubby Triola flashlights shaped like a large box of cigarettes, the dull glow from the lenses cutting weak tunnels into the blackness beyond the rock face.

Hildebrandt gave a curt nod and gestured toward the looming cliff. "We move now," he said in his precise German.

They climbed the rocky outcropping until they reached level ground, fringed with trees and thick brush. Faint trails branched away in several directions, some likely made by people, others worn by animals.

Hildebrandt stepped beside Philip and Thatch, pulling out the copy of the cipher now sealed in clear plastic against the rain. He tapped a gloved finger on the penciled notes beside its cryptic lines. "You said Levasseur was hiding navigational terms behind cooking phrases."

"Aye," Thatch replied. "The old Buzzard weren't talkin' about supper. 'Half covered' means the opening shows itself when the tide's out, hides when the sea's in. The first pigeon's this rock here." He gestured back toward the outcropping they'd spotted from the U-boat, its stony profile still facing the open sea.

"There must be a cave entrance if we're to find a forgotten treasure on this island," Philip said. "Levasseur wouldn't have used a building. If he had, then it would have been plundered or uncovered years ago."

"He speaks of a couple of pigeons," Thatch added. "So keep your eyes sharp, there may be another bird-shaped rock to find."

Hildebrandt barked orders, sending four teams of sailors fanning out along the cliff trails, combing every crack and ledge for a cave mouth. He kept Müller close, and together with two armed sailors, they pushed toward the sea-facing side with Thatch and Philip in tow.

An hour bled away in the rain. The tide continued its march lower despite the storm, hissing over black basalt as Hildebrandt's men found nothing—no opening, hidden or otherwise.

Thatch crouched low, rain plastering his hair to his brow, eyes fixed on the heaving surf. There, half swallowed by spray, jutted a jagged outcrop shaped like a single stone wing. From where he knelt, the wing lined perfectly with the pigeon's curved beak, the two forming a crude arrow that pointed toward a shadow at the tide line. Water surged and recoiled through it in rhythm with the waves, each swell revealing a low, black cleft no wider than a doorway.

His pulse kicked. That had to be it. Maybe, in Levasseur's day, the outcrop had a second wing that had been worn away now by a century of storms and tide. The old pirate's "pigeons" were still here, if you knew how and where to look.

Thatch gave a sharp whistle, drawing Philip's gaze along with Hildebrandt's suspicious glare. The Germans picked their way over the slick rocks until they stood beside him. He jabbed a finger toward the fissure.

"Someone needs to paddle out there, see if that's the door we're seekin'."

The approach would be ugly, knee to waist deep in churning water, footing on knife-edged reef. In daylight, it would be slow work. At night, with the storm swelling, it would be a gamble with the sea itself. Waiting for day may find the rising tide swallowing the opening completely.

Hildebrandt studied the shadowed cleft, then glanced at the exposed reef surrounding the point of the island. "Too shallow and narrow for a boat.

Wading out to that reef is the only way." His voice cut through the wind like a whip. "Müller, take our pirate friend."

Thatch gave him a slow grin, though inside he was already bracing for the wet bite of the sea. Müller didn't bother hiding his distaste as he stepped forward, removing the pistol and holster from his hip and slinging it and a coil of rope across his shoulder. He then shouldered his rifle on the opposite side.

Hildebrandt's flashlight beam stabbed toward the fissure, catching bursts of white-water surging in and out like the cave was breathing. "You've got ten minutes. If it's nothing, we move on. If it's something…" He let the sentence hang, but the greed in his eyes said the rest.

Müller followed Thatch down the rocks, each step slick and treacherous. The sea hit them in hard, cold bursts, swirling around their knees, then their waists. The closer they came, the louder the water and wind roared through the pigeon's mouth, spilling down into the dark. Every few seconds, a strong backwash sucked against their legs, tugging them toward the reef away from the safety of the shoreline.

Philip, watching from the rocks, caught the pattern—the mouth was feeding a channel that must lead deeper inside. If that channel ran all the way back through the cliff, it could be more than a hazard. It could be a trap to a watery grave.

Thatch felt it too. Levasseur had been cunning enough to use the sea as both guard and gate. If this was the way in, it wouldn't give up its secrets easily… and it might be just as dangerous when the time came to leave. The water swirled and rushed into the cave mouth. It was just under five feet high and was filled with a river of water rushing inside climbing to a third of the entrance's height. He looked behind him at Müller who crouched down to shine the light into its depths. His eyes found Thatch's and then he motioned for the pirate to make his way inside.

Thatch steadied himself against the dripping wall, eyes adjusting to the dim light of the Germans' flashlamp. The ceiling remained low enough that he and Müller had to duck, the Nazi's rifle angled awkwardly across his chest. The sound of the tide behind them was a constant, rhythmic roar, like the breath of some unseen beast. The water surged in and out of the cave at his knees. He shuddered to think what it would be like at high tide.

A few yards in, Thatch's hand brushed against something smooth amid the jagged stone. He squatted, wiping away a smear of wet algae with his sleeve. Lines emerged illuminated by Müller's light—carved deep, weathered but still clear—a pair of pigeons in flight, their wings crossing to form a crude "X."

"A couple of pigeons," Thatch muttered, recalling the first line of Levasseur's cipher. "Looks like we're in the right roost."

Müller leaned closer, his breath smelling of onions and stew. "What is it?"

"Mark o' the Buzzard himself," Thatch said, tapping the carving with a knuckle. "He's tellin' us we're on the right path."

They exchanged a glance, the unspoken agreement passing between them. Müller turned and strode to the mouth of the cave and shouted, waving his flashlight in broad arcs. Moments later, Philip and the rest of Hildebrandt's party picked their way over the tide-slick rocks and into the dark, their boots echoing off the stone.

The first dozen yards into the cave were slick and echoing, the tide still rushing and withdrawing through the jagged mouth behind them. Cold seawater pooled around their boots.

"This can't go far," Müller muttered, lifting his flashlight beam to the walls.

"The Buzzard wouldn't hide treasure where the tide'd wash it away," Thatch said, pushing ahead.

The tunnel began to slope sharply upward. The sound of the surf dulled, replaced by the drip of unseen water. They scrambled over a rise of black basalt and into a wide chamber above the tide line. Here, the walls were dry, the air still, and the floor thick with centuries of undisturbed dust.

Hildebrandt's light swept over shapes carved into the rock—spirals, crosses, and crude figures of birds. In the far corner, a narrow passage led deeper into the cliff.

"This is where we start watchin' our step," Thatch murmured. "Up here, La Buse's tricks might still have bite."

They began following the passage as it narrowed after the pigeon carving, forcing the men to walk single file with Hildebrandt leading. A moment later they came out into a chamber with another opening across the room. Hildebrant approached the passageway with the rest of the men filling out the space. The beam of his flashlight slid across the rough walls, catching on something carved into the rock beside the next entranceway—the snarling head of a dog, its stone jaws open in a silent growl.

Thatch froze. "Turkish dog…" he muttered under his breath, remembering the cipher.

"Yes, I think you're right," said Philip.

Müller glanced back. "What?"

But before Thatch could speak, one of the younger sailors, eager to impress, stepped forward and jabbed his flashlight at the carving. His boot scraped over a patch of dark, shiny stone underneath the statue—not wet rock, but hardened pitch.

The effect was instant. There was a grinding click within the wall, followed by a hiss and flash—a gout of flaming oil erupted from the dog's mouth, washing over the sailor's chest. The room erupted with light from the fire. He screamed, stumbling back into the others as the smell of burning cloth and flesh filled the tunnel. His rifle clattered to the floor.

The Germans shoved past Thatch, trying to smother the flames, but it was no use, within moments the man was still, his uniform smoldering. The room darkened as the fire died out.

Thatch's eyes lingered on the blackened carving. "Honey and sulfur," he said quietly. "That be the Buzzard's way o' sayin' 'Touch not the hound.'"

Philip took the cipher from Hildebrandt's shaking hand. Thatch looked over his shoulder in the glow of a flashlight. "To treat a Turkish dog, take a spoonful of honey and sulfur." He looked up at Thatch's eyes in the flickering light while he read over the clues.

"Clever bastard."

Hilderbrandt tore the cipher from Philip's hands and read over the next passage. "To stop a woman from snoring, you just have to whip together some oranges and oily olives to then spread just the oil on the pillow." He swung to face Thatch. "What does that mean? What is he saying?"

"He never had luck with women," Thatch remarked dismissively. "Perhaps it was his boar-like face, but it sounds like he was advising to poison your wife so that you may get some sleep." He chuckled.

Müller rewarded his quip with a jab of the rifle butt to his kidneys. Thatch grunted and went down on one knee. Philip helped the pirate rise and Müller raised his rifle to Thatch's face and made ready to smash it.

"Enough!" Hildebrandt's face was grim in the flickering light. "Mr. Thatch, stay out of the way. Müller, you keep an eye on him. Everyone watch where you step. And follow exactly in the path of the man ahead."

The echoes of their shipmate's screams still sounded in the sailors' ears as they climbed higher into the cliff. The walls narrowed, forcing them to move single file once again, flashlights casting nervous beams ahead. The floor grew dry and uneven, the smell of salt replaced by the damp, stale air of a place shut away from the world for centuries.

They turned a corner, and the left-hand wall was no more. The passage became a narrow ledge that ran upon an interior cliff face. The ceiling was too high for their lights to reach and the jagged drop on their left seemed unnaturally far. The ledge was thirty or so yards across from the next passageway entrance. From beyond it came a deep, rhythmic roar, like some slumbering beast exhaling in the dark. The sound rose and fell like the tide.

Thatch cocked his head. "That'll be the 'snorin' woman' Levasseur spoke of. And that much noise means she's got a temper."

The Germans spread out, scanning the floor and the dark chasm below. Flat steppingstones stretched toward the distant archway, their weathered surfaces marked by mold, the gaps between them slick with dark algae. Each stone had a worn symbol etched on its face. Hildebrandt motioned them forward. Five yards in, one sailor stepped on the wrong stone. It sank with a sharp *clunk*.

The roar became a shriek as seawater exploded from a concealed spout in the wall, slamming into the man like a cannon blast. His flashlight spun away in a glittering arc before he was hurled clean off the ledge into the blackness beyond. The man next to him made a grab to help his comrade but his efforts left him off balance and he slipped, screaming into the abyss. The sound of their bodies hitting bottom never came. Their shrieks faded into the distance until there remained only the rhythmic roar of the spouting water and the pounding hearts of the remaining men.

"We keep going, you lead now," Hildebrandt said strongly. He nudged Philip forward with Thatch following. Müller went next then the rest followed.

Philip looked closely at the stone the poor man had stepped upon as he ducked under the still spouting stream of water. It looked like a circle was carved into the surface. The next several stones and those just behind he noticed had a symbol resembling a two-handled jug or amphora, the kind used long ago to hold oil. Further up he saw more faded circles carved into the stepping stones. He tentatively stepped on the next stone adorned with an amphora, and it held his weight without sinking into the surface of the ledge.

He repeated the cipher to himself. "To stop a woman from snoring, you just have to whip together some oranges and oily olives to then spread just the oil on the pillow." What did it mean, he thought. He continued to step as lightly as he could. Thatch carefully moved in his wake, placing his boot only where Philip had. Several stones lay in front of him, cracked and weathered. The symbols were covered in dust, some completely void of carvings. He stood staring, not knowing where to place his foot. "Spread just the oil on the pillow," he pondered the clue.

"Move, little man," growled Müller from behind Thatch.

"Don't rush him!" barked Thatch.

Philip used his boot to rub the dirt from a stone in front of him, attempting to reveal a symbol. He thought he could make out another amphora in the stone. There were the makings of the rounded handles he'd seen on other carvings, if he could just get it clean. The ledge was now less than two feet wide, and he would need to leap over this stone to avoid it, but that leap could be his doom. "Whip together some oranges and oily olives…" He put more pressure on the stone to clear the dirt and sand away. The stone suddenly sank several inches.

WHOOSH!

Philip felt a blast of cool air a split second before a torrential explosion of water shot from a hole about waist high in the wall on his right. He lost his balance while attempting to spin away from the spouting water. He pirouetted and then the ledge was no longer underneath him, just the blackness of the abyss. One moment he was falling into nothingness, the next his body slammed into the side of the cliff face. Pain shot up his shoulder and arm as he realized Thatch had a grip on his wrist while he hung, feet bicycling against the slick rock face, desperately trying to find purchase.

Thatch was lying halfway over the side keeping Philip from falling. Water shot out over his head continuously from the hole in the wall where Philip had triggered the trap. Remarkably Müller and two sailors held fast to his legs.

"Give me your other hand," he told Philip as the man dangled by one wrist.

Philip tried to reach Thatch's outstretched hand but didn't have the strength to do it. Thatch's hand was losing its grip from the sweat and water that coated Philip's skin.

"Mr. Albert, you can do this. Stop thrashing about. Look at me."

Philip stopped moving his legs and looked up with eyes full of fear.

"Good, now reach up with your other hand and grab mine."

Philip was losing his strength; he tried but he couldn't seem to lift his body to reach Thatch's hand. He could feel the pirate's fingers slipping off his wrist. "I, I can't."

"Don't tell me you can't, you soft-bellied sow! Reach up and grab my hand, damn you!"

Philip used the last remaining energy in his body to reach up with all his might, pulling his shoulder down that attached to the arm held by Thatch. Pain shot through his muscles and joints as he reached up.

His reaching hand was rewarded with a vise-like grip as the pirate wrapped his rough and powerful fingers around Philip's own dainty ones. With the men holding his legs Thatch pulled his body back over the ledge, dragging Philip up to safety. Thatch sat back with his back to the wall, feet dangling over the side as the rest of the men carefully stood up and brushed themselves off.

Philip looked down at the sunken slab that had nearly ended his life and brushed away the remaining dirt. A circle was revealed where he had originally thought was the handle of an amphora. "Circle. Oranges, olives. Don't step on those. Those are bad. Spread just the oil. The amphoras are safe."

Thatch patted Philip on the head and rose to his feet, avoiding the gushing water from the wall. "Aye, Mr. Albert. Sound advice, mate."

Colette sat with Woodes Rogers while the sickly man did his best to keep down a bowl of broth she prepared for him. The crew was on alert but idle as there was nothing to do but watch the horizon and wait—wait for the landing crew to find a treasure that had been hidden for centuries. The boat moved with the swells but after months at sea she felt at home with the rise and fall.

"Do you think they will find it?"

Woodes wiped his mouth and set his bowl down. His body now ached from the inside out. "You've paired yourself with the devil. Why the world and tides turn for that man I'll never know. I feel my body faltering and desire nothing more but to be at home. And here I sit, after chasing Blackbeard and his ilk across the ocean, across time… to find myself, of all things—hoping for his success and safe return." He rubbed his stubbly face. "A charmed life the devil has."

Colette took his hand in hers. "Thank you."

He shook his head. "You won't take my advice, but it would be to stay an ocean away from that demon. Somehow, he is to blame for our situation but I'm tired of fighting, tired of chasing and wish just to rest."

Colette pushed the bowl closer to him. "Maybe after tonight. But now you need your strength. Finish your soup, Captain."

"Don't need more soup. I could use a drink. A strong one."

Colette raised her brows and smiled. "I have something for you then." She rose and searched a cabinet in the galley. When she sat back down it was with two bottles of German lager. She used a bottle opener to pop the caps with a fizz. "Several sailors brought beer aboard after our last stop at a fuel depot." She handed one to Woodes. "One poor lad lost his bottle to me with a bad hand of cards.

Woodes looked at the bottle with reverence. He tipped it to his lips and took a long pull. A bit of the brew trickled down his chin and he gulped down a good helping ending with a belch. "Ah, it bubbles," he said with surprise.

"Have you not had one before?"

Woodes shook his head and drank some more.

Colette smiled and drank from her bottle.

"It has been some time since I've drunk wine or its like."

"Well, let the spirits lift your spirits tonight, Captain." She leaned forward on the galley table and clinked the bottle in Woodes' hand with her own.

"Celebrating so soon?" Looff said in his commanding German as he strode into the galley. "Even now you steal from the crew, breaking rules of drinking on my ship."

Colette turned in her chair to face him, setting the bottle on the table. "It wasn't theft, but a lost wager. And why shouldn't we drink? We are not on duty, nor part of your crew."

SLAP!

Like the strike of a snake, Looff struck Colette with the back of his hand causing her to fall from her chair to the deck. Woodes, with a surge of strength, stood to defend her but Looff pushed him over the back of his chair to slam his head on the deck.

Looff took Colette's bottle and held it up to the light while inspecting it. "It is a fine German beer, that is true." He drank heartily from the bottle, finishing it.

Colette crawled over to Woodes where he lay unconscious. There was blood at the corner of her mouth where Looff struck her and when she cradled Woodes' head she found blood in his hair and on her hand. "Look what you've done, you bastard!"

Looff moved a little closer and kicked Woodes' boot. The man wasn't moving. Two sailors entered the galley having heard the commotion and stood waiting for an order. "Get this insolent Brit off my deck. Lay him in his cot for now. If he is dead, we will dump his body in the bay later." He then focused his stern attention on Colette. He knelt in front of her. "We shall see if Herr Hildebrandt proves to be successful in his quest, but your fate is in my hands." He took a lock of her hair and caressed it between his thumb and finger. "You will learn to be a good girl or there will be harsh punishments."

Colette swatted his hand away. He brought his hand up to strike her again.

"Captain!" his first mate shouted from the pilot house.

Looff stood up as the man rushed into the corridor.

"Two ships off the starboard bow."

Looff marched off and Colette got to her feet. She assisted the two sailors in carrying Woodes to his bunk. Once he was laid down, she listened to his heart and was thankful to hear it beating. The sailors left and she wet a cloth to tend to his head wound. When she wiped the blood from the back of his head he groaned and started to move.

"What happened?"

"Looff."

Woodes' eyes started to focus as he came to. "I remember. Damn bastard, I'll tear his arms out."

Colette laughed and helped him sit up. "You sound just like Edward."

Woodes looked at her with a mock glare on his scarred face. "That is the most hurtful thing anyone has ever said to me."

CHAPTER 32 – MUTINY

Anne Bonny shook out her hair before entering the corridor where a sailor stood at his post outside the armory. She sashayed on bare feet as she approached. His eyes couldn't help themselves as he watched her enticing form come closer. She smiled coyly at him.

"Did I get meself a bit turned in your big ship?"

"No ma'am, I mean yes ma'am, well, where were you headed?"

She sidled up next to him and leaned against the bulkhead, one hand twirling a lock of hair. "I was just looking for a storeroom where a girl could find a new shirt. You see, mine has been stained right here." She pointed to a smudge on her top that was unbuttoned to reveal a good helping of her cleavage.

The young man was staring now, distracted, and she tilted her head and put her arm on his. "Could you help find a new one?"

"It's just back a ways, sorta where you came from," he said pointing.

"Oh? I don't want to get lost or go where I ain't supposed to be. Can you just walk me there?"

He looked up and down the empty corridor. "Well, I guess it would just take a minute." He led her back down the way she came.

The ship was moving through the waves of the growing storm and Anne pretended to lose her balance, colliding with him. She wrapped an arm in his. "This is some storm, maybe I hold on to you before I hurt meself."

He smiled and his chest puffed out some and they came to the corner.

Jesse James was standing just around the turn with a big fist ready. WHAM!

Anne ducked, momentarily holding on to the man's arm so he couldn't defend himself and the sailor spun away after to land in a heap on the deck.

"Oh, I do like this jealous side of you," she said mockingly to Jesse.

"He seemed pleased as punch to escort you to a storeroom."

"Alright, enough flirtation. We gonna need those keys," said Frank with annoyance.

She bent down and fished out the sailor's set of keys from his pocket. Jesse followed her back to the armory door with Chester and Frank dragging the unconscious sailor. She found the right key and opened it to reveal a small room where racks of rifles, pistols, several machine guns and flare guns were stored along with boxes of ammunition.

Anne opened up a large metal box on a shelf and found the stash of their personal weapons.

"Well, we've hit the mother lode," Frank said taking his two .44-caliber Colt 1860 revolvers from the box. Anne, Jesse and Chester found their weapons.

Chester unslung a pair of navy duffels and began to fill them with rifles, pistols and ammo for the others in their party. He also slipped Charlotte's beloved kukri in his belt but as he loaded one of the .30-caliber Browning automatic rifles Anne swiped the blade from him. He turned to look at her in alarm.

"Don't worry yourself there, Mr. Chester, I just prefer to deliver this blade to her myself."

He looked nervously at the two cowboys, but Frank paid him no mind and Jesse just chuckled as he slung a rifle over his shoulder and carried a second in the crook of his arm.

"Alright. I guess this is where we split up." Chester hefted his duffel loaded with weapons and passed one to Frank. "I'll meet Vane and Black Caesar to take the engine room and when you hear them stop, you'll know it's safe to take the pilot house."

"Let's find a spot to tie this bilge rat, an store 'em where he won't be found," said Anne.

Anne relocked the armory and broke the key inside. Chester stayed to help as they searched for a storage room where they could stash the unconscious sailor and came to another locked door.

"Anne, see if you have a key for this on that ring," said Jesse.

"Sure, love." She tried several before she found the correct one and twisted the lock open with an audible click.

Jesse and Frank hauled the sailor into their arms while Anne opened the door and used the convenient switch to illuminate the dark space. They all had spent many minutes in wonderment fiddling with these things their first several days aboard the ship.

Jesse and Frank stopped in their tracks.

"What the devil?" Frank whispered.

Anne squeezed by to get a look.

"Bastards!"

They set the sailor to one side and each one entered to explore the contents. Anne picked up several Spanish coins.

"They stole our treasure?" Chester asked.

"Damn right they did!" Jesse said and began to open the chests and crates that contained the silver, gold, jewels and finery that had been stored in the hold of the *Queen Anne's Revenge.*

"That thieving bastard Outerbridge. I'm going to wring his God damn neck," growled Frank.

"What do we do now?" Chester asked looking from cowboy to cowboy to pirate.

Anne spoke up as she checked the loadout of her revolver. "We stick to the plan. Just not going to be as gentle about it as before."

Chester went below deck toward the engine room and Anne, Jesse and Frank moved midship to rendezvous with the rest of the crew. None stood in their way as they knew this hour had light staffing and shift changes were hours away.

Mary, Tom, Francis, Charlotte and Roberts were waiting just outside the galley. Two crew members of the *Ward* were already subdued and bound inside the mess hall.

"Looks like you found what we needed," said Roberts.

"Aye, that an more," replied Anne.

Roberts raised a questioning brow.

She flipped a coin in the air for Roberts to catch.

Mary looked over his shoulder as he held it in his palm.

"Is that ours? Where did you find it?" she asked.

"All our treasure is below, locked in a hold," Anne answered.

"They stole it?" asked Tom.

Roberts gripped the coin in his fist. "Tonight, we take it back and return the gesture in kind."

Jesse dropped the heavy bag holding the cache of weapons and unzipped it to reveal the plunder.

Tom was first to reach in, retrieving the two .45s belonging to his captain.

"Blackbeard's," he explained and stood back as the rest of them sought their own weapons and the US navy's upgrades.

Charlotte looked at her prized machete residing in Anne's belt. Anne had been waiting for her to notice and say something. A smile curled up her lips.

"Are we at odds over the rightful owner of that blade?"

Anne slowly pulled it from her waistband and twirled it in her palm. She approached Charlotte, brandishing the sharp edge near the glaring woman's chin. The rest of the room was silent, unsure of what was about to happen.

Anne held the blade near Charlotte's face. "I do like its hilt and weight…" She then flipped it antagonistically to spin around her wrist causing Francis to let out a gasp, but the hilt ended up facing the dark-skinned pirate instead of the pointy end. Charlotte never flinched. "But its edge is too dull for my liking."

Charlotte narrowed her eyes and took the offered kukri, sheathing it against her hip.

Frank let out an annoyed sigh. "Well, this night is about to get interesting. Everyone ready?"

"Aye," Tom was the first reply.

"We take the ship, maroon the captain and officers, and offer the pirate-life to any crew members that will take the oath," Roberts said.

"We need to conscript some gunners, the radio talker man, and the navigator," Mary responded.

"And the cook. Food is good on this ship," Tom added.

Several pirates laughed at that. Roberts set his hand on Tom's shoulder. "That be true, boy. The cook shall stay."

Anne checked the loadout of her revolver again and snapped the chamber shut. "Tonight, we mutiny."

Black Caesar waited with Charles Vane in a darkened corner just steps away from the engine room. There would be five men inside tending to the two boilers, a couple of machinist's mates, two firemen/boiler technicians and an engineering officer of the watch. Once Chester arrived, they would still be outnumbered but if he and the others had been successful, it wouldn't matter as they would be the only ones armed. The odds were also good that a few of the men working the boilers would be friendly. The past six weeks had brought the two diverse crews closer together. Sailing had a common language and ship-life, no matter what age you came from or what craft you sailed, brought out a sense of family that would bind a crew.

The two men waited in silence until they heard the footfalls of boots rushing along the corridor. The two big men stepped out of the shadows to find the wiry frame of Chester burdened by a pistol bulging out his waistband, a duffel heavy with weapons sagging one shoulder, and a rifle resting ready in his hands.

"There you both are," he said momentarily out of breath. He set down the tan canvas bag and wordlessly Vane and Black Caesar rummaged through taking several pistols and rifles each. They loaded the weapons with boxes of ammunition then Caesar shouldered the duffel, easily carrying it without effort.

"Quiet as shadows," Black Caesar warned. He saw them nod, then he opened the hatch and led them inside, Vane closing it behind them.

"Shut down the engines. Now." Vane's voice cut through the roar of pistons. He moved forward with his rifle and leveled it at two men.

The watch officer looked at them in confusion. At first, he didn't understand what they were doing, thinking this was a prank. For a heartbeat the watch officer only blinked at them, baffled. The pirates had been little more than comic relief these past weeks—spinning tales, gaping at the ship's machines. Surely this was another game.

Black Caesar and Chester spread out to guard the other workers as they gazed with shocked looks at the weapon-toting pirates. They slowly raised their hands.

"What the hell is going on?" asked the officer.

"What does it look like to you, mate?"

The man's face went white. "A mutiny?" he asked in almost a whisper.

"Aye." Vane's voice was iron. "Now kill the engines. Bring her to a stop."

Commander Outerbridge sat alone in his cabin, the clock edging past midnight, papers strewn across his desk, intel reports, intercepted messages, aerial sightings, fragments from civilian fishermen. For weeks they had been shadowing the German Type XB U-boat, always a few days behind, as it slipped from the Pacific into the Indian Ocean, steering toward the Seychelles.

Thanks to Bart Roberts, the gap had narrowed. The pirate's uncanny instinct for sea lanes and havens had pointed them toward Mauritius, known in his day as the Isle of France. It was there Roberts claimed he had once crossed paths with the pirate king, Olivier Levasseur.

Lieutenant Miriam Katz had confirmed the tale: Roberts had won a Catholic relic from Levasseur at the gambling table. A relic now suspected of being tied, somehow, to the pirates' impossible leaps through time.

Outerbridge exhaled, leaning back in his chair. His fingers pinched the bridge of his nose, pressing against the throb gathering behind his eyes. That relic was in the hands of the Nazis. There were two of those crosses known as the Sacred Lotus Twins of Goa and no one knew the location of the other twin. It seemed the Nazis were betting it languished with Levasseur's hidden treasure.

The *Ward* had arrived at Mauritius several hours ago and they were combing the coastline, searching for the U-boat while still towing the pirate ship in their wake. Another storm had suddenly overtaken them the last hour or so without warning and it steadily built in strength as they searched the nightscape for signs of the Nazis.

He set his spectacles on his small desk and reached for the lamp to turn it off. He would try to catch some sleep knowing that the watch would alert him if they found anything worthy of his attention.

Just then, his hand paused before pulling the lamp's chain as the *Ward*'s engines stopped.

He quickly slipped on his shoes and fixed his glasses back on his head. Something was amiss and his pulse rushed as he exited his cabin. The ship swayed as it slowed in the water. The developing storm rocked the hull as swells built in height and power. As he made his way to the pilot house, he heard shouting, and he quickened his step to a trot. When he exited the corridor he came to an abrupt stop to find a bayonet attached to a rifle stubbed against his chest.

His gaze followed the barrel of the M1903 Springfield to the crooked nose and squinted eye of one of Bart Roberts' crew members named Francis.

"You can hold right here, Commander."

"What in Sam Hill is going on here, sailor?"

Bart Roberts made his way through a small crowd of gun-toting pirates and crew members with their hands in the air.

"My dear Captain Outerbridge, good of you to join us this fine evening."

"Think carefully on what you are doing here, Roberts," Outerbridge told him without hiding the menace in his tone.

Roberts punched Outerbridge in his gut, sending the man down to one knee. He leaned down to speak threateningly in his ear. "You stole our treasure after your empty promises to set us free when this voyage was done. I should have your bare back keelhauled the length of this ship."

"I was under orders, damn you. And I didn't steal it, I just stored it!"

"You moved it without saying a word. Put it under lock and key deep in your ship's hold."

"Yes. To keep it safe. What if the *Queen Anne's Revenge* broke free or sank for God's sake?"

"Lies!" Roberts roared. He picked Outerbridge up by his collar and pushed him in front of him. "Assemble them on the quarterdeck," he shouted to the crowd.

The rain picked up as the pirates herded more than a hundred men at gunpoint. Charlotte moved a protesting and frightened Miriam by a fistful of hair to stand near Outerbridge and the officers.

Roberts stood on the raised platform of the .50-caliber deck-gun. His voice boomed against the wind. "The command of this ship now belongs to me. Mr. Outerbridge has been removed from duty after his crimes against the *Queen Anne's Revenge* have come to light. Whether it be known to you or not, our treasure, our property, was to be stolen away from us by Outerbridge and his superiors. We have taken back what was rightfully ours and seized this ship as a prize."

The crew listened with trepidation and Outerbridge started to protest but was struck in his kidney with the butt of Francis' rifle.

Roberts continued. "The captain and the officers will be put ashore along with any who do not wish to remain. I offer the rest of the crew that we have grown to admire and, dare I say, consider our mates, the option to take the vow of the pirate code."

He looked out at the darkened outline of the rocky northern tip of the island and pointed. "There lies the possibility of unfathomable wealth. Olivier Levasseur hoarded a massive treasure, and your German enemies search for it this very moment. Join us and we will conquer them and take what is ours, every man standing here earning a share of the plunder. I also offer a ten percent share that any takers will split of the treasure locked away on this ship."

He held back a smile as he let a murmur flow through the crowd. Outerbridge held his side where he'd been pummeled and watched in horror as many of the faces of the young men under his command considered the offer.

"You men are in the United States Navy! You'll be court-martialed and sent to Leavenworth if you join these—"

CRACK

This blow from Francis' rifle connected with his head.

"Time is short. Step forward to take the oath or make your way to the boats."

One of the Papa boats was dropped into the choppy water. Jesse, Frank and Mary ordered the officers at gunpoint to pick up Outerbridge and carry him to the boat.

A dozen scenarios played out in Miriam's head in the seconds after. She was petrified of staying aboard with these pirates, but it was an opportunity to further her knowledge of their history, and what brought them here, to 1942. She could be killed, certainly risked jail, but felt she would live a life filled with regret if she got on that boat with the officers. Would they make her fight, or could she convince them that her mind was what she offered in value? Would the pirates even take her if she stepped forward? On shaking legs, she strode frontward to a waiting Anne Bonny whose lips curled up in a curious smile.

"Welcome aboard, you naughty gentlewoman," said Anne.

Miriam's tongue felt too cumbersome in her mouth to respond, she just turned and faced the crowd of sailors, white-faced as the rain plastered her hair against her head.

Stanton looked over at Brockman and Kent, who were looking back at him for direction. He swallowed hard as he struggled to make up his mind. If he boarded the boat with his captain and other officers he would be shipped off to another destroyer, destined to fight the Japanese or even possibly this very ship and crew. He loved his country and wanted to serve, making his father proud, but something was calling him toward the pirates standing in front of him. He watched Lieutenant Katz cross over and felt a pang of envy. He had voiced his opposition about secretly taking their treasure from the pirate ship, but that didn't mean he would go against his commanding officer. Now, he was at a crossroad. If he joined the pirates, he would *still* be fighting against the Nazis. They were going to rescue Blackbeard and the others from the U-boat. The image of treasure flashed in his mind as well, treasure that was already held on this ship. Imagine what he could do with that wealth—for his family if nobody else.

He stepped forward and turned to look at Brockman and Kent. The two young men exchanged a look between them then joined Stanton on the other end of the quarterdeck. Within the next minute thirty-four more sailors crossed to stand with the pirates.

"Welcome aboard mates, huzzah!" Roberts raised his rifle in the air. The pirates and cowboys returned the cheer and several ex-*Ward* sailors tried it out. "Get the rest of these men off my ship and prepare for battle!"

It took two Papa boats to carry the departing sailors. Several essential crew members were forced to stay, and it took some convincing from the newly recruited pirates to set them on their specialized tasks.

Tom watched the coastline as they drifted closer. He narrowed his sharp eyes as he spotted an outline emerging in the shadows.

"Captain! Ship ahoy!" he called out.

Roberts rushed to the boy's side to see what he spotted. Stanton and several others joined him.

"That's her," said Brockman.

"Aye," affirmed Roberts. He looked out at the motoring Papa boats heading in the opposite direction further down the shoreline. "Call down to the engine room and tell Vane to get those beasts started. A battle is afoot."

All the crew scattered to their posts and duties. Miriam was left at the railing standing next to the stern young Chinese boy. She watched the boats carrying Outerbridge and the rest of the crew disappear south into the stormy distance. She shook her head and murmured to herself, "Now what are you going to do, Miriam, you just joined a mutiny… with a bunch of pirates."

She looked down to see Tom's face, now fixed with a wide grin as he watched the rise and fall of the U-boat's silhouette on the horizon.

CHAPTER 33 – TURKISH DOG'S MAW

The tunnel curved upward into a vaulted chamber where the path ended at a sheer wall of stone, with flush seams around a massive door made of the same stone blocking their way. It loomed high above their heads, twelve or more feet and immovable. To the right, half hanging from the top of the cliffside wall, was the snarling head of a dog carved from basalt, its jaws open wide, suspended on a chain so corroded it moaned as the head swayed gently in the cave's draft. Beneath it yawned a pit twenty feet deep, with a forest of iron spikes waiting to impale anything that fell. The opening spanning from wall to wall covered the entire length of the right side of the room.

In the center of the chamber sat a wide clay bowl filled with black lava stones, each the size of a fist. The men looked from the bowl to the statue and back again.

"What devilry is this?" muttered Müller.

Hildebrandt stepped forward, jaw set. He read the next line of the cipher. "'To make a Turkish dog eat well, throw some dry shit at it.' It's simple enough. We feed the hound." He grabbed one of the stones, hefted it, and hurled it toward the mouth. The rock clattered against the dog's open mouth and dropped into its jaw to fall inside the statue's head, causing the chain to descend a few inches. The chamber rumbled and the massive door ahead sank a few inches, grating down into the floor.

"You see," Hildebrandt told his audience. "A simple game."

Thatch kept his mouth shut. Levasseur touted that he was a master at architecture and proved to be quite the trickster thus far. What would be the penalty for missing?

Hildebrandt made a show of tossing the next rock in his hand several times in the air to himself before lofting it at the dog's maw. His second attempt caused the rock to clatter against the dog's carved teeth, deflecting away from the mouth, then vanished into the pit below.

The grinding sound that followed was not from the door. Instead, with a thunderous crash, a massive stone slab dropped behind them, sealing off the tunnel they had come from. Dust poured from the ceiling as the men shouted in alarm, trapped now with only one way forward.

"*Scheiße*," whispered one sailor.

Thatch spat dust from his mouth. "No turning back now, lads."

Hildebrandt, more nervous now, took another stone and tossed it at the dog's mouth. It bounced off its nose and clattered to the spiked chamber below. The floor groaned and shook. They all stood still as the stone slabs underneath them vibrated. Suddenly several slabs broke apart beneath two sailors' feet and they slipped into the open hole to fall screaming before being impaled on the spikes in a sickening crunch.

Philip held his ears as one man shrieked and thrashed momentarily before bleeding out into his death. The hole was near the opposite wall of the Turkish dog head. Philip's mind was telling him that it wasn't random. That the rock falling below triggered the trap.

Hildebrandt's face was white as a sheet. He handed Müller a stone from the bowl. The big German tested the weight of the lava rock and then stepped up to the edge of the pit and concentrated on the open mouth of the dog. He tossed the rock with a slight arch. It dropped past the teeth to roll into the jaw and sank down the statue's throat. The chain dropped several inches and so did the door with a noisy rumble.

The rules were now clear.

Hildebrandt nodded to Müller, and everyone watched as he threw another into the mouth. Cheers were voiced and again the statue along with the great stone door lowered a few more inches. One sailor, a tall lanky man with slick black hair, approached the door and attempted to leap up to grab its edge but it was still a good two feet beyond reach.

Müller let another rock fly, scoring again. The door lowered. The tall sailor stood next to the stone door and looked up as the top slipped down a few more inches though still quite out of reach. They all stilled as Müller took another rock from the bowl. He threw it toward the dog's mouth, but his aim was off, and it careened off the side to then drop below. They all stood motionless, waiting to see what would happen.

CRACK!

Several slabs of stone gave way beside Philip, dragging two men with them—including the tall one stationed before the door—down into the pit where they were shattered and impaled. Philip froze, the stones beneath his boots trembling, then settling into uneasy stillness.

"Stay still," Thatch ordered him.

"I shall not move, Mr. Thatch, even if I wished to run my feet refuse to obey."

Several sailors grabbed rocks out of fear that Müller would miss again. They began hurling stones, each man spreading across the chamber floor to avoid standing shoulder-to-shoulder—because no one knew which slab might collapse next. The sailors' faces glistened with sweat as stone after stone arced toward the dog's mouth. Some were swallowed, and the great door sank lower. Others missed, and the floor gave way in jagged squares, opening into the spike-filled abyss below.

A scream tore through the chamber as one unlucky German lost his footing when the slab under him dropped. He pinwheeled into the pit, impaled with a grisly slap. Two more followed in quick succession as the men's nerves frayed, missing their mark and dooming themselves to an iron death.

The floor was now a patchwork of cavities. Hildebrandt and Müller stayed near the center where the bowl sat. Philip was near the left side surrounded by gaping holes. Thatch stood near the right side with just one twelve-inch slab between him and the massive open space on the right side of the room.

Thatch watched as the bowl of stones was emptied fast. By the time the door had sunk low enough for a tall man to touch its upper edge, only a handful remained scattered across the chamber floor. The men scrambled to snatch them, each throw now made with trembling hands.

One by one, the last stones vanished into the maw—until only a single rock remained.

Philip stood alone on an isolated slab, every other path around him broken into empty air. The final stone lay at his feet. The others stared at him, frozen. He crouched, picked it up, and weighed it in his palm.

The pit below waited in silence. The dog's head leered. The chain groaned.

Philip drew in a long breath, adjusted his stance, and hurled.

The rock sailed clean through the air and clattered into the dog's mouth. The sound that followed was like thunder: the massive stone door ground downward, sliding deeper into the floor until at last the way forward yawned open in the rock face.

The chamber erupted in a mixture of relieved shouts and muttered prayers.

Philip exhaled slowly, the tremor in his hand betraying how close they had come to doom. He leaped over to the slab where Thatch stood, the pirate holding his arm to steady him. He clapped him on the shoulder with a grin.

"Well played, Mr. Albert. Seems the bitch's belly is finally full."

They hurried through before the chamber could claim any more lives, leaving the pit and its broken bodies behind.

Looff spied the two ships that sat out to sea off his starboard side through his binoculars. He could see the outline of both, recognizing the larger one as a US navy destroyer. It was an old one, likely built during World War I. The other was a wooden tall ship of some sort.

He called his crew to general quarters, and his three deck-guns were manned and waiting for orders. He cursed that half his crew were on the island somewhere searching for treasure, but they would make do. The landing crew had a radio but so far communication was lost, most likely due to interference from the land mass. They had had one message saying they were about to enter a cave structure, but it had been quiet since then.

Two troop-transport boats had departed from the destroyer, and he was prepared to fire upon them, but they headed south, away from their position. He tried to wrap his mind around the puzzle of what their mission might be. He wasn't even sure whether his U-boat was spotted but why else would they be here?

They could be sending those boats in order to flank them from the shore. *That must be it*, he thought. He gave an order to his radioman to tell Hildebrandt that he should expect company. They would continue sending the message every five minutes until they made contact.

He gave the order to turn the bow to face the enemy and ready the torpedoes. He smiled confidently that U-122 would have another kill to her growing list of victories. Rain poured off his slicker as he circled the deck, encouraging the men to be ready for battle.

He slid his feet down the ladder to land gracefully below deck. He entered the pilot house and barked orders to make ready to engage the enemy. He touted the strength and superiority of Germany and reminded his crew that the Americans were soft, with old technology. He marched through the ship toward the torpedo room to make sure the men on duty were ready to deliver death and destruction from their advanced munitions.

Looff couldn't resist the opportunity to rub salt into the wounds of the Brit and the American woman. He stopped at the cramped crew quarters where they sat next to one another on a bunk.

"Luck has found you again today. What a treat to bear witness to the superiority of Germany and the Führer. We are about to sink an American warship just off an island ruled by your country, Mr. Rogers. It pleases me that I have let you live to see this day. Just don't count on seeing another."

He strode off toward the torpedo room, laughing heartily.

Colette's jaw was set, and she stood to see the back of Looff disappear down the ladder at the end of the corridor.

"I only understood half of what he said, but it was enough to set my blood boiling. It will give me pleasure to watch that pig burn."

"And burn he will before this night is done," Woodes assured her.

The ceiling of the cave pressed lower as the party crept deeper into the narrowing corridor. Every man's nerves were frayed from the gauntlet of traps they had survived, even Thatch's iron composure beginning to show cracks. Müller shoved him forward to take the lead, while Hildebrandt lingered behind, poring over the cryptogram and their scribbled notes as if he might divine the next horror from its lines.

Thatch didn't need the parchment, he had the final line etched in his memory after weeks of staring at it:

To calm a woman who wants to get drunk, put sugared tea in wine. To put a man and his woman to sleep, you must take very strong and bitter African wine.

The words churned in his skull, taunting him. Some of Levasseur's clues had been literal enough, but this one… this one reeked of double meaning. La Buse was clever as the devil, and crueler still. His riddles might be nothing more than a pirate's joke, designed to mock those who sought his fortune. Perhaps there was no treasure at all. Perhaps the Buzzard had squandered it long before the hangman's noose snapped his neck.

Yet Hildebrandt believed. The German's pale fingers clutched the parchment in one hand while the other absently touched the cross at his throat. That damned relic had passed through more hands than a Nassau strumpet. Thatch had watched as Levasseur traded it from Bellamy. Later, Roberts had somehow come into possession of it, only to lose it to Woodes Rogers. Now the thing hung from Hildebrandt's neck like a prize.

The fool even believed its twin lay buried with Levasseur's treasure. That, Thatch knew, would be a bitter disappointment. He himself had once possessed the other. It had been tossed carelessly into a chest with the rest of Hornigold's plunder, collecting dust for more than a year. Thatch had no use for Catholic trinkets.

It was only later, when Black Caesar salvaged the *Queen Anne's Revenge* from the bottom of San Francisco Bay, that the cross had resurfaced. The quartermaster had taken a liking to it, and Thatch reckoned it still hung from Caesar's neck, somewhere near the Hawaiian Islands, thousands of miles away, provided that he was still among the living.

The passageway continued to shrink in height. Thatch crouched as he walked and when he looked past Müller and Hildebrandt he saw that Philip too was bent over as even he was too tall to walk upright.

"Pretty soon we'll be on our hands and knees if we continue this madness, Otto," Thatch growled at Hildebrandt.

"We are at the last. Soon we will have the treasure in our hands. We are close, very close. I can feel it in the metal of the cross. Its twin is near."

"Exactly what do you feel in the cross?" Philip inquired.

Hildebrandt clasped the base of the cross. "Power."

Thatch looked back at the German whose face was a mix of excitement and religious fervor. It was never wise to follow such a person when they had that glow. He looked further down the line of men to Philip and saw that he wore an expression of concern on his face mirroring Thatch's rising anxiety.

He bent lower and continued for some way until the light from Müller's flashlight illuminated a fork in the passageway. As they reached the divergence it was clear that crawling would be the method of entrance to either tunnel. There was enough room for Müller, Hildebrandt and himself to squat before the split.

There were only five sailors left alive to accompany them this far. They all crowded around to see which way they should go. The handheld light illuminated carvings above each doorway. The left side featured a woman holding a goblet, smiling, and the other was crude but depicted a grimacing man and woman drinking from a single jug.

Thatch sighed and sat back against the passage wall.

"What does it mean?" asked Müller, first looking at Thatch, then Hildebrandt.

"'To calm a woman who wants to get drunk, put sugared tea in wine.'" Hildebrandt pointed at the left-side opening below the smiling woman.

Müller nodded and pointed at the opposite carving. "'To put a man and his woman to sleep, you must take very strong and bitter African wine.'"

Thatch almost laughed aloud. He had taken Müller for a brute without intelligence but maybe he was mistaken. He was surprised that the man remembered the line verbatim.

"We should take the left path, toward the smiling woman. It must mean it's easier, safer," Müller suggested.

No, maybe not so smart, Thatch decided.

Hildebrandt studied the paper in his hands, reading over the text. He shook his head. "A false comfort. The man was a pirate. He would want us to be fooled by the smile. Isn't that right, Blackbeard?"

Thatch smiled. "Why don't you and your men wait here? Let Mr. Albert and I go in and make sure the path is safe."

Philip looked at him quizzically.

Hildebrandt thought about it and waddled forward to shine a light into the tunnel. The glow barely reached a few feet inside. He could see mold and muck covering the floor and walls. There must be water present inside. He inspected both passageways and each sloped down the further you went. He tried to guesstimate where they were located within the rocky cliff face of the coast, but they had twisted around and climbed and descended so many times that he was without a clue where the surface possibly was.

He looked back at Thatch and saw that he wore a clever smile on his lips. *What was he up to?* What if he ordered them to enter first and they were able to cut off the rest of them from reaching the treasure? *I must be close.* This was the last paragraph of the cipher. He shouldn't trust the pirate, he decided. He considered killing them both now as it was possible they wouldn't need them from here on, but what if something ahead stumped them from unlocking Levasseur's clues?

He pointed his flashlight at one of the U-boat's sailors. "You take the left entrance, make sure the way is clear."

The man looked frightened, and he turned to his crewmates for support or assurances. Their faces showed none.

"Move!" barked Müller and he pointed his rifle at the man.

Thatch and Hildebrandt made room for the man to squeeze by. He crab-walked to the opening under the smiling woman and set his hands on the edge. He pulled them back and there was algae smeared on his palm. The man looked back at Hildebrandt with dread but was given only a nod to proceed.

The sailor got down on hands and knees and used his flashlight to light his way as he crawled forward. After a few feet the slope deepened and the going became very slippery.

"What do you see?" Hildebrandt called out.

"It just keeps going down. I can't see that far ahead."

The man wiped his face from the strings of a spider web. His heart was pounding as his hands squished in the mush of the mold and moss covering all the surfaces. His hand clenched on a stone, finding purchase to pull himself forward with its aid. When his weight moved over the top of it the stone sank into the ground with a clunk. He froze and from somewhere in the dark he heard the grinding of a gear and the clank of something metal.

WHOOOOMPH!

The cave above the sailor collapsed and a thousand pounds of rock and rubble crushed him in a split second.

Hildebrandt was leaning into the passage when it happened and he flinched back in fear, landing on his backside as bits of debris and dust shot out of the entrance.

"I fear that might not have been the right path," Thatch chuckled.

Hildebrandt struggled to pull his pistol from its holster as he fumbled to right himself, face full of anger. Once he had it in his hand he shoved it at Thatch's head. "You first! Damn you! Get in there." He pointed at the right-side passage, then pointed the pistol at Philip. "You too! Now!"

Philip raised his hands and squeezed past a glaring Müller to kneel next to Thatch under the carving of the frowning man and woman. Thatch put his hand on Philip's shoulder then ducked to enter the tunnel.

The two men crawled through the mossy, algae-coated cave. Thatch had no flashlight, so he felt his way along. The smell of the sea was strong in the air, and he tried his best not to slip down the sloping surface.

Philip looked back, noticing the light shining from behind him. Müller was crawling, his bulk a few feet back, and it looked as though Hildebrandt was in his wake. He had spent many hours and days in caverns and caves similar to this one in his line of work. An expert in explosives would likely gravitate toward mining companies for employment. That experience cured him of being squeamish in small, cramped spaces. It was one of the few times he was grateful to be his petite size. He grinned upon hearing Müller curse while he struggled to squeeze himself through the tunnel.

Thatch felt he was making good progress through the cavern. He kept up a brisk pace so he could put a little distance between them and the

Germans so that he might come up with a plan. That is unless one of the Buzzard's pranks fried him to hard tack or crushed him to cornmeal. He could almost laugh at his thoughts but there wasn't enough room for him to do so.

He came upon a branch or something blocking his path. *It must be a root or branch growing through the cave walls.* It was too low to go under, so he climbed above it and started to shimmy past when something unexpected happened. One side of the branch broke free from the wall. The branch bent like a lever—exactly like a lever.

The floor lurched beneath him. One moment he was descending the tunnel, the next it felt as if the entire passage was tipping upward, pitching him backwards. His boots skidded, gravel scraping, and he feared he would crash into Philip behind him—only to see the scientist sliding away as well, carried helplessly down the shifting slope.

A sharp crack echoed. Hildebrandt spun at the sound just in time to see the floor give way behind him. A sailor's terrified face flashed past, then vanished into the void. It was as if the tunnel itself had split in half, the rear section shearing away while his own tilted and dropped.

He clawed desperately for purchase, reaching for Müller's boot—but his fingers slipped, and in the next instant he was pitched headlong into darkness.

Air tore at his face before he slammed down hard onto a slick stone chute. Water made the surface treacherous, and he rocketed forward at terrifying speed, his body twisting against the walls. His scream came out high and thin before he snapped his jaw shut, teeth grinding as he barreled down the incline like a cannonball. Behind him, Müller tumbled and kicked, scraping and skidding as his boots struck rock.

Then the chute vanished. Hildebrandt shot into empty air and braced for death—only to smash down on hands and knees into sucking mud. The impact drove the air from his lungs.

Müller crashed down on top of him, crushing his ribs further. Another body followed, then a fourth, the heap of men rolling and groaning in the dark. Hildebrandt struggled to move, but Müller's bulk pinned him. His pistol was gone. His flashlight too.

And from the blackness came the sound of laughter, low and hearty, unmistakable. Blackbeard.

CHAPTER 34 – HOG ON ICE

The sea was running high, swells crashing hard enough to send foaming spray over the gunwales of the *Ward*. Below decks, Chester stood watch in the engine room, keeping the ship's engineers honest under the pirates' new command. They'd all sworn an oath once Outerbridge and his officers were cast off, but Chester knew an oath only held as long as the man with the gun was watching.

The heat was suffocating, the air thick with diesel fumes and sweat. Chester didn't mind. Compared to the coal-fired brute he'd worked in 1873, these engines were a marvel. Two oil-fed boilers feeding a pair of Parsons geared turbines, driving nearly 25,000 horsepower into twin propeller shafts. He'd studied their workings for weeks, itching for a chance at the machinery. Now, with his sleeves rolled up and grease streaking his forearms, he grinned. Hog heaven, he thought.

On the main deck, Vane and Black Caesar had seized command of the gunnery crews. Three deck-guns and the torpedo tubes bristled in the salt wind, manned by sailors who glanced nervously at their new masters. The weather was turning foul—spray stung every inch of exposed skin, and the gale howled through the rigging like a banshee.

Stanton and his crew were manning their .50-caliber trying to keep the U-boat in its sights. The sea wasn't making it easy on them tonight.

Up in the pilot house, the cramped space was crowded. Roberts leaned over the chart table with Charlotte, Francis, and Miriam at his side. The

Ward's navigator and radioman, stripped of authority but not of usefulness, worked under their watchful eyes. The destroyer was no longer a US warship. Tonight, it sailed under the black flag.

Mary, Anne, Jesse and Frank were making their way to the bow of the ship where the forward-mounted .50-caliber waited to be manned.

"Again, no vote," griped Mary.

"He immediately declared war to stave off a vote," agreed Anne.

"I'm getting sick an tired of that pompous pretty-boy pirate," Frank said in his gravelly voice.

Mary chuckled at Frank's description of Roberts. "Ain't never heard him called that but it's fit'n."

The ship lurched to port as it crested a swell. Jesse was caught off balance and banged his knee on equipment that was protruding from the deck. "Damn it all to hell!"

Anne laughed at him. "You still ain't got your sea legs, cowboy."

"Don't want no sea legs, what I want is a damn horse and a trail to follow."

"I'd settle for a mule at this point," said Frank.

They reached the mounted 4-inch deck-gun and Frank moved to get into the gunner's seat.

"Not so fast, brother. I'm doing the shooting, you all are doing the loading."

"Why should you boys pull the trigger? Mary an me are the better shots!" Anne complained.

"You two got sea legs, remember? I need to sit, or I'll be slide'n around the deck like a hog on ice."

Jesse moved his brother out of the way and sat down taking the control wheels in his hands. The others got to work loading the gun by working the breechblock and setting the shell. Mary called out targeting details like she'd been taught by the *Ward*'s crew over the past several weeks.

"That ship is turning in our direction," Anne called out by the bow gunwale.

"Are we waiting for that pirate to tell us when to shoot?" Jesse yelled out against the storm.

"Screw'em," Frank said. "Fire when you got a bead on'm."

"What if Blackbeard's on the ship?" Mary voiced.

There was a flash from the U-boat, then the wind carried the boom a split second later. An explosive splash erupted just twenty yards off the bow. The concussion and water almost blew Anne off her feet.

"Blast them, Jesse!" she screamed out.

Jesse got a bead on the boat and waited for the *Ward* to settle back in the water after rising from a swell. He fired by triggering the lanyard pull and the gun boomed loudly and recoiled backward due to the force of the explosion. It then returned to its firing position by springs allowing the breech to be fast-loaded again.

Anne watched as the U-boat was slammed by Jesse's shot. The port side of the ship's bow exploded in a blast of fire and metal.

"Good shoot'n, brother!" Frank called out.

The second deck-gun manned by Stanton and his crew fired a round, scoring a hit on the U-boat's forward twin 2-cm Flak 30 rendering it useless and killing the two men manning the anti-aircraft gun.

The German's SK C/32 fired round after round at the *Ward* scoring several hits to the deck and the hull.

Anne held tight to the railing as the ship lurched to starboard and the winds and ocean swell became hurricane force.

Black Caesar was inspecting the damage done by the hits, but luckily the fires were quickly squelched by the driving rain.

"Ship!" Tom screamed out.

Caesar swiveled his head in the direction of the boy's cry. Tom was frantically pointing at the starboard side from his position midship. He followed Tom's finger and saw a huge shadow closing in on them. It was the outline of the *Queen Anne's Revenge*, and it was pivoting on its towline to collide with the *Ward*.

Caesar burst into action, brushing past Vane as he raced to reach Tom. "Get away, boy!" he boomed to be heard over the torrential winds.

Roberts screamed at him from the upper deck. "Cut lines! Cut her loose before she wrecks us!"

Caesar knew Roberts was right. He gave up the chase to help the boy and headed to the stern to release the *Ward*'s hold on the *Queen Anne*.

Tom watched Blackbeard's ship rapidly approaching. It was seconds from ramming them. It spun on its keel to smack against the hull on its starboard side as the towline reached its limit. He knew that Black Caesar was rushing to disconnect the two ships and that the safest thing to do was get the hell out of the way, but then who would man the ship? There was no one on board at the moment and the *Queen Anne's Revenge* would be lost without anyone at the wheel. He gritted his teeth and climbed up the railing to set his feet at the top. He crouched with one hand holding the metal and the other reaching in preparation.

Black Caesar slid on the wet surface to arrive at the stern. He worked desperately to disengage the towline. Vane arrived to lend him a hand.

"Faster, man!" Vane yelled at him and started to help.

"I've got it. Go make sure the boy's safe!"

"We'll all be dead if we don't cut this line!"

The line was released, and it snapped away from them to spiral into the sea. The two men fell backwards from the recoil.

The sound of the storm and the firing of guns was then overpowered by a resounding bang. They fell over and rolled on the deck as the entire ship rocked from the impact of the frigate crashing into the destroyer.

Black Caesar was immediately on his feet and running toward where Tom had stood. He could see the *Queen Anne* careening away from the destroyer. She still looked intact but, in the darkness and the rain, it was difficult to perceive her damage.

"Tom! Tom!" he cried out. He couldn't see any sign of the boy. He reached the railing and spun in place, searching. He leaned over to scan the turbulent sea but didn't spot the boy in the water. "Tom!" he screamed out, the wind swallowing his calls.

Looff watched through the periscope as the destroyer collided with the wooden tall ship. The impact sent them moving in opposite directions. He had ordered a torpedo to be fired just seconds ago and now the damn target was not where she was a moment ago. He knew the torpedo would pass harmlessly. The storm and damage from the enemy's guns were wreaking havoc on their ability to sink their ship. The tide was so strong that they were getting pulled out from their position at the headland ridge. Their engines were running at capacity to keep the bow facing the destroyer so they could continue their onslaught of munitions. One hull-breaching hit from a torpedo would end this encounter for good.

Colette hung on to the mounted bunk as she gathered up her meager belongings. She helped Woodes do the same, both putting on their boots and shoes.

"A hurricane, it has to be."

Colette nodded her agreement. "Out of the frying pan and into the fire once again for us. I wish to never set foot on a boat again if I survive this."

Woodes took her hand and squeezed it. "Survive you will. If it's the last breath I take, you have my word."

She returned the squeeze. "We both will."

They were knocked off balance by a blast rocking the hull. There was yelling and shouting throughout the ship. Looff's voice could be heard barking commands to his crew.

"Is it time?" she asked.

"We do this, and I don't know what we'll be throwing ourselves into," he answered with concern.

She nodded. "We don't have any other options."

Woodes gave a sign of agreement.

She stood and looked down the corridor. There were men steady at their stations and a few tending to steaming and smoking leaks and damage.

"Make ready," she said then casually set off for the ladder leading below.

Philip, Müller and Hildebrandt untangled their bodies and gingerly rose to their feet. Müller scrambled to his flashlight a few feet away and spun it around to illuminate the room. His light stopped on the tall figure of Thatch, grin attached to his face as he held Hildebrandt's Luger P08.

"What a fine adventure that was, me hearties," he said with a chuckle.

Hildebrandt stiffened, hands slowly rising.

Philip knelt and retrieved Hildebrandt's flashlight and shined it around the room. "My God," he whispered.

Thatch glanced to see what caught his attention and was stunned by the glimmers of light and luster sparkling in the beam of the handheld lamp. In one corner of the mud-strewn chamber lay an enormous treasure trove spilling out of rotted wood crates and chests. Most of the containers were nothing but rusted fragments after the centuries-old wood had disintegrated from the moisture and termites eating away at the lumber. Thousands upon thousands of coins glittered wet in the mud, unmistakably the Pirate Republic currency Hildebrandt had flaunted weeks before.

Hildebrandt's breath quickened, eyes devouring the sight. His hand slid to the silver cross at his chest, fingertips trembling. Could its twin be buried just steps away? Reverence drowned out fear. Forgetting the pistol pointed at him, he drifted forward, drawn like a moth to flame.

Thatch too had his eyes mesmerized by the prize.

Müller seized the opportunity. His rifle was several feet away, but his pistol was still stored in the holster on his hip. In one swift move he tore it free. Thatch whipped toward him, the Luger snapping up, but Müller already had Philip yanked tight against his chest, pistol barrel pressed to the scientist's temple.

"Drop it!" Müller yelled out.

Thatch took a step forward and turned his body to make a smaller target while aiming at Müller's large head.

"I'll kill him where he stands," said Müller.

"Aye. Then I kill you," rumbled Thatch.

The cavern rang with their standoff, heavy breathing and dripping water the only sounds.

Hildebrandt ignored the standoff, transfixed by the riches. He approached the piles and began rifling through the mounds, searching. He pulled piles of coins looking for the Sacred Lotus Twin of Goa, but no jewels, adornments or relics were present. His heart was pounding, frustration building as he realized the treasure only consisted of coins, *thousands of accursed golden coins.*

"Drop your weapon now!" roared Müller.

"You drop yours," Thatch said evenly and took another step toward Müller, increasing his chance of scoring with his first shot.

Müller jerked Philip back a pace, crouching low, using the smaller man as a shield.

"Mr. Thatch…" Philip stammered, terror rattling his voice.

"Don't worry, Mr. Albert, 'tis an easy shot." Thatch gently started to squeeze the trigger.

The two warring ships had begun to circle each other just off the island's northern tip. The sea was the cause of the dance. It churned and rotated with each in its grasp. Their engines roared and their screws toiled to break free from the current. Their gun crews paid no heed to their predicament, firing round after round, attempting to score the winning hit against their adversary.

The wind, along with the rise and fall of the heavy seas, complicated their aim. Roberts barked out orders but his inexperience with this craft and its abilities harmed their position. The *Ward* had begun to slowly spin on its axis. The effect reduced the accuracy of the two deck-guns causing frustration in the crew.

"Give up the seat, you horse-riding bilge rat!" screamed Mary.

Jesse was unable to score a hit in the last several minutes and his arms were growing weary adding to his poor aiming ability.

Frank grabbed his arm. "Let her in, Jesse! She might actually hit somethin' other than the sea," he yelled at his brother.

Reluctantly, Jesse leaped out of the seat and immediately Mary was situated in his place spinning the wheels to target the U-boat. Anne stumbled her way to help them continue loading. She and Frank called out the distance and heading to help Mary adjust her target.

CLANG!

The U-boat's forward-mounted gun scored a glancing blow on one of the *Ward*'s smokestacks, ripping off the top portion in a spray of metal and shrapnel.

Mary desperately lined up her target and fired, holding her breath during the second it took for her round to cross the distance.

BOOM!

The U-boat's forward deck-gun exploded, sending a blast of fire, twisted metal and body parts flying across the deck and into the sea.

Anne cheered and slapped Mary's leg in celebration.

"God damn, woman! I think I'm in love," Frank called out.

"Get in line, landlubber," Anne quipped.

Mary smiled and barked out an order. "Don't just stand there, you lily milkmaids, load me up!"

The three laughed and chambered another round for her.

While at another deck-gun, Stanton ordered Brockman and Kent to load the last round available to them. The storm they were caught in was like nothing they'd ever seen. The three men were soaked to the bone and only adrenaline was keeping their muscles moving.

"That's it!" Kent yelled over the wind. Brockman called out directions for Stanton as the ensign expertly navigated the barrel to target the U-boat by operating the wheels gripped in his hands.

Mary was also targeting, hand on the trigger mechanism.

The two gun crews fired their .50-caliber cannons at the same moment, just as the *Ward* tilted starboard, raising the port-facing barrels higher in the air then intended. Their munitions easily cleared the top of the U-boat and continued past, sizzling the air on their way to the cliff face just beyond at the tip of the island. The dual impact blasted the middle of the rock bluff with a huge explosion that sent shockwaves reverberating for half a mile inland.

The earth quaked violently underneath their feet and over their heads. Thatch pulled the trigger as a shockwave resounded through the chamber, and they all struggled to keep their footing. His pistol barked loudly, the sound echoing off the cavern walls followed by a ricochet as the round skipped off one rock to a second, then sizzled through the flesh of Thatch's thigh.

Müller took aim at Thatch the same instant, but the wounded man bent in pain causing the bullet to miss him completely. Philip struck out behind him connecting with Müller's ribs just hard enough to enable him to dive away from the Nazi.

Thatch twisted and took aim at Müller, firing two wild rounds as the man bolted to the side. The two men circled each other firing round after round as they moved and dodged from each other's shots.

Dirt and rock began to rain down into the chamber. One wall and the ceiling were beginning to crumble.

Philip ducked and wove around the room trying to escape the reckless bullets of the two shooters.

Hildebrandt, obsessed with searching for the treasure, cried out in frustration. "Where is it? Damn you, you bastard! Where is it!" He stood from his rummaging and turned to Thatch as he was shuffling by firing his pistol. "Where is the twin, you pirate bastard?" he screamed.

Müller in his own rage fired the last round from his pistol at Thatch but it ripped through his jacket to pass by and sliced through Hildebrandt's chest—ripping its way through rib, bone, lung tissue, then out the other side.

Thatch heard the click of Müller's pistol hammer and steadied himself. Müller looked at Thatch with anger and defeat and readied himself for the end. Thatch took several steps closer, no longer feeling pain from his own bullet-grazed leg. He aimed at the German's massive chest and pulled the trigger.

CLICK.

Müller smiled and leaped at Thatch. The two men grappled with each other, and Thatch repeatedly slammed the butt of the Luger against Müller's head and shoulder. The heavier man was in a fury and had Thatch in a bear hug trying to squeeze the life from the pirate.

Philip looked around not knowing how to help and saw that Hildebrandt was shot and hurting but scrambling to reach the lone automatic rifle that Müller had lost. Philip made a dash to get it first.

All around them the earth continued to quake. Dust was filling the air and the flashlights rolled around in the muck of the floor, casting shadows and making it difficult to see.

Philip and Hildebrandt reached the MP 43 at the same time. Hildebrandt outweighed Philip by thirty or more pounds but in his injured condition he struggled to overpower the small scientist. The right side of the room collapsed and opened to a chasm that fell into an underground river. They fought for control of the rifle, each holding the stock and barrel with both hands. Hildebrandt had his finger on the trigger and started to win the battle by pushing the muzzle closer and closer to Philip's head. A smile was creeping onto the Nazi's face.

"It is over, little man, you are weak," he taunted.

Philip pushed with all his might, but the black eye of the rifle inched closer to his head.

Philip let one hand slip away from the rifle and wrapped his fingers around the chilled metal of the sacred cross hanging from Hildebrandt's neck. He tilted the end and stabbed it into Hildebrandt's injured chest.

Agony shot through Hildebrandt's body causing him to convulse and lose his breath. Philip used his whole body to twist the rifle from his hands. Hildebrandt bent over in pain, letting the gun drop from his fingers. Philip held tight to the cross and it slipped over the Nazi's head as he stumbled back away from Philip.

He slung the cross around his own neck and gripped the rifle in both hands. He took aim at Hildebrandt as the man held his chest and backed away. Philip closed his eyes as he pulled the trigger. The rifle, in Philips unconditioned hands, was set for automatic firing and it barked out a dozen rounds in just over a second. The recoil sent the barrel waving wildly in his hands and he struggled to keep control as the powerful weapon pushed him back.

Two bullets exploded into Hildebrandt, and he flew backwards into the open chasm. The rest of the rounds bit into the ceiling and caused more damage to the already crumbling chamber.

Thatch was losing his breath as Müller squeezed tighter. He had lost his grip on the pistol and resorted to his fists when assaulting the iron-muscled Nazi. Their faces were close together and Thatch again smelled the foul onion-fragranced breath.

"Damn your rotten breath!" He tilted his head back in desperation and then slammed it forward to smash his forehead into the Müller's nose. The effect was instantaneous—the man's face was awash with blood, eyes watering and throbbing pain shooting through his head. He released Thatch and staggered backward, hands going to his face, Müller bent over while blood ran through his fingers.

Thatch stood and tried to catch his breath. Philip paced closer, rifle held at his hip, aiming the muzzle at Müller. Philip pulled the trigger, but nothing happened, the trigger seemed locked. He looked over the stock and trigger guard, finding a switch that he must have engaged unintentionally.

Müller made a guttural sound and turned to charge at them. His face was a horror with blood streaming down the sides of his mouth from his ruined nose, eyes already black and bloodshot from Thatch's blow.

Philip practically jumped out of his skin and fumbled his fingers to disengage the safety lock.

"Mr. Albert," Thatch said in warning.

Philip felt the click as the trigger lock switched to automatic fire, and he abruptly pulled the trigger of a gun for the second time in his life. The barrel moved sporadically as Philip held the stock and the trigger with all his might. He struggled to keep his eyes open, and they just told him that Müller kept running toward him without stopping. He realized after more than thirty rounds had been dispensed that the muzzle was pointing at the ceiling as he had lost control of the weapon.

KRRAA-KROOM!

The ceiling, riddled with bullets, suddenly crumbled and crashed in front of him to bury Müller in a pile of rocks and dirt.

"That's one way to do it, Mr. Albert," Thatch said in jest.

Philip sighed with relief. "Always my plan, really."

Thatch ignored him and looked around the room. The stability of the walls and ceiling were still in question. He approached the treasure hoard, and the rocks began to groan loudly.

"We need to leave here, immediately," murmured Philip nervously. He'd seen what cave-ins could do, how fast stone could turn into a tomb.

"And where shall we go?" Thatch picked up a fistful of Levasseur's coins and stepped into the light from the single flashlight still illuminating the room from the floor. He pocketed a few and held one up to the light, gold spilling between his fingers in a glittering cascade. "You did well, Buzzard. I must say I enjoyed your little games. Not as much as I'll enjoy spending your plunder," he mused to himself.

Philip looked around for a way out. He approached the edge of the raw fissure on the right side of the room. It was too dark to see far but twenty or so feet down he thought he could make out water flowing. He could hear it, he was sure. He turned to retrieve the flashlight in hopes of seeing a way down into the chasm but stopped as he watched a section of the ceiling tremor, dust sifting down. A jagged crack split open above Thatch's head.

"Move!" Philip screamed out.

Thatch had only a split second to look up and see what was about to happen. He took one long stride forward than leaped through the air at Philip. Thatch's body crashed into Philip's, carrying them both over the edge. Together they vanished into the abyss as the treasure and the chamber dissolved in ruin behind them.

CHAPTER 35 – TIME'S UP

Men rushed through the corridors, passageways and hatches as Colette glided through the U-boat. She was hell-bent on ending the career of this damned ship and its captain. Water leaks sprang from every corner and every pipe junction. Steam washed through the deck in streaming clouds of hot mist. The ship was pummeled by whatever force was attacking them. Looff had said it was a US warship, but the truth was it didn't matter to Colette. Her path was clear. She would trigger Philip's improvised explosive device and race to get captain Rogers off this ship before she sent them all to the bottom.

Looff had gone topside to see the damage his ship had taken. His calls for the guns to continue firing at the destroyer had gone unanswered. He stood on the ladder, half out in the storm to see his ship as well as his enemy caught in a whirling current several hundred yards away from each other. He glanced fore and aft to see the destruction that had been caused to his deck-guns. They were all in ruins due to direct hits from his foe's ordnance. The sound of cannon fire had ceased and he could see men rushing around the American ship.

He set his jaw and vowed to send them to the bottom of the sea.

There had been no word from his torpedo room after they had reported a malfunction that was yet to be resolved. *There are four damn tubes, how could they all be disabled?* He slid down the ladder and ordered his helmsman to keep the bow facing the destroyer. The man griped that he was doing his best, but the current was having its way with the ship.

Looff strode confidently through the passageways, unwilling to run. He would not show fear or concern to any crewmen that he passed. He barely glanced at the berth where the prisoners were kept but he noticed that only Rogers remained, and his face presented a worried look when their eyes met.

"Where's the girl?"

Woodes didn't answer but he gathered his strength to rise to his feet.

Looff looked nervously around. *What was she up to?* Now he was quick on his feet. He swung down the ladder and raced toward the torpedo room. He saw her climbing and standing on a pipe to reach something.

He could see the torpedo room open and three men moving one of the projectiles into the loading tube. *Good, they finally are ready to launch.*

Colette clung to the U-boat's pipework, struggling not to lose her grip as the vessel pitched violently. The ill-fitting German uniform tugged at her shoulders, but worse were the dainty heels from 1873 still strapped to her feet. The sailors hadn't had shoes small enough for her, so she'd been left clattering about in her bare feet. Her own delicate pair were utterly useless on steel decking. Every slip reminded her they were made for ballroom floors, not war machines. Her nerves crackled, and she managed a dark little joke to herself: *What kind of fool packs evening wear to travel through time?*

She kicked off the shoes and pushed herself higher to reach the kitchen clock Edward had placed in the ductwork. She saw the timer and its wire protruding from the back; she could see that it threaded through a hole in the bulkhead to the torpedo room. Even though the hatch was open, the gap was narrow enough that she was unseen by the men working to launch one of the propelled bombs. Her hand reached to grab the clock but before her fingers touched, she was abruptly yanked from her perch. She fell to the floor without a hint of grace, banging her hip painfully.

Looff loomed over her, his face twisted in anger. He screamed at her in German, words she didn't comprehend. He kicked her twice in the side and she curled into a fetal position to protect herself.

One of the torpedo men stepped out of the hatchway to see what the matter was, maybe to lend a hand, but he paused in his steps when Looff shot him a dark look.

"Destroy that ship or I will drown you myself!" he ordered the man. The sailor turned on his heels and went back to the gun crew to help prepare the torpedo.

Looff had no idea what Colette was up to, but he knew her plan was to interfere in some way with the torpedoes. He reached in and pulled the hatch shut to prevent anyone from entering the room.

He picked her up by the hair and slammed her against the closed torpedo room door.

"What mischief are you trying to cause, harlot?"

Colette spat in his face.

He wiped the spittle from his cheek and his eyes narrowed at her. He brought his hand back to strike her, but he was barreled over by Woodes from behind.

Colette was knocked away as the men grappled with each other. She quickly rose to her feet and climbed back up into the corner of the deck head. She reached the timer and twisted the knob to the agreed-upon ten minutes but thought better of it as she glanced back to see the two captains trading blows and wrestling on the metal deck. She carefully eased the dial to reset the timer while she steadied her trembling hand, hearing Philip's calm, precise voice in her memory: *When the hand strikes zero, the striker closes the circuit. The current hits the cap, the cap hits the charge—and then the warhead will do the rest.* She swallowed hard and left it at three minutes, unsure of the accuracy of the device.

She turned and leapt down to the deck, landing light on her feet. Ahead, Woodes and Looff were already grappling again—Captain Rogers' scarred hands locked tight around the German's throat.

Looff snarled, braced, and drove his boot up hard into Woodes' gut.

The blow hurled Rogers backward, ripping his grip loose. He slammed to the deck with a heavy clatter.

Before Looff could press forward, Colette rushed in. She swung the only weapon she had—her delicate heel—cracking it across the side of his head.

For a fleeting moment she imagined the point of her heel punching through the German's skull. But it wasn't to be. Looff staggered, shook off the daze, and turned with fury. His backhand came down like a hammer, smashing her across the face and sending her crashing into the steel bulkhead.

The impact rang in her skull, but she clawed back up on all fours, forcing air into her lungs. Across from her, Woodes was struggling up as well, battered but unbroken.

Looff straightened, rolling his shoulders, his breath ragged but his eyes burning with rage. He was readying for another attack.

Woodes looked sternly at Colette. "Go. Now, lass. Go!" he shouted at her.

Colette looked at him with concern and faltered with indecision.

"It is my fate," he said with renewed strength in his voice. "I welcome it."

Colette nodded and hesitated only for an instant as the two men squared off. She raced to the ladder and up to the next deck.

Woodes saw her disappear from view out of the corner of his eye. Looff stepped lightly and flexed his fingers as he made fists with his hands.

"What was she plotting, Captain Rogers?"

Woodes didn't take his eyes off him. He was barely on his feet, and his breath was ragged. He wanted to save every breath so that Colette could escape the death trap.

There was no room for circling or flanking. Each could either move toward their opponent or away. Neither was in the mood to give ground. They both lunged forward and struck out with blows. The two men had spent their adult life in worlds of violence and now they were certain this bout would end in death for one of them. Each was determined that it would be their adversary.

Colette raced through the ship passing sailors that knew nothing of what was happening below outside the torpedo room. Some of the sailors even showed manners and concern as she pushed by them on her way to the ladder that would lead to the top deck. She arrived outside Looff's quarters and a glance into the tiny space brought to her eye a relic that belonged to Thatch. She corrected herself as she darted in to confiscate it. It was the single-shot Derringer pistol that Thatch purchased for his cabin boy. Edward had squirreled it away in his sleeve since he had offered himself to Woodes in exchange for her release. That seemed like a lifetime ago.

She took the pistol and checked to see if it was loaded and confirmed the single round snug in the chamber. She shoved it deep in her pocket and tried to calculate how long it had been since she set the timer. Had it only been two or had those minutes passed?

She paid no attention to the sailors on duty in the pilot house manning the ship, trying to keep her afloat and moving. She knew where the life vests were kept and wrapped one in her arm. Colette climbed the ladder nimbly with her bare feet. One of the sailors shouted after her but she twisted the wheel on the hatch and swung it open and burst out from the interior of the U-boat.

She rolled against the water-drenched deck to find herself in the middle of a hurricane. She stumbled to the side amongst the tortured metal of the equipment and workings that had been damaged in the battle while she was below. Her hand grabbed onto the railing to allow her to gaze out upon the sea and the island nearby.

Her heart sank at the familiar motion of the sea they were caught in. It was the giant whirlpool that had swallowed them up in 1873. It was shallow at the moment, like it was just getting started, but she clearly remembered how it grew into a massive maw.

The sea spray stung her face as she saw the American destroyer that must have battled them directly across caught in the turbulence as well.

She heard and felt the launching of a torpedo from below the bow where she stood. She looked out and the projectile shot into view. It blasted through the swells and waves on its path to the other ship.

She heard a ringing in her ears, or imagined it more likely. Time was up. She leaped over the railing and into the roiling sea.

Woodes was taking a beating from Looff. He knew quickly that it was a fight he had no hope of winning. He just determined to drag it out for as long as his sick and damaged body could last. Finally, he was struck hard enough that he crumpled to the ground and turned over to see Looff, blood oozing from his lip, hovering above him.

Woodes had no strength to rise. He scooted back to rest against the bulkhead and started to chuckle to himself.

Looff stared at Woodes and considered finishing the man off with his booted heel. *Why was he laughing?* His mind flashed back to the woman climbing into the corner. *What had she been doing when he found her?* He turned away from Rogers and stepped over to where she had been perched. His eyes roamed the ductwork and pipes. *There.* He saw something hidden in the corner. He stepped up on a conduit to get a better look. His brow knitted in confusion. *A kitchen timer?* The hand ticked to zero and the buzzer rang.

CHAPTER 36 – VORTEX

Roberts screamed at the helmsman to get the ship under control. Charlotte even threatened the man with her kukri, but the ship wouldn't steer. They were locked in position with their bow facing the U-boat's bow across the swirling sea. They had used up the deck-gun's munitions and were unable to launch torpedoes at something dead ahead of them.

All this new technology at his fingertips and Roberts could do nothing but try to maneuver the ship for a broadside attack. Just like the cannons from his era, the torpedo tubes were mounted like cannon on each beam, port and starboard, located on the main deck amidships.

He stomped out into the fray with Charlotte and Miriam on his heels. The wind whipped their clothes and hair. The rain drenched them instantly.

"We need to escape the storm's grasp," yelled Charlotte.

"I know, love," Roberts answered as he descended to the main deck. "If you have an idea, don't be shy."

"We can't stay here. The fight is over." She grasped Roberts' shoulders. "We have enough treasure in our hold. Leave Blackbeard and the Buzzard's prize to their fates."

"Aye. You have the right of course," Roberts said with a nod. He looked around the deck of the *Ward* with renewed hope in his eyes. "If we break the storm's grasp and sail free, we'll need a new name for her."

Charlotte planted a soft kiss on his lips and whispered to him, "I trust you to choose a good one."

They were interrupted by the arrival of Anne, Mary and the James brothers.

"Isn't this ship powerful enough to break free of this horror?" Anne asked with an aggressive push to Roberts' chest, insinuating it was his fault.

"Back away, whore," Charlotte said putting the tip of her blade beneath Anne's chin.

Jesse and Frank quick as lightning drew their pistols to point at Charlotte and Roberts.

"Enough! We have to work together if we are to survive this ordeal," put in Miriam.

"The sea has us. We are running the engines at full power," said Roberts.

"It's the storm of time," Caesar said as he and Vane arrived to stand with them in the wind and rain.

Mary looked out at the growing vortex. Her blood ran cold as she understood what Caesar was saying. They were trapped again. She looked at the big African with concern. "Where is Tom?"

Caesar's eyes watered even in the face of the rain. "Lost."

Mary's face went white. "What? How?"

"When the *Queen Anne* struck the ship."

Mary couldn't hold in her emotions for the boy's loss. She pounded her fist on Caesar's chest. "How could you let that happen? Damn you!" Anger and grief raged inside her and she rushed to the railing to cry.

Frank watched her go and felt himself choking up. He hung his head then crossed to comfort her. Caesar watched her for a moment and the group mourned their young crewmate while the storm raged on. Caesar turned and walked off into the darkness.

Mary buried her head in Frank's chest as she cried for a moment. She raised her head to look at him and he gave her a forlorn smile. She turned her head to the sea, watching the distant ship across the swirling divide.

Lightning illuminated the water, and something caught her eye churning through the sea at them. Sorrow drained from her to be replaced by fear.

"Fish in the water!" she screamed out and pointed.

The group turned to see her pointing and rushed to the railing to see for themselves. Halfway between the two ships was the metallic projectile churning through the sea, cutting its way to deliver its payload to the *Ward*'s hull.

"What do we do?" stuttered out Miriam.

"If you're a Christian you stand and pray," said Vane.

"I'm a Jew…"

Vane looked down at her. "Then we run."

They turned as a tribe and sprinted away from the port side railing along with Stanton and his mates. They all saw it coming and even though there was no escape, they wanted nothing more than to put some distance between themselves and the deadly torpedo.

A flash and explosion lit up the sky, but it wasn't from their ship.

In the pilot house Francis watched as the U-boat exploded from within. The bow of the ship lurched out of the water, blasting apart in a fireball of molten metal, oil and flesh. The ship slammed down to the surface and the sea rushed into the open hull to claim its prize.

Philip and Thatch struggled in the rushing water to claim a gulp of air each time they miraculously surfaced in the underground river. Thatch had his feet in front of him the best he could, and hoped Philip was doing the same. He didn't have a moment to worry about the man's well-being as he was consumed with keeping himself alive.

There was no light anywhere. It was like he was completely blind, and his sense of movement was only present when his limbs scraped or slapped into something in the way, like rocks and reefs or possibly a scientist.

He felt Philip's hand grab the sleeve of his jacket after they collided with each other. They suddenly were airborne for a moment, and he realized they had just fallen over a waterfall below the surface of the island. *How far shall I fall?* Before he could answer his own question, Thatch was abruptly dropped into another body of water sweeping him away.

Thatch realized that the water was salty on his lips as he held tight to the breath in his lungs. He tried to swim to the surface, but he wasn't sure which direction was up. He let his limbs float limp for a moment and felt his body rise as he was pulled along the current. He now knew which direction was up and he started paddling again to reach the air. His fingers raked against the smooth surface of rock and his mind reeled as he understood he was now trapped in an underwater tunnel. His lungs started to burn as they starved for air. Swimming against the current wasn't an option, so he paddled and kicked to speed his journey along.

He slowly let out the remaining air in his chest and his eyes started to perceive shapes in the murk. There was a circle of dim light ahead where he was rapidly headed. He stroked his arms with all the strength left in his body and shot out of the tunnel into the ocean. He kicked and stroked to reach the surface. His lungs burned and he set his jaw to keep the water from flowing into his mouth. The sea was doing its damnedest to drown him once again. He wouldn't allow it; he must make it to the surface. His fingers clawed at the air before his head broke the water. He gulped in huge amounts before a wave crashed over him.

The sea was still angry with him, he saw. *Livid*, he corrected himself. Thatch took in another breath before diving back under the storm to search for Philip. He swam down and found the man flailing about, trying desperately to surface. He saw him swallow water and begin to choke. Thatch grabbed the back of the man's shirt and swam to the surface.

He pulled Philip into his arms and floated on his back with the man on top of him. He hammered his chest to expel the water and Philip coughed and threw up water from his lungs and the contents of his stomach. Thatch cradled Philip's chest in one arm and rode over the swells, searching his surroundings in the heavy surf and poor light.

"Boat," Philip said in a hoarse voice.

"I know we need a boat, you nit, but we're in the middle of the sea," he answered gruffly. The statement wasn't entirely true, Thatch conceded, as he could see the rocks and cliff face a quarter of a mile away from them. Swimming directly back in that direction would likely reward them with a smashing death on the rocks in this storm. The rock face that looked so much like a pigeon was now a craggy hole of blasted-out rock as if it had been hit by a giant cannon ball. He reasoned that that was the cause of their cave-in. The structure of the cliff face and underwater outcropping must be a web of tunnels and caverns winding under the water as well as the landmass. La Buse had chosen his hiding spot well. *To hell with the Buzzard.* His trickery almost claimed his life again. His legend had finally been buried under the earth along with his treasure.

"Boat," Philip croaked again.

"Mr. Albert, are we going…" Thatch halted his rebuke and followed Philip's pointed finger to see a small rubber boat just twenty yards away.

"Can you swim?"

"I can try," Philip answered and slipped out of Thatch's grasp. The two men swam their way through the rough sea and reached the boat. It was one of the Germans' that they used to paddle to the island.

Thatch helped Philip into the craft and started to pull himself aboard when the sea near them lit up with a flash of light followed by an explosion.

Philip pulled Thatch all the way into the boat and they both sat up to see what had happened. Thatch's heart immediately quickened as he worried about Colette. They could see it was the U-boat as its hull crashed into the water after being lifted up in the air from the blast.

Thatch grabbed the oars and forced one into Philip's hands and started to paddle toward the wreckage. He silently made a promise to Poseidon that he'd be a model sailor if the god would protect Colette from drowning aboard that hated ship.

KAAA-BAAM!

Another explosion lit up the storming skies further away. Philip stood up to get a look at the second eruption that shot up into the heavens. He almost lost his balance and would have toppled overboard had Thatch not pulled him down as a wave crashed over the side of their little boat.

He turned to Thatch with a confused look. "Another ship just exploded."

"Not our concern. Keep a sharp eye out for Colette and Woodes."

Philip nodded and did his best to aid Thatch in rowing the craft toward where the U-boat drifted, wrecked and sinking. He watched as the ship's location was quickly looking like it would pass them by before they arrived. It could not be under power in its condition, yet it was moving fast.

Thatch must have been having the same thoughts because he said, "She must be caught in a current."

Lightning flashed in the sky and Philip stood again, pointing. Thatch grabbed him again, forcing him to sit before he was swept overboard.

"I see her!" he exclaimed and pointed at a bobbing form in the water.

"Aye! Paddle, Mr. Albert, paddle!"

Colette raised her hand as she crested a swell, and she kicked her feet and swam toward the little boat. She was caught in the movement of the building whirlpool and worried that she would be swept past them. She struggled against the current pulling her away.

Philip leaned far over the rubber railing to hold his oar out for Colette to grasp as they approached. Thatch paddled madly to keep the boat near her. Her fingers touched the tip of the wooden oar, but she wasn't able to get a grip. It was slipping away, and she fought her way out of the life vest to be able to swim unencumbered. It would either save her life or doom her to drown in these treacherous waters.

Thatch dug the oar deep into the sea and pulled with all the strength he had. Colette kicked as her head went under and stretched her hand out as she submerged under a wave. Philip reached out as far as he could without going over himself and he saw her disappear in the water. He plunged the oar beneath the wave and felt resistance to the length of the paddle. He pulled the oar toward him, hand over hand and Colette's fingers appeared wrapped around the end of the wooden blade.

"I've got her," he hollered.

Thatch gave a final pull on the sea then launched himself next to Philip to use his long arms to grasp Colette. Her head surfaced, hair darkened by the water plastered to her face. Thatch pulled her from the water with renewed strength, and she fell into his arms. He brushed her locks from her eyes, took her head in his hands and kissed her deeply.

She coughed when his lips disengaged. "A moment, my love, I nearly drowned." She expelled more water as Thatch laughed gently, holding her.

"Aye love, nearly."

Philip sat back against the rigid rubber side and caught his breath, watching the touching reunion. Suddenly an arm was around his throat strangling him and pulling him over the side.

The boat rocked and Philip screamed out in alarm. Thatch turned in shock to see the bloody face of Müller rising out the water as he grappled with Philip. Müller was trying to climb into the boat while fighting to throw Philip overboard. Thatch picked up an oar and swung it down on Müller's shoulder, narrowly missing Philip's head. The strike connected with a loud crack and Müller's grip slipped on Philip's throat, but his fingers caught the necklace attached to the Sacred Lotus Twin of Goa that still hung from his neck. Müller pulled it tight, again choking Philip as the scientist tried to get his fingers between the chain and his skin.

Thatch swung the paddle again at Müller but the Nazi grabbed it in his large hand and pushed it away, sending Thatch off balance and over the side of the craft, splashing into the churning sea.

With Thatch gone Müller twisted the slack of the necklace in his hand and tightened the chain like a noose. Philip's eyes began to bulge, and his vision blurred.

BLAAAM!

Colette crouched over Philip, the Derringer in her hand smoking from the discharge. The tension on Philip's neck loosened and he twisted out from the necklace, the chain slipping over his head. He turned in time to see Müller gripping the cross in his hand as he sank under the water, a round hole visible in his forehead. The water around him turned red before he disappeared below.

They heard a cry from the other side of the boat and turned to see Thatch swimming his way toward them, but the current was still pulling them along at a fast clip.

"Edward!" Colette said with alarm.

"I'm here, love. Give me a hand," he called out.

"Edward! Behind you!" she called out as a large looming shadow rose in his wake.

Anne picked herself up off the deck and saw Jesse wipe blood from his nose having been slammed against the metal surface. She held her hand out and he gratefully took it, and she helped him rise to his feet. The storm raved on, but the ship felt different than before.

The impact of the torpedo had lifted the bow into the air and spun the ship one hundred-eighty degrees and the screws under full power had propelled the *Ward* away from the swirling vortex. Anne limped toward the stern, quickening her pace as she went. Jesse followed her. As they made their way, they passed Mary in the process of wrapping Frank's bleeding leg with a ripped sleeve of her shirt. He was smiling at her as she worked. Charlotte stood by Bart Roberts as he gave orders to a group of sailors gathered around him. He pointed to different areas of the ship, sending them on their tasks. The wind carried his voice away before she could hear what he was saying.

Anne's eyes met Charlotte's and the two women engaged in an unspoken argument that left no victor, just a stay until it would be resumed at a later date.

Further on she spotted Black Caesar sitting hunched over, head in his hands, Vane sitting quietly next to him trying to light a cigarette in the rain.

She turned as Jesse slipped his hand around hers and she smiled at him. Maybe the ship's hull was breached by the torpedo, but for now there were no fires on the metal ship and she'd seen several tenders still safely stowed about the main deck. The destroyer was still trudging away from the center of the tempest as they reached the aft gunwale. Jesse pointed into the night as lighting continued to light up the sky.

There, circling the outer edges of the swirling vortex, was a three-masted pirate ship.

"Well, I'll be damned," Anne said under her breath.

"She's just a ghost ship, taken wherever the current pushes her," said Jesse.

She watched the shadowy ship circle the whirlpool. A smile crept to her lips. The mizzenmast had a single sail set, giving someone steerage and influence of the bow's swing—should there actually be someone on deck to control the rudder.

Anne Bonny and Jesse James watched the *Queen Anne's Revenge* spiral down below the lip of the whirlpool.

Thatch looked over his shoulder as the hull of the *Queen Anne's Revenge* overtook his position. How it had arrived here was a mystery he would need to solve later.

He rose alongside it as they were lifted by a large swell. He trod water as he gazed up at her magnificent woodwork and ornamentation. He, it and the German rubber boat were being pulled along at a brisk pace, though his pirate ship seemed to be gaining speed. He searched for a way to reach her deck but her sleek hull offered no such access.

He was wary of being sucked underneath the ship and started to swim away toward Colette and Philip when a rope ladder dropped to splash just yards from him. He looked up but saw no sign of who dropped it down to him.

A quick couple of strokes brought him within grasping range. He wrapped the crook of his arm on one rung and waved Philip over. Colette reached out with an oar as Philip furiously paddled to keep pace. Thatch took hold of the oar's end and pulled them close. He held the boat steady while Colette started climbing up the rungs. Philip went next and Thatch let go of the little boat, watching it spin away into their wake. He looked ahead and stared in awe as the *Queen Anne* began to slip down into the maw of the vortex. The wind whipped his long beard and hair as he climbed the ladder, vertigo setting in as the water line rose around him to tower over the vessel. He did a double take as several sharks whizzed by just inside the wall of sea water. He hurried up the last length to leap over the railing and plant his feet on the most comforting of surfaces. Philip and Colette stood, looking exhausted.

Thatch gripped Colette's hand as the deck pitched under them, the whirlpool tearing at the Queen Anne's Revenge with a roar like the earth itself splitting apart. Relief that they had survived this far was dulled by a pang in his chest. Woodes.

"What of Rogers?" His voice was rougher than he intended.

Colette's lips trembled before she answered. "He… he gave himself up. So I could get away."

For a moment, Thatch said nothing. Spray stung his eyes, and he told himself it was only the sea. He looked out at the boiling horizon, though the U-boat was long gone beneath the waves.

"A hard man," he muttered, almost to himself. "Stubborn to the last. I'd have wagered him a snake… yet he met the sea better than most kings."

He fell quiet, jaw tight, and held the rail as the ship lurched toward the vortex.

"Captain!"

Blackbeard turned and found his cabin boy proudly holding out his leather belt, holsters and dual colt .45 pistols. Ignoring the wind and rain he buckled the belt around his waist and snugged the revolvers securely in their pouches. He put his hands on his hips and looked around, the ship empty of any other souls. *How did this one boy sail her to the Isle of France?*

"I see that ye been tak'n good care of her."

Tom's chest puffed out with the compliment.

"Well, truth be told, I haven't much need of a cabin boy no more."

Tom's face visibly fell as Colette and Philip silently watched the exchange.

"Seems what I might need is a solid first mate." Thatch looked around the deck absently than his eyes landed on Tom. "I'd be mightily lucky to have you fill that role, what do you say?"

Tom rushed to Thatch, and they embraced. He looked at Colette and saw her wipe a tear from her eye. Thatch dislodged the boy from him and patted him on the head. "Well met."

The ship lurched and ocean spray peppered the deck with foam.

"I'd ask you how you came to be here, but it seems we're in for another ride, so we'll save that story for later." He turned to address them all. "Follow me, lovelies." He led them to the aft castle and helped them wrap their wrists with rope to be tied to the railing surrounding the helm. He twisted a rope around his own wrist and attached it to the ship's wheel. They all gasped as the *Queen Anne's Revenge* accelerated and the bow began to point into the swirling mist of the vortex, spinning faster and faster as it descended into the abyss.

"Remember to hold your breath! Only Poseidon knows where we'll be spit out!" His laughter rang out as the sea swallowed the ship whole and everything went black.

CHAPTER 37 – PIRACY'S END

1971 Five Miles Southeast of Key West

Thatch opened his eyes to the blinding noon sun, squinting against its glare. Water dripped in fat rivulets from his soaked hair and beard, pooling on the deck beneath him. His back pressed against the sturdy base of the ship's wheel; his wrist was still bound to it. Blinking, he turned his head—and relief flooded him. Colette stirred first, then Philip, and young Tom. All alive.

With a grunt, he slipped free of the tether and rushed to them, kneeling. One by one he loosened their bindings, pressing fingers against throats, feeling the precious rhythm of breath. For Philip, he added a few light slaps across the cheek—half necessity, half for his own amusement.

Colette blinked awake, clutching his arm as he helped her to her feet.

"We're alive," she marveled.

"Don't be too sure," he said gazing into her entrancing eyes. "Feels like heaven to me."

She rose on her toes and kissed him, slow and deep, saltwater still clinging to their lips.

Philip staggered upright on unsteady legs and moved to the rail. The air was thick, heavy with humidity. Below, the sea shimmered in brilliant clarity. Fish darted just a fathom beneath the surface while overhead, gulls wheeled and cried, their shadows cutting across the deck.

On the starboard side, an island broke the horizon. It appeared lush and green, with the faint outline of another just beyond it. Philip narrowed his eyes, mind racing not only over where they'd surfaced, but when. Tom crept beside him, silent as always, until at last he raised a finger skyward.

Philip followed the gesture and froze. Far above, higher than he'd thought man could ever soar, a silver bird of the future cut across the heavens. It dwarfed the planes he'd glimpsed near Hawaii. A chalk-white trail made of cloud marked its wake, thin and perfect against the blue.

Thatch and Colette joined them at the railing, shoulder to shoulder.

"Ah," Thatch said, a rare smile tugging his lips. "The Atlantic. Good to be back in familiar waters."

"How can you be certain it's the Atlantic?" Philip asked.

"A sailor knows, Mr. Albert."

Colette tilted her head, skeptical.

He sighed and pointed. "That isle yonder, the last of the Florida chain. And back that way," he jabbed a thumb over his shoulder, "lies Cuba. Two days' sail at most. But we can't set foot there. Spaniards spy my ship or my handsome face, and we'll have every cannon from Havana to Santiago turned on us."

"That was a long time ago, Edward," she said softly.

He met her eyes, realizing she was right. Time had shifted beneath them all.

With a grunt, Thatch patted his pockets, searching for a cigarette. Finding none, he gave Philip a look.

"The Nazis took them," Philip reminded him.

"Aye. But I was hoping this time magic might have brought them back to me pockets or yours."

"It doesn't work that way."

"And how is it you've become such an expert?"

"I'm not but I've now traveled twice so I'm forming a scientific theory about it."

"Bah." Thatch dismissed his words with a wave of his hand. "I've traveled thrice so I believe I have a better lay of the land, Mr. Albert."

He raised his brows in challenge, but Philip let the matter drop.

"I suppose there will be no more threat of it happening again," said Colette.

Philip and Thatch both turned to her.

"Why's that, lass?"

"The cross," she said. "It's lost off that island in the Indian Ocean. Lying at the bottom of the sea with Karl Müller."

Philip nodded grimly.

"And the other, still with Caesar?" asked Thatch. They turned to Tom.

He looked at each of them before answering. "Black Caesar had it, but then he didn't."

They all stayed silent to let him finish; the boy hardly talked at all, and they didn't want him to stop.

"I asked him where it was. He told me safe, in a safe place, hidden in dear Anne's belly. I think he gave it to Anne to keep."

Thatch thought for a moment than began to laugh. "Ha! Caesar, that clever bastard. Come, follow me to Anne's belly and tell us your tale along the way." He strode off to the stairwell leading below, making a quick stop at his cabin.

When he entered it was in a state of disarray from either the wild journey through the storm of time or the disrespectful rifling that Woodes and Roberts must have given it when they occupied the cabin. *Maybe I should have waited a day or two before promoting my cabin boy*, he thought to himself with a chuckle. His feet squished on the wet carpet as he made his way to the oak desk. Thatch slid the drawer open and searched for his pipe and tinder box while the boy prattled on with his story. Thatch found the items he desired and set about bringing them into the ship's main hold.

Tom filled in the missing pieces of his adventure. His fantastical tale of pirates and cowboys aboard the *Ward*. The details came pouring out, building toward the mutiny that erupted when their fates once again crossed in the waters off Levasseur's island.

Thatch moved crates and boxes from the far wall of the near-empty main hold. Gone were the crates and chests of silver from the train heist, gone was the treasure housed in this very space when he arrived in Nassau to parley with all the pirate captains: Calico Jack, Jennings, Bellamy, Paulsgrave, Bonnet and all the others including his old captain, Benjamin Hornigold. A pang of guilt hit his heart as he remembered running his old friend through with a sword. *Traitor*, his mind corrected his heart.

He stood gazing at the bare back wall while the others watched with interest. His fingers traced the seam of a hidden door. He sprung the latch, and it swung wide.

Colette, Philip and Tom crowded around to see what was secreted away.

Thatch stepped back and as they pulled the stash of treasure out from the small hold, he pulled up a barrel and sat down to watch. Coins and jewels were the first. There were enough riches stored inside for the four of them to live like royalty for the rest of their years.

His eyes landed on Colette as she poured gold dust from a bag into her palm. She smiled at him, and he returned it with a wink.

He lit his pipe while they rummaged and savored the taste and sweet, pleasant fragrance of the tobacco. His rule against smoking aboard ship was disregarded as there wasn't a dry speck of timber to be found.

The riches of Levasseur were far out of his reach along with the hoard that lay aboard the *Ward*. He vowed to Poseidon himself that his pirating days were done, so long as the sea-god watched over the lovely woman now smiling at him. What he had in this room was enough. His battered body finally began to ease, muscles unclenching, pain giving way to a rare calm. For the first time in years, his mind felt clear, unburdened. *Whenever* they were, he would settle. He would spend his remaining days drinking rum, feasting, and dancing with the true prize before him—barefoot, draped in an ill-fitting Nazi uniform, and radiant all the same.

He saw Philip leaning in to pick something off the floorboards beyond the secret door. He slowly came out with something coveted in his hand. He turned and Thatch saw Philip's prize; the second cross of the Sacred Lotus Twins of Goa.

So, Black Caesar did hide it away in their secret hold.

Philip stepped toward him to offer it to Thatch but he held up his hand.

"I want nothing to do with that cursed Catholic relic, Mr. Albert. It's yours to do with what you will, and I'd like to never see or hear of it again."

EPILOGUE

Thatch folded the schematics he had been studying and pushed back from his desk. Rising, he crossed the cabin, passing the ornate bed, perfectly made with fresh cotton sheets. On the nightstand stood several photographs. He picked one up, heartened as his eyes lingered on it.

The picture had been taken on the garden patio of the house overlooking the serene ocean that he and Colette had purchased several years ago. None of them were smiling—still unaccustomed to the modern notion of showing joy for a photograph. His finger traced over their faces: Colette, radiant in an enchanting white dress; himself, Philip, and Tom in light-blue tuxedos, stiff and formal but together.

He set the frame down with care and climbed the stairs. Topside, the sky stretched wide, streaked with clouds turning orange and purple with the painting of the late afternoon's glory.

Two Cuban deckhands were finishing their chores. Thatch raised a hand in greeting.

"G'night, Captain."

"See you in the morning. Early," he reminded them. "Group of car salesmen from Miami, nine sharp."

"Aye, aye. Nine sharp," the younger one echoed.

"Nine for them, seven for you," Thatch shot back with a warning as he crossed the gangplank onto the long dock where the *Queen Anne's Revenge* lay moored.

He fished a cigarette from the pocket of his flowered shirt, struck a match, and lit it. Smoke curled upward as he strolled along the quiet inlet bay, the fading light catching in the ripples of the water.

A few minutes later, Thatch strolled in his flip-flops down the sidewalk, past the thriving shops of downtown Key West, the place he had chosen to call home.

In the three years since their arrival, they had adjusted to the new world. The world war had ended in 1945 with Germany, Japan, and Italy on the losing side. The newsreels and cinema footage of the city destroying bombs dropped on Japan shook him to his core. Governments wielded such immense power that the dream of a Pirate Republic now seemed nothing more than a romantic fantasy. It mattered little—he had given up that life, though he still followed the old codes when it suited him.

"Evening, Captain," called a hostess in distracting white short pants as he passed the outdoor patio of Tom's favorite cantina. With so many tanned young waitresses bustling about, it was no wonder the boy liked the place.

Tom had had his share of run-ins with the sheriff's department. Colette and Thatch had adopted him, signing paperwork at the courthouse making him legally their son. They had done their best to straighten his path. He'd grown into a scrappy teenager, quick with his fists when bullied for being one of the only Asian faces in town. Thatch had taken to drinking with the sheriff and his deputies to ensure the boy got leniency, though it sometimes cost him a few fishing trips on the *Queen Anne* to stay in their good graces.

Recently, Tom had taken to music. A girl had introduced him to a band named after some insect—ants, roaches, beetles? He had convinced Thatch to buy a record player for his room. The two teens spent hours locked away in his room listening to albums while Colette fretted about what else they might be doing.

"Good evening, Mr. Thatch!" called Margaret Ferris from across the street.

Thatch quickened his steps. Out of the corner of his eye he saw her crossing traffic, waving her hands like she owned the town.

"Mr. Thatch, I'd love to have a word with you and your lovely wife."

Damn these sandals, slowing me down. "We're very busy this season, lass, how about in a few months?" he replied, striding on.

"Well, I don't know if this place in Miami will still be on the market that long."

"Our loss then. We're quite happy in the home we have."

"But Mr. Thatch, think of the opportunity, oceanfront on Miami Beach!"

"I don't care for cities, Miss Ferris."

She prattled on about "other investment opportunities," but Thatch swallowed his frustration. "Should we be looking, you'll be the first we call." He turned sharply and crossed Duval Street before she could corner him further.

They hadn't seen Philip in more than six months. He had stayed with them for a time, but grew restless, fascinated with the new world. He flew in airplanes, explored New York, Boston, Los Angeles and San Francisco; reporting on its many changes. Eventually, he admitted he needed a purpose. He took a job with a company called International Business Machines. Thatch had wished him luck.

Their treasure had been divided evenly, though Colette had insisted Tom's share be locked away until he was older. She had a knack for such matters and spread their fortune wisely.

Philip had studied the surviving Goa cross, probing its rare metal and strange crystalline structure. Some nights, he confessed, it frightened him. He couldn't bring himself to destroy it though, nor cast it into the sea like its twin. In the end, he donated it to a famous museum in France, although in exchange he secured the right to see it privately whenever he wished.

For months they searched for word of their old shipmates but found nothing. The *Ward* was listed as missing, presumed lost in the Indian Ocean after an encounter with a German U-boat thought already to have sunk a year before. There was no official report of a mutiny by the *Ward's* captain who survived the night along with half of his crew members.

Every time Thatch sailed out of Key West and into the Florida Straits, he muttered a prayer to Poseidon to watch over his mates. He missed them all. Some days, he even forced himself to add a word for Woodes Rogers—not out of debt, but because the pirate hunter had given his life so Colette could live. On those days, Thatch almost respected him. On others, he cursed the man for the chaos and blood he'd sown, a shadow that still clung to their lives.

He stepped off the sidewalk and into the parking lot of the newest jewel in downtown Key West—a beautiful beachfront saloon, already half full this early in the evening. Above the wide-open doors hung the sign: *Colette's*.

Inside, the air was warm and full of laughter. The saloon gleamed with bamboo and teak, Colette's handiwork, and the wide accordion doors to the patio stood open, letting in the sea breeze and fragrance of tropical flowers. Locals and tourists crowded the place, drinks in hand, music drifting from the small stage where a new friend strummed lively songs on his guitar.

Thatch slid onto his favorite stool at the bar. His cigarette was gone, and he crushed the stub into the ashtray.

"Hey Blackbeard, how is you doing, mon?" asked Dante, the Jamaican bartender.

"Thirsty, Dante."

"Make you a daiquiri, then, Captain?"

Thatch shot him a sharp look.

"Rum it is, for the pirate captain."

"Aye."

He turned to survey the crowd, then back to the bar as a drink was set before him. He reached for it, smiled at the familiar warmth of good Caribbean rum on his tongue.

"What, no thank you?"

He looked up to see Colette smiling at him from behind the bar. She leaned in, kissed him, and wiped a bit of rum from his beard.

"There you are, lass."

"How far did you get today on the *Queen Anne*'s motor?"

He waved the folded schematics from his pocket before tucking them away again.

"I'll take that as a sign it still sits idle in the hold."

"Having that block of metal aboard feels like an insult to the old girl."

"Taking thirty minutes to limp in and out of the narrow harbor is a bigger insult."

"Aye," he admitted sheepishly. "I'll get after it in a few days."

"I've heard that before, love." She smiled and started to slip away to tend the bar's business.

He grabbed her hand before she could leave. "Dance with me later?"

She squeezed his hand. "Till the sun comes up."

He let her go about her evening business. The music ended and the musician sat down in the seat next to him.

"What is you drinking tonight, Jimmy?" Dante asked.

"Something with rum."

"Piña colada?"

"Perfect."

Thatch let out a groan. "Perfect way to ruin a good glass of rum."

"I think old Blackbeard just doesn't know how to have a bit of fun," said Jimmy.

"Aye, Dante, the bard might be right. What do you think?" Thatch asked the bartender as he mixed the tropical drink.

Dante pushed the colorful cocktail in front of Jimmy, complete with straw and tiny umbrella. "Ahh, I seen the man so jolly, he give Santa Claus a run for his money."

Thatch raised his glass to Dante and took another sip.

Jimmy laughed. "I imagine that's true. There is a rumor I heard that on the fourth of July you gave the sea a full broadside—with real cannonballs."

"He a real pirate, Jimmy, just born way too late," Dante said before moving down the bar to attend to several men in suit coats.

The two friends sipped their drinks. Colette passed by and patted Jimmy on the shoulder.

"Good set, Jimmy."

"Thanks for having me, Colette," he got out before she was out of earshot. He turned back to his drink and spun the little umbrella between his thumb and finger. "I've played so many dives throughout the East Coast but once I arrived here everything changed. This place changed me, changed my music… changed my soul. You've got a good life, Edward."

"Aye, that I do."

"What is the secret?" Jimmy asked sincerely.

Thatch lit a cigarette and the ember flared against the saloon's low light as he drew in slow, steady. He let the smoke curl between them while he considered his answer. At last, his voice came low and rough, carrying the weight of centuries.

"I think I've seen more of life than any man alive, my friend. Sailed more seas, plundered more ships, weathered more storms…" His eyes sparkled with mischief, but there was a sheen there too, memories pressing close. "But a pirate looks at forty and sees the waves in his whiskey, wind in his woman's hair, and home in the strum of a six-string."

Jimmy nodded, his guitar resting against his knees, the truth of it flickering in his easy smile.

"I think we were both born too late. Imagine what it was like during the Golden Age of Piracy. Now the treasure's all been plundered, and the cannons only thunder over oil or some claim to a patch of dirt."

He savored the rhyme, rolling it around in his head. His gaze drifted toward the open patio, lingering on the dark sweep of the sea. "There's a song in there somewhere."

Thatch lifted his glass, the rum catching the glow of lamplight as if it carried the last fire of the old world. He held it steady until Jimmy raised his own, their glasses meeting with a soft *clink*, almost lost in the hum of voices and laughter that swelled around them.

"Aye, mate," Thatch said, a grin tugging his face—half defiance, half sorrow.

"The song of two victims of fate."

ACKNOWLEDGEMENTS

First and foremost, I would like to thank my amazing wife, Janina. She is always the first to read my work, offering thoughtful feedback on both characters and story. A lifelong voracious reader, she and I don't always share the same genres of choice, but I trust her taste and insight more than anyone I know.

My daughter, Ava, has been my confidante since the very beginning—listening as I worked out the bones of this story and its sequel. She is always there when I need to bounce ideas off someone. These two wonderful women remain the backbone of any success I've achieved, even as they never tire of humorously poking fun at my pirate obsession. "Yo ho!" indeed.

To Robin Seavill, who edited each of my novels: I owe a debt of gratitude for your guiding hand, sharp instincts, and witty notes throughout our collaboration. From our very first exchange, your humor and warmth won me over, and your Bristolian perspective continues to bring authenticity and life to the many English voices in the pirate series. To you, my friend, I raise a hearty "Huzzah!"

Thanks also to my buddy Danny, for encouraging me to keep writing and for fueling the fire of turning this pirate obsession into something far bigger than I first imagined.

To Brent, my longtime friend and business partner—you've always supported the entrepreneurial spirit and dreams of those around you. There's no one else I'd rather have at my side when it's time to face the sharks.

And finally, to my fellow writers—your encouragement, camaraderie, and friendship mean the world to me. Our shared journey gives me energy every single day. I'm lucky to know and work alongside such talent, including (but not limited to) H.D. Scott, Dhara Parekh, Steven Prendergast, Marcy Mahoney, Bryan Mahoney, Graham Kirkham, and Joseph O'Loughlin.

Thank you all for being part of this adventure.

A LITTLE ABOUT ME BEFORE YOU GO

I grew up with a fascination for both pirates and cowboys. Born in Miami, with the Caribbean practically in my backyard, pirate lore was everywhere—woven into books, films, and the local culture. Later, my family moved to Tucson, Arizona, where I discovered a new obsession: the cowboy.

As a kid, I couldn't decide which world I loved more, so I mashed them together. Picture a boy in cowboy boots and shorts, a plastic revolver holstered at his side, an eyepatch crooked over one eye, charging down the street on his trusty Huffy bicycle with a banana seat. I'd wave a plastic cutlass at passing cars like they were galleons ripe for plunder. Looking back, I probably gave a few drivers heart palpitations, but my imagination was already steering me toward this very story.

When I began thinking seriously about a tale where pirates are unwillingly transported through time, I asked myself: what would they make of it? Drop them too far into the future and the world would feel like sorcery. But set them down in 1873, in the Wild West, and the world is different yet familiar—bridging their age of sail to the modern world. By the time of Book Two, you've now seen those same pirates clash with the marvel of powered flight in the midst of World War II.

I hope you enjoyed this adventure as much as I enjoyed writing it. If you'd like to stay abreast of what I'm working on next, sign up for my newsletter at: www.bryancantrell.com

There you'll find the other books I've written, updates on my other projects like films and podcasts, and a link to my pirate hub:

www.thepiraterepublic.com a place for pirate history, lore, merchandise, and my weekly newsletter.

And finally, if you'd like to do this pirate a mighty favor, please leave a review for *Pirates of World War II* wherever you found it. Stories live or die by their reviews these days, and I'd hate to see this one sink to Davy Jones' locker.

Thanks, matey!

www.ingramcontent.com/pod-product-compliance
Lightning Source LLC
Chambersburg PA
CBHW020331010826
48973CB00005B/1224